D0402729

THE
QUEEN'S CHOICE

Books by Cayla Kluver

from Harlequin TEEN

The Legacy Trilogy

(in reading order)

Legacy
Allegiance
Sacrifice

The Heirs of Chrior Trilogy

The Queen's Choice

THE
QUEEN'S CHOICE

CAYLA KLUVER

HILLSBORO **HARLEQUIN** LIBRARIES
Hillsboro, OR
Member of Washington County
COOPERATIVE LIBRARY SERVICES

ISBN-13: 978-0-373-21092-3

THE QUEEN'S CHOICE

Printed in U.S.A.

www.HarlequinTEEN.com

This book is dedicated to Grandma Bev and Grandpa Noel, whose support has made so many impossible things possible.

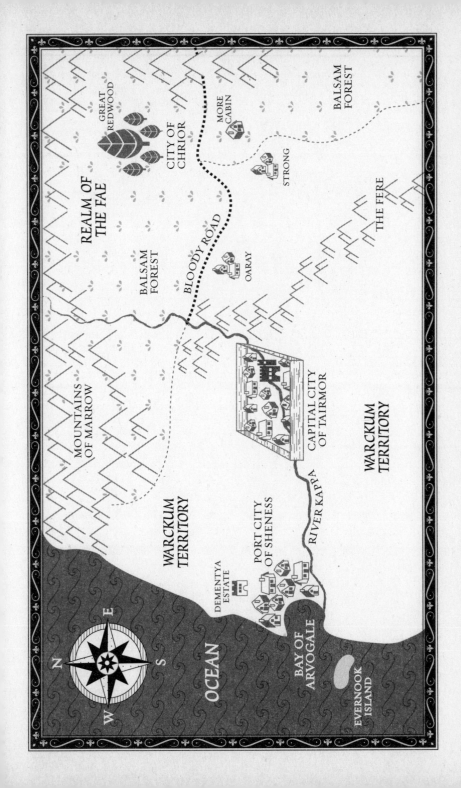

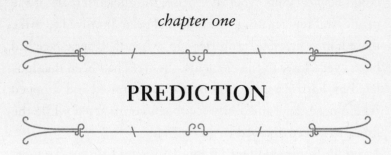

chapter one

PREDICTION

I stood at the end of the Road, feeling the frigid breeze and watching the leaves rustle in their dizzying patterns. I had a jerkin and cloak to keep me warm, a long-knife to protect me, but I knew how many souls haunted this place, and it was impossible to feel at ease.

The path and trees were white with snow, but in my mind I saw them red with soldiers' blood. It ran down the trunks like sap and flooded the walk. There was a legacy burned into the core of this place, and the passage of years could not see it forgotten. Fae and human alike were reluctant to set foot here.

It was not my first time traversing the Bloody Road, the site of the historic battle between human and Fae, so some of its mystique was lost on me. But as my legs were stroked by the hands of the lonely and the angry, of those who could not leave this place, a chill seeped into the marrow of my bones. I walked on, passing into the Realm of my people, for though the lonely and the angry of this Road had taken many, they could not capture me. The power of the elements that ran in my blood spared me.

Despite my long journey, my exhaustion fell away once the city came into view. The human world, though fascinating, could be wearying, whereas Chrior, the ancient cradle of Fae magic, was rejuvenating. Nothing had been destroyed to make these homes possible; centuries ago, when the Faerie race had been even closer to the elements, the trees had been manipulated by Earth Fae, the ground had been raised and dropped where necessary, and a city had been constructed while the forest had been allowed to go on living.

Snow shimmered around me, falling and filling my footprints. I dropped my magical shroud and unfolded my membrane wings, which glinted green, gold, and ice-blue like oil in sunlight. Hovering skyward, I let the thin cold air of winter test them as I flew to the Great Redwood, which had long ago parted its trunk for the royal Fae who protected and inhabited it, calling themselves the Redwood Fae. The ancient tree's orangey bark was coated with icicles, but I felt warmth radiating from inside. I ran my fingers over the love-carvings that surrounded the entrance—artistic tributes left by Fae, tiny designs across the surface of a bark that ran deep—and contentment filled my soul. It was good to see the world. It was better to come home.

Far beneath me, on the ground inside the Redwood, the Queen's Court was in session. Revelers with wings in myriad colors feasted and danced, their laughter, music, and conversation bouncing joyously around me.

On her throne of twined roots, Queen Ubiqua presided, and on both sides she was joined by her closest followers: my father, Cyandro, who served as her Lord of the Law; the eight members of her Council, among them my grandfather, the former reigning Prince; and Davic, the young man to whom I had entrusted my heart. Three chairs in addition to my own stood empty, but one most glaringly—the throne that belonged to Ubiqua's husband, who had never occupied it before his death.

I straightened my jerkin and handed my cloak and pack to a member of the royal guard, who would see that they were sent to my quarters. Then I hastened downward, following the spiraling ridge that ran along the inner walls of the tree until at last I came to the floor.

Almost immediately after I pressed into the midst of the Court—a jostling body of heat and fresh-spiced winter scents—arms were flung around my waist from behind, nearly knocking me into another Fae. I craned my head around and saw exactly who I expected to find embracing me. My best friend Ione, her blond waves adorably woven through a headband of scarlet berries, had playfully ambushed me.

"I was hoping you'd be back tonight," she exclaimed, beaming in her modest way. "The entire Court was. May the Queen's reign flourish!"

The cry was echoed by the Faefolk who now surrounded me, and I managed to return Ione's hug before shouts of "Sale!" floated from the crowd. A bark mug was thrust at me, and I happily accepted the drink that ran from our trees and nourished the Faerie kind more powerfully than any food.

Once I'd finished sharing greetings and toasts, I abandoned my empty goblet and approached the Queen. A long queue, monitored by the Queen's Blades in their bedazzling tunics, led to her throne of gnarled and ancient roots. My aunt smiled, kind and patient, as every member of her Court endured the procession to greet her and extend their respects. I drew up beside the line and walked its length, nodding to the Blades I passed.

The Queen's face lit up when I drew near, and I fell to one

knee, placing my forefinger upon her earthen perch. When I removed it, a droplet of dew was left in its place among hundreds of others frozen there in her honor, for tonight marked the twenty-fifth anniversary of my aunt's coronation. The droplets were gifts from Water Fae, sparkling amidst leaves and berries from Earth Fae, glowing embers like rubies from Fire Fae, and clearest crystals filled with whispers of fog and cloud from Air Fae. The elemental offerings would dissipate within the week, allowing room for the city's general public and not just the Queen's Court to pay tribute to her.

"Anya! How was your journey?" Queen Ubiqua effused, leaning forward to be heard above the revelry. Having her gaze upon me, as always, was like meeting Time—there was something incomprehensible about her, something infinite. She didn't suffer the same worries I did because her wisdom transcended them.

"Enlightening," I replied, rising, but I could not keep my eyes from drifting toward Davic. It was proper to acknowledge the Queen before the others around her, but it was he who was foremost on my mind. His gray-blue eyes muted the bedlam in the trunk, drawing me in as though nothing existed beyond the landscape of his elegant jaw, the black hair pulled into a ponytail at the nape of his neck, and the parting of his lips, an aphrodisiac in itself. He grinned at me, gripping the arms of his chair like he might propel himself upward at any moment and fly to my side.

"Go to him," Ubiqua laughed, tipping her head in Davic's direction, aware that she no longer held my attention. "You and I can talk later."

In need of no convincing, I hurried to my promised. He'd come to his feet, and he snatched the hand I extended to haul me onto the dais and into his arms. I laughed, wrapping my legs around his waist when he picked me up and holding his face for a lengthy kiss that was continually disrupted by our smiles.

"I almost forgot what you looked like," he teased, pushing our foreheads together. Our pose, somewhat unseemly for a royal and her partner, nevertheless charmed the assembly and drew a few shouts. We both turned scarlet and hid our faces in each other's shoulders, then Davic returned to his seat, taking me with him.

"I missed you, too," I murmured, settling against him and twining our fingers together. Soon I felt the heat of someone's gaze; I turned and exchanged a warm nod with my father, then took his hint that I should move to my own chair. I kept Davic's palm snug against mine while I scanned the empty seats, making note of who else was missing—Zabriel, the long absent Prince of Chrior; and my cousin Illumina, the orphaned daughter of Queen Ubiqua's brother.

Leaning close to Davic, I asked, "Where is Illumina?"

Though I could have guessed his answer from his resigned look, I waited for him to confirm it.

"She only stayed for an hour, maybe less. At least she was here for a while. Let's not dwell on her tonight."

I nodded, for Illumina's lack of participation was not unexpected. Quiet, studious and easily overshadowed, she avoided crowds to whatever extent possible. Still, I would have liked for her to be here. Not only was she a niece of the Queen, she was also heir to the throne due to the Prince's defection, and learning to connect with the people was an important part of her future.

Davic and I did not have much opportunity to talk during

the festivities, and we were glad when Ubiqua called her Court to a close and we could fly to the branches of the Great Redwood where I made my home. Davic also had an alcove in the mighty tree, though his family had no interest in Court life and lived far on the other side of Chrior. There was only one section of the Redwood that was unoccupied, a place where the branches were dry and dead and could hold little weight. The destruction was viewed as a tragedy and rarely discussed, but from what I understood, a fire had defiled our people's ancient refuge.

My residence was a small place, but practical. Davic walked the perimeter of the main room, focusing on the energy inside himself as he ran his finger along the love-carved indentation to spark and ignite it. Finished, he fell onto the sofa, putting his hands behind his head. The house warmed at once, and I curled up beside him, breathing in his familiar scent, musky with an undercurrent of Tanya flowers, which only grew on this side of the Road. The whole evening I hadn't given a thought to how truly tired I was, but now I relaxed, the heaviness in my limbs a reminder of how little I had slept the past few days.

"Well?" Davic asked after a bit. "How was the human world this time?"

"I made it to Tairmor before you called me back," I replied, offering him a smirk. "You're impatient, Davic."

He brushed my auburn hair behind my shoulder and kissed my forehead. "How long would you have been gone if I hadn't called you?"

"I wanted to see Sheness, the port city. A few more weeks."

His countenance grew wary, lips pursing and eyes slightly widening. He was the worrier of the two of us, and his expression was endearing in its predictability.

"Anya, your father has warned against Fae traveling that far west. He says there's been a resurgence of piracy over the past year."

"I'm aware of my father's warnings." I gave his hair a playful tug, making it difficult for a scowl to emerge. "But pirates surely don't lurk around every corner in Sheness, waiting to attack. They have their business, and I would have had mine. I do know what I'm doing out there. Anyway, it doesn't matter now. I didn't go near the port."

"You're not invincible, you know." He was looking at me sideways, not yet pacified. This was a variance we'd had before—he meant well, but he had a hard time trusting anything if it was beyond Chrior's borders, including me.

I chuckled. "Of course I'm not invincible, but Fae *are* more powerful than humans, and we have our elements to protect us. Anyone who tried to hurt me would be swept away by a wall of water before they could blink, while I flew away to the rooftops." My point stood even though that wasn't exactly how Fae connections worked. We had to rely on physically present matter that we could move and manipulate rather than *conjuring* our elements, but for me that matter could include blood and mist as easily as rain or river water, leaving me with a lot of power at my disposal. "Try not to be such a killjoy when everything is, at present, perfect."

He rolled his eyes, but I felt his body relax against mine. I plucked at the fabric of his shirt, nervous about the confession I was about to make. "I was a little worried, though, that something might be wrong when I felt your call."

Davic and I had been promised by a mage, the same mage who had wed my aunt and her husband, and the aura that bound us let us reach out to one another no matter how far apart we were. I'd felt the tug from Davic in Tairmor, the capital of the Warckum Territory, and had started home at once.

He chewed his lip, looking adorable as he made a bid for clemency. "Are you annoyed? I was thinking about you, and next I knew I'd signaled you before I'd even decided whether or not I should. If you're upset with me, I'll say I'm sorry it happened. Really."

"Aww, you'd say whatever I'd like to hear to save your own hide? You're so sweet." I shoved him, not upset in the least. Our bond was still fresh, and it would take time to adapt to its intricacies.

He let out a relieved breath, then played with my hair. His thoughts traveled over his face in what he believed to be a private course, though his ultimate expression told me he had landed on the matter I'd hoped he'd leave alone until the morning at least.

"Do you ever get homesick out there? I mean, you stay away for so long. I just wonder if…you don't like coming back."

Without fail, this conversation followed my returns and preceded my departures. Unlike me, Davic was content in Chrior, with no interest in journeying. He hadn't even been on his Crossing, the traditional rite of passage for young Fae. Following my Crossing, I'd developed a taste for the human world, a wanderlust that not even my promised's pleading could overcome, and certainly one that he had trouble understanding.

"The fact that I enjoy being in the Territory doesn't mean I *don't* enjoy being here."

"You spend more time in the human world than you do here." Preempting my response, he added, "I'm not trying to stop you from traveling, but it seems to me that spending time with me and your friends, with your father, is something you just tolerate until you can leave again."

Why couldn't we have a pleasurable reunion and leave it at that?

"It's not being away from you I enjoy, Davic. It's seeing what's out there, what's different about how the humans live. How the politics move and shift." I frowned, lost in thought. "For instance, there's something different about the mood in the Territory right now. I don't know what exactly, but I was seeing more Constabularies and military units. Maybe the Governor is just cracking down on crime. If he keeps it up, my father won't have much to warn about in a few months."

Governor Ivanova, elected conservator and custodian of the Warckum Territory, was known for the strict and swift enforcement of his laws. He was also known as King Ivanova by his detractors, because the governorship had been in his family for so long it was practically an inherited position, with no sign of change on the horizon.

"Then perhaps you should wait for the all-clear before you head out again. All right?" He kissed my forehead, then sought my eyes. At my grudging nod, a tease at last entered his voice. "You know, it *sounds* like I called you out of potential danger. Doesn't that mean I deserve a thank-you?"

"No, it means you're off the hook for cutting my trip short," I laughed, and he rolled over, trapping me beneath him.

"In that case, I should probably tell you that I didn't do it for me. The Queen asked when you'd be back and seemed disappointed in my answer. She didn't actually tell me to interrupt your travels, but it was clear that was what she wanted."

I pushed myself up on my elbows, Davic scrambling back to accommodate my sudden movement.

"Why?"

"She didn't tell me *that*."

"It must be urgent." My heart was thumping a little faster as I tried to imagine what could have led Ubiqua to summon me.

Davic shrugged. "I doubt it. She didn't try to talk to you at Court tonight."

"I should still go to her. At once."

Davic's brows shot upward, and he bent closer again.

"Or you could wait." He pressed his lips lightly to my neck, and, against my better judgment, I allowed my mind to cloud with the sensation, slipped my hands into his hair and slid back underneath him, indisposed to argue.

Davic and I slept in longer than we—or rather I—intended. Though he awoke when I rose and we spoke briefly, he was asleep again by the time I left, laying there still dressed from the night before. There was something about him that was angelic. Yes, he frustrated me when our differences came head-to-head, but my trust in him ran deep. He was solid and predictable, like a form of gravity. He would never hurt me, and his arms would always hold me whether my behavior was rational or nonsensical.

In the light of a new day, the snowfall had stopped, and everything was bright and glistening. Though it was cold, the air was crisp and fresh, not like in the human world where the people destroyed and polluted in the conduct of their lives. Many Fae feared that same pollution would seep like a dark fog across our borders and ruin our way of life. I figured if it came to that, it wouldn't be right to blame those who lived in the Territory; instead, the fault would be ours. The only chance for the humans to befriend Nature rather than dominate it was through us and our elemental connections, and we'd locked their race out of our Realm. They had to survive somehow. That was what Illumina and the others who were part of the Anti-Unification League overlooked: the humans' right to live.

I flew to the palm—the large knot that made a landing pad before the Great Redwood's main entrance—then hovered up to my aunt's private dwelling. I waved to the guards on the ridge, making sure they recognized me before I softly dropped to my feet.

Like closely stitched netting, thick green vines composed the floor of this part of the tree. To most looking up, this netting was the ceiling since no one passed beyond it without invitation. I took delicate steps, for the vines had give to them; despite our gift for flight, uncontrolled falls could be as deadly for Fae as for humans. Still, I knew the netting could hold more weight than it appeared; resiliency was strength, not weakness.

The Queen's companions were sitting around her throne, which was set back and framed by tied-away willow and lavender-leaf curtains. Catching sight of me, Ubiqua dismissed her Court, her smile and voice gentle. The last to rise was Illumina, her long black hair limp and sallowing her face. Still, her features were delicate, and her eyes, green like mine, were cheerless but sharp. She looked me up and down on her way by, and I had the feeling she was searching for changes in me since I'd been gone.

When the Queen and I were alone, Ubiqua motioned me closer, and I sat at her feet where her entourage had been. Silence hung between us, and I began to worry something was seriously wrong. Though decorum suggested I should wait for her to speak, I took the initiative and opened the conversation.

"Davic told me you were the one who wanted me to come home."

"I asked Davic not to make that known. I thought he might hold out longer than this."

We both knew my promised well enough to laugh softly at her remark. Davic had never kept secrets from me.

"I hope he didn't alarm you," Ubiqua went on, the blue of her eyes mesmerizing, like a calming tonic. "That wasn't my intention."

I searched her face for some clue to where this conversation might be going. "Aunt, if there's no cause for alarm, why am I here?"

"Because there is something I must tell you, and under the circumstances, sooner is better than later."

She smiled, although a deeper emotion seemed to be roiling within her. Her silver hair was loose in wispy curls, though here and there were braids—she treated the children of the Court like her own, and allowed them to play with her long locks. On such a glorious day, what could be troubling her?

"This Great Redwood I call my home has been alive much longer than I have, Anya, and it will outlive me by millenniums. We are friends. I talk to it, and at times it whispers back to me. And in its great wisdom, it has whispered that the end of my life is approaching."

"What?" Her statement rolled over my skin like a shock wave. I studied her in a daze—yes, she was aged, but her skin glowed like a young girl's, and her mind had lost none of its brilliance. There was no indication of illness about her.

"But that—that can't be right," I stammered. "You can't be dying."

"No, no, I'm not dying." Ubiqua placed a comforting hand

on my shoulder, where it settled without discernible weight. "Not now. For now, I have all the strength in the world. But soon it will forsake me, and there must be someone to whom I can entrust my legacy. Do you understand?"

"Yes, of course. You know I'll help Illumina in whatever way I can."

The Prince's defection from the Realm had transferred the line of succession to the lineage of the Queen's eldest sibling, Illumina's father, making Illumina next in line to the throne. But knowing this didn't negate my reservations about my younger cousin. I hesitated, wondering if I should speak my mind. While I expected Ubiqua would take my opinions in stride, it was nevertheless perfidious of me to raise them.

"I'm sorry, Aunt, but I…I don't think she's ready for this. She needs more time. She doesn't yet appreciate the value of peace with the humans."

To my surprise, no rebuke was forthcoming.

"I agree with you and am glad our thoughts align. Illumina will not succeed me." My aunt settled farther back on her throne, letting her words resonate between us, their meaning well within my grasp had I been disposed to embrace it. "I speak of an heir of my choosing and not just my bloodline. Someone who will honor my legacy and not pervert it. Someone who will finish the work I have begun, and bring humans and Fae together."

The Queen brought her blue eyes to bear on me, full of conviction and faith, and I was seized by an urge to run, not wanting to hear her next declaration.

"Will you accept this responsibility, Anya? This honor? Will you continue along the path I have set even after my death, just as you have followed in my footsteps during life?"

It was hard to hear her over the pounding of blood in my ears. Thanks to the order of my mother's birth, I had been allowed to live a privileged life without the real responsibility of being royalty, but that was about to come to a clamorous halt. It was true I had struggled in the aftermath of Zabriel's departure to accept the fact that, despite her idiosyncrasies, Illumina would be next to wear the Laura, the crown of laurels. But though the idea of her ruling had made me nervous, it had also been a relief. It meant no demands were placed on my future. Now the air around me felt charged with expectation, and my stomach burned as I felt the course of my life changing.

Coming to my feet, I crossed the room, as though that would permit me to escape the question. When I neared the edge of the netting, I paused, looking down at the spiraling ridge, my thoughts likewise twisting and turning in silent debate. I was sixteen, only two years older than Illumina, and not much better equipped than she to ascend the throne.

And what of my travels? Despite what Davic believed, I didn't just enter the Territory in search of adventure; my crossings were of assistance to my father, sojourns to gather information about human activities. But a queen couldn't be gone for months at a time. I would have to stay, and sit, and watch, and listen, always the voice of wisdom and the hand of equanimity. I would be domesticated…trapped in this city, charged with the responsibility of guiding an entire people to happiness regardless of my own.

Then there was, Nature forbid, the prospect of another war. I did not want to be accountable for deaths before I was even old enough to bring life into the world. No, the Laura would not fit me as it did my aunt.

"How soon?" I asked hoarsely, forcing myself to look into

the Queen's face. "When are you supposed to die? Can we stop it?"

"That doesn't matter," she responded, her eyes boring into me, uncovering my fears, their roots, and how deeply they coiled. But she persisted, for she put her people and her Realm before all else. "I believe the Redwood's prediction, but whether you choose to or not will make no difference in the end. I will die one day, and when that day comes, I have to know that someone…someone with a strong and pure heart will be stepping up to rule in my place."

"What makes you sure I have a strong and pure heart?" I put a hand against the Redwood's wall and tightened my fingers, its heartwood sliding under my nails. "I understand your reservations about Illumina—I have them, too—but Aunt, I want my *life*."

Though I felt childish saying these things, her eyes were sympathetic, and she reached out to me, summoning me to her side.

"There is only you, Anya. Only you share my ideals. Only you can continue leading the Fae toward peace with the humans." She took my hand, lightly touching the white gold band with a ruby center that I wore around my right middle finger. She held it up to catch the light, reminding me of who I was, for the ring signified that I was a member of the royal family, the ancient Redwood Fae. "On the one hand, you deserve your life. On the other, the Faerie Realm and the human world deserve your dedication. What is your answer?"

I tugged on a strand of my hair, trying to ignore the warmth and compulsion in her eyes, trying to concentrate on the question and not on the prospect that she might be dead in what—a few years? Months? Mere weeks? The possibilities were enough to break my heart.

"Who else knows?" I asked. "About what the Great Redwood told you?"

"No one. I wanted to resolve things with you before I told your father or the Council."

"Then you will talk to Illumina." My spirit settled into a state of numbness and resignation. I had a duty to fulfill that was of greater importance than my own desires. "You will tell her...that I am going to be your successor."

Ubiqua smiled gently, pleased by my decision but more compassionate than ever. "Yes, today. And I will immediately send the news to Cyandro."

Although my father was her Lord of the Law, I couldn't fathom the reason it was imperative to tell him so quickly. But the Queen continued to lay out her plans, not permitting me time to dwell on the question.

"I would like you to bring Illumina to me, and to stay with us when I inform her of my decision."

I agreed, despite the fact that this was not a conversation I wanted to witness. My nerves were already raw, and I didn't think I could handle hearing Ubiqua's news a second time. While no one, including the Queen, was immortal, she had held me after my mother, her sister, had died following a long illness. She had helped my father to carry on. She had given me reasons to smile when I'd thought there were none. I loved her deeply, and the thought of losing her was devastating.

I went to find Illumina in accordance with the Queen's request, taking my time for the sake of my churning emotions. My cousin also lived in the branches of the Great Redwood, though she more so under the guidance of our aunt. She was fourteen, an orphan of just two years. Having experienced the death of my mother, I felt for her, but my empathy did not stop me from recognizing that the girl was strange.

Illumina's small shelter was sprinkled with books, odd items she had collected, and blankets, all of which were acceptable enough. But the walls were splattered red and black with whatever images or limericks entered her mind to paint, and sheets of parchment with beautiful but macabre charcoal drawings were strewn across her table. When she found or concocted a message she especially liked, it was no secret that she would use a small knife to carve it upon her body. Her arms were scarred; across the crest of her right breast was engraved: *Keep silent your screams and never look back.* When she wore a corset dress, she made no effort to hide this particular disfigurement, as though the sentiment would impress others. In my case, it only turned my stomach, and pushed my thoughts toward the sad horror that she had once sat alone with her tool of choice to work her art, blood dripping down her chest, ignoring the pain, and felt proud in the aftermath. Sometimes I tried to envision committing the act myself, the dedication it would take, and the idea kept me awake at night. Illumina frequently disappeared, probably to some hideaway in the Balsam Forest where she found the privacy she needed to mutilate herself, and I wished I knew where, in the hope that I could stop her.

"Hello?" I called, opening the door, then adding a firm knock upon the wood.

"Anya," my cousin responded, coming into the living area from her bed chamber, which was set off by a curtain of leaves. She had such a high, sweet voice, and once she'd pushed back her black hair to reveal her face, I could tell she was delighted to see me. She was a true study in contradictions.

"Aunt wants to meet with us both," I told her, my hand still on the door.

"Yes, of course." She dropped the book she had been reading, and it landed on the floor with a thump. "She'll want to tell me herself that you're to be Queen."

She went to a cupboard for a bark cup, still seeming happy. After sprinkling herbs into it from a small container, she extended it to me, and I obligingly ran a finger around the rim, filling it with water I derived from the air. Illumina blew on the liquid, amplifying her body heat until it began to steam.

"You're not upset?" I asked, thrown by her dispassionate attitude. To my knowledge, Illumina had always aspired toward the throne in her own way. She was a lonely girl; to her, the Laura would have been a constant companion.

"I'm not," she said, now blowing on the drink to cool it. "Honestly, I couldn't have expected it to be any other way. The line of succession has been a bit irrelevant in our family ever since my father was passed over for the throne and Aunt became the heir. And just like then, you have more to offer than I do, at least in the Queen's mind. You've always been a step ahead of me."

I couldn't disagree, and the moment that followed was one of the longest of my life.

"I've become quite addicted to this tea," Illumina resumed, her soft giggle inconsistent with the seriousness of her words. "I can hardly make it a day without a cup. Just let me drink this, and then we can go."

I waited with her in stilted silence, trying to figure out what went on in her head. Her upbringing had been unusual; that was inarguable. Having been under the influence of both a generous, peace-loving queen and a human-hating father, I could understand the confusion with which she went about her daily life. But sometimes she reminded me of a boulder rolling down a mountain, bounding this way and that, no one quite sure where she would land at any given moment.

Finished, Illumina set down her cup and flew with me to the palm, then up the ridge to the throne room.

"Aunt was keen for you to return," my cousin remarked along the way. "I knew it had to be official business. But why now? And why so urgent?"

"The Queen will tell you that herself."

It wasn't my intent to be short with Illumina, but I didn't want to talk about the Redwood's prediction, for telling another person would somehow make it more real. And if it was real, then my life was careening toward inalterable change.

chapter two

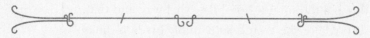

THE WINTER SOLSTICE

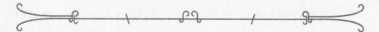

The news of Ubiqua's impending death was as much a blow to Illumina as it had been to me. Perhaps more of one, after the loss of her parents, her mother in childbirth and her father so recently. She fell to the ground at our aunt's feet and cried, gripping her hand. It was painful to watch; I didn't want to be present and didn't know why I was.

At last, Ubiqua motioned for Illumina to stand. "You must be strong, child. I am not leaving you today. And Anya will need your help in time to come, when she rules."

Illumina took a few gasping breaths, then her green eyes darted to me.

"How am I to help Anya? Unless it is that you doubt her."

Ubiqua's eyebrows drew together, mirroring mine. "I have never doubted your cousin in anything. She will be a great ruler."

"Then you must doubt me. You want me to be an aid to Anya so that I'm not left to my own devices. Is that it?"

"No! I want you to be an aid to Anya because the two of you should stay close, always."

"We have never been close." Illumina sounded sad now, though an underlying tone of suspicion lingered in her voice.

"You know we've always disagreed on important issues, issues that, in your opinion, make me unfit to rule or be any sort of aid. Don't patronize me, Aunt."

She turned her back, seeming so hurt by the end of her speech that I would have called out to her had Ubiqua, her voice unexpectedly stern, not done so.

"I am not patronizing you, Illumina. In fact, I have a task for you, if you will accept it. One that more than proves my faith in you."

The Queen's words triggered a warning inside my head, but I did not speak out. It wasn't my place to question.

"I'm sending you into the human world to find someone for me. Someone very important."

Like an angry wind it hit me—what the Queen was going to ask of my cousin—and my lips parted in shock, my poise shredded. A task to preserve Illumina's dignity was one thing; one that endangered her life was quite another.

"I need you to find my son and tell him about the Redwood's prediction. Ask him to come home, if only long enough to say goodbye. I want to see him one last time."

Other than the initial efforts to locate Zabriel after his flight from the Faerie Realm, no attempt had been made to track him. My father's ambassadors in the Warckum Territory would have kept their eyes and ears open for news of the Prince, but the risk of alerting the humans to his identity and presence had been considered too great for any other action to be taken. Ubiqua had thus been forced to accept that her son's destiny lay in his own hands. If he returned, it would be of his own volition.

Illumina appeared awed by the Queen's request, her eyes wide and unblinking, but she quickly acquiesced.

"I'll do it, Aunt," she said, voice solemn as if she were taking an oath.

"Thank you. I've already told the Lord of the Law to expect you. He will advise you about matters relevant to your journey. But I must caution you in one regard. Above all else, you must remember not to speak of your quest to anyone associated with Governor Wolfram Ivanova. He will not be a friend to you in this endeavor."

Illumina's brow furrowed. "Isn't Ivanova for Fae rights? He outlawed hunting. He wouldn't want Zabriel hurt."

"The Governor will not be a physical threat to either of you, but he may nonetheless be an enemy. He doesn't know he has a grandson, and I fear he would not easily relinquish his progeny if he found out."

My cousin processed this information in silence. I was already privy to the knowledge that Zabriel's birth had been kept secret from his deceased father's family. He had learned of the decision his mother had made shortly before his departure two years ago, and had confided in me, needing to express his pain and confusion. I suspected her long-concealed action had been added to his list of reasons to leave Chrior.

"I won't seek help from the Governor or those who work for him," Illumina promised. "I can find Zabriel without help from the humans. When shall I leave?"

"When can you be ready? Time is of the essence."

"I'll report to the Lord of the Law at once."

Her purple-and-pink wings aflutter, Illumina ran to the edge of the netting and took the jump to seek out my father. She was in a hurry to claim this most vital of responsibilities, and our aunt was in a hurry to give it to her. I now understood the reason the Queen had immediately notified Cyandro that I was to rule, and anger bubbled inside me. I couldn't help feeling deceived, manipulated—Ubiqua had not fore-warned me of the request she intended to make of her younger niece. With a sense of sisterly protectiveness toward Illumina, I turned to my aunt.

"What are you doing?" Though my tone could be viewed as inappropriate, I made no attempt to disguise my disapproval.

The Queen stood, her shimmering dress swishing across the vine floor. "I'm trying to make sure I don't die with an estranged son."

"That's not what I'm talking about. You shouldn't be send-ing Illumina on an errand like this."

"Should I instead let her feel useless?"

"Of course not. There are plenty of arrangements to be made in preparation for a new ruler. Give her something she can handle. Send *me* after Zabriel if you want him to come back."

"Anya, I doubt anyone will succeed in convincing my son to return, so what difference does it make who I send? Illumina's odds of success are no worse than anyone else's."

I rubbed my hands over my face in exasperation. "I *know* Zabriel. We were friends before he ran away. He's far more likely to listen to me, and I'm already familiar with the human world. I would at least have a chance."

"So does Illumina. She knows the precautions to take, and she's of age to go on her Crossing. She's cleverer than you're willing to acknowledge. Besides, I believe if I don't give her a purpose now, she may never be your ally."

"That's a lost cause, Aunt. She's hated humans all her life. It's the way your brother raised her."

"Don't bring Enerris into this," Ubiqua snapped, and I wondered what nerve I had struck. She came forward, standing over me so that her superior height was apparent.

"Then *send me*," I reasserted, not about to be intimidated.

"I think perhaps you are envious of an opportunity to travel without having to appease Davic over your absence."

My eyes narrowed. First she reprimanded me for involving Enerris in our argument, then she dared to suggest a strain in my relationship with Davic. A rush of defensiveness came over me.

"Fine. Let Illumina go. But if she fails to return, you and no one else will be to blame."

I stalked off and leaped from the edge of the vines, twisting and turning my way down to the palm. Floating was a favorite sensation of mine, letting my wings battle the air and seeing what shapes my shadow made while I fell. Today's shapes were as broken and disjointed as my thoughts, and as convoluted as my loyalties, which were torn between my aunt and my own heart.

I knew Davic would be waiting, his curiosity piqued, exactly where I'd left him, in the main room of my alcove. But if I stalled a bit longer, he would understand the message—he was good at reading my mind—and return to his own place. I couldn't yet discuss Ubiqua's decisions with him, for it was his reaction I dreaded most, perhaps because I suspected he would be happy. And why shouldn't he be? We would be together in Chrior, we would have a life and a future laid out for us, and it would provide the stability he craved. But until I had come to terms with these changes, I was afraid I would see his happiness and resent him for it.

Instead of going home, I slipped through the branches of the Great Redwood to land above my father's dwelling, the nook of the tree where I had grown up, and waited but a few minutes for Illumina to depart with a bounce in her step. She thought she was ready for the outside world, but she was too naive to even make that judgment. And she couldn't pass unnoticed, not with her scars and her outspoken opinions, not unless she made an effort to disguise her appearance and her character, something she had never been willing to do. Though I made the argument to Davic that the Warckum Territory was safe for Fae, it was really only safe for Fae who could pass for human.

I fluttered to the stoop once my cousin was out of sight and crossed the threshold without knocking. My father was an Air Fae like Ubiqua, so without my mother, who had been a Fire Fae like Davic and Illumina, he had to light the house manually. This wasn't difficult for him, but it was dispiriting for the rest of us to watch. In her absence, he was forced to think about things he'd never had to before, and even though the sunken border of fire tracing the alcove walls was bright, the house felt a little colder for that reason.

My father, his hair graying but his beard dark, was rolling maps at the wooden table in the main room. At my entrance, he looked up with a weary but genuine smile. I vacillated near the doorway. While it was expected that those who traveled in the human world would make a report on their experiences and observations to my father, the task often made me ill at ease. Cyandro was known throughout the Realm for his kindness and fairness, but the sorrow that had entered his eyes upon my mother's death three years ago had not faded. And my resemblance to her led him to avoid me at times, making me less reliant on him and more independent than most Fae my age.

"I'm glad you're home, Anya. I worry when you're away."

He carried his armful of maps to the cupboard where they

belonged, hidden from me when I was a child but not so well hidden that he could not enjoy watching me struggle to remove and replace them when I thought he wasn't near.

"There's no need to worry," I said, compelling myself to step forward. "I'm always careful."

"Ah, but that young man of yours." My father's voice was tired, as if it had spent too many years talking. "He worries."

Having cleared the table, he took a seat and motioned for me to join him. I obliged, perching on the stool across from him.

"Davic doesn't worry," I said with a grin. "He pouts. There's a big difference."

My father wagged his head in amusement. "You may have a point. Still, there's no denying he has a good heart. There isn't a young man I would trust more with your life than Davic."

"You ought to see him when he's with his friends. Your opinions might change in a hurry."

He laughed. "Regardless, I know him, perhaps better than I know you, my dear."

The relaxed atmosphere that had briefly existed between us flitted away, and I looked down at my soft leather boots. As my auburn hair fell forward, I wondered if my father were wishing for a glimpse of the green eyes that were identical to my dead mother's. The resemblance was painful for him most times; other times he considered it a gift; at present, I only desired to hide my face from him.

"Anya…" There was a touch of longing in his voice, and I counted the awkward moments that trickled past. Then he cleared his throat. "Illumina is happy about her assignment. So am I."

"Why?" I demanded, irritated with him and Ubiqua for being so eager to see my cousin off.

"Come, you must know the answer to that. She's young, but…so are you. I would rather Illumina be at risk than my own daughter."

It was a blunt statement, and rather heartless. I hated the sad truth it suggested about Illumina. Had there ever been someone who'd wanted to keep her safe above all others?

"When will she depart?"

"Tomorrow morning."

"She's not ready for this, Father. I'm afraid she won't make it back. And this is an especially bad time to send her. The human world feels more unsettled than usual."

"Maybe that's part of Ubiqua's plan." His tone was matter-of-fact, and I squirmed in my chair. "Illumina shows more similarities to her father than anyone wants to admit. You knew Enerris, and have some idea why he was passed over for the throne. And you know what his fate was, in the end."

I swallowed with difficulty, wishing Davic was here with his skill for language to interpret these words for me, to find a meaning in them that was less awful than what I imagined. Perhaps Ubiqua was willing to put Illumina in harm's way out of a belief that when she returned, she would have a better appreciation for humankind. Or maybe my father was implying exactly what I thought he was, and the rarely revealed harsh side of Ubiqua had made a decision for the betterment of her Realm.

"Now tell me about the human world," my father invited, fulfilling his duty to gather information from those of us who traveled. He reached for his record book in preparation for taking notes. "What do you mean when you say it's unsettled?"

"It's more a feeling than anything else. But there are certain signs—humans lock their doors earlier at night, and I heard rumors of children going missing. There are also more patrols in and around the outlying towns. I don't know how to explain it, but the atmosphere in the Territory is tense, more wary."

"Perhaps piracy is to blame? The criminal they call Pyrite has been making a name for himself in Sheness. Other Fae who've returned tell tales of him and his crew."

"I've heard nothing of him beyond mutterings in public houses. I'm starting to think he's just a myth. A story to tell children at night and keep them close to home."

"That's not what Governor Ivanova believes. My ambassadors write that the murder of a government employee has been credited to Pyrite, which suggests that the influence of piracy on the coast has started to move east. I don't like what that could mean for Fae in the Territory. Right now there are a number of our people who are late in returning from their journeys."

His brow furrowed, my father scratched a few notes in his book with his quill. "I'll bring your observations to the attention of the Council. There are precautions we can take. Perhaps Crossings should be temporarily postponed."

At last he returned to the problem before him—me.

"Be all of that as it may, Anya, the atmosphere you're describing provides more than enough reason for you to stay here. You're the Queen's chosen heir, and that means your safety is more important than Illumina's. But I won't pretend I'm upset about that."

It was clear I would not sway my father on the issue of my cousin any more than I had Ubiqua, so I took my leave, the thought of Illumina navigating the human world on her own weighing on my mind. Equally disturbing, Ubiqua's actions seemed to contradict her assurances to both Illumina and me that she had much time to live.

Instead of returning home, I spent a restless, thoughtful day wandering the city, seeing it in a new light. Most of the Faerie population lived in the sprawling city of Chrior, although our Realm included a large section of the Balsam Forest, where we hunted and kept a few animals; gathered berries, nuts, and medicinal plants; laid to rest our dead; and held celebrations. The idea that I would be expected to rule these people and this land was paralyzing. I tried to convince myself that it wouldn't be so difficult to adjust to the responsibility of being Queen, that I could embrace the new lifestyle that role would entail. But I couldn't shake the portent of trouble that gripped my heart, the same portent that gripped me when I thought of Illumina. Neither of us was ready to undertake the tasks the Queen had set before us.

When darkness fell, I went to visit my cousin, needing to see for myself that she was packed and ready. Though the hour was late, she was not asleep. How could she be with such a daunting mission resting upon her shoulders? Instead, she was going through the scant things she intended to take with her—she would have been told not to carry much—and checking her weapons. The travel satchel beside her was imprinted with the royal seal, and was identical to mine, for they had been gifts from Queen Ubiqua.

"I expected you eventually," she said, looking up from her seat in the corner, where the heating furrow that ran along the walls created an especially cozy space. "I know you're not happy with Aunt for giving me this charge."

"I don't want anything to happen to you." I pulled up a deadwood stool of my own and sat opposite her.

"I thought it might be that you don't want Zabriel to come home."

My eyebrows drew close, narrowing Illumina's view of my eyes. "Why would that be?"

She shrugged, running a polishing rag over her long-knife. "Well, once he's here, he's the rightful heir to the throne, isn't he?"

This hadn't occurred to me. Zabriel seemed so distant lately, more of a dream than a person, that I hadn't really contemplated his claim to the Laura. I shook my head, dismissing the thought before it had the chance to morph into a hope.

"Zabriel doesn't want to be King of this place. His actions have more than established that. He has a wanderer's spirit, not a politician's. Aunt says he takes after his father in that way."

"That human Aunt married. That's what she gets for involving herself with them."

My gaze darkened. "Just so you know, not only did Aunt love William Ivanova, it broke her heart when Zabriel left. She tried to make him feel connected to our Realm, to see that he belonged here, but Fae like you drove him away. Watch what you say, for Nature's sake, Illumina."

"Sorry," she muttered, adding a few medical supplies to her pack.

I took a deep breath and slowly exhaled, releasing my irritation.

"Anyway, I came because I wanted to see if you had any questions, any concerns. It's your first time in the human world. Things are going to be different from the way they are here."

Illumina smiled sweetly. "Thank you, Anya. I can always trust you to look out for me, can't I? But no, I prefer to learn from experience."

I bowed my head, no longer in the mood for conversation. If she didn't want my help, I couldn't very well give it to her.

"Then I'll merely wish you luck." Vaguely dissatisfied, I stood and moved toward the door. "Don't forget to bring Sale with you, but keep it well hidden. It's illegal to have in the Territory. And watch for hunters. The human world can be dark for Fae."

"I'm not naive, Anya. My father schooled me better than you know."

I ignored my cousin's comment and departed, stepping onto the branches of the Great Redwood and into the freezing air. But the chills that assailed me weren't only related to the temperature—whether with purpose or not, Illumina had mentioned something I had ignored, and that was Zabriel's right to his inheritance. He *was* the Prince. And prior to his exodus two years ago, he had been a good one, a compassionate young man who had been born with wings but no elemental connection. After struggling for fifteen years, he'd decided he belonged in the human world, put up his shroud and run away, across a Road that had been cursed by the Fae to end the war and separate the races; a Road that might have killed him because of his paternity.

If he could be persuaded to come back, he would make a better ruler than I would. He would be a better bridge to the humans since he shared blood with them. He would not feel like a usurper, like the Laura didn't belong to him. The line of descent said he should be given the option of claiming the throne.

Illumina might not want to give it to him. I trembled at the conviction I felt—she could calmly reconcile herself to my ascendance to the throne, but it would be another thing for her to see the Faerie Realm under Zabriel's authority. He was an outrage in Illumina's eyes, his right to rule illegitimized by his human heritage. Sending her after Zabriel was a bigger mistake than even I had appreciated, for if she found him, she would not want to bring him home and risk that he might take back what was rightfully his.

My cousin left without fanfare the following morning; I only knew she was gone because she was absent from the Queen's Court as we went about our business.

The day marked the official start of winter, and in anticipation of the approaching solstice, there were festivities throughout Chrior. Ubiqua's Court toured the sights, I beside Davic, clutching his hand for warmth. It was hard to feel frightened about the future when I was with him; the challenges of the world seemed far away. Up ahead walked my father, his wizened wings deep blue and glimmering in the sun, while the younger members of the Court surrounded my promised and me. Davic's friends laughed and jostled him, while I exchanged amused glances with my soft-spoken best friend, Ione. She was stunningly beautiful, but lacked confidence—she assumed the worst of people's stares when in truth they merely could not look away.

"Where is Evangeline?" I asked, referring to our mutual friend who had for years lived with Ione's family. Evangeline's home life was unhappy at best, her parents among those who made me thankful for my father's kindliness.

"She hasn't returned from her Crossing yet," Ione revealed, tying her long blond curls around her neck like a scarf. "I thought she'd be back around the time you left on your trip."

"She's probably enjoying her newfound independence in

the world outside Chrior. She's always been a bit adventurous. Remember when we were younger and she would disappear into the woods overnight? And the scary tales she'd make up about her encounters with mystical creatures like Unicorns and Sepulchres? Well, her Crossing is a chance to come home with some *genuine* stories, and she's going to chase after them long and hard."

"Some Fae don't come back, you know." Ione cast her eyes downward in ill-supported dejection. "Some choose to stay in the Territory."

"Evangeline wouldn't do that."

"I'm not so sure, Anya. What reason does she have to return?"

"She has more than enough reasons. For one, everything she owns is here. And her family is here—her *real* family." I took Ione's hand with my free one. "Your parents, and friends like us. And the human world is much bleaker than ours, even considering Evangeline's troubles at home."

I looked around me at the tall trees, their boughs curved like drapes from the weight of a healthy snowfall, meeting each other in a pretty pattern that framed the street. We were in a paradise, where soft lights twinkled at us from houses and businesses on all levels of the city without effuse. Slender catwalks constructed out of deadwood denoted the roadways above our heads, fittingly resembling the rings inside a tree, as far as could be seen. The city of Chrior was taller than it was wide.

"We're a more contented race than the humans. They quarrel and compete with each other, hoarding money and possessions. The Warckum Territory is an interesting place to visit, but it isn't home. For most of us, it never could be. So don't worry. Evangeline will be back."

Ione smiled, reassured, and joined me in surveying the beauty around us. But my father's words from the previous night crept to the forefront of my mind. *A number of our people are late in returning from their journeys.* Could Evangeline be in trouble? Could some injury have befallen her? Humans hunting Fae for sport was a danger in the Warckum Territory, despite Governor Ivanova outlawing the practice, and there were always the perils posed by wild animals and unknown terrain. But these were risks we always ran when entering the human world; they were no greater for her than for anyone else. Taking a deep breath, I forced myself to heed the words of comfort I had just offered to my best friend.

Our tour continued, though it was interrupted several times by spontaneous revelry about which we could hardly complain. When a line of Fae came dancing in front of us wearing booties with curled toes, loud laughter erupted. The shoes were a stereotype taken from the artwork of humans, with no basis in reality. My fellow Fae looked ridiculous in their matching outfits, chanting drinking songs and tossing elemental gifts into the air. A gust of snowflakes, harmless embers, and leaves that ought to have been dead this time of year came floating around us. Queen Ubiqua, smiling unreservedly, was the first to applaud. Davic chuckled and kissed the back of my hand, then pulled a leaf out of my hair.

A deafening *crack* interrupted the crowd's exultation, and gasps traveled like a wave through the assembly. Davic pulled me closer and I instinctively looked up, thinking that a tree branch had broken, or a rare winter thunderstorm had taken over the sky. Instead, the sea of people parted from a focal point ahead of us. I glanced at the Queen and saw her face darken, her shock replaced by malice.

In the center of the walk was a scarecrow, a vulgar manne-
quin dressed in a human military uniform and smeared with
crude oil. As the wind snaked its way down the street toward
the Queen's party, it carried with it the acrid smell of the
thick black substance, one of the resources the humans used
to power their factories. A Faerie stood proudly before the effigy he had built, while others tossed hand-sized boxes in an
ever-steepening pile at its base. In the leader's hand was the
cause of the sound we had heard—a flintlock pistol pointed
at the sky, reeking smoke.

Words like *sacrilege* and *atrocity* were murmured around us,
and I made to storm forward to Ubiqua's side, only to be
yanked back by Davic.

"Don't," he warned, turning to shield me with his body.
"Your father will handle this."

I clenched my fists around my promised's jerkin, knowing he was right. The Lord of the Law was already holding
his right arm up to signal the Queen's Blades, Fae who were
trained to use conduit blades to concentrate their elemental
magic in defense of the Realm. A dozen gathered round, wearing the colors of their elements, three each dressed in green,
red, blue, or white. My father awaited the Queen's directive,
for she had yet to speak.

"Falk," she called, addressing the man with the pistol. "Surrender yourself at once. Spare your children this shame."

"The shame lies with you!" he screeched in return.

The high and grating pitch of Falk's voice helped me to place
him. He was an outspoken member of the Anti-Unification
League—commonly known as the human-haters—and had
historically been more of a nuisance than a problem. The AUL
was an extremist group, not able to curry favor with the average

citizen, the majority of whom trusted and supported Ubiqua whether their politics stood here or there. The men stacking boxes around the effigy were Falk's sons, allies by blood, and they scrambled to the sidelines when their work was done.

Falk brandished the gun wildly, causing the Blades to tense and the citizens of Chrior to scream and cower.

"You call this an atrocity? You'd best accustom yourselves to the sight of it! Accustom yourselves to savagery, barbarism, and all manner of destruction, for they are synonymous with *humanity,* with the scum our Queen would welcome into this city!"

"Get rid of him," Ubiqua snarled to my father, and he nodded at the men and women who stood ready to carry out her orders.

The Blades advanced, and Falk, a Fire Fae, thrust out his hand, shooting a burst of flame from his palm at the effigy's head. The straw caught, and fire spiraled in a furious rush to follow the track of crude oil down to the bottom.

"Unification will be the end of the Fae!" Falk shouted, over and over until the Blades wrestled him to the ground. Then the onslaught began.

A hundred more *cracks* rent the air, only this time something was different—this time, people at the front of our ranks were falling, and people near me were on the ground. And blood was spilling onto the snow.

Despite the chaos that surrounded me, my brain organized what I knew about human weaponry, the details clicking into place like swords slotted into their sheaths. In the boxes were bullets, and the bullets contained gunpowder, gunpowder that had ignited, sending the bullets flying. Oddly, this realization sent a momentary burst of hope through me as though fate might reward my intellect by putting an end to the carnage. Then the hottest burn I'd ever felt ripped through the muscles of my upper arm. I cried out and clamped my hand over the offending area, staring in fascination at the blood weeping through my fingers. My hand slipped over the wound, and the true searing set in.

A battle cry heralded a tremor in the ground, and the crashing of water overpowered the sound of exploding bullets. Torrents washed over the crowd, knocking a number of us into the rapidly forming mud, but the shots ceased. When the volume of water slowed to rivulets, I looked toward the remains of Falk's prideful effigy and saw one of the Blades in blue kneeling with her head bowed, but it wasn't in deference to the scarecrow. She had thrown her hands upon the ground to call upon her elemental power, and had summoned the water to save us.

Only soft crying and the lowing of grief remained of the commotion. The boughs of nearby trees were bent across the street; Mother Nature had heard the call of an Earth Fae and hunched close in an effort to shield her children. Several of the Blades—those who had been closest to Falk—did not stir from their facedown positions on the ground. Falk himself lay still beneath the body of one of the Queen's men. I drew in a cold, ragged breath, but my lungs refused to work properly and forced the air back out, making me gasp. Vertigo flitted around me like an insect. I pushed myself to my feet, the mud's suction fighting to restrain me. It clung to my celebration dress, adhering the fabric to my legs and making it difficult to walk.

I searched the ground for Davic, and found him not far off, struggling to stand. Turning my head in frantic motions, my icy wet hair whipping across my face, I sought out Ione. She was also nearby, sitting on her bunched skirt, coughing and spitting out filth. My gaze went to the Queen, who had been protected by her Blades, their remaining number having moved her away from the site of the incident. My father broke through the guards and into my line of sight, his eyes manic.

"Anya! *Anya!*"

"Here!" I shouted, voice hoarse.

He rushed to my side, pulling me into a fierce embrace, and I yelped, my injury more serious than I'd realized. As he ripped open my sleeve to take a closer look, Davic and Ione joined us. Soon medicine mages and more Blades arrived on the scene to deal with the damage and the injured. Though it was clear the peril had passed, my body was levied with tremors. I tried to sit down, but my father picked me up with the ease of a young man, jerking his head for my friends to follow. I rested my head against his shoulder, for once content to let him care for me.

chapter three

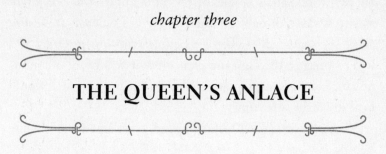

THE QUEEN'S ANLACE

Ubiqua was an emblem of righteous anger. There had been only three casualties besides Falk as a result of the previous day's protest, a miracle considering the number of bullets that had been fired, but that was three too many. The solstice celebration was supposed to represent a new beginning, not signal the end of lives. It was supposed to be joyous, and yet even now thirteen Fae, including me, lay injured in various states of severity.

My arm had required stitches, but not much fuss beyond that. While Ubiqua paced before her throne of roots in the Court Room of the Great Redwood, I sat at a long table with my father and the members of the Queen's Council, a group of eight who kept their ears to the walls and floors for rumors and mutterings in the Realm. They knew the people's thoughts, feelings and plans, and made sure my aunt stayed ahead of whatever turbulence might be brewing. Unfortunately, foreknowledge of an attack like the one we'd endured yesterday, which the people had taken to calling Falk's Pride, was hard to come by.

I sipped a mug of Sale, its primordial warmth coursing through my body with every swallow. The heat would seek out my wound and strangle the potential infection as one might wring water from a rag. The fresher the wound, the more acute the sensation—when I'd begun drinking yesterday, I'd had to breathe through the pain; now it was more of an annoyance, a tingling sensation like I'd hit my elbow. I would heal in hardly any time at all.

"The culprits?" the Queen snapped, her clasped hands white behind her back.

"Falk died during his own assault," my father replied, shuffling some documents on the tabletop. A ceremonial fire pit crackled and hissed at his back. "One of his sons was a fatality, another has been arrested, and the third is missing."

"A search is being conducted for the third?"

"Of course, but I have little hope of finding him. The bedlam across the city after the incident would have granted him more than enough opportunity to disappear. In my opinion, we won't hear from him again."

Ubiqua nodded solemnly, jaw and lips tight. She was regal in her simple brown gown, worn to honor the dead in their return to the earth, but beneath her composure roiled an anger the like of which I'd never seen in her before. It was cold and hard, the will of Nature that might at any moment quake the ground.

"Question the young man in custody," she ordered. "Find out where the missing brother may have gone. Do not stop the hunt until he is located, arrested, or driven from our Realm. So help me, I will never see innocent blood on the streets of Chrior again."

Respect emanated from everyone at the table. I watched Ubiqua closely for emotions and subconscious expressions, clues about how she was coping on the inside that might help me become as fit a ruler as she. Aside from granite conviction, I detected very little.

"The people look to us for guidance," she continued. "They are gathering at the palm in accordance with my request?"

Tthias, Envoy to the Public, confirmed this. "They await the Queen, the Lord of the Law, and her Court."

"Good. We shall meet them."

Ubiqua descended her dais and all stood. Abandoning my Sale, I followed her and the members of the Council to the ridge, only pausing once when my father placed his hand on my shoulder. I turned to him, my gaze traveling upward to meet his blue eyes, and he pulled me aside.

"You've hardly spoken since you were injured."

"There hasn't been much need."

He nodded, though his furrowed brow told me it was not due to agreement. "I don't care who you talk to—me, your aunt, Davic, or Ione. But open up to someone, Anya. Talk about what happened yesterday."

I ran my fingers over my mending injury. "Father, I'm fine. This is hardly a wound at all."

"It's not the physical I'm referring to, my dear. When mortality rears its head, no one emerges 'fine.' No one."

He squeezed my good arm and stepped past me, and I watched him go in bewilderment. I truly did feel fine, on the inside as well as the outside, but he evidently did not expect that to continue.

The Court joined us at the palm and we sang to honor the solstice and comfort one another, reinterpreting the melodies and verses of our ancestors' joyous holiday cants to infuse lamentations…eulogies. Some of us could not carry a tune, but the observance was not about perfection; it was about embracing the imperfections in each other and in our world, imperfections that had been shown in sharp relief the previous day.

The citizens who had gathered on the walk below bowed their heads until we were finished. Then, in accordance with tradition, the Queen removed the Royal Anlace from its sheath at her hip and moved to the trunk of the tree, where love-carvings from every occasion surrounded the entrance. She would add something now to honor this solstice and remember the dead. But she stopped before touching the blade to the wood, contemplated, and looked to me.

"Anya," she said, extending the Anlace. "You do the love-carving. This year, I feel it should be you."

The Court, the Council and the citizenry were all still, waiting for my reaction to color their own, but I could muster none beyond a blank, stupid stare. No one but Fae rulers had carved the Great Redwood in the past—no one but Fae rulers had ever held the Anlace. But its ruby-studded pommel winked at me, expecting my fingers to close around it and shield it from the wind. I wanted to back away, but I couldn't refuse the Queen's offer, no matter how many centuries of tradition it shattered. Superstition aside, this was a distinction bestowed upon no other. Ubiqua was telling her people to follow me, to believe in me, alas before I'd been given the chance to decide if I believed in myself.

"Anya," Davic murmured, a subtle prompt, while Ione reached out to touch my hand. Their presence gave me courage, reminding me that I would not be alone in facing my new future.

Ubiqua was compelling me with her eyes, and the Anlace still glinted in the bright winter light. Bolstered, I went forward and accepted it. In my hand, it felt diseased, as though the queasiness spreading through my body was punishment from the knife itself for seizing this power before it was due to me. Nonetheless, I went to the trunk and left my mark: half a snowflake, the top obscured by the crescent moon. The winter solstice was a long and frigid night that broke unto a fresh dawn, perhaps one with no more fear and no more needless death.

"Thank you," Ubiqua said with that tender smile of hers.

The look she received from me in return was less than friendly. She had, without warning, put me center stage in what was sure to be a controversy. I hadn't even adjusted to the idea of taking the throne; I didn't need all Faefolk discussing the possibility, wondering what the Queen's gesture meant. I held out the Anlace to her, wanting it gone, but she wrapped her hand around mine, trapping the knife in my fist.

"Keep it," she whispered.

A painful throbbing began behind my eyes, the tension spreading its tendrils to my temples, and then, like a thorned vine, to my heart, squeezing slowly. Ubiqua gave an address, but I couldn't make out a word. I left as soon as I could, not wanting to be in the presence of so many questioning gazes, not wanting to feel the anxiety and pressure they created. The Council especially was examining me, seeming to wonder how this daughter of a youngest child had risen to wear the Queen's dagger on her hip, to pilfer it away from its owner and from Illumina, its rightful inheritor.

With the sun setting, I withdrew to my alcove and closed the door behind me. Though I wanted to believe I had shut out the world, even here I could not hide from the burden my aunt had handed me in the form of a gold-pommeled Anlace.

I stalked back and forth across the main living area, covering my mouth to keep near-hysterical gasps from razing my throat. Instead, they came short and fast through my nose, and dizziness threatened to overtake me. My life was no longer mine to control. By a single deed, I had become something more than I wanted to be in the people's eyes. My aunt had known that I was, consciously or unconsciously, keeping a back door open, and without hesitation she'd closed it.

My desire to protect my voice lost out to frustration, and I screeched—one long, harrowing note that threatened to shatter mirrors and glassware, as well as my own eardrums. With a forceful but ill-conceived sweep of my arm I knocked the nearest object from the tabletop. I drew up short as it shattered, and, suddenly subdued, tiptoed around the table, glass crunching beneath my boots. Fragments in white, scarlet, and gold sparkled at me, and I slipped to my knees to survey the wreckage. The ruined decanter had been a gift from my father upon my betrothal to Davic; it had also been a much-beloved possession of my mother's, the blown red glass matching the sinuous patterns in her wings.

"No," I moaned, cradling a piece with golden inlay. I wanted to blame Ubiqua for inciting my temper, or my father for entrusting the piece to me in the first place, but my heart refused to accept excuses. I alone had broken this precious keepsake.

Filled with remorse, I had a sudden urge to go somewhere, anywhere that wasn't here. Recalling Illumina's comments about Zabriel, my self-pity transformed itself into grim determination. I could not let this change happen in my life until I had exhausted all other options. The broken decanter was an omen of the dreams that would be lost to me if I stood passively by.

I hurried to the bedroom, pulled out my leather travel satchel and shoved in the essentials—a small flask of Sale, jerky, a change of clothes, herbs, bandages, and other minimal medical supplies, an extra blanket for warmth, and my money pouch. I stripped off the brown dress I'd worn for the memorial in favor of warm leggings, a woolen tunic and my heaviest jerkin. The last thing I grabbed was a cloak. Looping the strap of the satchel across my chest, I started for the main room, but my eyes fell on the Anlace I did not want lying atop my dresser. I halted, allowing my gaze to linger. Without understanding why, I picked it up and pulled my long-knife from its sheath, replacing it with the Queen's weapon. After adding my own blade to my pack, I stepped through the doorway.

"I knew you'd be doing this."

Davic was sitting on the sofa, having come in while I was preoccupied with packing, tacit disapproval written on his face. I sighed and grabbed my bedroll, my mind searching for words that might appease him.

"I know you don't understand, Davic, but I have to go."

"You don't have to go anywhere—unless you believe there's nothing worth staying for in Chrior. For Nature's sake, you're hurt, and you just got home from your last trip! Why won't you let us help you? You ought to be here with your family, with *me,* for more than a few days. Or is that notion so insufferable?"

"This isn't about you," I snipped, wishing he wasn't between me and the door. Deciding this wasn't the time to argue with him, I made my voice more placating and tried again. "I'm sorry, but you don't know what's going on."

"I'm not stupid, Anya." He stood and crossed his arms over his chest, toeing the mess I'd made of my mother's decanter. "It's obvious Ubiqua overwhelmed you today. But is it too much to hope you might try to make sense of it around the people who love you?"

"Is it too much to hope you might trust my judgment?" My spine stiffened in irritation. I wanted his boot out of the broken glass. I knew he wasn't doing any more harm than I'd already done, but I couldn't reason myself out of an irrational reaction. Instead, I pointed at the shattered pieces.

"Stop it. Leave the decanter alone. I'm going to fix it. I'm going to fix it, Davic!"

He withdrew his foot and watched me with more concern than ever.

"I'm going to fix it," I repeated more calmly, enunciating clearly. "When next I'm home. There's just something I have to do first. I want to be with you, but there's something else I have to do."

Now that I sounded less crazed, he rolled his eyes. "Sneak out in the dead of night without telling me or your aunt or your father where you're going? Stay away for Nature knows how long? Is *that* what you have to do?"

"No!" I dropped my pack at my feet, its thump indicative of how angry I was at the assumptions he was making. "I'm going because Queen Ubiqua is dying."

The lines in his face fell away, and he paled. "What?"

"Yes. She's dying. And she didn't send Illumina on her Crossing, she sent her after Zabriel. Only Illumina doesn't have a chance of finding him—it's her first time in the human world, after all. She's essentially been set up to fail. I'm going to find him instead, bring him back here if I can and remind him what it means to be the Prince. That throne is Zabriel's, not mine. It shouldn't be mine."

"You're scared of it."

"Is that so hard to comprehend? Is that so wrong?"

"No. But you should be realistic, Anya."

He took a step toward me, and I backed away, troubled by his words. He halted, his arms falling limply to his sides.

"What do you mean?" I demanded.

"How long might it take to find Zabriel? What are the odds he'll even consider ascending the throne? I think you could better spend this time preparing for what's coming. Maybe... once you understand your duty better...it won't be so daunting."

I took several deep breaths, trying not to show Davic my true reaction to his words, his sensible, oh-so-typical-of-Davic words. He always walked the easiest path, always let everyone around him dictate who he was and what he would become. It would be easy to succumb to the way things were, easy to surrender my hopes and dreams in the face of resistance. But fighting would show me how much power I had over my own life. Maybe, just maybe, I had enough power to alter my future. Fighting to find out now was better than never knowing.

"Give me three months. I'll find Zabriel, and if he's unwilling to be the heir, I'll do as you say. I'll accept it all."

Davic studied me for a long time, aware of the finality in my tone, then released a humorless laugh.

"Three months. I know I can't stop you, so if this is what you have to do, by all means go. But after three months, be ready to give up your travels. *Please.* Be ready to stay with me and the Fae as our Queen."

I nodded once, then hoisted my satchel and went around him to the door. He stopped me with one last question.

"What should I tell Queen Ubiqua? Your father?"

"Tell them I needed time away. Don't say what I'm really

doing. And when you see Ione, tell her I'm sorry I had to leave again. I wish it were different." I smiled wistfully, willing him to understand that this last message was for him as much as it was for my best friend.

I looked at the open door before me, then backtracked to touch his face, drawing him close for a kiss. This was the last we would see of each other before my fate was decided. His hands drew our bodies together, compressing us into one being.

"I'll be waiting for you," he whispered.

I pulled away and walked outside, about to begin the most important journey of my life.

Chrior was alight with lanterns, and the square where the massacre had occurred was decorated with gifts, elemental and otherwise. People were still assembled there, singing and seeking each other's consolation. The Queen wove among them, taking her subjects' hands, offering words of sympathy and encouragement, and acknowledging their respectful bows. With her silver hair flowing behind her, she was the living embodiment of a spirit of comfort. Keeping to the fringes, I bypassed the crowd, and, in my earth-toned garb, vanished into the trees.

It wasn't long before I was alone in the darkened woods, with only faint echoes of music and voices reaching my ears. Much louder were the snapping of sticks and the rustling of bushes caused by animals that hunted at night, and animals that were hunted at night. Without daylight to show the sprawling landscape, the walls of the forest could have trapped and confused me like a maze. But this was the route I always took to leave Chrior, and I knew it well enough to trust my feet to follow the path, despite the unsettling thoughts that were chasing around in my head—Evangeline's stories of the supernatural creatures known as Sepulchres, together with images of Falk's missing son, who could be hiding in these woods, waiting to inflict vengeance for the deaths of his family members.

Snow crunched beneath my boots, and it was impossible to move quietly, which grew more vexing the closer I came to the Bloody Road. I had warned Illumina about hunters, a far more realistic danger than the ones I was envisioning. Just as humans mounted the heads of bucks on their walls like trophies, so had the wings of Fae become badges of accomplishment for some of them, and near the Bloody Road was a popular place for such brutes to stalk. I could put up my shroud, but if I were seen crossing the Road, any hunter who happened to be looking would know I was no human. Humans could not survive the Road.

My heart beat faster than normal, and it was futile to try listening to logic instead of my darkness-fueled imagination. This was the reason I tried not to travel at night. It was good Illumina had departed in the morning; hopefully, she would not have been plagued by such fears.

Fed up with the way my footsteps reverberated, I took off my cloak and shoved it in my pack. With my wings uncovered, I flew to a branch, opting to hover tree to tree in silence until I had passed the Road. I looked down on the battle site as I went, seeing how pure and undisturbed the snow was, and listening to the wind. It always whistled strangely through this part of the forest. I scanned the area ahead of me, my Fae sense of sight, like my hearing and smell, heightened in comparison to the abilities of humans. Observing no signs of danger, I dropped to the ground, relieved to be past the crossing. Now I could leave the forest and its secrets behind.

The next instant I would relive for years to come. Had

I adopted my shroud and hidden my wings before falling, things might have been different. Had I been quicker, or less eager, I might have been spared.

I heard the whipping of an arrow and turned toward the sound an instant before the weapon pinned my wings, both of them in one sharp strike, to the tree I had just vacated. Gasping, I tried to tug free, succeeding only in tearing the membrane of my wings. As excruciating pain seared through me, I shrieked and braced against the tree, trying to keep the strength in my legs. If my knees buckled, I would hurt myself further. My vision was darkening, filling with spots, but then fingers gripped my chin, turning my head, and my eyes focused once more. I was staring at a human, a broad, grimy, stringy-haired man. "Got one," he muttered.

There was movement behind him—more humans, one woman amongst four men, her feminine aspect revealed by her manner of dress and her slight silhouette in the moonlight.

The man holding my chin pushed my head against the tree. He fitted something made of leather around my wrists and snapped it tight so I couldn't move my hands. My arms felt weak under the immobilizing pressure of the shackles. Then he nodded to one of his comrades.

I knew what they were going to do. Frenzied, I tried to draw on my elemental connection to the water, asking the snow, the ice, the sap in the trees, the water in the earth, to rise up and shield me. But unlike the waves that had rushed to the aid of the Queen's Blade to extinguish Falk's Pride, no response was forthcoming. Usually, a Faerie's pain and distress alone summoned an elemental reaction, but I had nothing. Not a single bead of sweat answered my call.

I cowered, waiting for the second man to deliver fortune's

justice. I was helpless, so completely helpless in that moment. All the independence I was so proud to possess, all the dignity and potential others saw in me was gone. I was no one in the eyes of these humans, and I could not stop them from degrading me, defiling me, robbing me of what made me Fae.

A halberd the comrade carried.

A halberd he brought down on me not once, not twice, but three times in order to sever my wings from my body. Cutting through the bone near my back to make sure he didn't miss a shred of the light and delicate but fiercely strong appendages.

I didn't feel the pain especially. I was numb. Shocked. Agony was like an echo, loud and close, but strangely detached from its source, strangely detached from me. I fell to the ground, staring at the Road I had been so careful about navigating, aware that the hunters were leaving with their prize. Someone was wailing; no, I was wailing. The woman approached and I rolled away from her, not knowing what else she could do to harm me, but clawing at ice and snow in an effort to avoid her. She leaned down behind me and stroked my hair.

"Shhhh," she whispered in my ear, and then she, too, departed.

I was bleeding. Nature, I was bleeding. Not only from my back, but from my chest, my arms and my bound hands. Magic was seeping out of me, black and excruciating. I could see it drifting away. The magic that would let me pass the Bloody Road to reach home again.

Leaving dark red smears in the snow, I kicked and flailed, trying to catch the intangible substance, my one unrecoverable hope. But only unconsciousness came to me, and when it did, I prayed it would hold on to me forever.

chapter four

TRAPPED

"Zabriel, what happened?"

"Nothing."

"Then I suppose you woke up with your wing torn like that."

"Maybe I did."

"Just because your father was a human doesn't mean you can lie to me."

Whether the Queen had intended it as an insult or not, it was clear from Zabriel's stormy expression that the comment had stung. Fae nature was complex: we could confuse, evade, and conceal the truth, but we could not tell an outright lie. It was the price we paid for our magic. Dishonesty was a trait reserved for humans.

The medicine mage had already departed, having stitched the wing, leaving Zabriel hunched on the edge of his bed, his arms wrapped around his legs, hugging them against his bare chest. I sat on the floor in the corner of the room, wishing to be invisible. But I couldn't leave, for I was the one who had brought this injury to my aunt's attention. I was the one who had been frightened.

"Mind what the mage said, Zabriel," she warned, watching as he rose to find a shirt. "You're not to fly for two weeks."

"I don't care."

He shrugged on a tunic, wincing as his bandaged wing found its way through the fabric.

"Well, I do," Ubiqua responded, tone biting. "For Nature's sake, Zabriel, what is wrong with you?"

My cousin's dark eyes shot to his mother. His eyes were his father's, but he had the unusual silvery-blond hair with which Ubiqua had been blessed when she was younger, only his was wild, reflective of the apathy of a lonely soul.

"What's wrong with me?" He laughed humorlessly. "What's wrong with you?*"*

"What do you mean?"

Zabriel slammed the door of his clothing cabinet shut, the color high in his cheeks. "You married a human! That's what I mean. How could you do that to me?"

Ubiqua was taken aback, and her incredulous laugh showed it. "Is that what all of this has been about? Love, if I hadn't married your father, you wouldn't even be here!"

At Zabriel's volatile silence, she abandoned sarcasm and continued, "I loved your father. And I was—and am—trying to bring two cultures together. That *is why I married him."*

"Selfish reasons. Political reasons. Did you ever think about what kind of life I would have? Growing up with no father, belonging nowhere?"

"You belong here."

"I belong nowhere. *And certainly not here."*

My eyes widened as he headed for the door, but Ubiqua summoned a great wind using her connection to the air, and the door slammed shut before her son could storm out.

"I knew life would not be easy for you," she seethed, her jaw tight in an effort to suppress her anger. "I knew controversy would follow you, and no part of me thinks it's fair. But there's a greater purpose at

stake here, and you represent that cause. It's what your father wanted. It's what all the people want, even the ones who are afraid. You have to be brave enough to face that!"

Zabriel swung around, his eyes burning. "Brave? You don't think I'm brave? I was brave enough to try cutting off my wings, Mother. I would have succeeded, too, if Anya hadn't been so afraid to see me in pain."

Ubiqua's mouth opened in horror, and I cringed in my corner though she wasn't looking my way. But Zabriel was unrelenting. He was fifteen, no longer as intimidated by a parent's power, and his gaze bore into hers, his fists clenched at his sides.

"I'm tired of it," he said, shaking his head. "I'm tired."

Ubiqua, still stunned by what she had learned, didn't immediately respond. But it soon became clear from the straightening of her shoulders and the tilt of her head that she would react as a Queen, not as a mother.

"You don't have the luxury of being tired, Zabriel. You have sacrificed so little compared to what I have done, and what your father did for you. He died trying to cross the Road to be with you. He wanted to raise you in a land where he would have been a foreigner, an enemy. He would have endured all that for this cause, and for the love of you. Have you no respect for his memory?"

"I don't remember him, Mother. There's nothing to respect. He died before I was born trying to reach an empty throne in a place he never belonged. This Realm was not his, and it isn't mine, because I am not a Faerie. Nor do I want to be!"

"Zabriel! Zabriel!"

He was gone. And I didn't think I would ever see him again, because I knew he had decided. He'd talked about leaving for long enough, and now it seemed the time had come. No ties of blood or of magic could *keep him here, just as even the wedding mage's aura had not been able to see Zabriel's father safely across the Bloody Road.*

And that aura had been stronger than the one Davic and I shared.

Without magic in one's soul, one could not enter the Faerie Realm.

Now the hands of the lonely and the angry that had caressed me harmlessly so many times would take hold if I went near them.

Davic could not bring me home.

Ubiqua could not bring me home.

Unless I found Zabriel, Illumina would rule. And her hatred of humans would be fiercer than ever. With men like Falk as her lieutenants, she would bring us once more to the brink of war.

Everything we peacemakers had accomplished would be as waste, and the Faerie people would be corrupted.

I woke with a gasp, one side of my face pressed into something soft and wet. Disoriented from the vision, from memories and reality forced upon me in sharp relief, my breath came fast. Clarity, unfortunately, did not.

At first I lay motionless. My head ached, my body burned and I didn't know where I was or how I had gotten there. Slowly I comprehended that I was in a room instead of outdoors: a room with a wardrobe, a bookshelf, a rocking chair, and a bed; a bed on which I was resting. And my pillow... It was wet with tears.

I never cried—when emotional, I broke decanters and argued with people and ran away from the things that scared me. I hadn't cried since my mother's death three years ago. Yet the proof was in front of me.

Unable to get my bearings this way, I pushed myself up, lifting my chest and stomach from the mattress. The movement set torture upon my back, and it all returned to me—the attack, the halberd striking me again and again. I was feeling the pain now that had felt so distant then.

I collapsed, a moan slipping through my parched lips. The sound drew someone's attention, and the door into the room opened, light breaking in like a beacon, but with my hazy vision I couldn't make out the person who entered. I fumbled to protect myself, hoping to somehow go unseen, only there was nowhere to hide, and no way I could run. The person's weight depressed the mattress, and I heard a female voice.

"Mother, she's roused!"

Dropping her volume, she whispered to me, "You'll be all right. We're taking care of you."

Unable to fight the pain, I lost consciousness, once more wandering in fevered dreams.

I stood at my mother's side, her body already prepared for the funeral pyre, and said one last goodbye. Her red hair was as beautiful as ever, and had far more life than the rest of her. Slowly I reached out to touch her hand, then squeezed it hard enough to bruise, not believing she couldn't feel it. When she didn't respond, I lost the grounds to protest her burning. She'd been a Fire Fae in life, and it was fitting to return her to the element that had chosen her. She was wrapped in a white cloth so the assembly wouldn't have to watch her skin blister and slip away from her skull like petals spreading from the heart of a flower. I knew it was happening anyway. I'd once accidentally burned myself, and the sting had remained far longer than any cut. The licking of flames against flesh was agonizing.

My lips were dry with cold as my father put his arm around me, blocking the wind, and led me back to the Great Redwood from the assembly's gathering place in the distant woods where we Fae said farewell to our dead. Our party was quiet, Ubiqua walking in front, her hand on Zabriel's back, Illumina and her father behind us. My cousins and I were now equal—there were three parents between the three of us. We had each lost one.

When the bittersweet reception was under way in the Redwood, I left my father's side to sit alone on the ridge, watching Faefolk below console one another with food, drink, and warmth. Before long, someone came to sit beside me—someone with whom I could talk.

He handed me a mug of hot Sale, as usual having none himself. He wasn't allowed to drink it. I took his offering gratefully, the gesture enough to bring tears to my eyes on a day when tears desperately wanted to come. But I sniffed, bit my lip, and dried my face of the few that escaped.

"I know," Zabriel said, leaning against the bark wall behind us with one arm resting on his knee. "You're not supposed to be sad. You're supposed to be strong for your father. Being sad will make things worse for him."

I nodded, not stopping to digest what he'd said. Thinking was what gave birth to self-pity, and self-pity served no purpose.

"That's stupid, Anya," he said, and I turned to him in instant agitation, one powerful emotion easily transforming into another.

"And what would you know about it?"

He hung his head, thick hair falling forward. I shouldn't have snapped at him. He was a year older than I was, and the heir to the Faerie throne. For these reasons and more, he deserved my deference and respect. But rather than put me in my place, Zabriel's big dark eyes met mine of green and he scooted closer to embrace me.

"It's okay to be sad, Anya. It's okay to be angry, even at your mother. People leave us when they have no business leaving. And your father can handle himself. He's got the Queen, the Council, and his friends to look out for him. He doesn't need you to be strong."

I tucked my head against my cousin's shoulder. Maybe he was right.

Maybe for just a minute I could let the weight of my own loss settle suffocatingly on my chest. Maybe I could take a moment and gasp and sob.

I gazed ahead, my eyes dead like my mother, tears leaking down my face and onto Zabriel's jerkin.

"What's it like to only have one parent?" I stammered, my emotions inhibiting my speech. "I want to know before I wake tomorrow."

"The rest of the world doesn't change. Only your world. And you wonder why this happened to you and not to somebody else. For a while, people will treat you like you're a puzzle with a missing piece, until they realize the piece missing was just part of the background, not part of the actual picture." He rested his chin atop my auburn hair, and I waited, hoping he would say more. "You don't need that background piece to be what you're supposed to be, Anya, even though it looked nice and everything. You're still whole. Even though it doesn't feel like it."

Struck by a realization, I sat up and gazed into his face.

"Then you don't feel whole, either?"

He was silent for a long time, his thoughts unreadable.

"No, I don't. My father shouldn't have died. If he loved me so much, he shouldn't have risked his life by trying to cross the Bloody Road. He should have known I would need him, and taken better care of himself. He should have known that without him, I'd be alone here in the Faerie Realm, singled out as the only person with human blood. But you, Anya, you're not alone. You'll never be alone."

I clung to him and believed his words because I needed to, not caring whether or not they were realistic.

And now I'd become one of those people who, like Zabriel's father, should have known better. But that insight had arrived too late, leaving me at the age of sixteen trapped outside my home, wingless, broken, and very, very alone.

★ ★ ★

I was calm when next I broke through the fog of my misery and came to full wakefulness; perhaps my subconscious mind remembered the pain that movement had caused me earlier. I glanced around the room, still lying on my stomach, again taking in the simple, almost meager furnishings. Hand-knitted throws and pillow covers were the only bursts of color, and the blankets that warmed me were threadbare in places.

It took me a moment to notice the young woman sitting in the rocking chair near the foot of the bed. She looked to be about my age, her dark brown hair tied into a ponytail with a ribbon of navy blue to match her tunic. One leg was tucked up beside her, and she was holding a book, its cover obscured by a paper wrap. I wondered what she was reading—and from whom she was hiding the title.

"What are you going to do with me?" I rasped. I didn't know how long I'd been slipping in and out of awareness, but the dryness in my throat and mouth suggested I hadn't had a good drink in days.

My visitor startled and looked up.

"Nothing, unless you have something to suggest?" With a wry smile, she stood from the rocker and approached, nestling her book in the crook of one arm. "How do you feel?"

"Like you're lying."

I couldn't afford to be civil. The human world was a notorious place, and for all I knew, she could be the woman who'd stroked my hair, condescending to offer me comfort after my wings had been taken.

"My father found you when he was hunting," she patiently explained.

"Is that the story he told you?"

My eyes darted toward the door. It was evening, and faint light drifted through the cracks between it and the frame. This young woman's father might be waiting for me in the next room with his halberd. I tensed, yearning for the Anlace, for the power I felt when I held it. But my body was so weak I doubted it would have provided me with a viable defense.

She laughed. "It's not just a story. My father hunts deer and rabbits. *For food.*" Noting my glare, she sobered. "Sorry. I shouldn't make fun."

She was looking at my back, though the blankets and the light fabric of a nightgown hid my skin. The humans must have removed my jerkin and shirt to cleanse my wounds. Where were they now? Where were the Anlace and my satchel?

"I'll get you some water." The young woman turned to the bedside table and filled a glass from a pitcher, and I gingerly propped myself up, though water wasn't the drink I desired. What I needed was Sale. "You must be hungry, too."

I didn't have much of an appetite, taut as my nerves were, but I let her think what she wanted. I downed the water, however, which felt like sand as it made its way through my constricted throat.

"May I have a look?" she asked, taking the glass from me. She meant at my back, where my wings had been, and she was hesitant about her question.

"Why? Curious?"

"No. My mother and I have been caring for you since my father dragged you home."

She was curt, and I lay down again, feeling rebuked. After setting her book on the table, she peeled back my coverlet, lifted the nightgown and removed a bandage moist with blood, pus, and, from the smell of it, alcohol.

"It's not as bad as it could be," she announced, not a hint of revulsion in her voice, slightly increasing my confidence in her skills as a healer. "Let me get a new bandage."

She left the room, but I hoped she would return and light the lamp on the bedside table. The sun was setting and would soon leave me in darkness, something I didn't want to face, not with my heart and body feeling so unwieldy. I clenched my jaw as apprehension filled me, bubbling toward panic at my circumstances, and I sat up, not wanting to suffer the pain but needing something upon which to fixate. While the hot flare that shot through my body was enough to make me gasp, I was thankful to discover that this time it did not bring me close to tears. My caretakers knew what they were doing. Grasping the blanket, I held it in front of me to cover my breasts, and consciously slowed my breathing.

The moments ticked past, and I glanced at the bedside table and the book with the paper wrapping. I picked it up, lifted the paper cover and glanced at the title: *Crime and Punishment in the Warckum Territory*. Not what I'd been expecting, and probably "borrowed" from the man of the house. For some reason, humans tended to view women as less capable than men, while Nature—and by extension Fae—made few such distinctions. Hearing the creak of the floorboards as someone approached the room, I replaced the cover and returned the book to its former position.

When the young woman entered with a basket of medical supplies, she was not alone. A girl, perhaps eight or nine years old, carried an armful of wood, which she stacked next to the hearth. She wore a constrictive dress that was not conducive to such work, reaffirming my previous thoughts on human conventions.

"My name is Shea," the older of the two girls said to me. Their matching brown hair and brown eyes left no doubt they were sisters. "And this little helper is Marissa."

Marissa smiled at me as she stirred the flames back to life… flames that Davic could have summoned to his palm in an instant, that would have glowed before his sharp features; added hints of gold to the silvery color of his eyes; created a halo around his head of black hair. Hair through which I loved to run my fingers. Hair that I might never touch again.

"If you're feeling well enough," Shea resumed, oblivious to the deep sense of loss that was coursing through me, "we can wrap these bandages around your chest and you can join us for dinner. What do you say, um…?"

"Anya."

"Anya. What do you say?"

I needed to eat before I withered away. With the depletion of my magic, my body felt heavier, more cumbersome, and even this short period of alertness had sapped my energy. But I shook my head, huddling against the wall.

"I won't go out there. And I'll hurt anyone who enters this room aside from you."

Marissa froze, then finished her work by the fireplace and scurried out the door. Shea examined me, eyes dark as flint.

"I understand you have no reason to trust me, but no one in this house wants to harm you. You would be dead if it weren't for my father, Anya."

She said my name like a challenge, and we continued our staring contest until she broke eye contact to set down the basket, her hard words and attitude in stark contrast to her youthful appearance. She lit the lamp at last, illuminating the side of the room where I sat, then pulled up a chair and silently rewrapped my wounds. The alcohol stung, but thankfully the process was short.

"I'll bring your meal to you," she offered, coming to her feet. Before I could decide on the right words to thank her, she retrieved her book and departed.

The room was somehow colder without her, and lonely, even though it was only minutes before she reentered to deliver my food. Still, I did not ask her to stay. The humans didn't need to know that I was mentally as well as physically weak.

Shea left to join her family, and I ate. Then with the feeble burst of strength the food provided, I stumbled to the wardrobe. My footsteps felt thunderous, and every time my body swayed, its momentum felt impossible to stop. It yearned for the floor, and a near-silent moan of misery escaped from me. Catching the door of the wardrobe, I hauled myself out of my hunchbacked posture, my arm smarting where Falk's bullet had struck me. It was by far the lesser of my injuries, but it felt like barbs hid beneath the skin regardless.

I swung open the wooden armoire door and fell to my knees before my pack. Reaching farther back, I found what remained of my bloodstained clothes. Beneath the washed but warped cloth lay the Queen's Royal Anlace, solid, sharp, eight inches long and easy to conceal. I took it with me as I crawled to the bed, dragging along my satchel, and I tucked the blade under my pillow. Then I sorted through my possessions to see what supplies, if any, the humans had left untouched. Except for my travel papers, which I would need to venture farther into the Warckum Territory, everything was in its place: my jerky, my medical supplies, my long-knife…and my flask of Sale. I held it in a shaky hand, watching the firelight take stabs at the small container's metal exterior as if attempting to drain what it contained. Sale—the drink that rejuvenated my people, speeded our healing and made us warm inside and strong out. I struggled with the cork, then put the bottle to my mouth, ready to endure whatever it took to regain my vitality. But at the last instant, I stopped and frantically scrubbed my lips clean of the amber liquid. Sale killed humans. The elemental magic of the Faerie drink overpowered their systems and poisoned them. Without my wings, was I now human? Would Sale kill me, too?

Wanting to test my nature, I held my hand over the pitcher on the bedside table and concentrated my life force, reaching for the water it contained, trying to connect with it; but there was no kinetic tingle in my fingers, and no accordant ripple on the water's surface. If it weren't for my eyes, I would have believed the pitcher empty.

"I'm right here," I keened, my voice an urgent whisper. The liquid continued sleeping, as though I didn't exist. Was this how it felt to be dead? Not a part of anything, cut off from your soul? Was this what it was like to be human?

Biting my lip, I buried the flask of Sale in the bottom of my pack, trembling at the possibilities it held. That drink could either heal me or leave me dead, and I wasn't yet willing to take that bargain.

I lay down in bed, my fist clenched around the hilt of the Anlace in readiness to attack or defend. The vile thing—it was the reason I'd left Chrior. It had frightened me away. Hot tears stung my eyes. I never cried. *I never cried.*

I needed to return to the Road, now stained with my blood as well as the blood of the humans and Fae who had died in that final battle. I didn't know how many precious drops of magic might still be inside me, but I had to try to get home before all of it was gone.

★ ★ ★

I woke after only a few hours with a pounding head and a body-wide ache—even in sleep, my muscles had been tensed to fight. I unclenched my jaw, rubbing my cheeks and temples, and scanned the humble room. Everything was gray in the morning light. It was so early even the colors were asleep.

A clock was ticking somewhere in the house, but there were no other noises. To all intents and purposes, I was alone. Reflexively, I tried to unfurl my wings to hover to the wardrobe, only to be met with intense pain—the nerves in my back were reaching out to make contact with appendages that no longer existed, and the resulting spasms, while they could probably have been called phantom pain, felt as real as the stabs from any blade.

I stepped softly, not wanting to wake anyone. My balance remained uncertain, forcing me to concentrate on my footing as though I were a young child. Teasing open the wardrobe door, I shuffled through the clothing stored inside—dresses of wool and linen in bland colors hung side by side, none of which would do for traveling. I knelt and slid open a drawer to find leggings and warm woolen tunics.

I threw off the nightgown the humans had lent me, thinking too late of my injuries as my shoulder blades protested the movement. Nausea undulated through me, and I swallowed hard, closing my eyes and steeling myself to vomit. Luckily, not enough remained in my stomach from the previous evening's meal for me to suffer this indignity. I heaved a few deep breaths, then stood before the mirror to get dressed.

Bandages still swathed my chest and back, bandages I nervously unraveled before the looking glass. Part of me thought it would be wiser not to know, but the dominant part wanted to see the evidence, to see what those hunters had done to me, as though my fortitude in facing the reality of their actions might be some revenge against them. But at the first glimpse of my stitched and broken skin, the sickening proof of an involuntary amputation, I hurriedly rewrapped the wounds. *Not now.* I couldn't deal with it now. Getting home was all that mattered.

I put on the clothes from the drawer, assuming they belonged to Shea, for they fit me reasonably well. She was shorter and stockier than I was, but my boots came far enough up my calf to cover the few inches of bare skin left by her leggings, and the bagginess of the tunic was negligible. After gathering my weapons and my bag of supplies, wincing away the ache of every minute addition of weight, I crept out the bedroom door.

In the main room of what I had deduced was a simple house, the ticking I'd heard was amplified. The tall clock that stood across from me was made of rough wood, but it had been carved with care, and had probably been built in the same space it occupied. Chairs sat before a barren fireplace, a rickety table took up most of the room and a kitchen crowded the only available corner. The floor was of raw wood, uneven beneath my boots.

The light outside was growing warmer, and I hastened to the front door. This was my best chance to return to Chrior. But before I could touch the handle, the door swung inward and a cold wind gusted over me, it's prying fingers finding every fault in my woolen armor while it ushered in a man so tall he cast me into shadow. I could smell blood on him, blood and gunpowder, and the memory of Falk's Pride flashed in my head as though I were in the square again, shaking in the mud, counting the fallen. I cowered and stumbled away from him, losing the more feeble balance I had without my wings.

As my shoulder hit the wall, my back revolted, and I screamed. I would not pass out; I would not give up this opportunity to reach my homeland.

The man was growling something in a deep voice and coming closer, looming over me. I fumbled to protect myself, and my hand fell upon the Anlace just as his fist closed around my arm. I lashed out, and his yowl told me I'd made contact. Taking advantage of the moment, I scrambled to my feet, abandoning my pack. My heart was rising into my throat, and I gagged as I lurched through the door. There were more voices emanating from the house now, and I thought I detected the sounds of pursuit. Without looking back, I fled for my life in a direction I hoped would lead me to the Bloody Road.

chapter five

BLACK MAGIC

I ran and ran, winter birds cackling above my head, the snow turning my hands and wrists red with cold every time I stumbled and collapsed. My eyes fought for clarity as the pain in my shoulder blades stretched and intensified, but I pushed on through the maze of trees and the pristine white ground. There was pressure in my skull, and a persistent buzzing that after a time muted my hearing and reminded me of how little I'd eaten in the past— What had it been? A few days? A week? Nature forbid it had been more.

When I recognized a cluster of saplings, my energy was renewed, and I pulled myself up a slight incline, certain I was going the right way. Footprints soon marked a path, and that path led me to the eerily vacant Road, bookended on either side by walls of inhospitable thicket. I stopped, panting heavily, listening to the wind as it whistled a warning song through the hollow tunnel of trees.

My blood, perverting the snow, was the sole aspect of the landscape that was not gray or white or muted green like the needles of the trees, making its color all the more horrific. In a frozen, crimson grin it engulfed the base of the balsam against which I'd been pinned and stained the trunk, leaving me to surmise that it could not have been long since I'd been injured. Not the weeks I had feared, at any rate. It hadn't snowed since I'd been attacked.

I dropped to the ground and gazed across the Road, squinting into the heatless sun. I saw a glimmer on the other side, a haze of beauty I would have called an illusion, except that magic was visible to those with a sharp enough eye. This gave us an advantage in recognizing one another in the Territory, for even a Faerie's shroud was not imperceptible if one looked closely enough—light reflected from the supposedly empty space at Faefolk's backs. Rarely could a human identify us, not with their diminished senses, but a few were gifted enough to spot the signs. What I saw across the Bloody Road were the lissome currents of Nature's purest creation, currents of magic I longed to feel against my skin.

My heart seemed to pitch forward, and I stood, allowing my feet to follow. I lurched onto the Road, concentrating my thoughts on Davic, urging whatever magic remained in my body to trace the path of our promise bond and bring him to me. Although something fluttered under my skin, it was trapped there, stretching its fingers but unable to claw free. My bond with Davic may have still been in existence, but it floated without direction, just as my steps took me no closer to that beguiling sunrise in which everything was discernible— Ione's diamond-blue eyes, my father's gentle, reserved voice, the halo of righteousness that Ubiqua wore like a crown, Davic's easygoing smile. My body was weakening, my hope and resolve with it, and the very essence of my being wanted to emerge from my chest. How easy it would have been to let it, to sink into obscurity and give myself back to the earth and its elements.

Then a tingling sensation invaded my arms, beginning in the tips of my fingers and growing in strength. It wasn't painful, even as a similar sensation conquered my legs, and I watched in awe while my hands fell away like sand slipping through an hourglass. But when the sensation invaded the core of my being, striking me with the weight of an anvil, fire roared up my throat. I threw myself backward, but I was too far from the human side of the Road. I would die here on the frozen ground, and though I had contemplated death moments before, facing it in truth now was the surest proof that I wanted to live.

Through my terror, I felt pressure under my arms, and then, miraculously, the burning receded, and I was left a shuddering heap in the snow. Magic, black and cloudy, leaked from my pores, called back to the Road and its home in Chrior. I looked up to see Shea sitting beside me, examining her hands as the elusive substance slithered between her fingers, her disgust and confusion unmistakable. She tried to wipe her palms in the snow, her pallor a reminder that she, too, would have felt the retribution of the Road.

"It's magic," I murmured, watching the inky film evaporate from her skin. "It's leaving me. Forever."

"What the hell were you thinking?" she erupted, startling me with her vehemence as she snatched my collar with both hands. "You can't go home. If I hadn't followed you here, you would be dead, do you understand that? Home is *gone,* Anya. There's no going back."

Her dark eyes were red rimmed, and she pushed me away to swipe at them. Underneath her cloak she was in her nightclothes, and she was shivering uncontrollably despite the sweat beading on her brow.

"Why do you care?" I bristled, crawling to my knees, guilt

spurring my raging emotions. "Why would you risk your life for me?"

"Maybe I'm stupid! I mean, I don't even know you. But you must be important to someone. Or at least, someone is important to you. You kept saying his name in your sleep."

"Davic," I whispered.

"No. The name you said was Zabriel. Now tell me, would *he* want you to do this?"

Shea stood and offered her hand to help me up, and the heat of shame blazed across my face. How could I have forgotten, even during these dark days, even for a moment, the reason I had left Chrior? Ubiqua's throne was not mine. Now it could never be, and the need for Zabriel to be found was greater than ever. With no way to communicate the new urgency of the situation to my friends and family in the Faerie Realm, the task was mine and mine alone. I had to locate Zabriel and convince him to return or else intercept Illumina and enlist her aid.

I trudged through the snow behind Shea, the two of us no longer speaking. Despite the pangs that afflicted my back, I dreaded our arrival at the cabin. The man I had injured was probably Shea's father, and he would likely not be pleased at my return. He confirmed this the moment I walked in the front door. Half a foot taller than me, he made me feel insignificant as he gripped me around the arm, tightly compressing the abrasion left over from my bullet wound. I winced but said nothing. He escorted me to the bedroom I had been occupying, his lined and weathered face wearing a glower that warned me not to challenge him. With a shove, he sent me inside before closing and locking the door.

Rooted in place, I listened to his footsteps recede. My breath came fast and short, swirling about me in the stagnant room, and I resisted an urge to hammer on that door and break it down. I wanted Shea's father to know I was a fighter, and not anyone's prisoner. The irony was that my own actions had made me a captive—this morning, the lock had not been in use. Dragging my feet, I paced, ignoring the ache in my back and the hunger pains in my belly for as long as I could. Eventually, I noticed my satchel near the wardrobe—thankfully the man of the house had let me keep it.

I stuffed myself with jerky and stale bread, then, overcome by fatigue, I dozed for a bit. When I woke, I resumed my pointless pacing, on occasion considering the window as a way of escape. But I ultimately discarded the idea; I was not yet well enough to be on my own. If this morning's misadventure hadn't served as enough proof, I could feel sticky discharge—blood, pus, I couldn't be sure—fighting through my bandages. I needed to recover here for several more days before I'd be ready to travel. Then I could run far away from that man whose dubious intentions fed the wellspring of dread in my chest.

As the day crept toward night and the shadows lengthened, the bedroom walls seemed to close in on me. Just when I thought I could stand the isolation no longer, the lock clicked and the door swung open, revealing the man I had injured. He considered me, then moved aside, inviting me into the main room with a sweep of his arm. I stepped past him, the heavy, appetizing smell of cooking meat combating my wariness, though I remained conscious of every shift in my host's formidable form.

An entire family sat around the table, attired in pristine dresses. Their soft murmurs of conversation fell away at my approach and all eyes came to rest on me. There was Shea, of course, her chocolate hair pulled away from her face, and Marissa, the little girl who'd brought firewood to my room. There was another girl, a middle sister, and a blond-haired, blue-eyed woman whose fork and knife shook from the tension in her hands. Her lips trembled, but no words came forth, giving the appearance of extreme cold despite the heat from the fireplace and stove, which made the house almost overly warm. The raven-haired man, who was no doubt her husband, stepped around me to retake his seat, the strength he radiated more than enough to make up for any frailty in her.

Shea stood, her chair grinding against the floor. Her tightly fitted blue linen dress struck me as impractical, although a pouch and knife at least hung securely from her belt. Motioning to each family member at the table in turn, she made introductions.

"Anya, this is my sister, Magdalene. Marissa, you remember. And these are my parents, Thatcher and Elyse More. Everyone, this is Anya."

I forced myself to smile, the expression feeling stiff and unnatural, as though the corners of my mouth needed to be oiled. This was not surprising, considering the day's events and the dearth of friendly greetings I was receiving. Marissa gave a tiny wave, but it was clear from her wide, watchful eyes that she still thought I could hurt her, and Magdalene glanced between her parents as though she might get in trouble for acknowledging me. Elyse wouldn't meet my gaze, while Thatcher, the only one among them with probable cause to distrust me, stared at me unrelentingly. I was grateful when Shea dragged an extra chair into place at the table—standing made me feel overly conspicuous, a target for fear and hatred. I sat down, perched on the edge of my seat—ironically as if I could take flight.

"I believe I owe you an apology," I said, catching sight of a bandage wrapped around Thatcher's thick forearm, his crisp white shirt rolled above it.

I concentrated my attention on my hands, not pleased with the timidity my discomfort was breeding. When no response was forthcoming, I braved raising my eyes to his. They were dark like Shea's, though there was movement within them, calling to mind rolling fog, his traveling thoughts practically visible. It might have been wise to show deference to him, but I sensed a test to see if I could be intimidated. Pride swelled, and I refused to give ground. I was royalty, and fortitude was inbred. He could stare forever, and I wouldn't look away.

At last, Thatcher More smiled—not widely, but it was a smile nonetheless.

"It's all right. I might have done the same in your position." He shifted his gaze to his food, stabbing some venison with a knife, his manner a touch too nonchalant. "That's an interesting weapon you used against me. It burns as much as it cuts."

I braced myself, his reference to the Anlace making me uneasy, although the rest of the family obliviously began to eat.

"An irritant of some sort, I presume," he went on. "Derived perhaps from poison sumac or ivy?"

I neither confirmed nor denied his assumption; I couldn't have addressed it even if I had been disposed to do so, for I wasn't sure of the answer. The blade could have been infused when it was forged with the sap of a poisonous plant—Fae knew how to construct weapons in that manner. But the secrets of the Queen's Anlace were known only to the Queen, and I did not occupy the throne.

"I should also thank you for saving my life," I said, redirecting the conversation to insert a small test of my own. "Although I'm not sure why you did."

"You needed help, and I was in a position to give it. There's nothing more to be said on the subject. You can stay with us until you're well enough to travel. I assume you had some destination in mind at the time you were ambushed?"

"Yes, I did." I glanced around the table. Shea alone showed interest in our exchange, reading my expressions and her father's with subtle looks. The rest of the family was engrossed by the food on their plates, the younger daughters mirroring their mother's behavior. At risk of pushing my luck, I forged ahead with Thatcher. "But I won't get far without my travel documents."

Thatcher cocked one eyebrow, then reached into the pocket of his coat and tossed the leather envelope containing my passport onto the table in front of me. I reached to pick it up, and caught him examining the ring I wore on my right middle finger. The likelihood was slim that he would recognize it as a royal ring, but it was obviously valuable. What if he demanded it in payment for his kindnesses?

"Forgive me for going through your things," he said as I drew my hand and passport beneath the table. "It's important for me to know who is in my house, so I took your papers."

My eyes narrowed. "And did they put your mind at ease?"

"Yes, despite the fact that they're falsified. The forger's work was excellent, and those types of illicit documents usually come with prudent priorities."

Everyone stopped eating, stopped moving, their forks poised in midair. Thatcher, however, merely reached for more bread, signaling that the meal should continue.

"Forgery doesn't bother me, Anya, assuming that's your real

name. I expected it. The law may be pro-Fae, but that doesn't mean the people of the Territory are. It's safer for Fae to have documents that say they're human, just like it's safer for some humans to carry papers that don't reveal their true identities or professions. Mind you, I'm not talking about criminals here. But the fact that your passport is such a good forgery tells me you're well connected. And I can see now that you're well-enough raised."

I bristled at the condescension in his tone. "Why wouldn't I be?"

He settled back in his chair, one hand forming a mighty fist. "Faerie."

The word rolled off his tongue like a curse, and whatever tenuous trust I'd begun to develop in him vanished. *Fae-hater,* my brain insisted. But that couldn't be the case. Not only had Thatcher's family kept me alive, they'd been regarding me as a guest, providing me with a bed, fresh clothing, and food. Yet something in this man's background made him mistrustful of my people. Though common sense screamed that I let the matter rest, I responded in kind, my tone a match to his.

"Human."

Again the world seemed to come to a grinding halt, the only sound the clock against the wall, its ticking absurdly loud. Then Thatcher laughed, pushing back the heavy hair that fell to his cheekbones.

"Well, I'm glad that's out of the way." He raised his glass to me in salute. "Feel free to move around the cabin and join us at the table for meals. Shea can lend you some suitable clothing for dinnertime. But keep in mind, knives should only be wielded when eating."

The jest broke the last of the strain between us, and though

I still felt like an unexpected and not entirely welcome guest, the family's usual dynamic emerged at last. Marissa and Magdalene, it turned out, were little chatterboxes who enjoyed sharing the events of their days. Thatcher doled out the next morning's chores to his daughters as though they were gifts, and Elyse smiled and nodded politely along. Discarding caution, I ate hungrily, Shea sending encouraging looks my way. I was certain she had vouched for me with her father, and while I was appreciative, it did not erase the reservations I held. If she hadn't endorsed me, how would he have dealt with me?

When everyone had eaten their fill, Thatcher rose from the table to settle into a worn-out armchair by the fire. As he packed and lit his pipe, Shea cleared the dishes, and Elyse herded the younger children to their bedroom. I stood uncertainly by until Thatcher took note and called for me to join him. I grimaced, thinking the interrogation that had started at dinner was about to resume. Nonetheless, I obliged, pulling a kitchen chair close to the fire.

"Did you get a look at who hurt you, Anya?" he asked, motioning toward my back.

My jaw tightened, his interest resurrecting my fear that he might be a Fae-hater. Perhaps he was worried I might be able to identify one of his friends.

"No, only that it was a group of five men and one woman."

Thatcher took a pull on his pipe, considering. "I've on occasion seen a group of men in this part of the forest. I've never thought of them as Fae hunters, though. They do contract work for clients, but I suppose if the client wanted a unique trophy..." He trailed off and tapped the stem of his pipe against his chin. "I've never seen a woman with them. I imagine it could have been the client. Some want to experience the thrill of the kill, if you know what I mean. Fetishists and the like."

My stomach churned at his choice of words. Were we Fae viewed as no more than animals on this side of the Bloody Road? How could someone take pleasure in the agony that had been inflicted on me? The notion was faith-shattering. Maybe the Anti-Unification League's rhetoric that we should keep this kind of evil locked outside our borders had more validity than I had been willing to consider.

"I don't know any of the men personally, mind you," Thatcher continued, showing no sign he was aware of my reaction. "Not the sort of folks I choose as associates. But it is a group of five, related in some way, brothers or cousins, I think."

Silence fell, for I did not know how to respond. His matter-of-fact tone sounded a hollow note against my painful reality.

"Dad," Shea interjected, coming to lay a hand gently on my shoulder. "Can we talk about something else?"

Thatcher sat up straighter in his chair and cleared his throat. "Of course. I don't suppose it does any good to rehash the past. But I am sorry, Anya, for what those men did to you."

His expression was sincere enough, confusing me all the more. He was a difficult man to read, and I couldn't determine if his inquiries came from a desire to know because he was somehow involved, or if he was trying to help. In the end, I remained guarded and on alert.

"Go on to bed," he finished. "I'm sure you're tired." Meeting Shea's eyes, he added, "I suggest you and your mother redress Anya's wounds. Her outing this morning won't have done her back any good."

With a nod, Shea went to retrieve the medical supplies

from a cupboard over the stove, and we walked together to the bedroom.

"This is your room, isn't it?" I asked upon entering, drawing my conclusion from the clothing I had found in the wardrobe.

"Yes, I'm sleeping in with Marissa and Maggie for now. Dad thinks it's best this way."

"Afraid I'll devour you in the middle of the night?"

"Good guess."

"I was joking."

"So was I." She grinned and pulled out some fresh bandages. "Let me have a look at you."

I sat on the bed, turning away from her so she could methodically re-dress my wounds. At some point, Elyse came in to observe Shea's progress. After a few minutes, she set a vial on the nightstand.

"For pain," she explained, not quite meeting my eyes. "Two sips should dull any discomfort you might have."

"Thank you."

A smile flitted across her lips. "You're quite welcome. Now get some rest. It's important to a speedy recovery."

She gave her daughter a nod to tell her she was doing fine work, and departed.

"There," Shea declared, coming to her feet. "Now be a good patient. Even with that juice from my mother, this is going to take a while to heal. Every time you tear it open, you set yourself back."

"Got it. And thank you."

She went to the door, then turned about with an impish smile. "Just so you know, I expect you to return every stitch of clothing you take from my wardrobe."

I laughed, and she disappeared from sight, leaving me feeling relaxed for the first time all day.

I was awake early enough the next morning to hear Thatcher leave the house. I scrambled to my feet, dressing as quickly as I could given my sore muscles and ungainly movements. After grabbing my cloak, I passed through the cabin and out the front door, wanting to take a look around. My excursion to the Bloody Road hadn't allowed me much opportunity to scout the area. Seeing tracks that led into the woods, I assumed Thatcher was gone, and trekked around the side of the cabin.

It was cold, the morning light so faint it appeared to cast a shadow. I stepped slowly, cautiously, the crunch of my boots resonant in the still woods. I rounded the corner to reach the back of the home and came to a stop, eyes on a shack nestled among the trees. It was roughly built, giving the impression it had been erected in a hurry; it stood as though its knees were drawing together. I approached, my senses on full alert. If Thatcher knew more about the hunters than he had revealed... what might be hidden inside? Were my wings or those of other Fae tacked along the walls?

The door was locked. Glancing upward, I saw a small window set below the eaves. Without thought, I flexed the muscles that would have unfurled my wings, but instead of rising off the ground, I doubled over in pain. As the agonizing stabs in my back diminished, I mentally berated myself. Straightening, I spotted a sturdy branch that overhung the building. If I could drop from it onto the roof, I could lay flat and lean over the edge to get a look in the window. Plan in place, I scaled the tree, gritting my teeth against the stretching and tightening of my back muscles. When I was high enough, I inched out onto the branch and swung down, hanging by my arms as I prepared to drop.

"What the hell are you doing up there?"

My fingers went to jelly and I barely managed to maintain my grip on the branch. Thatcher stood ten paces from the shed, holding a string of rabbits in one hand, his hunting gun in the other. His expression was a blend of incredulity and displeasure that made him look like he'd taken a drink of sour milk.

"I, um…I can't fly, so I climbed the tree." Unable to lie, I told the truth, although not the complete story.

"I see." He rested the butt of his gun against the ground and rubbed his brow. "For what purpose?"

"To get higher?" My arms aching, I let myself drop onto the roof. I landed more heavily than I'd expected, gravity apparently the only element that had an interest in me, and I nearly tumbled backward into the snow below.

Thatcher snorted. "Looks to me like you wanted to get on top of my shed."

I gave him a sheepish shrug. "There's a good view from up here."

"A view of what exactly?"

When I didn't respond, he hoisted his hunting gun so the barrel rested against his shoulder and took a few steps closer.

"In case you're interested, that window's too dirty to see through. So I'd suggest you get down. There's nothing of interest for you here."

Embarrassed, I slid to the edge of the roof and dropped to the ground, wincing upon landing. As the cold wind erased some of the heat from my cheeks, I labored over what to say. Did I owe him an apology? Should I risk asking him about the things that troubled me?

"Just go back inside," he ordered, stepping past me to un-lock the shed.

I nodded, but didn't move, trying to perceive his character, to understand his motives.

"Out with it," he abruptly directed, hand on the door latch. "What is it you want to know?"

I bit my lip hard and met his eyes. "Are you or were you a Fae hunter?"

He laughed shortly. "I won't hold that question against you, Anya, but no, I don't hunt your kind. I find the sport, if you want to call it that, barbaric."

I offered him a weak smile, for I believed he was being hon-est. "Thank you. I'm sorry for doubting you."

"No harm done." He gave his string of rabbits a shake. "Now go inside so I can skin these."

I headed back to the house, knowing I should feel better about Thatcher in the aftermath of our encounter. But some-thing about his behavior still made me uneasy, and I finally realized what it was—he hadn't opened the door of the shack while I was there.

Everyone else was up when I reentered the cabin. Shea cast me a quizzical look, but did not ask where I'd been, nor did I volunteer any information. I simply began to help with break-fast preparations. Human cooking wasn't much different from Fae cooking, despite the ridiculous gossip in Chrior that they ate their food raw, drank blood and cannibalized one another when their hunger grew too great.

Thatcher came inside in time for the meal, and we all ate to-gether, though I made no attempt to participate in the family's small talk. When I was finished, I retreated to my bedroom and kept to myself the rest of the day, wanting to concentrate my energy on healing. I was recovering more slowly than I had from any previous injury, and I could feel the anxiety this bred building within my body. My attempt to cross the Road had made me acutely aware that I was in a race against time. I needed to find Zabriel and bring him to Chrior before Queen Ubiqua died; and I needed to do it before the last of my magic was gone. The Bloody Road would kill me—that much was certain. Likewise, the Sale tucked in my pack would kill me if my nature was fully human. But if I had a sufficient trace of magic left in my being, the healing power of the drink might be enough to see me safely back to Davic and the Faerie Realm. My plan was to find Zabriel, then consume the Sale, leaving my fate to the amber liquid in my flask.

In the late afternoon, after preparations for the evening meal were well under way, Shea took me into her bedroom and offered me a choice of two dresses to wear for dinner. While I didn't have a problem changing out of my leggings and shirt, I wondered what was behind this particular convention.

"If you don't mind my asking, Shea, why does your family change into fancier clothing for this one meal?"

"It's my dad's idea. He wants us to end the day in a more civilized fashion. And my mom says it's a way to remind us of our manners and how we should behave in polite company."

I stared at her in confusion, wondering what *polite company* they expected to encounter out here in the wilderness.

Ignoring my expression, Shea smiled and tossed me the dress at which I was pointing. "You might say it's one of our little quirks."

She returned the garment I had rejected to the wardrobe, selected a different one for herself, and headed for the door.

"I'll leave you to change, and then you can join us. Don't

worry—you'll get used to our traditions. Besides, it's actually kind of nice to feel like a princess, however briefly."

Shea departed, and I lay the dress down on the bed to examine it. It had more buttons and ties, ruffles and bows, than anything I'd ever worn before. Celebratory gowns in the Faerie Realm were loose and flowing, although they were often decorated with beads or bits of colored stone.

I scratched my head, not even sure which side of the garment was the front. Putting it on was sizing up to be more challenging than learning to read the night sky. Eventually I managed it, and I was pleased that my biggest worry hadn't materialized—the dress wasn't too tight around my chest. I'd pictured having to face the family the entire meal, maneuvering my body in order to hide the open back that was necessary to keep pressure off my injuries.

I went to examine myself in the mirror on the wall, and hardly recognized the young woman staring back at me. The hair and eyes were correct, but I looked more like a doll than a living, breathing person. I combed my fingers through my loose auburn hair, then entered the main room to take my place at the table.

This evening's meal consisted of a delicious rabbit stew served with thick slices of bread. The younger girls talked animatedly, and the overall conversation was punctuated with murmurs of "please" and "thank you." Maybe this custom wasn't such a bad one, after all.

When everyone had eaten their fill, I helped Shea with the dishes, while Elyse did some mending and Thatcher drew his younger daughters around his fireside chair to entertain them with card tricks and shadow puppets. When Elyse rose to usher the girls to bed, Shea cast several glances at her father before finally posing a question that I sensed ran counter to her better judgment.

"Dad, will you be hunting again soon?"

"Yes, I want to fill the shack before the weather gets harsher. Why do you ask?"

"I want to go with you. We'll bring back twice the game."

Thatcher perused his daughter while he slowly exhaled his pipe smoke, and the tension in the room ratcheted upward. Knowing my presence was no longer needed, and likely not wanted by Shea's father, I stole to the bedroom. I left the door open a crack, however, and peered out at the argumentative pair.

"You haven't held a gun in months," Thatcher asserted, giving Shea the same look I had received from him before he had locked me in the bedroom the previous morning: an assiduous stare that suggested something precious to him was being threatened. "I only taught you to use a pistol in case of an emergency. Besides, your mother needs you here."

"She can get by without me," Shea replied with a touch of belligerence, taking a few steps toward him. "Maggie and Marissa are old enough to help her with the cooking and the laundry. You can easily teach me to shoot a hunting gun— I'm tired of being in the house all the time."

"The alternative would do more than tire you." There was danger in Thatcher's voice, and I had the impression he was no longer talking about hunting.

"It might *interest* me. But never mind that. What is it you always say? *You can't put a price on my safety.* But you can put one on my freedom. You don't have any problem with that."

Agitated, Thatcher shifted position as though to get up, only to decide against it.

"Shea, you're not coming with me. If you're bored, I'll ask your mother to find more for you to do."

With a disgusted groan, Shea stormed toward the bedroom. Remembering at the last moment that I occupied it, she halted, her face scrunched with deliberation. Then she knocked upon the wood. I waited a few seconds before inviting her in, not wanting her to know I'd been eavesdropping.

She closed the door and strode to the bedside table, where she struck a match to light the lamp. I watched her carefully constructed expression for signs that I could broach the topic. Then I realized she wouldn't have come in here if she didn't want to talk.

"How much is the price on your freedom?" I ventured.

Shea laughed bitterly, the emotion not really directed at me. "I knew you'd be listening. I kind of hoped you would be, if I'm honest."

"Then...what do you want from me?"

"I want to know if you've ever thought someone—someone who's always been right before—was wrong. About a very important matter."

I laughed more loudly than she had. Buying a little time, I went to my pack and unsheathed the Anlace, examining the blade. Had I ever questioned someone who was wise and powerful? Ubiqua had handed me her crown. Yet where was I now? Lost in the woods, lodging with human strangers, unable to return home. I should have trusted my aunt's judgment when she had commanded me to stay in Chrior; I should have listened to my father and Davic. All of which made me the last person who should be giving advice on this subject.

"Why are you asking me?"

"Do you see anyone else I can ask?"

It was a fair point. The Mores lived an austere and solitary life. "Yes, I've thought that. It's the reason I crossed the Road. It's the reason I ended up that bloody mess your father found."

Shea paused, digesting this information as she chewed on a thumbnail. "Where were you headed before the hunters attacked you?"

"Nowhere, potentially everywhere. I'm looking for a cousin of mine. He ran away two years ago, but his mother is dying and she wants to see him before she does."

I stopped, deciding Shea didn't need to know that the stakes were higher than this, that my cousin's mother was the Queen and that the fragile politics of two races hung in the balance.

"What did she do to chase him away?"

It was a blunt question, and a rather bizarre reaction to my story. Shea assumed automatically that Ubiqua was to blame for Zabriel's flight, while I'd never considered that the Queen might be at fault. Feeling it wasn't her business, I didn't respond.

"Sounds like an important task," Shea continued, undisturbed by my evasiveness. "I hope your luck improves from here on out. Lord knows, this family has little to spare." She laughed self-consciously, as though she had revealed something she should not. "But thank you for being honest, Anya. I haven't had someone be straight with me for a while now. And I haven't had a friend in even longer."

I didn't bring up the fact that, discounting the time I'd spent unconscious, she'd known me for a total of three days. But then, who was I to reject her offer? She'd saved my life but a day earlier, at risk of her own. There was hardly a better foundation for building trust.

"You can have your bed back," I volunteered, thinking it

no longer fair of me to inconvenience her. "I can sleep on the floor."

"No," she said, almost recoiling at the thought. "For one thing, you're hurt. And for another, you're a guest. Now let me have a look at your wounds."

I carefully removed and hung the dinner dress, then let Shea care for my back. After her departure, I crawled into bed, though I left the lamp lit, suspecting she might claim the floor in here rather than her sisters' room. I heard her come in a little while later, and allowed myself a tentative smile. The barriers between us were falling away. And maybe I needed a friend as much as she did.

chapter six

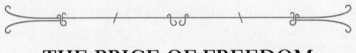

THE PRICE OF FREEDOM

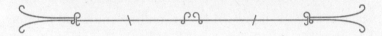

Over the next few days, I joined in more of the family's activities, helping with meals, playing with the younger girls, and assisting Marissa with her reading and letters. While I had never before spent such intimate time among a human family, I couldn't help but think their lifestyle peculiar, even for their species. They lived far away from any human settlement, from any neighbors, ostensibly preferring to keep their own company. Thatcher, in particular, continued to make me nervous. From what I could tell, he hunted, cleaned, and repaired his weapons, chopped firewood and prowled the area around the cabin as though on alert for intruders. He appeared to have no livelihood, and even when he relaxed in his armchair with his pipe in the evening, his gun was never out of reach.

My initial assessment of Elyse as timid was a gross understatement, though the reason for her meekness remained unclear. I had assumed she was afraid of her husband, but he never raised his voice or hand to her. Instead, it seemed she was afraid of life itself.

Even though I was on the road to recovery, my body felt heavy and sluggish. I probably weighed less without my wings, but my inability to hover made me feel rooted in a way I never had before. It felt like the earth was working against me, like it was trying to prevent every step I took. This sense of discontinuity with the natural world was demoralizing, and never more apparent than when I bathed and was surrounded by water—water that, when I'd been in possession of my elemental connection, had hugged my skin gently and kept me warm like a silken coat. Now it pressed on me, pulling at me and making it hard to breathe. Before long, I dreaded submerging myself in the treacherous substance. With no ability to communicate with it, the water's raw power was evident, and I feared the element that had once been my closest ally.

I was outside one afternoon with Shea, fetching firewood, when three sharp *cracks* punched through the air, startling us both.

"What's going on?" I asked, clutching the Anlace that was sheathed at my hip. I scanned the trees, which hugged the More house almost constrictively, on alert for a threat.

"Gunshots," Shea said shortly. "But not from my father. He doesn't hunt this close to home. Something's wrong."

She patted the pocket of her coat as though to check its contents, then rushed into the trees. I sprinted after her, suspecting I would be more effective in a conflict than she would be—I wasn't wearing a dress, and would be calmer if Thatcher was injured. Besides, she'd saved my life when I'd run off.

Shea was faster than I expected, or else I was slower, and again I bemoaned the loss of my wings for handicapping me. I caught up to her when she halted, confused about which way to go, for snow was falling and the footprints Thatcher had left on departure were gone.

"Follow me," I said, mentally re-creating the gunfire in my

head. The shots had so abruptly broken the quietude that I could still hear them ringing in my ears, and I thought I could guide us closer to their point of origin. Eventually the sound of a male voice reached us, and we jogged toward it, taking care in case there was peril ahead. We broke into a ring of trees, but heard no sounds other than the dull rustling of an animal in the distance.

"Dad!" Shea screamed, forgetting caution, and I rushed to quiet her, pressing my palm across her mouth. I'd already been attacked once in this forest. What if the voice we'd heard belonged to one of the contract hunters about whom Thatcher had told me? She tore my hand away, her eyes darting frantically about.

"What are you doing out here?"

Thatcher pushed his way through the underbrush and into the small clearing, dragging a dead buck. Close on his heels was a burly, bearded man with blank eyes and a hunting gun resting against his shoulder.

Shea pressed her hands against her cheeks. "I heard the gunfire. I thought something bad had happened."

Thatcher's heavy brows dove toward his nose. "And if something had happened, what were you planning to do about it?"

Her jaw clenched tightly, Shea withdrew a silver pistol from her coat pocket. "I came armed."

Though I instinctively shied away from the weapon, I looked at her with new respect. I did not know how much skill she had with the gun, but at the very least she was willing to defend herself. Thatcher glanced at the burly hunter, who was stroking his beard as though he was bored or hard of hearing. Somewhat more relaxed, he then shook his head at Shea, although he did not otherwise address his daughter's readiness to do battle. Instead, he motioned to his companion.

"I ran into Gray here. He was tracking this buck and I helped him. We're going to split the meat back at our place. Let's get going."

Thatcher and the hunter headed off, Shea trailing without objection, but I hesitated. Our flight from the cabin had taken us in a direction opposite the Bloody Road, into a part of the forest with which I was not familiar, and a strong sense of apprehension stole over me.

I stood still, barely breathing, the hair on my arms and the back of my neck prickling. Glancing around, I soon found the reason for the feeling. Every tree in the ring that surrounded the clearing was scratched, as though marked by a wild animal. I pressed my memory, but couldn't recall the markings being there when Shea and I had arrived, though my senses, lacking magical enhancement, didn't pick up peripheral detail in the same way they once had. Even more disconcerting, each set of scratches was level with my head. Shea was shorter than me, Thatcher and Gray taller, and no scratches announced their heights. It was as if some creature had made me a crown.

A drop of icy water landed between my shoulders and slipped down my spine, and I jumped, breaking free of the trees' bewitchment. Trying to will away my misgivings, I followed the trail of deer's blood until I caught up with the others.

Once back at the More residence, Thatcher and Gray took their kill to the shack that stood behind the house. Shea and I went inside and sat before the fireplace in the main room, warming ourselves in silence, and I tried to assess the damage I might have done to my back with today's exercise. While I couldn't be sure, it felt like I was bleeding, and I wanted to scream in frustration at the sluggish rate of my recovery. Behind us, Elyse busied herself with dinner preparations.

"You two are quiet," she said, and I jumped at the sound of her voice. She was so meek that I never really expected her to have one. With a huge sigh, Shea came to her feet, leaving her coat and pistol on the chair.

"It's nothing. Just Dad. He wouldn't take me hunting with him and now he's angry because I followed him."

Elyse nodded, curling her body around the stove as if she wanted to become part of it, to disappear entirely. What was it about this family? Shea was brash and defiant. Elyse acted like a horrible fate awaited her every time she spoke. Thatcher continually scrutinized me, presumably thinking I had an ulterior motive for being there, when he was the one who had saved my life. If all humans lived like this, they were a stranger species than even Illumina or anyone in the Anti-Unification League realized.

We washed and changed into dinner dresses, then ate without Thatcher, who was still helping Gray divide the meat. The younger girls had already been sent to bed by the time he entered, and Elyse hastened to prepare him a plate of food. But it wasn't food that interested him. Waving his wife away like she was a buzzing fly, he called for his eldest daughter.

"Shea, grab your coat and meet me by the shack."

Shea's head jerked in her father's direction as he once more left the house, and she quickly obeyed his bidding. Elyse, looking uncomfortable, went to check on the younger girls, while I retreated to the bedroom, leaving the door partway open in case father and daughter returned. I was determined to find out what was happening, and didn't trust that Shea would tell me. Crossing the room, I carefully opened the window in the hope that my sharp Fae hearing would enable me to catch their conversation. I knew Shea was in trouble, but I wasn't sure why.

At first, all I detected were rumblings; then Shea's voice became strident.

"I want out of here! You can't keep us locked up forever."

"Locked up?" Thatcher's voice rose ominously. "You think this is a prison? Try hard labor, Shea. Try servitude. Try paying back a debt to society."

"A debt to society? No, you owe a debt to that government man. And I could respect you for fighting that debt. But you're not fighting. You're running, and you're dragging your family down with you."

"I will not have you speak to me like that! I have done everything to keep you safe—"

"Everything except own up to what you did."

A long silence followed Shea's acidic response, then I heard the cabin door open and Thatcher's thunderous footsteps upon the floor. The door closed, telling me that his daughter had likewise come inside. I hastened to the other side of the bedroom, intent on continuing to eavesdrop, this time watching, as well, through the crack in the door.

Thatcher saw his daughter's gun out of the corner of his eye, still lying on the chair. The fire at his back was feeble, and I could hardly see what he was doing as he strode across the room. Then he handed the silver pistol to Shea, the bullets clutched in his fist.

"You don't need these," he growled. "I'm letting you keep that gun because it was your grandfather's, but don't push me, Shea."

"Take the bullets. Take whatever you want. That doesn't change a thing." Shea tore off her overcoat and flung the gun on top of it. "You're not listening to me. I told you—I want out of here. Stop being a coward."

Thatcher stared, openmouthed, and I tensed, thinking he might strike her.

Shea hoped he would hit her. I knew it the moment Thatcher chose to admit defeat, stumbling away from her, and her posture shrank with telltale guilt. Still caught up in her anger, she looked to be on the verge of tears, but managed to whisper an apology. Turning from her father, she strode into our room, opening the door so forcefully she nearly knocked me over, then closing it with purpose.

"Why doesn't telling the truth feel better than this?" she demanded, gripping the handle with a white-knuckled fist, the slam of the front door in the background telling us Thatcher had left once more for the shed.

"What is the truth, Shea?" I thought I needed to know—both for my protection and for her sanity.

She bit her thumbnail, deliberating, then words poured from her mouth like a dam had broken.

"My father crossed someone in Ivanova's pocket. It was a while ago, over two years now. When he ran, he made his family collateral—any of us can serve his sentence, seven years in the Governor's service if we're caught. My father sold our freedom to keep his own."

"What did he do?" I asked, struggling to grasp the situation. What could anyone do to earn seven years of servitude? This explained why Shea had been eager to be friends with me—a family on the run had no chance to form bonds.

"It's no secret that Ivanova is a narcissist. There are three social classes in Warckum—the Governor's friends, the surviving, and the slowly dying. His friends sleep on feather beds and eat imported delicacies, while the lower classes waste away. We thought fortune was at last smiling on us when one of the *feather beds* commissioned work from my father. He was a woodworker in Tairmor, and all it takes is a smile from one of Governor Ivanova's men to change your entire existence in that city. But then Dad objected to some part of the project and didn't deliver. I've never known exactly what went wrong, but it's obvious he didn't make a wise decision."

I remembered Illumina's rants against humanity, and was filled with a new appreciation for my aunt. Ubiqua had never punished my cousin for disagreeing with her. She could have. Certainly Illumina's words had never been welcome, and her father's ties to the AUL had always been of concern. The Queen could have silenced my cousin's opinions and objections, just like Thatcher More's had been silenced.

"So your father was convicted of some offense against the government?"

"Not convicted, just sentenced," Shea scoffed. "When we heard a warrant had been issued for his arrest, we fled to Sheness. We hoped to bribe our way onto a ship and leave the continent and the Warckum Territory for good, but the port city was handling an influx of armed forces. So we headed inland, all the way east to the Balsam Forest, where people worry more about crossing the Fae than the Governor's laws. Here there are no patrols. But here there is also no *life,* at least on this side of the Road."

She slumped to the floor on her makeshift bed, tossing one arm across her forehead.

"I can't stay here any longer, Anya. You're the first person I've seen who's my age in over a year. You can't imagine what that's like. Stagnating. No friends, no community, no opportunity to grow up. I've been thirteen in my parents' eyes for two years now. I feel sick here. I'd rather die than stay."

I couldn't blame her for resenting Thatcher. My thoughts went to my own father, the Lord of the Law in Chrior, not a man who lacked for courage. He wanted nothing more than for me to be happy, regardless of the cost to him; he'd said as much the night of Illumina's departure. And yet I could find reasons to be bitter toward him. He'd distanced himself from me after my mother's death. He'd supported Ubiqua in choosing me as her heir, even though he knew how I would react to it. He hadn't been a perfect father. But he would never have forced me into isolation, into loneliness and inertia the likes of which Shea was describing.

"But exactly what punishment is your father fleeing?"

"My father's never been open about his crime or the potential punishment, so I don't know what they'd do to him if they managed to arrest him. But I can't bear the thought of my sisters enduring punishment in his place." Her voice was harsh, anger once more rising. "How can he claim he's protecting us when his actions have made us all vulnerable to imprisonment?"

"I can't answer that, Shea. He must think keeping the family together is the right thing to do."

She sighed heavily. "Maybe with the right sum of money, the Governor would consider my father's debt paid. But what do you pay a man who already has everything?"

A long screech interrupted our conversation, and we both jumped. Realizing its likely cause was a tree branch brushing across the window, we broke into laughter, as though that would prove there was nothing to fear. The diversion was welcome to me—I had no answer to Shea's question. Could Zabriel's grandfather really be so pitiless? Or did he just go along with whatever recommendations his advisers made?

As tiredness took hold of us, we prepared for bed, and I finally had a chance to examine my wounds. To my dismay, my back was once more crusted in blood. While Shea applied salve to the injury, I satisfied some of her queries about my life in Chrior. I described to her the way the city was constructed and told her how it felt to have an elemental connection: that the earth was your friend when you had none, that it was there to protect you and you it. I tried to bring Ubiqua, my father and Illumina to life with my words, leaving out the detail that we were royalty. The only person I didn't mention was Davic, for I doubted I could speak of him. The ache in my heart was too great for words. All that was left of our promise bond was a curiously vacant sensation, a void in my chest that was ever growing, expanding, trying to fold me up inside it. Maybe Davic felt something, too, but he was safe in Chrior, and I didn't think he would identify the feeling unless he attempted to contact me, something he had sworn not to do for three months. He was my best hope for help from my people, and he might not apprehend I was in trouble until a quarter of a year had passed.

A rattle of the window interrupted my ruminations, and Shea stood to check that the latch was secure.

"That's odd," she said, brushing aside the curtains and peering through the glass. "There's no wind tonight."

I went to her side and gazed into the darkness, scanning the trees and the shadows they cast. Everything was peaceful and still, the snow sparkling in the brilliant light of the moon and stars. There wasn't even a whisper of a breeze to explain the noises we'd heard.

"You're right. No wind. Maybe it died down."

"That fast?" Shea's voice was tight, and worry lines furrowed her brow.

"I don't know." I opened the window and glanced beneath it for tracks, but couldn't make out much in the gloom at the base of the house. "I don't see anything."

"Do you think I should tell my father? Maybe that hunter—Gray—told the authorities where to find us."

"It's not someone coming after your family, Shea. Humans can't cross the snow without leaving footprints."

"A Faerie?"

Though my first reaction was to say no, for there was little reason for my kind to travel this far into an unsettled part of the Warckum Territory, I hesitated. Falk's missing son, for one, might have a desire to leave inhabited areas behind. I squinted and leaned farther out the window than before, my eyes darting back and forth to examine the ground. Might he be stalking me? I was a perfect target for his revenge, which he was sure to be pursuing. Trying to banish the paranoia that roiled inside my chest, I reminded myself that Fae looking for medicinal herbs might likewise travel far afield. At last I answered Shea, who was watching me with furrowed brow.

"I doubt it was a Faerie, although it's not impossible. Most likely it was just an animal. We can have a look around tomorrow if you want."

Shea nodded, though the fear did not fade from her eyes.

"There are some Fae who work for the Governor, you know," she warned.

After refastening the latch and tugging the curtains into place, we slid into our respective beds, and quiet descended upon the room. But try as I might, I couldn't fall asleep, for an unexpected resentment of Zabriel was growing inside me. Why had he left the Realm of the Fae? How could he have voluntarily abandoned the things for which I was yearning, the things I would miss forever if I couldn't get home? And since his decision to desert the Fae had at least been voluntary, why couldn't it have been *him* to lose his wings and *me* to retain the option of returning to Chrior? Unable to reconcile the morality of these thoughts, I closed my eyes, my head beginning to ache. I wasn't aware of falling asleep when a memory so vivid it felt like a living experience exploded across my mind.

The Great Redwood was filled to capacity with warm bodies and joyful noise, so full that not an echo could be heard despite the tree's magnificent size. It was our beloved Queen Ubiqua's birthday, and she celebrated with food and revelry for all Faefolk, preferring to give rather than to receive. Her blue eyes scanned the crowd, and she smiled graciously, nodding greetings here and there. But when her gaze landed on a particular individual, her smile became as bright as a sunbeam.

At my side, Ione tracked my aunt's line of sight. We were holding hands, and she tugged at my arm to draw my attention to Zabriel. His grin was vivid and contagious; he loved celebrations, the opportunity to meet new people. His dark brown eyes were alive with the fever of excitement, and his presentation was exquisite. Some of the Fae doubted he would be able to command our people because of his lack of an elemental connection, but it was times like these I realized how wrong the naysayers were. To see him was to want to be near him; to speak to him was to fall under his spell. He needed no magic for that.

Ione's face was flushed, but not from the warmth or the Sale. My cousin was trim, well dressed, and well-groomed, undeniably handsome with a crown of berries around his head, and Ione was in awe of him. In the spirit of the evening, I shoved her toward him; to her mortification, she bumped into his shoulder.

Zabriel steadied her, glancing automatically behind her. When he caught my eye, I winked, and he loosed his warm, rich laugh. He took Ione's hand and spun her in a dance. Her halo of blond hair shone in the light. Girls watching whispered and fidgeted enviously.

A moment later, hands playfully covered my eyes, blinding me. A kiss to my cheek and an arm that spun me into an elegant twirl left no question who was responsible—in Davic's hands, it was impossible not to dance well.

Dipped into a graceful back bend, I gazed upside down at the line of thrones and chairs against the wall of the Redwood. My father raised his eyebrows at me, and I giggled, pointing him out to Davic when he pulled me up and into his arms. My dance partner grinned shamelessly and sent a dramatic bow in my father's direction. The Lord of the Law chuckled and waved a hand of dismissal toward us.

The chair next to my father's was empty, though it had earlier been occupied by Enerris, Queen Ubiqua's brother, who was probably mingling with the revelers. One more seat down, my cousin Illumina watched the party with wide, cautious eyes. She would not leave her chair, let alone dance.

"Anya!"

Immediately recognizing Ione's voice, I took Davic's hand, leading the way through the crowd to my best friend. Though she hadn't been particularly loud, something in her tone had pierced through the gleeful noise and struck a chord in me. She needed me.

At first glance, everything seemed fine, but as I came closer, I saw that Zabriel was in conversation with Enerris. The Queen's older brother was silver haired and wizened, taller and more physically imposing than my cousin, and his presence cast Zabriel's untouchable glow of youth into shadow. I didn't know what was going on between uncle and nephew, only that it was unlikely to be good.

"You're not a boy anymore," Enerris said to Zabriel in his deep rumble. "The people are beginning to remark upon your qualifications as a ruler."

"I'm aware of that," Zabriel replied, irritation in his voice. Enerris seldom let him forget.

"Then take the opportunity to show that you are one of us."

Zabriel's face grew suspicious. "And what would you suggest, Uncle?"

Enerris smiled and extended a bark mug to my cousin, and I knew with a seizing of my heart that Zabriel would not refuse. I glanced wildly about for someone who could stop him, then moved toward him myself. Extending an arm to ward me off, my cousin took the mug in his elegant, long-fingered hands. Before I could speak, he raised it in a toast and put it to his lips, downing the Sale in one draught.

"Zabriel!"

The scream cut through the celebrations, bringing the music to a discordant halt. Confused murmurs whirred through the Redwood, and a ripple began in the crowd as Faefolk made way for the Queen and her Lord of the Law. Enerris backed away from his nephew, but Ubiqua caught his movement.

"Seize him!" she ordered, and my father obeyed, twisting Enerris's arms behind his back while the Queen hastened to her only child.

"Mother, I'm all right!" Zabriel averred, horrified by the scene.

Her eyes wild, Ubiqua struck him across the face with the back of her hand. Zabriel staggered, his dark eyes shocked and betrayed—his mother had never, never hit him before. But this time he had gambled with his life. Queen Ubiqua had forbidden him ever to consume Sale, afraid that with his human blood, the drink would poison him. In an hour, or two, or twelve, he could be dead.

Ubiqua clutched at him in a panic; then her wrath found Enerris. I saw in her cold expression that forgiveness of her brother would never come, and I leaned against Davic as his arms encircled me protectively. This night, the world had changed.

chapter seven

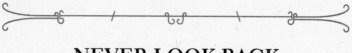

NEVER LOOK BACK

.I rose early the next morning with determination in my heart. I would drive myself mad with thoughts like the ones I'd had last night. If I didn't give myself a purpose, I would sink into bitter despair, and there wasn't time for that. Fully healed or not, I needed to leave.

I dressed in the dim light of the sunrise, knowing I would have to obtain two things for my journey from Thatcher More—food and a map. With this in mind, I approached the shack behind the house where he so often disappeared. The door stood ajar, and I could hear him moving around inside. Not wanting to give him a chance to deny me entry, I took a breath and crossed the threshold, steeling myself for what I might find. But nothing looked horribly amiss, and my fluttering heartbeat settled into a normal rhythm.

Thatcher stood at a wooden table littered with animal hides and bones, cutting venison into strips with a hunting knife. The table's surface had absorbed enough lifeblood to emanate the sour odor associated with these activities, and yet the scent was vague, suggesting the workspace was frequently cleaned. A variety of tools hung on the walls, and a smaller table held

what looked like partially finished carvings and other wood-
working projects.

"Excuse me," I interrupted. "Are you turning some of that
venison into jerky?"

Thatcher jumped and spun toward me, knife at the ready.
My body automatically locked into a defensive posture, Anlace
in hand even though I didn't remember reaching for it. It hadn't
occurred to me that Thatcher might not hear my approach—
I'd assumed my skill for silence had been lost with my wings.

"It's you," he growled, wiping newly formed beads of sweat
off his forehead with his sleeve. "You shouldn't be out here."

With Shea's confessions fresh in my mind and annoyance
bubbling in my chest, there were many retorts that sprang to
my lips. But I bit them back and returned the Anlace to its
sheath. Antagonism would get me nowhere.

"I'm sorry. I wanted to talk to you in private."

An unremitting stare was his only response, and it felt like
he was trying to push me out the door by sheer force of will.
I stepped farther into the shack, doing my best to ignore his
attitude.

"I'm planning on leaving soon. I wondered if I might have
some meat for my travels?"

"When will you depart?"

"In a day or two, I hope."

With a grunt that I took as a yes, he returned to work. I
shifted from foot to foot, waiting for him to say something
more, to ask how much food I'd need, where I would be going,
anything that would ordinarily be asked, when my gaze fell
on a pair of leather fetters that looked disturbingly familiar.
Frowning, I picked them up from the smaller table and rubbed
them between my fingers, only to have Thatcher snatch them

away. When I looked down, the crusty, dark russet substance that stained the leather now stained my hand.

"Distinctive souvenir," I said pointedly, my wrists stinging as though the straps still encircled them, immobilizing me for the halberd to *strike—strike—strike*. My surroundings grew fuzzy for an instant, my memory dragging forth that dark night, each deafening blow still able to create a throbbing in my temples.

"Not a souvenir," Thatcher grumbled, clutching the cuffs in a thick fist. "You may not place much faith in me, but don't do me a disservice. I just wanted to see what the hunters are using these days."

"And what have you determined?" I asked, banishing the belligerence from my voice.

"They're getting more sophisticated. And they're well funded. See these studs?" He pointed to the manacles, and I nodded. Between bloodstains, the leather held bits of a shimmering black mineral. "That's sky iron. Very hard to come by, and very expensive."

I paled. From the Fae perspective, sky iron was what humans called an old wives' tale. Said to fall from the heavens, it contained the only substance in Nature that was inherently harmful to my people. According to lore, it grounded us, taking away our ability to fly and to communicate with the elements. Its existence was laced throughout our histories, but with its earthly source unknown, the accounts were largely accepted as allegories rather than fact.

I was face-to-face with a myth, and I understood now why the water hadn't answered my call when I'd been attacked by the hunters; but that wasn't the most terrifying part. No, the most terrifying part was how many other myths I'd dismissed throughout my life, and how the tide slunk in over sturdy ground when I lent them credence.

"What will you do with the leathers?" I pressed.

"Sell them, if I can. Might bring a tidy sum, and I can use the money."

Disgust washed over me. "You mean you'll sell them to hunters?"

"This isn't personal, Anya. I need the money, and I'm not interested in asking questions."

"It's personal to me."

To my surprise, he laughed and examined the fetters more closely, as though realizing for the first time that the blood forming the stains belonged to me.

"Yes, I suppose it is. I guess I can afford to be poor a little longer."

Without another word, he opened the base of the smoker and tossed the leathers into the fire.

"You're a good man, Thatcher More," I said, perplexed by his shifting priorities. "At least I think you are."

"There aren't many these days who would agree with you. But that's neither here nor there. You're welcome to all the jerky you want. There are plenty of deer in these woods. Anything else you need?"

"A map of the area, if you could draw one. I'm not familiar with this part of the forest."

"Simple enough. I'll have it for you in the morning."

"One last thing. What about acquiring a horse?"

"You can rent one in Strong. It's the closest town to us and it has a government-sponsored livery stable. If you return your mount to any of the company's locations, they'll refund half your investment."

"Thanks," I said again, resisting the urge to ask him about his problems with the Governor. He was being cooperative, and I doubted that would continue if I delved into his personal affairs. I didn't have the right to pry, no matter how curious I was.

I turned to go, but Thatcher arrested me with a warning. "You're not to take Shea with you."

"What?"

"Shea is unhappy here, no point in pretending otherwise. I suspect she'll want to go with you. But the outside world poses a threat to her that she is too young to appreciate. I want your promise you'll turn her down."

I gave my auburn hair a thoughtful tug. This possibility had not yet occurred to me. Then I gave him the best answer I could.

"It's not my intent to take her with me. I'll do my best to discourage her, but that's all I can promise. She has the right to make up her own mind."

Thatcher's return expression was not in the least satisfied. He took a deep breath, gripping the edge of his worktable so that the muscles all the way up his arms flexed.

"Fair enough," he grumbled, for there was little else he could say to me.

I left him alone in the shack, wishing there was something I could do to make the Mores' lives easier. Perhaps if I found Zabriel and he took his rightful place on the throne, I would ask him to assist the humans who had helped me when I was at my most vulnerable.

Instead of heading to the front door, I walked around to the back of the cabin. It was so cold that the snow had crusted over, and I was practically able to walk on top of it, only occasionally breaking through. When I came to Shea's window, I scanned the ground, not really expecting to see any tracks. The immaculate snow confirmed the likelihood that the noises we'd heard had been those of an animal—nothing heavier than a fawn could have passed here without breaking the crust. While a Faerie could have hovered, I would probably have heard the hum of wings last night. Fae wings in motion made a distinct sound recognizable by those whose ears were attuned to it. I also scrutinized the surrounding space for glimmers of magic in the air that might have been left by one of my people, but found nothing. Satisfied, I returned to the house to help with the day's chores.

After supper that night, Shea and I put her sisters to bed, an activity I had come to enjoy, for the four of us would gather in the younger girls' bedroom and share tales. Shea was the primary storyteller, although occasionally Magdalene took on the role. I knew from legends within my own land—and from Thatcher's identification of sky iron—that old tales often had a core of truth, and hearing human versions might give me extra insight into their world. A few of the stories existed in the Faerie Realm, as well, and these I took to have more credibility than the others. If a fable commanded the belief of two separate races of people, it was bound to have deep roots.

"So you see, the woman destroyed herself by trying to become more beautiful," Shea explained to Magdalene and Marissa, who were sitting on their beds, listening intently. "We're made the way we are for a reason. You can't go against nature."

"Or you'll end up uglier than before," Marissa offered, and a round of giggles followed. The girls had been outside during the day, and the clothes we'd hung to dry by the fireplace fractured the light, casting eerie shadows across the floor and walls.

In the spirit of this atmosphere, Magdalene made a request. "Tell us a scary one, Shea. We know about ending up ugly."

"*You* do," teased Marissa, prompting Maggie to playfully smother her with a pillow.

"You don't need to hear a scary one," Shea said with a roll of her eyes. "You should go to bed."

"No!" Marissa implored, breaking free of Magdalene's assault. "I want a scary one, too. Please, Shea?"

"Fine. Let's see…. Oh, I've got one. Have you ever heard of a Sepulchre?"

Marissa and Maggie shook their heads, while I sat up straighter on the floor. This was yet another myth the Fae shared with the humans; Evangeline had frightened me and our other friends with stories about Sepulchres when we were younger.

"Long ago, before the Faerie War, there were these creatures, these beautiful creatures. No one was sure if they were men or women or even what color they were, they shone so uniquely," Shea began, separating the girls and moving to sit on Marissa's bed. "The Fae were friends with them, and used to share their magic so the creatures could stay beautiful. But then the war erupted, and the curse of the Bloody Road stopped anyone who wasn't Fae from crossing into the magical Realm. So the creatures, in order to survive, had to feast on the next best thing—children, the younger the better, because they were so pure."

This was met with the expected gasps and shivers, and Marissa pulled her quilt up to her chin.

"It's said that these creatures, called Sepulchres, slip through windows and cracks in doors and steal children away to their dungeons somewhere beneath the ground. No one knows what happens then, except that the children are never seen again."

There was silence for a moment, then Marissa whimpered, "That's not true, is it?"

"Don't worry. Even if it is, Sepulchres never go after big girls like you and Maggie." Shea tweaked her younger sister's nose, drawing a weak smile.

"Shea," I admonished. "Your sisters are scared."

"I know that."

"Then tell them the truth."

"I did!"

I sighed, feeling presumptuous for challenging Shea in front of her sisters, but hating the fear in Marissa's enormous dark eyes.

"Not completely."

"Then by all means, straighten me out! What is the truth?"

I turned to the little girl, ignoring Shea's tightly crossed arms, and told the story as it was repeated in Chrior.

"A long time ago, when humans and Fae shared the lands now occupied by your race, there were these creatures called Sepulchres. They were nourished by Fae magic, but they never attacked children. And when the Faeries left the human world, all the Sepulchres died. So, you see, it's actually a sad story, not a scary one. There's nothing to worry your pretty head about."

Marissa grinned and curled up on her side. After kisses and good-nights, Shea and I returned to the bedroom we jointly occupied, my mind mulling over her version of the tale.

In Chrior, Sepulchres were just another story told to demonize the humans, who had viewed us as heathens, reprobates, and usurpers, and driven us out of their lands. The Sepulchres had been trapped on the human side of the Road and condemned to death without access to our magic. Humans apparently believed the creatures still existed, while the Fae believed them to be extinct, their species one massive casualty of the war.

"So you really don't believe in Sepulchres?" Shea demanded as soon as our bedroom door had closed, hands on her hips. "Because I've heard of children going missing, back when we lived in Tairmor."

"Tairmor is a big city, and I have no doubt children go missing. But I don't think Sepulchres are to blame."

"How can you be sure?"

I flipped my hair over my shoulders, exasperated. "I'm not *sure*. But I do know that as long as monsters and demons are taking the blame for kidnappings, they're providing excellent scapegoats for *real* criminals. And I'm Fae, remember? I think I know more about magic and magical creatures than you do. Besides, Marissa and Maggie would have been lying awake all night waiting for some horror to slip through the window if I hadn't told them what they needed to hear. Isn't that what's important?"

Shea scowled but said no more, though she prepared for bed with a vengeance. I could tell she was still irked, but I didn't give her the satisfaction of acknowledging it. I was plenty irked myself. Children didn't deserve to be scared. Illumina wasn't much older than Shea's sisters, and she'd lived most of her life in fear. It had led to her bizarre habits, her unpredictability, a desperation, perhaps, to be more frightening than the things that frightened her. It had taken more than a scary story to subvert Illumina's mind in this way, but the thought of Marissa or Magdalene slinking into the woods to injure their own bodies the way Illumina did was enough to caution me against beginning the pattern.

Other than collecting the promised map and jerky from Thatcher, I went about my usual business the next day, occasionally ruminating on the best way to find Zabriel. My cousin, according to Queen Ubiqua, had his father's spirit. I'd seen it in him, though I hadn't known the human Prince of the Fae whom some had viewed as an interloper, others as a blessing. Zabriel had always been focused on the next thing, the lands he wanted to travel, the people he would meet or, in the interim, the worlds he invented in his mind. There was always that elusive adventure up ahead. Now I wondered if it had been a way for him to escape his painful present. In any case, the current day had never mattered as much to him as *someday*.

Ubiqua had been afraid to let Zabriel cross the Bloody Road in the aftermath of her husband's death. Her son had no elemental connection, a deficiency that had been obvious from a young age. Most Fae manifested their element within days of birth and learned to communicate with Nature at the same rate they learned to talk, but young Zabriel had feared water, abhorred the dubious flickering of flames, and been helpless against the cold wind. There had been hope for an Earth connection, since he'd loved the feel of dirt under his nails and the sun on his skin, but an incident with poison berries dashed that hope. Even as toddlers, Earth Fae instinctively knew the difference between kind plants and cruel ones, and Zabriel was oblivious. It was normal in light of the evidence that Ubiqua should fear for her son's life against the curse of the Road. In her zeal to protect him, she'd forbidden him to go near it, and had kept Zabriel's birth a secret from his human relatives. She wanted no incentive for him to leave the Faerie Realm, no eager arms awaiting him on the other side of the boundary. As a result, he'd believed they didn't want him, maybe even that they blamed him for his father's death.

Had Ubiqua suspected Zabriel harbored these fears, she surely would have told him the truth sooner, but she hadn't done so until he was fifteen, at which point chaos had ensued, and her son's reckless abandon had steered him to brave a Crossing of his own accord. When he'd gone missing, the entire Realm had been searched; it was ultimately assumed he'd gone into human lands when not a trace of him was found, even on or near the Bloody Road. No news of him had since reached the Queen or my father's ambassadors in the Warckum Territory.

Would Zabriel have tried to find his father's family? It would have been an easy task considering their prominence, another fact I had not shared with Shea. She didn't need to know of my cousin's connection to the man she viewed as responsible for her family's strife. I ultimately rejected the idea that Zabriel would have sought out the Governor—when he'd abandoned his claim to the throne, he'd been tired of expectations and being defined by the blood in his veins. He had no memories of his father, a fact he never hesitated to share with anyone who happened to ripple the surface of his deep-rooted bitterness toward the human for siring him. I couldn't picture Zabriel pursuing a history and a legacy he did not want.

Where, then, would he have gone? A place where he would blend in, where he would be difficult to track. A large city. The capital? Tairmor was busy, but it was also the seat of the Governor's power, and offered little excitement once one adapted to its curiosities and pace. Sheness, however, brimmed with foreigners, trade, new technologies, and adventure, or so I'd heard, and the port city was as far from the Balsam Forest as the continent allowed. It was more likely Zabriel would have traveled there. After all, he saw himself as an abomination, neither human nor Fae, and one was likely to find many abominations in Sheness.

A shudder passed through me at this thought. Was I now an abomination, too? Shaking off the notion, I forced myself to concentrate only on Zabriel, settling on Sheness for my destination. Two years had passed since his disappearance, and I had to start somewhere.

I waited until evening to tell Shea of my decision to depart, when we were together in her room. A significant part of me wanted to just steal away, avoid goodbyes and potential trouble with Thatcher, but Shea and I had become friends, and I owed her an explanation. She would be lonely without me, and the resulting guilt I felt was more intense than I had anticipated. I was prepared, however, to deal with her disappointment. To my consternation, when I finally forced the confession past my lips, I encountered resolve rather than disappointment, and I realized how well Thatcher understood his daughter.

"I'm going with you," she proclaimed, a stubborn set to her chin.

I shook my head, but Shea wasn't put off.

"What are you going to do, Anya? You have to find a way to live among the humans now. Do you think that's going to be easy? Maybe in your Realm people respect teenage girls, but they don't here. We're bothersome and in the way, too young to be taken seriously and too old to be innocent. The world doesn't want us, and if we don't have each other, we have nothing. I need to leave this place, and you're going to want a friend out there in the Territory. You might even need one."

I rubbed my temple, my feelings aligning with hers—I didn't want to be alone. But how could I say yes when I'd promised Thatcher that I'd turn her down?

"What about your family?"

"They'll be fine without me. I haven't been here in my heart in a long time."

"Your father doesn't want you to leave."

Shea slowly blinked her chocolate-brown eyes, pondering the meaning of my statement.

"Did my father talk to you?" She read the answer in my expression, and her eyes narrowed. "He has no right to forbid you from taking me with you. This isn't his decision, it's *mine*."

I laughed, impressed by her spunk. "That's exactly what I told him. But there are other things I have to consider."

"Then consider. I'll wait."

I sighed, trying to weigh the complications of having Shea with me against the advantages she might present. I wasn't afraid to leave the Balsam Forest—I'd done it often enough the past couple of years. Still, how many times had I crossed the Bloody Road without incident prior to the loss of my wings? All it took was one time, one unfortunate circumstance. I was less likely to encounter such a circumstance if another person was looking out for me. On the other hand, I'd end up spending part of my time looking out for Shea. She was inexperienced, sheltered, and angry, a surefire formula for trouble. And having her with me would no doubt slow me down, although in truth, so would my sluggish transition to humanity. I wasn't fully healed and wouldn't make exceptional time anyway. And then, of course, there was Thatcher's potential reaction. I was more wary of him than was Shea. To him, I was a meddler, an outsider, someone *expendable*. Shea was precious to him, while I was a threat.

"All right, you can come," I ultimately concluded, the scales tipping in her favor when I remembered how she had saved my life on the Bloody Road. "But dress warm and pack light— we've got a lot of ground to cover."

Shea grinned, excitement pinking her cheeks. "Thank you, Anya. You won't regret this."

Without another word, she prepared for bed, humming to herself, and I hoped she understood the gravity of our mission. This wasn't a game or a lark. The fate of the Faerie people might very well rest on my shoulders, and as for Shea, she would be risking her freedom every time someone laid eyes on her.

I woke with the sun and roused Shea. Without speaking, we packed the supplies we would need, then dressed in thick leggings and boots, topped by woolen shirts to which I added a jerkin and Shea an overcoat. We grabbed heavy cloaks as our final layer; they would double well as blankets at night. Light snow was falling, and I pondered the murky sky through the window, hoping the snow would stay light. According to Thatcher's map, we were ten miles from the nearest town, a small cattle-ranching community called Strong that was barely considered part of the Warckum Territory. There we would spend the night and arrange for transport to the west.

By the time Shea and I were ready, the rest of the family had awoken. We entered the main room to double takes and falling faces.

"Shea, what…?" Elyse queried from her position at the stove, wooden spoon slipping from her grasp. Thatcher looked up from his seat by the fireplace, setting aside the gun he had been cleaning.

"I'm leaving," Shea told them without any preliminaries.

Elyse blanched, while Thatcher stood, his ominous glower compelling Marissa and Magdalene to sidle closer to their mother.

"No, you're not, Shea," he contradicted, his hands raised as though to catch her if she darted for the door. "You have no idea how dangerous it is out there."

"I'm not stupid, Dad," she said, though a touch of regret prevented the words from being defiant. "I know it's danger-ous. But I'm not going to live the rest of my life this way."

Thatcher turned toward me, about to redirect his anger, but Shea stepped between us.

"Don't you dare blame Anya. You asked her to try to dis-courage me, and she did. This is my choice, understand? But don't worry. I won't put the rest of you in jeopardy. If I'm caught, I'll accept that it's my own fault and serve the sentence."

Their dark eyes met, and Thatcher's shame at seeing bravery in his daughter that he himself did not possess became detect-able in the slump of his shoulders. He strode past her down the hall, and Shea's lip trembled in an effort to hold back tears. Then Maggie and Marissa rushed forward and embraced her.

"You'll come back, won't you?" Marissa asked, too young to arrive at the conclusion that was etched on everyone else's face.

"I don't know," Shea whispered. "But I believe I will see you again someday."

Elyse was next, clinging to her daughter until I thought the two of them had melded into a tragic statue. They separated at

Thatcher's unexpected return. Embarrassed, Elyse wiped the tears from her cheeks.

Thatcher took Shea's hand, closing her fingers around a leather pouch.

"Get a belt in Strong and set these bullets. I've tucked a bit of money inside for you to use."

At his daughter's nod, he extended a necklace, reaching around her to fasten it underneath her hair. It draped a third of the way down her chest, the gold chain culminating in what appeared to be a small, upside-down looking glass. The necklace was beautiful and no doubt expensive, but obviously meant something more to him than money.

"Wear it always," Thatcher intoned, his voice thick. "Don't ever take it off, not even when you sleep or bathe. It will bring you luck. And if they catch you, tell them where to find me."

Shea dropped her gaze, but he grasped her chin, lifting it to reveal the tears she could no longer restrain.

"Shea, tell them where to find me. Promise you will."

She sniffed and brushed a hand across her cheek. "I won't."

"You *must.*"

"I won't. I'm sorry. I'm not about to put all of you in danger. Besides, you don't deserve that sentence any more than I do. And I don't trust that the Governor's men won't hurt you. That's not a chance I'm willing to take."

Thatcher sighed and shook his head, his disappointment eclipsed by the pride that was written all over his face.

"Stubborn girl," he said, voice husky, then he gave Shea a light embrace. "Take care."

Extending his hand to me, he made a request. "Keep her safe. You have more experience on your own than she does."

"We'll keep each other safe." I met his firm grip with one

of my own, feeling the weight of his faith settle on my chest. It was heavy, but within my strength to carry.

We did not spend much longer on goodbyes, for Shea's expression revealed that if she did not leave soon, she might change her mind.

"Let's go," I said, when we stood outside among the trees that cradled the More house.

"And never look back," she responded, sending a prickling sensation down my spine. An image flashed like lightning in my head, an image of Illumina with a small, sharp knife, cutting into the flesh above her right breast, painstakingly carving words of special importance to her: *Keep silent your screams and never look back.*

chapter eight

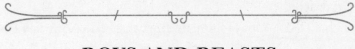

BOYS AND BEASTS

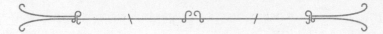

For miles beyond the border of Strong stretched pastureland occupied by cattle, fuzzy with the cold. Their unique stench rolled over Shea and me as we neared the town proper. It wasn't the kind of scent that made travelers cover their noses, but it wasn't pleasant, either. I could see how someone who had grown up there might remember it fondly, but to foreigners it was less than endearing.

No guard or gate blocked our passage as we crossed a quaint bridge over a frozen lake, so we strolled into town in the late afternoon like invited guests. The cobblestone streets were muddy and hay strewn, but the thatched buildings were well kept. Strong was a ranchers' hub, where folks came for supplies, trade, and company. Of course, at this time of year, most cattle sales had already taken place, so we were likely to encounter only locals. A single inn, the Morrow Bend, offered accommodations to travelers, and I secured a room with the money I'd provisioned myself from previous trips into the human world. After dropping off our packs and cloaks, we settled at a table in the small but welcoming pub that made up the inn's first floor. Snow had dogged our steps the entire day, and a hot meal would help chase the chill from our bones.

"I always thought Fae would be vegetarians," Shea remarked while we sipped steaming mugs of cider, awaiting the food we'd ordered.

I chuckled. "A lot of humans think that. Too many bad fantasy stories, I guess. We need meat as much as you do."

She was no longer listening to me, her eyes instead absorbing the activities of happy drunks, gregarious waitresses and swarthy bartenders like they were a newly discovered species, leaving little doubt she'd never before visited an alehouse. I hadn't thought about how green she was to the world outside her father's hideaway. It was like she'd slept away the past two years.

We settled in to relax, Shea jabbering more than she ever had around me, asking an endless stream of questions until our food arrived and gave her mouth something else to do. To me, this was a good sign; she had more stamina than I had expected.

At a pause in our conversation, I pulled my leather passport folder from inside my jerkin and laid it on the table. Shea opened the flaps and removed the thick, distinctive sheets of paper stored inside. The parchment was made from a combination of unique materials, an inimitable mixture designed to resist replication.

"Travel papers," I explained. "Forged, as your father surmised. We need to obtain some for you if you're to venture into the heart of the Territory. I assume the ones you had prior to the issuance of the arrest warrant for Thatcher are useless."

"Of course." She slid my documents back across the table. "I'm sure my name is on every wanted list at every checkpoint in the Territory."

"Shea, I'm sorry, but we can't fix that. I'm just out to find my cousin and bring him home."

She was nodding like she understood, but her discontent

made me nervous. If she decided to try to get back at Governor Ivanova out of spite, there was no way I could protect her. She'd land herself in prison.

"We rest tonight, then go north," I continued, tucking my leather folder back in my jerkin. "The man who supplied me with these works out of Oaray. He'll provide us with what we need."

Shea cast her eyes around the room and red dots appeared in her cheeks. Not sure what had embarrassed her, I glanced over to see a boy at the bar raising his mug to her.

"You'll have to get used to that," I chuckled. Shea was rustic and still a little chubby from childhood, but her large dark eyes were alluring and her wavy brown hair shone. She would draw the attention of men whether she wanted it or not.

She gave me a slight smile and went back to her meal, her heart seeming to fill along with her stomach. Before long, her spirits had recovered and she waved to the boy at the bar. In another minute she was up and talking to him. I clutched my mug of cider and curled into a corner of our booth. Let her have fun for a night; she wouldn't have too many of these opportunities. And I needed to work a few things out in my mind.

Though I'd said nothing specific about our next stop to Shea, my thoughts were now on Oaray, my least favorite of the human cities I'd visited, only because I was aware of its true nature. The smiling faces and respectable businessmen were a front for a town famed for its illegalities. The place teemed with whores, of both the male and female variety, but by day they were delivery persons for the grocery or performers at the local playhouse. Accountants funded the transportation of illegal citizens to and from the big cities by filching a cent here, a dollar there from their clients. Nothing tax officials would notice without scrupulous examination, but everything to a few unlucky souls who needed passage.

Of course, not everyone deserved passage. Sometimes the motivations of Oaray's proprietors were so buried even their cohorts didn't know the full purposes of the businesses. As harmless and kind as Oaray's citizens were to prospective customers, they made possible the breaking of laws both frivolous and imperative. And they were such a cohesive unit, so good at hiding their crimes, that they couldn't be stopped through any sanctioned legal process. Because of all this, Oaray had been nicknamed the City of False Smiles.

Taking a long swill of lukewarm cider, I let my thoughts drift to Illumina. My younger cousin had a good two weeks' head start on me, but she would also have needed travel documents. She would have been sent to Oaray by my father to get a forged passport. Once Shea and I reached the city, we might be able to pick up her trail. I would have less trouble tracking her than Zabriel if it came down to it, and I could revamp my strategy as needed.

Then a new worry arose. What if Zabriel had made sure he could never return? What if he'd removed his wings like he'd tried to once before, and was now as powerless to cross the Road as was I? My dinner threatened to reemerge, and I covered my mouth with my hand, taking several deep breaths. There was no point in dwelling on this possibility. In my mind, he would remain Zabriel, Prince of the Fae, the same person I used to know, unless I found out differently.

Thinking it time to retire, I looked across the pub for Shea. There was no sign of her. Disconcerted, I sat up and surveyed the room more thoroughly. Strong was a border town—there was no reason we should have encountered trouble with the authorities this soon. Nevertheless, she was not in sight. In desperation, I headed to the bar, flagged down the server and described Thatcher More's daughter to him.

"Brown hair and eyes, wearing brown leggings and a blue tunic. Last I saw, she was talking to some boy."

The barkeep nodded and pointed toward the side door of the Morrow Bend. "Saw 'em head out that way. They both had a bit to drink."

I clenched my jaw against the rising irritation in my chest. While there was no reason we *should* have encountered trouble, I'd apparently released a starving wildcat in the land of plenty. Problem was I couldn't afford to have a starving wildcat along with me on this trip.

Making for the side door, I knew what I would find even before I opened it to the cold wind. A snow-crusted alley stretched left and right, but footprints and laughter brought my attention to where Shea was pressed against the wall by the boy she'd met at the bar. He was kissing her neck, holding her hips, pinning her with his body. Grinning, she opened her mouth to his and pulled him closer.

In two swift strides, I pulled the gent away from her and gave him a shove. Though I hadn't intended for him to land on his rear in the snow, the result was nonetheless satisfying. Shea giggled and covered her mouth. If she was embarrassed, it was only because some fuzzy, faraway recess in her brain told her she ought to be.

Dismayed, I pointed to the door. "We're going inside. Now."

"What if I don' wan' to?" she mumbled in protest, her words slurred.

The young man stumbled to his feet, his coordination poor in his drunken state. He crashed into the opposite alley wall before righting himself, and I cocked an eyebrow, wondering if he'd remember in the morning how he'd gotten his bruises. At last getting his bearings, he lurched forward, his momentum allowing him to push past me and put an arm around the girl he hoped to seduce.

"Who's this bitch, honey? Tellin' you what to do. You wanna stay with me, don'cha? Maybe I should do yah a favor and shut her up."

Shea's eyes widened, perhaps realizing through her inebriation that her partner in lust had more in mind than she did. She tried to remove his arm, but didn't have a good angle or leverage, and ended up feebly swiping at it. Viewing her actions as a request for help, I grabbed him by the collar and slung him once more against the alley wall, hoping he would crack his head on the stone and be incapacitated. But he put his hands out in time to catch himself. He turned around and raised his fists, his manhood apparently challenged. He was broad-shouldered and tall enough that I could have hidden behind him, and a sardonic, fatalistic part of my brain acknowledged that this was going to hurt.

More as a reflex than anything else, I called on my elemental connection to the water to help me, but all I felt was a strange, dilating hollowness in my core—I no longer had the ability to make the wet snow slippery and knock my adversary out cold. Neither could I hover into the air to confuse him or attack from above. I was left with no distinct advantage aside from my sobriety, and his threat suddenly carried more weight. I dug my nails into the palms of my hands, for this sort of weakness was a new feeling, one that made me want to run even though I'd never retreated from a lone combatant before. I detested the boy for making me feel afraid; at the same time, I was too afraid to provoke him.

In the end, only one thing occurred to me. I likewise balled my fists, reluctant to pull and potentially lose possession of the Anlace, and when he was close enough, drilled him in the crotch with one of my boots. He yelped at a soprano pitch and went down faster than anyone I'd ever seen.

"Hurry," I shouted to Shea, snatching her arm and tugging her back inside the pub, letting the door slam behind us.

Though Shea swayed on her feet, I kept her moving, past the bar and tables, and up the staircase to our room, fuming inside. If she hadn't come with me, I would have been tucked away in bed already, warm and sleeping, and not worried about pursuit by a man who I could only hope was still clutching himself between his legs in agony. This was how she thanked me for taking a chance on her?

After forcing all the water I could down Shea's throat to reduce the likelihood of illness in the morning, I cracked open the window, hoping the cool air would help to sober her up. Then I tucked her into bed. She was asleep within fifteen minutes, but the same peace eluded me. Seeing Shea with that boy had reawakened thoughts of Davic. What was he doing in Chrior this night? Cavorting with friends? Visiting his parents and sister on the other side of the city? Or was he reading a book, safe and warm in his alcove? I closed my eyes at that image, aching to be warm in his arms, to lay my head on his shoulder. A lump rose in my throat, and I rubbed my hands over my face, refusing to wallow in longing. It was time I accepted the simple truth. Even if Davic realized something was wrong, convinced Ubiqua and my father and Ione, and they all came looking for me, there was nothing they could do to change my circumstances.

I continued to toss and turn, dozing in and out without really resting. The darkness did not lift, only shifted, and I knew in the morning this night would seem surreal and distant.

Shea was sniffing between her heavy breaths, and though that wasn't the reason I couldn't sleep, the repetitive noise irked me. Worse, now that I'd noticed it, I couldn't get it out of my head. I snugged my pillow against my ears, then sat up and threw it at her, realizing too late that I'd have to get up to retrieve it. With a sigh, I rolled out of bed to snatch it back, and froze.

The wheezing wasn't coming from Shea.

My breath caught, magnifying the earnest beating of my heart. As unobtrusively as I could, I swiveled to check the room, trying not to imagine what might be behind me. The light from a street lamp fought its way through the ratty curtains, casting knotted shadows across the floor. A creature—luminescent yet deathly gray—was slipping from underneath my bed, using the foot post to hoist itself up. It wasn't facing me, and I praised Nature that I'd gotten up. It sniffed at my mattress and groped about with its glowing spearlike fingers, its emaciated body following waiflike behind those strong digits that were slithering up the coverlet. It had neither the size of a human adult nor the smallness of a child, and its legs, if legs they could be called, were bound together by intricate spider webs of skin, stretched to their limit. The lower half of its body was almost useless, but nevertheless the thing moved with a perverse grace.

I shook Shea violently by the shoulder.

"What?" she murmured.

The creature's head whipped around, and I choked on the cry in my throat—the same shredded skin adorned its face, looking like bruise-colored scars across its pallid cheeks. Its eyes were pupil-less, nothing more than phosphorescent orbs of sickly green, and my insides twisted as I saw that it had no mouth or nose. How was it making that ragged noise? Through its pores?

The ghastly visitor made a high-pitched keening noise and threw itself from my bed to the floor, where it crawled toward us at an uncanny speed, its long fingers reaching well in front of the rest of its body. Shea scrambled to her feet, letting out the scream that I could not. My weapons were on the other side of the room, past our intruder, but Shea lurched toward her coat, searching through it with frantic hands. She needn't have hurried for her own sake—the creature had no interest in her.

I bumped into Shea's bedpost, almost losing my footing as I retreated backward until I was pinned against the wall, the creature never more than a few inches away. It grabbed my ankle, my calf, the hem of my shirt, finally coming face-to-face with me. I could feel the tug and release of its breathing, its hungry inhalation, cold exhalation. It was near weightless, but its odor was sweet like death. I knew what it wanted, why it was interested in me and not Shea. It wanted magic, and it had followed my trail in the same way a hound followed a scent. How it would go about draining the little magic I had left was the true mystery, the true terror. I flattened myself out as much as I could, eyes shut tight, afraid it would rob me of my very soul.

At the report of a gun, the creature squealed and retreated, and I fell to my knees. Out of the corner of my eye, I spied Shea, the silver pistol shaking alarmingly in her hands, and the muscles of my chest threatened to strangle my heart. That bullet could easily have hit me.

Rolling and writhing, the wounded creature crashed into my bed, Shea following it with her outstretched arm. Once more she fired, but the weapon clicked hollowly, for only a single bullet had rested in its chamber. Thatcher had removed the rest, and Shea had not thought to reload.

Further violence wasn't necessary, however, for the spindly thing was no longer interested in us. It had knocked over my bag, spilling its contents across the floor, and had picked up my only hope of returning home—the flask of Sale that might kill or save me. I tried to reclaim my feet to take back what was mine, but my trembling body gave out. Shea inched toward the door, one hand on the wall for support, the other gripping her gun and shaking so hard the weapon continually bumped against her leg.

I shrieked, but there was nothing I could do to stop that unnatural being from using its tendril-like fingers to remove the cork from my flask and pour the Sale over its head. The liquid dripped down its body, hissing and creating a steam through which I couldn't see. But I heard its deep, pleasured sigh. Next instant, the room was empty except for Shea and me, the creature having left the way it had entered, through the open window.

"No," I moaned, crawling to the remains of my belongings. "No, no, no!"

But it was too late. Nary a drop of Sale remained. Breaking into staccato sobs, I crumpled to the floor, hating the thing that had stolen my only chance of living a life with Davic and my family in Chrior, hating the hunters who had reduced me to a single, feeble hope, hating myself for being so, so stupid.

If I had followed my own advice to Illumina, I would never have been a victim. If I had listened to Davic and stayed with him, I would never have been in the vicinity of the humans who'd maimed me.

I felt more than heard Shea's approach. She wrapped her arms around me, and I leaned heavily against her. The immediate fear for my life had dissipated, but a greater, overriding terror was moving in. A long time ago, before I'd lost my wings, I'd thought that bravery could be attained with an open mind and heart, by pursuing and facing my demons. Now I considered that fearlessness was the luxury of the cloistered and the blind, and that it was too late for me.

"You were right, Shea," I whispered. "About the Sepulchres. The curse didn't kill them. It turned them into monsters."

"You couldn't have known those…*things* exist. You're not superhuman. Er, super-Fae, I guess. And we don't know for certain it was a Sepulchre."

"It wanted *me*. It wanted the magic from my wounds, and when it couldn't—" I broke off and fumbled for my empty flask.

"What was in there?"

There were simultaneously too many words and no words at all to explain to Shea what had been in the flask. But without Sale, I had neither the hope of reclaiming my old life nor the possibility of neatly ending my current one. And if all else failed, that had been my plan. I blinked back a wave of tears and forced myself to breathe.

"It was a form of medicine."

Though Shea frowned, she asked me nothing more. I was thankful she didn't berate me for the way I had dismissed the cautionary tale she had told her sisters. I'd been a fool. There had been signs that something was watching me...the scratch marks on the trees in the clearing, the rattling of the window latch in Shea's bedroom. That creature must have followed us all the way from the Balsam Forest. If I'd just sacrificed a little pride and considered that Shea might be right, perhaps I could have prevented this.

There were voices sounding in the hall, and the door shook with someone's weight thrust against it again and again. Startled, we scrambled to our feet. Two men broke the lock and burst into the room, a posse of curious faces gathered behind them.

The barkeep had led the charge, and his troubled eyes fell on us. "We heard a scream and what sounded like a gunshot."

"I thought I saw someone in our room," Shea smoothly lied. "I guess we both had too much to drink."

I attempted to smile in confirmation. "Sorry for the alarm."

"You're paying for that door," the other man, presumably the innkeeper, scoffed.

Ignoring the mess on the floor and the tears on my face, the irritated pair scowled at us and headed back into the hall, waving the onlookers on their way. Luckily, the door remained on its hinges, permitting me to jam it closed. Shea plopped on her bed while I lit the lamp, then I went to sit next to her, having no inclination to be near the window.

"Why lie?" I asked. "I thought humans believed in Sepulchres."

"Not everyone does. Besides, what would you do with two hysterical girls claiming they opened fire on a glowing spectral creature?"

"Toss them in the street. And take away their liquor and guns."

Shea giggled, adrenaline and alcohol undoubtedly fueling her emotions. "That would have been a much worse end to this than paying for damages."

I smiled despite myself. "Very caring gentlemen, those two. No offer to look around, no 'Are you all right?'" I adopted a gruff, over-the-top voice. "Just, 'Fix the damn door!'"

Shea laughed once more, and this time I joined in, the relief welcome. Only our first day journeying, and already our adventures were beyond anything I could have anticipated.

After breakfast at the Morrow Bend, during which Shea and I studiously avoided conversation about the events of the previous night, we went to the livery stable and paid the rental fee for two horses. As we led the animals into the sunshine—a pleasant change from the weather the day before—I drew Shea's attention to a tannery.

"Over there," I said, pointing. "See that leather shop? I'll hold the horses if you want to get a belt."

"A belt?"

"For your bullets. And you might want to load your gun."

"Oh, right. I guess my brain isn't fully functioning yet. I'll just be a minute."

She headed to the tanner's, and I was thankful the alcohol she'd consumed hadn't made her physically ill; a muddled mind I could handle. She returned with a gun belt strapped around her hips and over one shoulder, the spare bullets Thatcher had given her already in place. After securing her pistol at her side, she buttoned the overcoat under her cloak to hide the evidence.

"Now, how do I get on this thing?" she asked, taking the reins to her mount from me.

"You don't know?"

"Nope. Not the slightest idea."

"I thought all humans knew how to ride horses."

She laughed. "We're not born on horseback, you know. Most men learn, but I've only ridden in wagons or buggies."

I laid a hand on my mount's neck to calm the animal, who had taken to pawing the ground. "It doesn't look that hard to me."

"Hold it. You mean we just paid for two horses and you've never ridden before, either?" Shea was gawking at me in disbelief.

"Well…no," I admitted. "We have horses in the Faerie Realm, along with deer, bear, and other large animals, but few of us ride. We're light on our feet and don't tire easily. And we fly, remember?"

"Don't suppose you've ridden deer or bear, either," Shea groused, and I gave her a pained smile.

"Look, we've got a lot of ground to cover, and this is the best way to do it."

Shea turned away from me to examine the bay gelding she had been given, and I did likewise, scratching my head as I tried to figure out the best approach to take to this riding business. I'd seen people mount before, so I tried to mimic the movement, placing my left foot in the stirrup. My action was apparently of great interest to my horse, as he turned his head to observe me, shifting his body away from me at the same time. I hopped on one foot to stay with him, and I could have sworn he sneered. An experienced rider would probably have guffawed at this notion, but it seemed clear to me that the big bay was taunting me. Animals usually beheld Fae with a certain amount of respect, but either I was no longer Fae or this horse was wicked.

To my credit, I finally swung my leg over my gelding's back and settled into the saddle. A glance at Shea told me she had also gotten this far, and was looking rather proud of herself. Ready to move forward, we tapped our mounts on their sides with our heels, but neither horse budged. Mine pinned its ears back and turned its head to nip at the toe of my boot. I yelped, though I had not felt the horse's teeth, startling the animal into jigging sideways. Shea's horse rumbled and spun in circles, and she ended up gripping the saddle with a nauseous expression. Then it ceased, its rump aimed at me, and began to back up.

"Your horse is growling—he's growling!" I slammed my heels against my mount's side, frantically trying to avoid a collision, or worse, a kick.

Laughter broke out behind us, and I swiveled in my saddle to see a young man standing in the door to the livery stable. He was perhaps seventeen or eighteen years old, and over his clothing he wore a leather apron with an assortment of metal tools poking out of its pockets.

"Horses don't growl," he said, earning a scowl from me. "They aren't wolves. You'd think the two of you are Fae, the way you ride."

"Fae can ride," I snapped. Just because I wasn't among them didn't mean I had to abide his bigotry and know-it-all attitude.

"Then you're definitely not Fae," he responded with a grin. "But since you rented the horses, I assume you want to get somewhere. I'd be glad to give you a few pointers."

"That would be very nice of you," Shea jumped in, cognizant of my foul mood.

The boy spent the next hour explaining how to rein, move forward, change gaits, halt, and dismount. He also instructed us on how to saddle and bridle the geldings, as well as basics like how to tie them and how much grain to feed them. He spent more time with Shea than he did with me—her smile was pretty under any circumstances, but especially so in comparison to my irritable countenance. I didn't like looking foolish, but there was no denying I had been served a plateful of humility.

When the boy finally deemed us somewhat competent, he slapped our horses on their rumps, sending us off at a teeth-jarring trot. For the next couple of miles, we changed between the walk and various trot speeds, trying to find one that was comfortable. At length, our horses settled into a ground-covering jog that we could sit without feeling like we were going to be catapulted across the plains. Pleased with ourselves, Shea and I shared a grin.

Now that we had the hang of horseback riding, we made good time on our way to Oaray. It was a two-day trek, during which we twice came close to military troops. I grew numb upon seeing them—I'd never encountered law enforcement or peacekeeping forces this far north. Fortunately, here on the fringe, they weren't too concerned with checking papers. If they had, Shea could have been arrested on the spot for not having proper documentation. Still, it was worrisome, and I wished I could hover into the air for a better view of what lay ahead in order to steer clear of such encounters. Given the fresh, crisp breeze at our backs, I also longed to float on the currents for the pure pleasure of spiraling to the ground. But such delights were now lost to me. Annoyed at myself for focusing on the things that had been stolen from me, I urged my horse into a faster pace. There was more than one way to feel the exhilaration of movement.

chapter nine

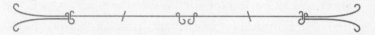

THE CITY OF FALSE SMILES

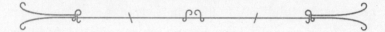

I paid for my eagerness to stretch my horse's legs and feel the wind rush—my legs were stiff and sore by the first night, and by the time we saw our destination on the horizon, it felt like my tailbone had been forced partway up my back. My entire rear resented the notion of movement in equal measure to its resentment for sitting still, and there was no muscle I could stretch to relieve my discomfort. Shea, I determined from her tart expression, was experiencing much of the same.

We arrived in Oaray in the early evening, while the town still looked like a happy, safe place to raise children. In truth, it was—but only if parents wanted their offspring to establish themselves as successful deviants come adulthood.

As I had been in the City of False Smiles before, I knew where to go and what to do. I led Shea on horseback through a few narrow streets, then into a main plaza, where the night was awakening. Greetings flew everywhere. The people of Oaray knew one another well, and visitors were welcomed whole-heartedly because they were the source of the city's income. There were nice buildings in the plaza, shops and the like, but only one remarkable structure. An open stable was attached to one side of it, and we tied our mounts before entering the peculiar bookstore-inn-restaurant-church that beckoned to us.

Every sort of person lounged inside the place, which was named The Emporium. There was drinking, but not to excess; the crowd seemed sober enough. Long fainting couches accented the floor-to-ceiling bookshelves that had the attention of a few children. On the other side of the establishment, chairs were arranged like pews and a man preached. In a corner to the preacher's left, I spotted an exchange taking place: a bible for quite a bit of gold. I wondered what treasures the undoubtedly hollowed-out book really contained.

"Can I help you?" asked a woman with a bright accented voice that told me she wasn't a native of the Warckum Territory. Truth be told, she probably didn't have the papers to leave Oaray. She stood behind the counter straight ahead of us, and I smiled back, Shea close on my heels.

"Room ten-twelve," I said, and the woman, blond hair braided with twigs and pretty berries, pulled out her register.

"What was the room number you requested?"

"Four-six," I replied, ignoring the confusion in Shea's dark, penetrating eyes.

"You're all set." She flipped her book closed and handed me a key. "You know the way?"

At my nod, she finished, "Sleep well! Service will be up in a few."

I thanked her and turned toward the stairs that curved behind the entry desk. But before I could take more than a few steps, Shea caught my arm.

"Care to explore a bit?" She glanced around the establishment, clearly intrigued by its atmosphere, and my stomach clenched, wondering how many young men might be on the loose in Oaray. At the concern on my face, Shea tentatively added, "I mean, this looks like an interesting place."

I sighed, feeling like an overly strict guardian. "Not now. Business to attend to first. We'll see if there's time after."

She nodded and followed me to the staircase. Up, up, and up we went until we found the third floor, which was nothing more than attic space. Unlocking the only door, I ushered my friend inside a tiny, dingy room stuck under the eaves that held but a couple of chairs and a table. Its smell was rancid, a mixture of spilled alcohol, cheap food, pipe tobacco and blood.

Shea wrinkled her nose against the odor. "Anya, what the hell? I know we're on a tight budget, but there's no bed up here, and this room is not labeled ten-twelve. That *service* the girl mentioned had better be good."

"It will be. Just relax."

We sat around for half an hour or so, Shea occasionally parting the dusty curtains to peer through a small window, until finally there was a knock on the door.

"The person you're expecting?" she asked, and I hopped to my feet with a nod.

But the person who came through the door was not Deangelo, the trustworthy Faerie with a despicable attitude who had sold me my forged papers when I'd gone on my original Crossing. This was not Deangelo, to whom we Faeries were sent for aid, to whom Evangeline would have gone for travel papers stating she was human, the man Illumina would have been told by my father to see. This was a new man, young, small in frame and height, but with sharp hazel eyes. He wore suspenders, a top hat, and heavy eyeliner, probably so he could blend in with the night crowd of Oaray, although the clothes suited him better than a costume of convenience should have.

Behind him came an older man, large, bald, and carrying a wooden box.

"Who are you?" I asked confrontationally, but the fellow in the suspenders was neither insulted nor surprised.

"I'm not Deangelo," he drolly admitted, tapping a cane he didn't need on the ground to punctuate his words. "A blessing from the perspective of some of his customers."

"Not from mine."

The bald man carried his box to a beat-up desk and set it down amidst a cloud of dust, and Suspenders spun to flop dramatically into a moth-bitten armchair. I scrutinized him—he was not much older than Shea and I.

"There's no way around this, darling. I do the papers now. Deangelo got taken away about two months ago."

"Taken away?" My gaze drifted to Shea, hoping she was keeping an eye on the bald fellow. She didn't disappoint. Her hand rested on the pistol at her hip.

"You're not going to trust me unless I'm straight with you," the suspendered fellow went on. "I respect that. If you worked with Deangelo in the past, then you have to know it's dangerous, what he used to do, what I do now. Every once in a while the Governor decides it's time to raid Oaray. The rumors about this place finally get to him or something. Who knows? But Deangelo went down in the last sweep."

"Well, where is he now?" I demanded, thinking not only of the aging Faerie, but of Evangeline, who might have wandered into the middle of this *sweep*.

"How should I know?" The cane tapped a few times, whether out of impatience or nervousness, I couldn't tell. "The Governor's laws protect the Fae, but they sure as hell don't protect criminals, not even magic ones."

For the first time, the bald man spoke, muttering something in a language I couldn't understand. At his partner's quick shake of the head, he went back to the wooden box.

"You want papers or not?" Suspenders drawled.

Though I wasn't happy about things, I nodded. We needed travel documents for Shea, no way around it.

"Tell me your names," I grumbled. "So I'll know who I'm dealing with in the future."

"Haruspex by first, Eskander by last. But you can call me Spex—the rest just gets in the way. That big guy over there is Hastings. So what name are we putting on these papers? I guarantee they'll look as official as if the Governor himself put his seal on them."

"Mary Archer," I said, giving the name only a moment's thought. Shea could pass for a Mary, and the last name was common enough not to draw questions. "We just need the one set."

Hastings pulled up a creaky chair and opened his box, re-moving a few materials. The basic papers were already made up, but he mixed together some ink that had a distinctive shine in the light, and made careful swoops with his hand to draw out the necessary print. When he was finished, he waved Shea over, handed her the quill, and instructed "Miss Archer" to sign her name.

"That's everything you need," Spex said, standing with the same sort of flourish with which he'd sat. "Now, about what I need."

"I know, twenty gold," I said, pulling out my money pouch.

"Fifty," he corrected, and I froze, trying to make sense of his unyielding expression.

"That's more than twice Deangelo's rate!"

He shrugged unapologetically. "So you can do math. Doesn't change the price."

"But it does make you a thief. Especially when I don't know if your work's any good."

"Forger, thief—any more compliments and I'll blush. But here's the bottom line. After what happened to our mutual acquaintance, rates went up. The risk factor is greater. I can't justify putting my neck on the chopping block for twenty pieces." Spex sauntered toward the door. "If you don't like the price, don't take the papers. If you don't trust the product, that's all the more reason to walk away."

Shea muttered something to Spex as Hastings closed up shop. From her tone, I guessed it was an insult, but the words were in the same language the illicit duo had spoken earlier. His heavily lined hazel eyes shifted from smug to cautious; the bald man, on the other hand, appeared not to have heard.

I counted out the coins Spex wanted and handed them over.

"If these papers don't deliver," Shea barked at the departing men's backs, "you'll hear from us. You can count on it."

"Just stay out of trouble, dolls," Spex called as he descended the stairs, then the businessmen were gone.

I tossed Shea my travel documents and she compared them to her new ones. "They look good. Hard to believe, but I think they'll pass."

"I want to know what really happened to Deangelo."

Dust floated around our heads, and I was about to suggest we leave the attic and find a real place to sleep when Shea stopped me with a question.

"Deangelo was your friend?"

"Not really a friend. He was old, sort of hated all living

things. But he was dependable. A Faerie who fell in love with money and settled out here after he went on his Crossing."

"Because Spex and Baldy—they were trying to decide if you were Fae."

"What?" I sputtered, the leather folder she'd returned to me slipping through my fingers. It flipped open, and the documents broke away from each other in the manner of grown siblings.

"I speak a little Bennighe," Shea affirmed, helping me to gather the papers. "It was my mother's first language. The big guy asked what Spex saw on you. If you flickered or something like that. I don't know all the dialects. But he meant did you have wings."

I stuffed my passport into my jerkin and ran to the window. Evangeline would have come this way on her Crossing, and Illumina almost certainly had encountered these two. I was lucky enough—if it could be called luck—to be wingless, but my friend and my cousin would have been exactly what Spex was looking for. What did he and Hastings want with Faeries?

Through the coats of dirt on the pane, I could see citizens lighting gas lamps along the street. I surveyed the scene and caught a glimpse of the distinctive pair with whom we'd just done business vanishing around a corner.

"Come on," I ordered, grabbing my coat and pack. Shea did likewise, and we fled the room, eager to see where the forgers were headed.

Leaving The Emporium, Shea and I headed onto the streets, which had the atmosphere of a perpetual holiday despite the cold—everything was prepared and kept to impress guests, including decorative pine wreaths on doors and lampposts that brought sparks of life to the city in the dead of winter. We jogged in the direction Spex and his partner had been going, and identified their destination with relative ease. There was a second inn, this one home to a large and raucous pub, a few blocks away.

The inn was named The Illusion, presumably a jab at the blindness of the Governor's Constabularies to Oaray's under-belly. We went indoors, Shea in the lead, since Spex had spent more time talking to me than to "Mary Archer." I pushed back my hood, not wanting to look suspicious, then tied my reddish-brown hair into a bun to draw less attention to its vi-brant color.

With little searching, we found the pair we had followed at an out-of-the-way table, engaged in a discussion with two other men. I examined the faces of the four conspirators and my palms began to sweat. Spex and Hastings were meeting with Fae hunters. I knew because the tall, stringy-haired man who had bound my hands was among them. I hadn't expected to remember any of their faces, but now that he was before me, his features were as recognizable as my own reflection. Based on what Thatcher had told me, the other men were likely his brothers or cousins. Besieged by trembling, I shrank into the shadows along the wall, images of a halberd flashing behind my eyes. My temples pounded, and my body jerked in an at-tempt to escape the phantom weapon.

I took a few deep breaths, tightening my fists at my sides, part of me wanting to rush forward and attack the culprit and part of me wanting to disappear. Shea said nothing. Her eyes were on our prey, making her oblivious to my struggle.

I gradually regained control of my emotions. There was nothing I could do about the past, however potent it was in my mind, but this meeting made it more imperative than ever to find out what Spex and Hastings might be doing. Their choice of associates left much to be desired.

Feeling tense and short-tempered, I waited with Shea at a dimly lit table near the door until the meeting broke up. The Faerie-hunters departed first, followed shortly thereafter by the odd duo we were trailing. Drinks in hand, Spex and Hastings sauntered by us, though their eyes never flicked in our direction. I frowned, for they stood at a deliberate distance from one another, their demeanors no longer that of friends or even associates. In fact, Spex stared at Hastings with unmistakable animosity.

Not wanting our presence to be detected, Shea and I delayed a bit before trailing them, stepping outside in time to see Hastings snatch the mug from Spex's hands. With a nasty laugh, he dumped the hot drink onto the street, melting the light layer of snow down to the cobblestone.

"What makes you think you get to keep that?" he sneered. "Just 'cause we had a generous customer don't mean you're one of us."

In an effort to listen without being seen, Shea and I slipped into the adjacent alley as the bald-headed man threw the mug away, obviously unconcerned with The Illusion's property. But rather than fight back, which would have been in accordance with his attitude, Spex hooked his thumbs in his suspenders and ignored the insult.

"And by the way," Hastings continued, starting once more down the street. "You keep up this farce of being in charge, me being your stupid sidekick, and I'll make you regret it, boy."

"I'm doing my job," Spex retorted. "Why change the farce when it's working? Besides, you aren't exactly customer friendly."

"Put some respect in that tone or I'll feed you to those ghouls myself."

Fear gnawed at my belly. Had I heard Hastings correctly?

"They're not attack dogs, Hastings. They're Sepulchres. They feed on purity and magic, neither of which I have in abundance. And you say people are supposed to believe you're *not* my stupid sidekick?"

The bald man's temper flared too quickly for protective measures, and one large hand wrenched Spex's black hair, knocking his hat off his head. I winced, afraid I would hear the snap of the young man's neck. Hastings thrust his associate into the alley wall, and we pulled up our hoods and shrunk farther back, out of range of the streetlights. Alarmed and confused, we watched Spex sink into the snow and wipe at the blood that trickled from his brow.

Hastings guffawed, shaking his head. "Come on, then. Get up."

To my shock, Spex obeyed. He grabbed his top hat and cane before stumbling after his partner as though on a leash, his posture completely devoid of dignity. Hefting my pack, I took a step after them, but Shea grabbed my sleeve.

"Anya, this isn't smart. Something's not right with these two, and I don't want to get in the middle."

"I don't have a choice," I snapped, jerking free of her grip. "I have another cousin, only fourteen years old, who would have come here not long ago. They might have hurt her."

I once more started after Hastings and Spex, only to have Shea throw her arms around me. With a burst of energy, she tugged me backward, and we stumbled over each other in the darkened alleyway.

"Let me go!" I fumed, twisting and turning in a struggle

to go after the pair of criminals that was getting farther and farther away.

"Listen to me," Shea gasped, pulling me down beside her in the snow. "If Spex and Hastings think we're onto them, they could hurt *us*."

"I don't care. They were talking to one of the hunters who hurt me." My tone turned vicious as thoughts of revenge inflamed me. "I'd like to track those men down one by one and truly make them understand what *hurt* means."

"Then it's a good thing my head's on straight," Shea scoffed, yanking on my collar to snap me to my senses. "They were talking about Sepulchres, multiple Sepulchres. Remember that thing that tried to kill you for your magic? Well, I'm disposed to avoid more of those creatures. Besides, if Spex and Hastings are hunting Faeries, then this operation has to be bigger than just the two of them. There's probably a whole network out there, and it'll take more than you and me to bring it down."

I stared at her, her words pricking me like bee stings. At last grasping her logic, I gazed at the muddy snow beneath my folded legs.

"The sad truth is this, Anya. If your cousin's been snatched, she's not in Oaray anymore. There's too much risk of discovery here. We won't gain anything by playing our hand this soon. We have to hold on to the information until we have more to go on."

I sunk into myself and sprawled on my back on the cold ground, letting the fight drain out of me. My temples were throbbing, and in the center of my forehead there was a tug, urging me down some deep tunnel I instinctively dreaded. I squeezed my eyes shut to chase away the sensation, only to be flooded with vivid images of a place and time I thought I'd left behind.

★ ★ ★

"I'm sorry if I offended you earlier," said the little girl, her shape so frail and tiny that I couldn't help thinking her a child, though she was but two years younger than me.

"It's all right," I assured her, watching her brush a hand along the indentation in the walls to ignite it. "You didn't offend me."

"I realize that you and Aunt share the same views. But I know why my father believed what he did, and I'm honoring him."

"What do you believe, Illumina?"

She looked up at me, her green eyes almost afraid, though I couldn't fathom the reason. If one of us was to be afraid, it should have been me in light of the things Illumina had said that afternoon in argument with the Queen. Human-lovers were traitors, she had asserted, not peacemakers. If we wanted to ally ourselves with humans, we should leave the Realm of the Fae and roll in the mud with them. Faeries were the elite species, and humans were oxen, and human-lovers floundered in between, not deserving what either side had to offer. She had practically said we pacifists didn't deserve to live. Her words might have given me pause when she'd asked me to come and see her, had I not known that her vehemence in speech was rarely linked to action.

"What are you really asking?" Illumina astutely countered.

"How would you feel if you saw a human in need? A child crying, or a man or woman drowning and calling out to you for help?"

"It doesn't matter what I'd feel. What matters is right and wrong. Humans make ruins of everything they touch. They're a stupid, vile race that should be eliminated like vermin, whether or not they could incite sympathy in me under the right circumstances. That's what it means to be a real warrior—to be able to put aside feelings in favor of the greater good. That's how the world is changed."

"There's no such thing as the greater good if you're busy killing and destroying along the way," I argued, appalled by her logic, the logic *instilled in her by Ubiqua's brother, my own uncle. "Besides, who said it was your calling to be a warrior? You're only thirteen. It's not up to you to change the world."*

She homed in on me like a bird of prey, coming around the love-carved bench between us with such determination that I backed away.

"Age doesn't matter," she spat. "All that matters is belief, strength, power, and letting nothing stand in your way."

Illumina was breathing heavily, her eyes glistening with angry tears; then she gasped in a lungful of air and her mood abruptly changed. In the blink of an eye, she was the same girl I'd seen upon entering her shelter: a petite, kind, sweet-voiced angel.

"I'm sorry, Anya. I can be so rude sometimes. I don't mean it."

She turned away from me to contemplate the images that covered her walls.

"Why, Illumina? Why do you believe these things?"

Glancing over her shoulder, she smiled a little half smile. "Because."

She took hold of the hem of her tunic and lifted it, slowly and purposefully so that her bare back was exposed to me. Scarred into her skin were the words: belief, strength, power, perseverance.

My clearest thought was that she could never have reached to do this to herself.

"Anya, what's this other cousin's name?" Shea asked, shaking my shoulder. Her tone implied this wasn't the first time she had asked the question. She was kneeling beside me, brushing back her snow-dampened hair, concern written all over her face.

"Illumina," I croaked, propping myself up on my elbows. I felt hazy, like I was recovering from too much Sale. I glanced around, trying to clear my confusion. Where exactly was I?

"Well, I hate to be the one to say this," Shea went on, "but it seems you need to decide which cousin is more important to find—Zabriel or Illumina."

Oaray. The alley from which I'd watched Spex and Hastings disappear. I covered my face with my hands, the bitter snow trying to burrow beneath my knuckles, my faculties restored. I needed to find Zabriel, even if it meant abandoning Illumina to some unknown fate. Queen Ubiqua's desires were paramount.

"You're right," I sighed, shifting into a sitting position. "Zabriel is our priority."

Shea nodded and rose to her feet, then extended a hand to pull me up beside her. Clammy and frozen, we trudged back to The Emporium, where I retrieved an actual room key from the berry-crowned blonde at the front desk. As we climbed to the second floor, neither of us in a mood to explore our surroundings, memories of a conversation with my father surfaced, ominous and unsettling. He had hinted that Ubiqua might not have intended for Illumina to return to Chrior. If my young cousin had come into contact with Spex and Hastings, I had an unproven but firm belief that my aunt may have gotten her wish.

I felt ill the entire night we spent in Oaray, suffering from both chills and flashes of heat. The sensation was bizarre— even during my on-and-off recovery at the More house, I hadn't thought of myself as sick. Fae were all but immune to traditional human illness, but Zabriel had described something similar to me. He said fever was like inhospitable weather that got *inside* you—no shade or water could relieve you.

After dragging myself out of bed in the morning, I dropped off our room key at the front desk, then Shea and I found a little restaurant in which to have breakfast. Thankfully, my symptoms had abated enough that my hands were no longer shaking.

We took seats at a corner table, Shea taking care not to remove her overcoat—her belt full of bullets would have drawn immediate attention since the people of Oaray were so fond of their facade of joviality. The one person who probably wouldn't have noticed was the owner of the restaurant, for he was too busy bickering with another patron to pay us much heed, even as he took our orders.

"I told you," he called over his shoulder while he set down our plates. "I won the bet! I got the goods to prove it." Looking at us as though we were an interruption, he blustered, "Anything else?"

"I'll tip you five pieces if you take that man and show him your winnings," Shea murmured, and I cocked an eyebrow at her, not understanding her purpose. "But just him. Not his friend."

The proprietor examined us with a confounded expression, and I stole a glance behind him. My eyes landed on Hastings and Spex at a far table, and I gave Shea an appreciative nod.

"Oi!" the owner called, turning away from us, apparently having decided he could use some extra jingle. "You come and see what I got right now. I don't have time for all this sniveling and arguing."

With a gruff laugh, Hastings stood, stretching his bulky arms before gripping Spex by the back of his shirt.

"Leave the kid, Hastings," our new accomplice barked. "If anything goes missing from my stash, I want to know who to gut."

Hastings scowled and pushed Spex back into his chair.

"Stay put," he ordered, then he followed the proprietor up a narrow flight of stairs.

I sprang to my feet, not about to waste time, and hastened to the seat Hastings had vacated. Shea followed, taking up the spot on Spex's other side.

"There's a reason he's nothing but a lackey," Spex remarked, referring to his absent companion. "I saw you two come in. I knew what you were going to do before you did."

"What's your interest in Faeries?" I demanded, my voice conspiratorial. "Tell me quick, before your keeper comes back."

Spex's eyeliner was smeared, his hair unwashed. He hadn't changed clothes since last night, whether for lack of an opportunity or for lack of caring, I didn't know. In the morning sunlight that streamed through the windows, he struck me as pathetic. In his defiant eyes, however, was a rejection of my judgment. I didn't know anything about him.

"You got your problems, I got mine, honey," he said, taking a stab at the floor with his cane. "Just leave it alone."

He pulled on his cloak, making to leave, but Shea slammed her hand down on his hat before he could pick it up, crunching the brim. With her other hand, she tugged aside the corner of her coat, revealing a section of her belt. Bullets winked at Spex warningly, and I gave him my best glare. This was quite a game into which we were wading.

Spex pursed his lips and sat back. "You want the truth? I don't give a shit about Faeries. All I do is spot them." He pointed at me. "You used to be one. Lost your wings. I can tell because the magic is floating around you. I'm a resource for some important people, and that's all. If you want real answers, talk to Hastings. Good luck, mind you."

"What happens to the Faeries you identify?" I persisted.

Spex had answers he wasn't giving up. I glanced at the cut on his forehead from when Hastings had thrown him into the wall, wondering if reopening it would encourage his cooperation. Normally, I wouldn't have considered violence, but I'd hit the man lusting after Shea in Strong, and this fellow disgusted me even more. He'd described himself as *a resource,* as though that were an honorable profession. He was nothing more and nothing less than a hunter's accomplice.

"I don't know," he replied, the words punctuated, and I had the impression he'd read my mind. "Now get out of here before he comes back. Unless you want to get me killed."

"Why should we care?" Shea sneered.

"Because Hastings will kill you, too." Spex was growing desperate, hazel eyes darting about the room, body bent toward the staircase from which Hastings would emerge as he strained to listen for footsteps. "What is it you want from me?"

I took a breath, abandoning my frustration with him. He was a prisoner of some kind, not the threat I imagined him to be.

"I need to know if you identified two Faeries, both female. One has long black hair and is small, younger than us. You might have noticed scars on her body. She would have been through here about three weeks ago."

Spex shook his head. "Haven't had a Faerie besides you in the last month. Doesn't sound familiar."

This was a relief, although it begged the question of where Illumina would have gone besides Oaray, especially since my father would have stressed the importance of falsified travel papers. Then my heart faltered—maybe something had happened to her before she'd reached this city.

"The other one is tall, white-blond hair, probably tied with different-colored ribbons. My age. Her name is Evangeline."

This time, Spex nodded. "Yeah, I identified her."

I gulped for air but could produce no sound, prompting Shea to speak up on my behalf.

"Where do they go? The Faeries you spot?"

"I don't know. Really, I don't. Look, it's not just my neck I'm risking by talking to you...." He trailed off, then focused his gaze on me. "You care about this girl, don't you?"

He was seeking a reason to be honest with me, and I could tell he needed a good one. Whomever he was putting in jeopardy by talking with us was important to him, and I had to show that Evangeline was just as important to me. I nodded, the tears in my eyes an unintentional boon to our goal.

"We keep Sepulchres," Spex murmured. "Hastings takes the Faeries to them because the creatures can identify their type of magic. You know, fire, earth, whatever. After, some of them are let go, thinking they drank too much and had a wild night, and some of them I don't see again. My best guess is they go to Tairmor. Maybe. It'd be a logical stop, anyway."

Shea stood, pulling Spex along with her, surprising me as much as him.

"Come with us. We'll find out if you're telling the truth, and you'll be rid of Hastings."

Spex jerked violently away from her, drawing a few stares from other patrons in the restaurant.

"No! I can't. I can't go with you. I told you, I'm not the only one in danger here. I have a debt to pay."

Shea paled. "A debt to whom?"

"Who do you think? Now get out of here. I don't want to know your names, and I don't want to see your faces again.

And if you open your mouths and get me killed, damned if I don't come back to haunt you. Go!"

We hurried back to our table, leaving Spex to reclaim his seat mere moments before Hastings and the restaurant owner returned, laughing with one another. We devoured our food, putting our heads down as Spex and Hastings departed. After giving them time to clear out of the area, we gathered our meager belongings and left the promised tip on the table for our server. Ready to leave Oaray behind, we headed to the livery stable, only to discover a familiar, large, bald-headed man inside the building, talking to the owner.

"Excuse me, but we'd like our horses," I boldly interrupted. The livery owner mumbled something beneath his breath, then led our geldings into the aisle to saddle them.

"Nice-looking animals," Hastings remarked, stroking one of them on the neck. Turning to the owner, he offered, "I'll lend a hand. Can't expect much help from the girls here."

I resented the way he referred to us; I also resented his involvement in preparing our mounts, though I couldn't come up with a reason to object. When the men had secured our bedrolls and packs behind the saddles, I nudged Shea and we walked outside, letting the livery owner lead the horses. Swinging aboard much more smoothly than our first attempt in Strong, we nudged the geldings forward, leaving Hastings in the dust. I sincerely hoped we'd never have the displeasure of seeing him again.

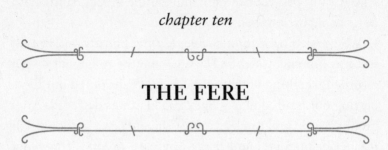

chapter ten

THE FERE

I had no doubt that the next leg of our journey to Tairmor would be the most taxing. There was a mountainous stretch between the east and west sides of the Warckum Territory called the Fere, most likely a shortened version of *interference*, for its sole purpose seemed to be to hinder travelers. While there was a path carved through the Fere, and a few tiny mining towns where Shea and I could have stayed, we opted to make our own camps off the road. After our dubious encounters with the locals of both Strong and Oaray, we preferred to be safe rather than sorry. My travel funds were also drying up faster than I would have liked, the inflated expense of Shea's travel papers having delivered a bit of a blow.

Shea was restless on our first night in the wild, mountainous country we were now crossing. She tended the fire, continuing even after it was energetic enough to heat our sleeping space under a gray stone outcropping. Having traveled through this part of the Territory before, I made a snare and went hunting for small game, wanting to conserve our jerky. When I returned, Shea was standing and staring out into the void, a lit piece of wood held high. She jumped when I stepped out of the darkness, and I could no longer ignore her state of mind.

"What's the matter?" I asked, retrieving my long-knife and sitting down to skin the animals I'd captured.

"Nothing. I guess I'm just nervous about being followed."

I chuckled. "Who would be following us? Spex and Hastings have a business to run. And the Sepulchre that broke into our room in Strong stole what it wanted and got a bullet for its trouble. I hate to tell you, but we're not all that interesting. So what's really going on?"

Shea sighed and came to sit beside me, poking at the fire. "My last trip through the Fere wasn't an easy one. It's messing with my head."

I thought about this for a moment, putting our meat on a spit to cook. "When your family fled Tairmor?" At her nod, I pressed further. "I don't quite remember—what was your father involved in?"

"He was a woodworker and a machinist, specialized in clocks. We used to have the most beautiful clocks all over the house."

"He built the one back at the cabin," I surmised, picturing the tall clock that stood in the main room of the Mores' house. It had been simple but beautiful, with etchings around the face.

"He did." She smiled, reflecting. "He was a very fine craftsman—still is, I suppose. He found his own raw materials and made everything from scratch. His work was always of top quality. And he was careful about the projects he undertook. He knew the specifications of an order before he decided whether or not to accept it. That's why I don't understand what went wrong when he received work commissioned by the government."

A nervous discomfort began to build in me as she spoke. "Did you ever see what he was making?"

"Once—it looked like a magician's box. You know, where the magician makes someone disappear? I'd seen a magic show in Tairmor when I was younger and was excited about the project. But he got angry at me for poking around and said it was just a fancy wardrobe. All I know is he didn't finish the work, and ended up owing the government a large sum of money."

She hugged her knees to her chest, and I could see the descent of her mood in the dropping of her eyes and hollowing of her cheeks.

"When we found out we couldn't leave the Territory from Sheness, we came through here—through the Fere. We stayed off the path, traveling mostly at night, and it was horrible. It was cold, and we were afraid of pursuit. And if my mother hadn't known her plants and herbs, we probably would have starved to death."

Shea hesitated, distractedly toying with the necklace Thatcher had given her. "One time when we were resting, I got up the courage to ask my father about his debt. He didn't really want to talk about it, but he ended up saying, 'Sometimes the people we're supposed to trust do bad things. And even if we respect those people, their actions are still wrong, and something has to be done about it.' I always thought he was talking about himself, telling me I shouldn't resent the government for trying to find us. Now I think maybe he was defending his own decisions, and trying to explain politics to me."

"Politics can be complicated," I acknowledged, feeling I had some experience in the field. "I'm sure your father had good reason for abandoning the government's project, whatever it was. He wouldn't lightly take his family on the run."

Removing our sizzling dinner from the spit, I offered a portion to Shea. "No one's going to bother us tonight. And hot food in your stomach will make it easier to sleep."

She nodded and took a bite. "This is delicious. Better than jerky."

"You sound surprised. I think I've been insulted."

Shea grinned. "Not at all. I just didn't know how good a cook you'd be. After all, you didn't know how to ride a horse."

I reached behind me, grabbed a handful of snow and flung it at her. Before long, we were both laughing, her jest giving me confidence that she would be fine.

We continued our difficult journey through the Fere, and by the third night, I was shivering far more than could be attributed to the bitter weather.

"Sit close to the fire," Shea told me, and I inched toward our source of warmth, allowing her to remove my blanket and cloak. My body felt incapable of functioning normally—my movements were choppy, as though my muscles had to break free of thick sap.

I shuddered in the breeze that made its way into our makeshift pitched-blanket enclosure, and turned my back to Shea so she could look at my injury. She lifted my shirt and gasped.

"What is it?" I asked, my jaw barely unlocking for speech.

"When did you remove the bandages, Anya? I didn't say you could. Never mind, it doesn't matter now. But the way this looks, I'm going to have to lance the wounds. The infection is deep, and I need to draw it out."

She went to her pack to retrieve a hunting knife and the necessary supplies, leaving me longing for Sale, which I realized now was a miracle drink. Not only did it speed healing, ward off illness and increase energy, it also took the edge off pain.

I knew of nothing like it in the Warckum Territory. It was beginning to feel like being human was akin to being cursed.

"I'll try to be quick," Shea said, heating her blade over the fire to sterilize it.

I nodded. "Ready when you are."

She came to my side, and I buried my face in my knees, clenching my jaw against the flare of pain I knew would be forthcoming. But when Shea touched me, I lurched forward, seized by the certainty she intended to harm me. I turned around, my hand slipping to the Anlace, and fear dashed across her face.

"Anya, are you all right? I thought you wanted me to help you."

I stared at her, whatever I had felt fading. "I did. I mean, I do. I'm sorry, Shea. I guess I'm just not feeling well."

Shea chuckled nervously. "That's obvious. So am I going to have to knock you out to get this done?"

"No, but thanks for the offer." I gave her a weak smile. "I promise to be a good patient."

"Then let's try again."

I returned to my earlier posture, and this time I permitted Shea to minister to my wounds.

"All right, that's good for now," she finished. "But I'm going to have to keep an eye on you. We're probably in for a long night."

She was right, of course. Between my intermittent discomfort and the medical attention she had to continually administer, neither of us slept much. I lay facedown on a bed of blankets, and when Shea wasn't attempting to clean and redress my fractured skin, the rest of the blankets were on top of me, including those that had cushioned the horses' backs beneath our saddles.

Despite my mound of coverings, I was cold, and I worried about Shea in her modest cloak. The one time I mustered the energy to offer her some of the warmth I was hoarding, she stubbornly refused.

"Patients come first," she said, appeasing me by sitting close to the fire. "Besides, what would I do if you died out here? This adventure we're on would be no fun at all."

"Did your mother teach you that?"

"What? To value my friends?"

I was pale and sickly, but nonetheless, the sound that came out of my mouth resembled a chuckle.

"No, I meant about the patients. Didn't you tell me back at the cabin that she was teaching you to be a healer?"

"*Trying* to teach me. I know enough to get by, but I was never that interested, to be honest. I think she hoped I'd become a nurse one day. That's what she used to be."

Shea gazed off into the distance, and I was thankful she missed my wince as I readjusted my position. I couldn't resist my next question, since our upcoming stop was the capital city.

"Are you excited to be going to Tairmor again? Or scared?"

"I'm not anything really," she responded with a shrug, though I could see the lie in her eyes. I waited tolerantly, my silence inviting her to continue. "There's this naive part of me that wants to see the city again, walk around like nothing ever happened, nothing changed. But that's stupid. It won't be safe for me in Tairmor. It's the most likely place someone will recognize me." She sighed, poking at the fire with a stick. "The capital's not my home anymore, Anya. It's a trap waiting to spring. Knowing that, I shouldn't be eager to get there."

"But you can't help yourself."

"Nope," she said with a reckless sort of cheerfulness. She came to her feet and tossed the stick into the darkness. "I'll walk into the trap smiling. Can't be helped."

I laughed, but it turned into a cough, which turned into another grimace.

"I'm fine," I said, sensing Shea was about to hand over her cloak.

She frowned at me for a moment, then changed the subject. "So you have two cousins lost out here in the human world?"

"It looks that way."

"Zabriel is the runaway you told me about, and..."

"Illumina is supposed to find him."

"Then what are you doing out here?"

The tale was taking on a humorous ring, and I bit my tongue to keep from responding, "Who knows?" I opted to try to explain instead.

"Illumina's only fourteen. And she's troubled. I don't really understand why my aunt sent her in the first place. So I decided to come after Zabriel myself and, if I can, make sure Illumina gets home safely."

"And I thought *my* family was messed up," Shea joked, bringing a wry smile to my face. She had a point. The royal family of Chrior was made up of human-haters and human-lovers, runaways and seekers, those who wanted the throne and those like me who absolutely did not. "I'll help you look for Illumina, too, if you like."

I nodded, concern wrinkling my brow. "I hate to say it, but if Illumina had run into Spex and Hastings, we'd have an idea how she's faring. As is, something could have happened to her before she even reached Oaray to get travel documents."

"I can't imagine how I'd feel if it was Maggie or Marissa who was missing. You must be going insane."

"If I let myself dwell on it, I want to throw up. I'm worried about both of them. It's been two years since Zabriel's disappearance, and I have no idea how he's doing or who he might have become. He'd be seventeen now, and might not have any interest in seeing me. And Illumina has never been in the Warckum Territory before and really shouldn't be out here on her own."

"And Evangeline? Who is she?"

"One of my best friends. She hadn't returned from her Crossing before I left—that's when we go into the human world for the first time. She was later than she should have been, and I knew something was wrong. I just didn't want to see it. I don't know why people think things are better if we pretend they're not happening. Pretending certainly didn't make anything better for Evangeline, wherever she is."

"This territory is a wilderness for you Fae, isn't it?" Shea mused, unable to argue or even comfort me on the point I had made. "Just like the Balsam Forest is for humans."

"Yes, I suppose it is."

Our conversation dropped off. Expressing my concerns to Shea had done nothing to ease them, and a sick feeling had now crept into my stomach. Eventually, I noticed her biting her thumbnail, a sign she was restless, too.

"Is there something else you wanted to ask?" I prompted.

"It's just curiosity, so you don't have to answer if you'd rather not. But I was wondering if you have any brothers or sisters? Or do you only have cousins?"

"I'm an only child, which is pretty typical of Fae families since the war. We live long lives and have somewhat limited space in our corner of the forest. I only have the two cousins, and like me, they have no brothers or sisters."

"What about your parents?"

Shea's line of inquiry was taking me down an uncomfortable road. I didn't want her to know of my family's connection to the Queen. But she had told me about her family; it seemed only fair to tell her about mine. Besides, I hadn't talked to anyone about my mother and father since Zabriel had run away, and there was a surprising longing in my heart to do so. And so I gave an honest, but incomplete, answer.

"My mother died a few years ago. She was sick. My father monitors news from the Territory and offers advice to travelers."

"I'm sorry about your mother, Anya."

"No need to be. I have a good life in the Faerie Realm."

The words came without thought, but I could tell from Shea's expression that she was feeling the reverberations of my mistake. *Not anymore* seemed to echo in the air between us.

"We should try to get some sleep," I mumbled, my mood sinking. I no longer wanted to discuss my situation. Things that had been kept locked away for two years could remain unsaid for a while longer.

Shea settled down on her bedroll, while I fought to keep my anxiety in check, reminding myself we'd soon arrive at the capital, where we were bound to find some answers. We'd have to be careful, of course, and avoid the Governor's men, a task that wouldn't necessarily be easy since Tairmor was the seat of his power. I didn't know much about Governor Ivanova, except that he was supposedly pro-Faerie rights, yet Spex was paying off a debt to his regime by helping to identify and abduct Fae. That discrepency, coupled with my aunt's warning that Ivanova did not know he had a grandson and should not be viewed as a resource to us, ensured that I had no intention of going near the man. Not to mention the risk he posed to Shea.

Though finding a comfortable position was difficult, I tried to get some rest, knowing it was essential to regaining my strength. I could not afford to be sick; I could not afford to slow down. My straightforward mission to find Zabriel was becoming complicated, and the complications presented by Illumina and Evangeline were dangerous. I needed to find out who was hunting Faeries almost as much as I needed to bring the Prince of Chrior home. And the longer I delayed, the more Fae would potentially be hurt, and the more in jeopardy the throne would become.

By the next morning, I was fevered, and when we stopped at one of the mining towns, Shea was insistent that we find a doctor. I refused. No one in these parts needed to know that I was—or had been—Fae. The people here spoke in short, lazy sentences, looked at strangers with suspicion, and in general didn't radiate a sense of open-mindedness or caring. No one even paid my obviously severe condition a glance. Instead, we took advantage of a little market and restocked our supplies, including bandages. These would have to see us the rest of the way to Tairmor.

Our dealings completed, we retrieved our horses from the stable where we had left them to be fed and watered. There wasn't much food available for them in the Fere, especially not in the winter. We paid more for their grain than for our own provisions, but we didn't have a choice. We needed the horses to make any sort of time.

We walked our sated animals down the raw, stone street—

the only street in the whole place—until we came to the edge of town. A gated tunnel greeted us, guarded by a handful of military men. After exchanging an uneasy glance, Shea and I approached.

"Halt," ordered one of the men, jumping from the outpost beside the gate. "I need to see your papers."

I removed my travel documents from my jerkin, Shea likewise producing hers. Though I noticed a tremor in her hands, the man either didn't see it or chose not to remark upon it. He took our passports and examined them carefully, in particular eyeing the seal in the bottom right corner. Satisfied, he returned them to us, which more or less established the quality of Hastings's work.

"Raise the gate!" he shouted, motioning us ahead.

The gate was so rickety the raising of it could have caused its destruction, and I ducked my head protectively as we rode beneath it. Still, the existence of the obviously hastily constructed checkpoint was bothersome, for it was another sign that things were changing in the Territory.

The horses fussed during the initial minutes of darkness inside the tunnel, reminding me again that I was a nominally proficient rider, but they soon settled down. My eyes also adjusted quickly to the dimness—perhaps I still possessed certain Fae characteristics. Shea, with her human senses, rode behind me, her horse's shoulder to my mount's hip, as though afraid she would get lost.

We camped that night under an open sky. I'd done my best to hide my pain throughout the day, but now my shoulder blades ached with every pulsation of blood that passed through them. The bandages around my chest felt soaked, and I could hardly tolerate a shift in position. Despite my hope that Shea's ministrations would have been enough, I could no longer deny that I needed a doctor.

Though Shea was inclined to backtrack to one of the towns for medical help, I wouldn't entertain the idea. We were closer to Tairmor at this point and traveling downhill. Retreating would mean a more arduous journey for me and the horses, one I wasn't sure I could make. I didn't share this last thought with Shea, however, suspecting it would have made her even more insistent. Instead, I put on a brave face and promised to call for her if my condition worsened. While she wasn't happy about the situation, she mixed some herbs from her medical supplies in a cup of warm water, assuring me it would help me to rest.

I lay on my bedroll, floating between awareness and un-consciousness, between the heat of the sun and the chill of the moon. Faces and shapes kept flashing through my mind, jerk-ing my limbs as though I were a marionette in some lurid pup-pet show, and each time I moved, my back ached and stung. First there was Zabriel, but his warm, dark eyes had turned pale green and glowed ominously, warning me that he was not the same Prince I had known. Next was Ubiqua, sitting on her throne of twined roots, her hair matted and tangled but long enough to trail across the floor of the Great Red-wood. Circles cleaved to her eyes like men aboard a sinking ship, and she gazed through me, begging me to understand. Understand what? That she had sent Illumina to die, she told me, that the sacrifice was necessary. I fled from her in horror.

Then I met my young cousin, her black hair and pale skin unchanged from the way I remembered her. The only differ-ence was that she was happy to see me, and Illumina was rarely happy. Just when she broke into a smile, figures loomed behind her, and a man wrapped his overgrown hand across her mouth.

"Got one," he murmured, and I lurched forward, wanting to save her from the hunters, but she had faded into shadow, intangible and ghostly.

I couldn't breathe. I was hot and cold at once, my body fevered, my lungs screaming for air. It was part of the dream, part of the illness, my mind maintained; then clarity came to me, and my eyes flew open.

I screamed loud and long, though the sound was muffled by luminescent fingers. A pistol went off, but the suffocating grip around my chest and throat only tightened, and I struggled against arms that were at once weightless and as strong as iron. Then my thoughts clicked into place, and I groped at my hip for the Anlace. With my legs threatening to give out, I ripped it from its sheath and struck at my assailant with a blade instead of bare hands.

A spine-tingling screech tore through the darkness, evidence of the effectiveness of my defense. Again I struck, the Anlace sinking deep into flesh and sinew, and the creature released me. I fell to my knees, then scrambled toward Shea, the horrific sounds of my attacker's death throes echoing in the foothills of the Fere. I cowered, feeling like I was still trapped in my nightmares, that any direction I ran, walls of glass would contain me like a figure in an orb.

Shea was suffering no such delusions. Loading and reloading her pistol, she fired a steady chain of shots that hit their mark more than once and eventually forced our enemies to withdraw. When at last the only sounds were the wind and the frantic stamping of horses' hooves, I raised my head and dared to look around.

On the ground near my bedroll lay a corpse—only one, despite the number of bullets Shea had sent flying. But the body was no longer white like the hands that had tried to strangle me; it shimmered green, blue, red, and gold in the manner of Faerie wings. Gradually a black fog corrupted the skin, then dissipated into the air.

"What...?" I stammered, unable to process the sight. "What...?"

"Sepulchres," Shea supplied, kneeling beside me. "There were four of them. They went after you first. But this time, they came at me, too." A shudder passed through her body, perhaps from the memory of those long fingers reaching for her throat. "I—I thought they were going to kill me, but then they backed off. I suppose because I have no magic. When they began to tear through our packs, I drew my gun and started shooting."

She was pale and shaken, and I looked to the Royal Anlace in my fist—the weapon that had killed a once-magical creature when bullets could not. Perhaps it wasn't such a bad thing that Queen Ubiqua had given it to me. I thought back to Thatcher's assessment that the blade had been imbued with poison, but I couldn't quite embrace that idea. The weapon was a relic, forged by our ancestors, the Old Fae, and using the riches of Nature for dubious purposes like crafting poisons would have been even more proscribed historically than it was now. I had a stronger sense that the Anlace was imbued with an ancient power long since out of my people's reach. Our smiths could craft conduit swords for the Queen's Blades to augment their elemental magic, but making a weapon with independent magical properties was unheard of. Maybe the Old Fae had possessed skills we lacked.

"We've got to get out of here, Anya," Shea urged, rising to her feet. "They could come back, and my gun doesn't do more than scare them."

Too weak to be of much help, I watched my friend haphaz-ardly gather up our things. When she went to get our packs, it became clear the Sepulchers had only gone after mine, for hers was still tied closed. It didn't take long to discover the reason for the creatures' interest.

"What's this?" she asked, holding up a small vial filled with an amber liquid that glistened in the firelight.

"It looks like...the same drink the Sepulchre took from me back in Strong." I doubted Shea knew much about Sale other than that it was a dangerous and illegal substance, and I didn't want to get into a discussion of it now.

"I remember." Shea's face puckered in bewilderment. "Why is it in your pack? I thought that flask was all you had."

I tugged on my hair, trying to sort things out, and the an-swer hit me with the force of an arrow.

"Hastings," I gasped. "He must have planted it when he was helping saddle our horses. It would have attracted the Sepulchres."

"You mean he sent those creatures after us? On *purpose?*"

"I've never encountered a Sepulchre in my travels in the Territory before, not even when I had my magic. We know Hastings keeps them—he must have found a way to control them, too. That vial would have left a scent for them to follow."

Shea launched into a string of profanities that would have done a sailor proud, ending with, "I'm going to kill that fat, ugly, balding swine someday!"

I gave the only response that came to my addled brain. "I've never encountered a balding pig in my travels, either."

She gave a short laugh and finished the work, deftly rolling our bedding. After helping me to my feet, she approached the horses intending to saddle them, only to discover that the geldings had fought their ropes during the attack, and one of them had fallen and broken its neck. It was eerie to see an animal so large and powerful motionless, its eyes partially open and glassy with fear. Shea did the only thing we could for it, removing the horse's halter and lead to let it lie upon the ground as it had been born—unbound.

When we were at last ready to go, Shea helped me into the saddle of our remaining mount and climbed up behind me. With the sun just breaking over the horizon at our backs, we continued our journey down the other side of the Fere, believing our destination within reach this day. I clutched in my fist the vial with which Hastings had fortuitously supplied me—Sale was extremely difficult to come by in the Territory, and what he'd stowed in my pack wasn't much. But it might be enough.

chapter eleven

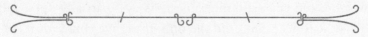

FRIEND OR FOE

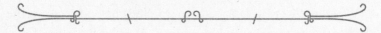

Tairmor was built to make an impression. The capital of the Warckum Territory was a fully walled marvel of a city, with massive stone dams to accommodate the river Kappa at its western and eastern borders. Shea and I followed the path of the river to the solid metal gate, around which curtains of water fell according to the dam's directions. The structure of the city was more than architecture; it was art.

The gate was open, seeming to invite us in, but we were stopped by guards whose demeanors were not entirely friendly. Considering the number of people they had to deal with each day, and the volume of documents they had to examine, their brusqueness was understandable, albeit annoying. It wasn't our fault that the Governor's men had increased security tenfold since the last time I'd been here. Not only were our papers scrutinized, but we were required to record our names and state our business, which we listed as touring, in a massive logbook before being granted passage. Shea had the presence of mind to ask the guards for directions to the nearest doctor's office, while I clung to our horse's mane, letting the blanket that was draped over my quivering form brush against the animal's flanks.

Though the beauty of Tairmor was lost on me at this moment, it had made quite an impression when I'd seen it a couple of months ago. The fountains and snowbirds' nests, which the nonmigratory birds strikingly insulated with dragon's blood sedum flowers, always reminded me of Chrior. The river gorge that cut through the center of the city created a perpetual gentle spray of water, while the falls that fed the Kappa down the side of the chasm were stunning. Of course, the city was still human—clouds of smoke puffed from homes and factories on the horizon, trees were killed and mutilated rather than negotiated with to make dwellings, and the earth's natural ground was paved over for streets. The way humans settled and claimed an area was by erasing what it had originally been, and the Fae in me resented Tairmor for these things, despite its magnificence.

Shea brought our horse to a halt, and I was assisted from the saddle and taken inside one of the buildings. All I felt was heat, despite the unrelenting shake in my bones. Someone removed my travel clothes, peeled away the soiled bandages that clung to my back like drying mud and put pressure on my screaming wounds. I cried out, and that was all it took for me to lose consciousness. My last sight was the silver pistol at Shea's hip, my accompanying thought the meager hope that she would keep up her guard while I was in a hapless state. These were neither familiar surroundings nor familiar people, and the question remained whether we had landed among friend or foe.

I awoke in the same sort of pain I'd been in when I'd opened my eyes at the More house, my body so fussy and restrictive that if I moved the wrong way, I'd damage myself all over again. The best thing I could do was lie still, even though my neck hurt from being craned to the side while I'd slept on my stomach.

I closed my eyes, trying to remember how I had ended up here. Then curiosity got the better of me and I examined the room, or what I could see of it from my position on the bed.

To my left was a curtain, while on my right, set into the brick wall, was a window with brilliantly clean glass. Judging from the voices that floated in the air, there were other people beyond the curtain, and when a woman in a soft blue dress that looked like a uniform came to check my pulse, I caught a glimpse of a row of beds behind her. I was in a human hospital. But where was Shea? Though I longed for an answer, I didn't make inquiries of the hospital staff, desiring no attention beyond what was necessary to care for my back.

As the day went on, restlessness set in, and I pushed myself up to look out the window. A short distance from the pane of glass was a brick wall—the space was hardly large enough to be an alley, though that was its purpose, and snow and leaves were gusted into piles along the ground like whitecaps. My gaze fell on a flyer posted a few yards down from the window, and I stared at it, unsure whether to laugh at the irony or appreciate the sentiment.

"FAE not FOE," it read above a drawing of a winged person with, fittingly enough, the same curly-toed boots we rigorously mocked in Chrior. At the bottom it announced: "Faerie Rights Are Human Rights." I was aware of the Governor's somewhat poetic penchant for slogans around which to rally his people, although I wasn't sure how well they worked. Some even asserted his efforts were child's play, the result of a weakening mind. Nonetheless, the flyer served as confirmation that the official position in Tairmor was staunchly pro-Fae.

It was evening before the curtain that divided my room from the larger hospital ward was pushed aside and Shea blessedly entered, glancing behind her as if to ensure she wasn't being followed. In true fugitive fashion, she'd probably been hiding during daylight hours. She jerked the divider back into place, though the thin fabric couldn't possibly shut out sound.

"Thank God you're awake," she exclaimed, moving to claim the chair at my bedside. "How are you feeling?"

"Better. Don't worry. I'll be able to travel tomorrow."

The skeptical lift of Shea's dark eyebrows told me she thought otherwise, and I sat up straighter to demonstrate my strength and stamina. I could tell she was still dubious, but at least she didn't belabor the point.

"Whether you can travel or not, I think we're safe for the time being. It's been three days and no one's recognized me or taken issue with you." Flashing a grin, she leaned closer to me, and it was clear she had also been treated well—her hair was clean and brushed, lying loose about her shoulders, and her clothing had been laundered. "Then again, I haven't left the hospital. I acted like I was starving and won several good meals and quite a bit of sympathy."

I chuckled at her self-satisfied expression, but couldn't share her casual attitude. We'd already lost precious time and I didn't want to lose more.

"I really can travel tomorrow, Shea. They injected me with some medication a while ago, and it's helping. I promise I'll take it easy, but there *are* a few things we need to accomplish."

She rolled her eyes. "Maybe letting yourself heal ought to be the first thing you do. Look, this hospital has so far been a good place for us. After all, you're not dead, and I haven't been arrested."

"I suppose I can wait and hear what the doctor has to say. But as soon as I'm discharged, we'll nose around the city for Evangeline and try to find out if Zabriel's been here." Diverting my gaze, I added, "I don't think there's much hope for word on Illumina.... I mean, she has no travel papers."

"At least we have a plan," Shea replied, trying to sound upbeat—she understood that my cousin might be dead or injured. "The best thing we can do right now is get a good night's sleep."

"That raises an interesting question. Where exactly have you been sleeping?"

She grinned mischievously. "On a cot in the doctor's lounge. I curl up after I've finished my patient rounds."

Shea ducked out of view around the curtain before I could retort, and I lay down on my side, settling into the comfort of my pillows. As I stared at the lights of the city filtering in through the window, my thoughts traveled to the events leading up to Queen Ubiqua's marriage to William Ivanova. From what I understood, the Governor had desired a lasting peace with the Faerie Realm along with an exchange of information. He understood that there was much to be learned from us, and that our elemental connections could be used to benefit both of our races. But I wondered if, in the aftermath of his son's death, his devotion to the cause was fueled by yet another motivation—to ensure the human world was welcoming to Fae in the hope that his grandchild would eventually cross into the Territory. He had known Ubiqua was pregnant, after all, and perhaps anguished over whether the baby had been born alive after crossing the Road in its mother's womb, whether it was a girl or a boy, and whether he would ever have a chance to get to know his eldest son's offspring.

It was early morning when I was roused by a man softly repeating my name, and I forced my bleary eyes to focus on him. He was gray-haired and bespectacled, with neatly trimmed facial hair. On my other side, Shea was rising from the chair with a tug at her rumpled clothing, flustered that he had come in without her notice. I wondered when she had returned to the room.

"I'm Dr. Nye, and you've been in my care since your arrival," the man said, his watery blue eyes kind. "I'm happy to say the infection in your wounds has dissipated promisingly, and you're doing quite well. We're in need of beds, so I'm willing to discharge you, but you must stay on the medication I've prescribed. And I'd like to recheck your wounds three days hence."

Shea stood and took my hand, laying claim to me for the stranger's benefit.

"So we can leave?"

"Well, you can leave *here*." He was hedging, and my stomach lurched. Shea let her tension show in her jaw, clenching it so tightly the tendons in her neck stood out. "You see, there's one other matter, Anya. You do realize you were the victim of a crime?"

While I wasn't sure what I had expected—maybe a bill for hospital services or a visit from the director of a children's home—this was not it. Taken aback, I warily nodded. Of course I was a victim, according to the law of the land. But surely it was far too late for me to file a report—I couldn't imagine that an effective investigation was still possible.

"As a medical practitioner, I'm required to report evidence of crimes to the Governor's Constabularies. Please don't let this alarm you. All they want to know is what happened when your wings were removed. We would all like to see the people responsible caught and punished. We don't want them to hurt anyone else."

Shea, looking nauseous, was holding her head in her hands, though thankfully she had faded into the background where Doctor Nye couldn't see her. Something in the man's tone had revealed a terrible truth.

"The Constabularies are here, aren't they?" I inquired.

"They're waiting outside."

Judging from the doctor's apologetic tone, he didn't enjoy entrapping his patients in this way, though he wasn't hesitant enough about the Governor's methods to have given me a ten-minute head start out the door. *Bureaucrats.* Wasn't it my business whether or not this crime should be recorded, examined, disseminated? Hadn't my experience been amply traumatic? I could have made a thousand political arguments, but my true horror lay in the thought that my own carelessness in tending my wounds during our travels might be responsible for Shea's discovery. Seven years her father owed for his crime. Seven years to repay a debt just like whatever debt Spex was repaying. Who knew what she might be forced to do if she were imprisoned?

Dr. Nye stood and moved to draw back the curtain. Shea's reaction would have been comical, if not for the jeopardy we faced. She stumbled to the corner of the room and out of the light streaming through the window, as though it would burn her. Then, realizing her behavior might draw more attention than it would divert, she plopped into a chair and tried to relax her posture, turning her head to the side and directing her eyes downward.

The men who entered didn't even glance Shea's way. Both

wore crisp double-breasted, brass-buttoned red uniforms, and carried two pistols and an assortment of knives around their hips, strapped in their sheaths with leather clasps. Though this armament was in keeping with their jobs, it made me nervous. Judging from the way Shea's hand slipped beneath her coat toward her pistol, it had the same effect on her.

While snowbirds chirped outside, the younger of the men knelt at my bedside, forsaking the chair. He had gray eyes and soft brown hair that reminded me of Davic. My heart lurched, and I swallowed hard, trying to force my promised from my mind.

"It's Anya, right?" queried the gray-eyed officer.

His partner crossed his arms in the background, tapping his foot impatiently. Judging from his insignia, he ranked higher in Tairmor's police force, but he wore a hard, authoritative expression. The Davic look-alike was probably here for his bedside manner. He had the social skills to deal with victims.

At my nod, the younger man continued, "I'm Officer Matlock. You can call me Tom. I'm so sorry for your troubles, Anya. Could you tell me what happened?"

I told him the little I cared to repeat, not wanting to dwell on the details. I'd crossed the Bloody Road and immediately been attacked. Almost as if the hunters had been waiting for me. No, there was no way they could have been expecting me. The trip had been spontaneous. No, I couldn't describe their faces. It had been dark. But they were a group of five men. And there had been a woman with them. In the end, I told him, I was just glad to be alive.

Officer Matlock impelled me with his argent eyes to elaborate, and my throat stung from the effort to hold back tears. For some reason, I wanted to obey those eyes, though there was little else of importance to tell him. He didn't need to know that I was glad to be alive only because I had a purpose to fulfill; that I had to find Zabriel and make sure Illumina and Evangeline were all right, but that beyond that, I wasn't sure I had anything to live for. The blank my mind drew when I tried to imagine life after the completion of my mission was emotionally hollowing, and I hoped the Constabularies would leave before my inner emptiness caused a cave-in.

"Thank you," Tom said when I did not continue. "I can only imagine how difficult this has been for you. You're very brave."

"I'm not," I blurted, unwilling to let him turn my ordeal into a noble act. "I had no choice in the matter. Surviving something that's forced on you doesn't take bravery. It just takes willpower."

A smile briefly flirted with his lips. "Let me apologize for my word choice. You're very strong, Anya. I admire that."

I wished I'd kept my mouth shut—this conversational segue had been unnecessary. I felt the color of my cheeks deepening. He appeared not to notice, or was kind enough not to draw attention to my reaction, simply rising to his feet to let his superior step forward.

"Constable Marcus Farrier," he abruptly introduced himself, not extending a hand or offering a nod. "I'm here with Officer Matlock on the Governor's behalf. Your hospital bill has been paid, and you are owed compensation for your suffering. Dr. Nye says you are well enough to travel, so if you would kindly accompany us, we'll see you to the Governor's manor."

There was no room for refusal—Farrier made his request in such a way that to object would have been uncouth. Besides, who would turn down money? I made the mistake of looking to Shea for help, prompting him to amend his offer out of politesse.

"Of course, your friend is also welcome to come."

My face paled as quickly as it had reddened, but I gave a stiff nod. "Give me a moment and I'll get dressed."

The officers bowed their heads, then went to stand on the other side of the curtain like an armed guard, and Dr. Nye went to obtain my medication. Shea rushed toward the bed from the corner where she had been cowering, mouthing profanities at me.

"How can they force you to do this?" she hissed as I crawled out of bed, woozy from the painkillers I'd been given.

"I don't know. I suppose for most people, this would be a good thing, an honor even, but for us? Nature."

Steadying myself with a hand on the bedpost, I examined the tiny room for an alternate exit. There was none. We could make it out the window, but it was a long drop to the ground. While Shea might stand a chance of escaping that way, I'd be caught before I could make it out of the alley. If the Governor wanted me brought to him like a delinquent under guard, he was going to have his way.

"What are we going to do?" Shea whispered.

"I'll go with them. You find a place around here to hide, and I'll come back for you."

"No! I thought we agreed that we didn't trust Ivanova. You can't go by yourself, and if that means I have to go with you... well, then, I will."

I appreciated her devotion, but shook my head so vigorously I stumbled under the medication's influence.

"The Governor just wants to look at me, moon-eyed and compassionate, and say he wishes things had happened differently. His men have no reason to suspect me of anything. There's no need for you to risk arrest."

"Oh, to hell with that," Shea huffed. She went to the dressing table to retrieve my laundered clothes and hurled them at me. "We're not splitting up. Your logic and reasoning aren't going to comfort me if something happens to you, and I'm sick of hiding. Besides, we've come this far together. If one of us is going down, we both are."

Her loyalty was emboldening, and I grinned. In my heart, however, I knew that the risk we were disregarding was much greater than either of us wanted to admit.

When we were ready, the doctor wished us well, gave me a vial of medicine and saw us to the foyer, where our cloaks and packs were stored in a large closet. Without a word, Officer Matlock hoisted my satchel, letting Shea carry her own things, then he and Constable Farrier escorted us to a fancy carriage parked on the street outside. After assisting us to enter, Matlock tucked fur blankets around my legs, and I felt a flutter in my stomach at his chivalry. With a warm smile that I returned, he settled on the bench opposite me with our packs at his feet, while Shea curled up beside me, taking a tight hold of my hand.

The journey itself was enjoyable. Hidden beneath expensive covers so that not even winter could affect us, we were like queens being transported to our castle, and I imagined the cold was annoyed at not being able to reach us. Shea seemed exhilarated with her decision to accompany me. It was as though she'd spent so much time being afraid that this was the greatest relief of her life. She pointed out landmarks to me, many of which I'd seen in my previous travels. But I let her go on—this was her city, and she hadn't been there in a long time.

We fell silent as we passed the heart of the capital, draw-ing the concerned gaze of Officer Matlock until he noticed what we were staring at: the beautiful marble bridge spanning the gorge to connect the north and south halves of Tairmor. The bridge commemorated the lives of every human soldier who had died in the battle of the Bloody Road. The Fae had cursed the Road in a desperate attempt to save our city, and in so doing had destroyed beyond recognition or reclamation the bodies of every human soldier in the vicinity. The monu-ment had been painstakingly etched with the names of all who had been found and identified, an overt reminder of why some humans would have sanctioned—even celebrated—the brutal removal of my wings. My eyes did not leave the bridge, which I thought more incredible than anything in existence in the natural world, until we had left it far behind.

By the time we arrived at the Governor's residence, Shea was no longer giddy with daring and our queenly accoutrements had lost their charm. There could be nothing good awaiting us inside that mansion, despite how splendorous it was. Radi-ant light emanated from every window, while river spray cre-ated a pleasant fog. White pillars upheld a second-floor porch, and the overhang housed a front step with cherub statues on either side. Given the Governor's pro-Fae stance, I wondered if this meant he subscribed to the belief that Faeries were de-scended from higher beings. Human religions often employed winged creatures as messengers of the divine, while Fae be-lieved that all things spiritual resonated from the earth—there was no need for extraworldly beings when every living thing was a component of the Spirit of Nature.

We descended from the carriage to stare up at the high peak of the roof, which seemed to jut at a self-righteous angle. I hesitated, filled with foreboding, afraid that the building's architecture foreshadowed the attitudes of the people we were about to encounter.

The Constabularies ushered us through the front doors of the Governor's mansion and into a cherry-paneled vestibule. Straight ahead, across marble floors, rose an elegant, arching staircase decorated on every step with yellow-and-blue-flowered plants that should not have been alive this time of year. Pine garlands wrapped indoor pillars and an impressive chandelier.

"This way," Constable Farrier decreed, not waiting for a servant. He headed up the stairway and down the left corridor, motioning for Shea and me to follow. More solicitous of my condition than was his counterpart, Officer Matlock offered his arm, guiding me up the steps. Shea stayed at my other side.

"I'll be downstairs when you're finished," he informed us upon reaching the landing.

"Thank you," I murmured, then turned toward Farrier, who stood in front of a door at the end of the corridor, the tapping of his foot revealing his irritation at our snail's pace.

Shea and I approached, and the Constable opened the door, ushering us into a sitting room instead of the office I was expecting. I took several deliberate breaths as I steeled myself to meet the Governor for the first time—this was Zabriel's grandfather, the bane of Shea's existence, a person about whom I'd heard both wonderful things and terrible things, and nothing in between.

The man who awaited us on the other side of the room held a letter in one bejeweled hand, his opposite forming an elegant steeple as it supported his weight on the mahogany desktop. He was younger than Governor Wolfram Ivanova should have been—he looked to be in his forties, whereas the Governor would be nearing seventy, and his dark hair did not even hint at gray. He was fit, clean-shaven, and over his dress tunic were strung thick gold necklaces with apophyllite stones in triangular designs. The stones were a close match to the blue of his eyes, which flicked from object to object and person to person as he sized up the situation in a businesslike manner. Shea glanced at me, and it wasn't difficult to determine the nature of her thoughts. Not only was this one surprise too many this day, but it threw into question the purported reason we were there.

"Thank you, Constable," the man said with a tight-lipped smile, and Farrier took his leave with a smart salute.

"Please, girls, have a seat," our host continued, and the hair on the back of my neck bristled. Yet again, a human was calling me *girl,* a diminutive that in my estimation implied I had no skill or intelligence worth recognizing. I was royalty in Chrior, yet considered little more than an ingenue in the Warckum Territory. At a nudge from Shea, I sat beside her on an embroidered sofa, while the man settled into an armchair across from us, a narrow table acting as a buffer in between.

"Which of you is Anya?" At my nod, he leaned forward to lift a hefty pouch from the tabletop. "Take this, please, with my apologies."

I accepted the pouch, despite the fact that payment for a part of my body struck me as ghoulish. We could use the money, and whether out of pity or not, anyone who lived in this mansion could afford to spare some funds.

"You told the Constabularies everything about your injury, in detail?" the man continued, astute eyes fixed on me.

"Yes," I said, still trying to figure out his identity. I knew the Governor had a living son, though I had never seen him. Might he be the man sitting across from us? Shea solved the problem in her inimitable fashion.

"Who are you?" she demanded.

Our host laughed, an odd yet somehow pleasant cackling sound; then he shook his head at his own thoughtlessness.

"Yet again, I apologize. Allow me to correct my oversight. I am Lieutenant Governor Luka Ivanova, Commissioner of Law Enforcement in the Territory, and the Governor's son, naturally. I'm afraid my father is feeling ill today and is unable to meet with you. Please believe me, Anya, when I say he wanted to be here."

Turning from me, he cast his eyes on Shea. "Since we're sharing identities, who perchance are you?"

Shea tensed as Luka's gaze drifted to her hip. There was no doubt he made out the shape of her pistol, but his expression did not change, nor did his good humor abate, leading me to the conclusion that her armament didn't worry him.

"Mary," Shea offered at last. "Mary Archer."

Luka gave her a sly smile. "An honest enough name, I daresay. Although I must admit, I expected something a bit less common."

It was clear from his tone that he knew Shea was lying to him, yet he didn't pursue the topic. Did he think he had the power to condemn and pardon as he pleased? Or did he know his father's laws weren't always fair, and think it a shame Shea had to use a fake name? Either way, he wasn't interested in causing us trouble. Maybe we were lucky the Governor was sick.

"Now, if it isn't too difficult for you, Anya, I would like to hear the story of your injury myself."

Luka had returned his attention to me, his hands folded neatly together and his expression sympathetic. I shrugged and flatly gave him the same details I'd shared with Officer Matlock and Constable Farrier. Repeating the words wasn't hard as long as I detached my heart from their meanings.

"How did you get to Tairmor?" he pressed when I had finished. "By all accounts, you were injured in the Balsam Forest. Did you travel here wounded? That would have been an extraordinarily difficult trip."

"I allowed myself a little time to recuperate first," I said, squirming inside. He was pulling more information from me than I wanted to reveal.

"Did you come by way of Oaray?"

My mind spun as I tried to determine how to dodge this question. In the end, he spared me the necessity of a response with a wave of his hand.

"No need to worry. I know Fae sometimes shy away from obtaining legitimate papers here in the Warckum Territory. And Oaray is the best place for Fae and human alike to get travel documents with no questions asked. So please, go on. Tell me about your journey to Tairmor."

The Lieutenant Governor was surprisingly astute, for he hadn't examined our passports, and yet knew they were forged. But more importantly, he wasn't interested in arresting us for this offense. On the contrary, he was very understanding, and it was beginning to seem he was as staunchly pro-Fae as his father.

"Well, I thought I was all right, but in the Fere..." I trailed off, uncertain what I wanted to say. Queen Ubiqua had warned against getting involved with Zabriel's human relatives, and if I told Luka about the Faerie-spotting operation I'd started

to uncover, I might become entangled in the issue. Fighting
the impulse to glance at Shea lest I give away that I was hiding something, I decided to tell him a small piece of the story.
"We were attacked by Sepulchres."

Ivanova sat back, the lines on his face deepening into creases.
"Sepulchres... But they're legend. I'm sorry, I don't doubt
you—but they're only supposed to haunt the Balsam Forest,
aren't they?"

"They feed off magic. They could have followed me after
I was injured."

"I'll have my men investigate at once."

Luka stood and walked to the sideboard to pour himself a
glass of wine, his tall, graceful body obeying his mind's com-
mands with an elegance that was rare. It was an elegance that
Zabriel had always possessed. The Lieutenant Governor was
his uncle, a member of the side of his family that didn't know
for certain whether or not he existed. They ought to be told,
I suddenly felt, though I knew better than to blurt out the information. Still, I wondered what it was about this man that
made me want to confess my secrets.

After offering a glass of wine to Shea and me, which we declined, Luka returned to the subject of my injury.

"There's a place I'd like you to visit, Anya. We have a shelter here in Tairmor for Fae in your position. It offers a chance
to start over, help integrating into human society, that sort of
thing. And it would give you lodging while you recuperate.
You could stay as long or as short as it suits you, but I think it
would be worth a look. I'll have Constable Farrier transport
you there."

He strode to a desk in the corner and beckoned me to approach. As I did, he penned a short letter, signing it with a flourish before tucking it into an envelope.

"I'm acquainted with the woman who runs the shelter," he said, extending the envelope to me. "She's a Faerie herself, name of Fi, and this will let her know of my referral. You'll receive the very best treatment—I swear it."

Luka was being extraordinarily kind, but I wasn't paying attention to him any longer. On the wall by his desk hung a board with wanted posters nailed to the wood. Thatcher More's face was on one, sketched crudely in accordance with his importance to lawmakers. But on a much larger poster in meticulous detail was a face I knew well—high cheekbones, slightly upturned eyes, his mother's lips, his uncle's nose.

Zabriel was smirking at me from a wanted poster on Luka Ivanova's wall, and beneath his face were the words:

30,000 gold pieces for information leading to the capture of the pirate, thief and murderer known by the alias William Wolfram Pyrite.

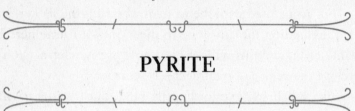

chapter twelve

PYRITE

I continued to gape, dumbfounded, at the wanted posters, and Luka stepped to my side.

"See anyone you know?" he asked, his tone only half joking.

My laugh was so forced I wanted to slap myself. Scrambling for recovery, I dodged his question by going with the first notion that entered my mind.

"I didn't know you had such handsome criminals in the Territory," I said, pointing to the sketch of Zabriel. I hated myself for embracing the role in which Luka had automatically cast me—that of a young, shallow girl—but I could see no other way out of the situation.

Shea came to join us, her inquisitiveness getting the better of her, and the Governor's son shook his head with the same tight-lipped smile he'd given Farrier. It wasn't disapproval, but it was a close second.

"Don't be led astray by his looks," Luka cautioned. "He's a dangerous sort. Do you know what *pyrite* is? Fool's gold. Just like the shine this boy has. He appears to be a treasure until you get close and realize he's a worthless criminal, no better than the rest."

"Thirty thousand gold pieces," Shea noted, cocking her head with a smirk. "Sounds like a treasure to me."

Luka laughed, Shea's quip resetting the mood, and I slowly released the breath I'd been holding. I wasn't sure what words might have come forth if our host had pressed me further. Yet again, I was thankful Shea was with me. Though I had been dubious at first, she and I had become more than friends—we were good partners.

"He's rather young, isn't he?" I ventured, hoping to glean a little more information.

"That he is. Young, handsome, daring, some would even say philanthropic—all qualities that capture the imagination of the populace. Sometimes I think he has more admirers than I do." A scowl crossed Luka's face like a twisted cloud, and he stared up at the drawing of my cousin. "Unfortunately, the citizens don't realize the heartlessness of what he *really* does. They don't see the businesses ruined by his robberies, or pay to repair the vandalism he and his crew perpetrate. They don't have to look upon the bodies of the people who get in Pyrite's way, attend the funerals, or console the families."

As though remembering that he was entertaining guests, Luka gave his head a quick shake, breaking his entranced gaze. But I couldn't shake the chilling realization that catching Pyrite was more than a goal for him—it was an obsession.

"My apologies once more," he said in true gentlemanly fashion. "Where have I left my manners? I do believe I've extended more apologies to you two in the short span of our acquaintance than to most people in my entire lifetime. But please understand, I oversee crime control in the Territory, and I take all of this very personally. Rest assured, we will bring Pyrite to justice."

The Lieutenant Governor took my hand and pressed the envelope containing the letter he had penned against my palm,
holding on just a bit longer than was necessary. Becoming
aware of my ring, he pulled my hand a little closer to examine it.

"That's an interesting ring you're wearing. Quite stunning."
He frowned and rubbed his chin, and it took all my willpower not to pull away. "I've seen one similar to this before,
although sadly I can't remember where or when. Not that it
matters, I suppose."

My heart thumping against my rib cage, I met his light blue
eyes, but did not see any suspicion within their depths. He was
a rich man, and it made sense for him to have an interest in
beautiful and valuable objects. But I didn't like the notion that
if ever he remembered where he'd seen that other ring, he'd
realize I was one of the royal Redwood Fae. I didn't want to
consider where that road might lead.

"Take care, both of you," he said in dismissal, escorting us
to the door. When his gaze fell on Constable Farrier in the
corridor, he added, "Send Matlock to me for a moment."

"Yes, sir," the Constable barked, once more snapping a salute.

With a sharp turn on his heel, Farrier shepherded us back
to the entry, where his counterpart waited for us. With a jerk
of his thumb toward the staircase, he indicated to the younger
man that he had been summoned. After paying Shea and me
a nod, Officer Matlock jogged up the steps, then continued
down the hallway, his pace brisk. Despite the kindness Luka
Ivanova had exhibited toward us, I doubted he was someone
to keep waiting.

We settled ourselves on a settee, and Shea began to chew on

her fingernails. I took her hand to halt the nervous habit; years of royal upbringing had left me with few of my own. When Matlock returned a short while later, he and Farrier escorted us to the carriage. Shea and I didn't speak during the ride, although she was grinning, and for obvious reasons. We'd just walked into enemy territory and come out unscathed. It was nothing short of a miracle: Thatcher's daughter was a wanted person; Ubiqua had warned against having any contact with the Governor and his associates in the search for Zabriel; and our encounter with Spex suggested that someone powerful, perhaps even with influence in the government of the Warckum Territory, was plotting against my people. Yet here we were, alive, well, unshackled, and quite a bit richer than we had been that morning. Even my royal ring had gone unidentified.

I tried to concentrate on thoughts of Zabriel and ignore Shea's impatient fidgeting. She knew me well enough not to have fallen for my remark about Pyrite's good looks and was no doubt dying to ask me what my interest in him was really about. She wouldn't raise the question while Matlock was present, giving me a blessed little time before I would have to clarify. Shea might have already put together the pieces available to her, but there were significant gaps in the picture I had painted her of my family—gaps I would soon need to fill.

Our journey ended in a lower-class district of Tairmor, nowhere near the gorge, which, by all accounts, was the preeminent place in the capital to live. Nonetheless, the rush of the Kappa echoed all around us. I smirked as I stepped down from the carriage—despite the Governor's pro-Fae stance, the wounded of my kind had been stuffed away among the discarded of the human race. There were no riverfront properties or water views in the area to which we had been delivered; rather, we were relegated to the gutter district, where the water and filth ran down from the homes of the wealthy and from Tairmor's major business areas. But at least we had a roof over our heads, and that was sufficient to maintain Ivanova's political reputation.

The Fae-mily Home appeared to be in decent condition, despite its location and its dreadful name. Tom Matlock offered to help us carry our things, but we refused, waving the Constabularies on their way. The carriage clattered down the street, looking like a show horse among oxen.

"Now what?" Shea asked, glancing around as she hoisted both of our packs. "They didn't exactly leave us in tourist territory, did they?"

"Inside, I guess." I motioned to the shelter, and Shea pursed her lips, questioning my judgment. "You just pointed out we're in the middle of nowhere, so I don't think we should start wandering. This looks like a good place to stay the night, maybe even better than most in this neighborhood. Besides, someone here might have information about Evangeline and this Faerie-spotting business. It's worth checking out."

"Are you sure *I'll* be welcome here?"

I grinned. "Well, you're *fae-mily* to me."

Shea swung her pack and hit me in the rear end, and I hopped away toward the shelter's entrance. She was quick to follow, despite any lingering reservations.

As Luka had said, the shelter was run by a Faerie named Fi—Fi the Fae, I realized with a twinge of sympathy for the woman. She had both of her vibrant orange-and-yellow wings, which she did not shroud within the Home, telling me she had voluntarily stayed in the human world to establish this place.

She read the letter I gave her with wide-set blue-green eyes and an ever-widening smile.

"Luka Ivanova's a good man," she said, laying a hand tenderly on my shoulder, not wanting to irritate my injuries, of which she had already taken stock. "He monies this place almost single-handedly, and he's always sending his officers around to make sure we have what we need. And that takes some doing—donors for a place like this are few in number and generally have bigger hearts than pocketbooks. Please, come in."

We followed Fi past the admissions podium and into a dining area that was filled from wall to wall with wounded Faeries. A lucky number of them were recovering from simple injuries—a broken wing or bone—but an unsettling majority of them were like me, wingless and desolate. They limped and slouched about the tables like bodies without minds. If not for my mission, I would be similarly lost and dispirited, and this shelter would be my best hope for salvation. I scolded myself for my initial cynicism about this place. Fi was saving lives with her Home, however embarrassingly christened it might be.

Shea and I ate until we could hardly move, she enjoying the view of the city out the large window, I perusing faces. I sought out white-blond hair, shimmering blue eyes, any number of smiles that could have been Evangeline's, but there was no sign of my friend. Just as there had been no sign of my cousin Zabriel in that heartless smirk on the wanted poster in Luka Ivanova's meeting room. I frowned, thinking of my father's ambassadors within the city. It was difficult to believe none of them had seen the wanted poster and recognized their Prince—so why hadn't word been sent to Chrior of his infamy in the Territory?

Seemingly reading my thoughts, Shea drew me from my reverie. "So that poster. I'm guessing you're not really out to flirt with William Wolfram Pyrite."

"No," I laughed, deciding to start with the simplest of the revelations to come. "That sketch was of my cousin. Zabriel is a wanted man."

I massaged my temples. I hadn't even begun to ponder the ramifications of this development.

"I'm wanted, too," Shea reminded, poking at me with her soup spoon. "Remember, this government doesn't always have its head on straight."

This was a heartening thought, and for a moment, I considered leaving things there, just finishing the meal and continuing the journey for Zabriel with Shea in the dark, but definitely at my side. I couldn't conceive of the reaction she might have to learning my cousin was an Ivanova, and that I'd been withholding this information from her. But the truth had to come out. If I left it to chance, I had a feeling fate would choose the worst possible moment to unleash the news.

"Shea, listen," I said, going for the guts of the matter. "The name Zabriel's using—"

"I assume it's a joke," she interjected, still in a mood that reflected the day's good fortune. "The pyrite, of course, then Wolfram for the Governor. I'm not sure about the William. Whatever the case, he's mocking the system, and that's fine by me."

"I know why he chose William," I mumbled, half hoping Shea wasn't paying attention. But she was, and the way her eyes skirted the room told me she detected my hesitancy.

"Anya, what is it?"

I wrapped my hands around my mug of cider, clinging to its

warmth. Shea had been extremely forthright with me through-out our short friendship, and I feared my coming words would seriously erode her faith in me. Were our positions reversed, I would have been hard-pressed to forgive her or trust her again.

"He's making fun of his lineage, Shea." I stared at the knots in the wood of the tabletop, not quite able to meet her eyes. "Zabriel is the son of William Ivanova. He's probably using the alias as some kind of dare to his mother to try and find him."

When at last I raised my head, Shea was gaping at me, the sudden paling of her skin making her chocolate eyes all the more intense.

"You mean by looking for Zabriel…we're helping the Governor find his grandson?"

"No!" I cried, grateful for an honest answer that was also good news. "I mean, Zabriel is the Governor's grandson, but we're not helping Ivanova to find him. The man doesn't know Zabriel exists. They've never had any contact."

"But we're playing in Ivanova's backyard. If anyone figures out who Zabriel is and sees us nosing around, we'll become a lot more interesting to the one person who absolutely cannot find out who I am."

"You're right." Though I longed for a way to defuse Shea's rising anger, there was nothing else I could say.

"And you let me risk my freedom like this?"

Her lips peeled away from her teeth in disgust, and shame slapped me like a wave; but just as quickly as the tide had come in, it changed, and indignation rushed to fill me. I wasn't a creature deserving of revulsion. I was a Faerie, and a royal one. I had reasons for the things I said and did. A vicious defensiveness stole over me, and unweighed words spewed from my mouth.

"What freedom? You talked about being a prisoner when you lived with your family. You said anything would be better than that. If I'd told you this back then, it wouldn't have made any difference. You would still have come with me, and you'd still be sitting here with me now."

Shea stood, throwing her tableware down with a clatter. "Maybe it wouldn't have made any difference. But those were my choices to make, not yours. And if you're so sure it wouldn't have mattered, then I really don't understand you not telling me."

I winced, and a hot flush crept up my neck. There were so many holes in my justifications that I was in danger of falling through them. But Shea had one more barb to toss my way.

"And I'd always heard Faeries couldn't lie. Just further proof that you aren't one anymore."

I stared at her, my hands balled into such tight fists that my fingernails were cutting into my palms. I wanted to hit her, to leap across the table and knock her to the ground. Whatever I had said or left unsaid, how dare she mock what had been done to me?

Shea knew she'd crossed a line. She shrank in on herself as I'd seen her do when she'd argued with her father about his reasons for taking his family on the run. For better or worse, she tended to say exactly what she was thinking. Not always an endearing quality, but at least the people around her were sure to know where they stood with her.

"Everything I've told you has been true," I responded, each word enunciated. "There were just...parts I left out."

Shea's eyes darted toward the front door, and for a moment, I thought she was going to storm off. But rationality prevailed. However fortunate we'd been up until now, it was dangerous for her to be seen on the streets of Tairmor. Instead, her furiously working brain landed on the next bit of information I'd neglected to share.

"William Ivanova married the Queen of the Fae. It was a huge controversy. I wasn't even alive and I've heard every last detail. Which means Zabriel is a prince—*the* Prince. So we're chasing down the Governor's grandson, who's the royal heir in the Faerie Realm, and who will probably be the most notorious individual in the Warckum Territory once people learn he's half-blood." She stopped, her brows furrowed, then latched on to the final piece. "And since he's your cousin, you must be royalty, too. How many steps away from the throne?"

I brushed a hand over my face, wishing I could say I was leagues away from wearing the Laura, as had been the case at the time of my birth. A memory flashed in my mind of a field turned golden with the sunset, my mother spinning me around. I couldn't have been more than three years old, happy, safe, carefree. Back then, the Queen's son, her siblings, and her brother's daughter had formed a buffer between me and the throne. How could so much have changed in a few short years?

"What difference does it make?" I stammered. "I'm only royalty in Chrior, and I can't go home again. Let's face facts— I have no more chance to take the throne than you do. I'm just Anya now."

Shea huffed and stiffly retook her seat. "Right, you're just Anya. Just Anya with a hell of a lot of secrets. I've been going about with my life in your hands, you know."

"I do know. And I haven't done anything that might hurt you. In the beginning, I thought it would be dangerous for me, for Zabriel, if I told you these things. I was wrong."

I hoped my tone was penitent enough to convince her. I

could understand her anger, but in reality, I'd kept my promise to Thatcher. I'd been looking out for her.

We sat in silence for a few minutes, Shea's posture and the tension between us gradually relaxing.

"What about you?" she asked at last. "What's it like finding out your cousin's a criminal?"

"It doesn't feel real. It's like a game. Something Zabriel and I might have played at as children. Fugitives from the law, surviving in the human world in whatever way we can. Only it's not a game, and according to that poster, my cousin, the Prince of Chrior, is a thief, a pirate, and a murderer. A *murderer,* Shea."

My lips moved with difficulty, resisting the formation of the words. Who could Zabriel have murdered? And why? The young man I knew had never been inclined to hurt anyone. The most damage he'd done as of turning fifteen had been to his own body, when he'd tried to sever his wings. How much could he have changed?

Shea was watching me carefully, and I had the impression she wanted to offer consolation, even though five minutes ago we had been at each other's throats. But there was nothing to say. Finding Zabriel was still my goal, whatever he'd become. In the end, she offered a practical assessment.

"It also said he's a pirate. If that's true, then we'd better head for Sheness. It's hard to be a sea devil without a sea, and it's the only port in the Warckum Territory."

"But what if he's not at port?"

"Then we'll wait and ask around about him in the meantime. We can't follow him onto the water."

"And if he doesn't make port in Sheness?"

She tied her dark hair back in its usual fashion, automatically assuming a more businesslike air.

"You worry too much, Anya. With that big a reward on his head, you can be sure he's hitting the ships in and around Sheness, and hard. Besides, the city's practically a paradise of women and liquor. Where else would he go?"

I grinned and rolled my eyes, quite able to imagine Zabriel indulging himself. He rarely did anything in moderation. "So that's what pirates do with their free time?"

"It's all well and good to plunder loot, but the reward is in spending it," she explained with a grudging smile.

"I hope they spend some of it on baths."

"I wouldn't count on it."

We both laughed, slipping back into a familiar pattern with each other. As Shea made final adjustments to her hair, I studied her, suddenly thinking this quest very unfair to her. She was going to a lot of trouble to find a Faerie she'd never heard of before I'd crawled, bleeding, into her life to take advantage of her family's hospitality.

"You don't have to come with me, Shea. You could stay here in Tairmor. This is where you're from, after all."

Her eyes met mine. "We've been hiding in Tairmor for all of four days and you think it's safe for me here? If I stayed, it would only be a matter of time before I ran into someone who recognized me and was willing to turn me in for the reward money I'd bring. Besides, I couldn't settle down to a comfortable life while my family wastes away in the Balsam Forest. The best thing is to keep traveling, and you're the best way for me to do that."

I wasn't entirely appeased, but I didn't argue with her. She'd proven herself reliable, and in my heart of hearts I was loath to lose her companionship.

I started to stand, but Shea laid a hand on my arm. "If I stay with you, Anya, I don't want any more surprises. So is there anything else you're not telling me?"

"I think that's it."

"You *think?*"

I sighed. "I'm not purposefully hiding anything else from you. But let's face it. My life's been nothing but a series of surprises this last month. I can't guarantee there won't be more."

"Well, at least being on the road with you isn't boring!"

We had been given a double bunk in one of the more private rooms at the shelter—Luka Ivanova had indeed requested we receive the best accommodations Fi could offer. We shared the room with a few others, but it was far less crowded than the rest of the sleeping areas, and the well-stoked fire provided more than adequate warmth.

Shea was asleep before I could say good-night to her, but the crashing sound of water that permeated Tairmor kept me awake, reminding me painfully of my lost ability to connect with my element. Too sore to have claimed the upper bunk, I lay on the bottom one, contemplating the dying embers in the fireplace and trying to sort things out in my head. Thatcher More was wanted by the law, I reasoned, and he wasn't a bad person. Technically, Shea was a criminal evading capture, but that didn't make her morally bankrupt. Zabriel couldn't be a different person, not the way I feared. It just wasn't possible.

My thoughts wandered, and I tried to picture my life once this journey was over, once Zabriel had been found and hopefully returned home to become King of the Fae; once I knew whether or not Illumina was safe, and what had happened to Evangeline. Where would I live? What would I do? I didn't know which Davic loved more, the Faerie Realm or me, but either way, I couldn't ask him to leave it to keep me company. He had a family to consider—a mother, a father, a little sister. Though my stomach tightened at the thought of letting him go, I couldn't expect him to join me. And his happiness would be fleeting if he did, for his very spirit was anchored in Chrior.

Indisposed to sink into self-pity, I focused on Shea. Maybe she and I would set up somewhere together and find a way to help her family. My past was irrecoverable, but hers did not have to be. Given her devotion to my cause, she deserved that same support from me. Although a stable, loving future with a human family was as ethereal as a child's daydream, it was comforting enough to still my mind and allow me to drop into slumber.

chapter thirteen

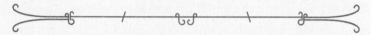

THE STREETS OF TAIRMOR

Early the following morning, I approached Fi at the front desk to inquire about Evangeline. My spirits dropped when the founder of the Fae-mily Home shook her head, her short dark hair bouncing incongruously with her regretful expression. But then she paused, one hand rubbing her forehead, and my hopes rose again.

"There was a girl," she said in her soft, high voice. "The hospital brought her here—she just wandered into their care, so they passed her along. She was tall like you say, with pale blond hair. The right age, too, though you wouldn't have known it by looking at her." The wide space between Fi's brows creased sadly. "Such a waif she was. And sorely confused. Never even told us her name."

"Do you remember what happened to her?" Despite the grim description Fi had given, excitement flushed my face. If Evangeline were alive, I would find her.

"I don't. She was here for a few days—maybe two weeks ago—then gone without a word. I can't wrap my mind around her injury, either. There are just so many faces and tragic tales that come through my door…. It's hard to keep track of them all. But like most who find their way to me, she was in no shape to be on her own." Fi offered a rueful smile that tugged at my heart. She was among the sacred few in this world who devoted their lives to helping others, yet never viewed themselves as doing enough. "You can ask the other guests, though. Someone might recall her better than I do."

"Are there any other shelters around here?"

"None like this one. Mine's the only recuperation home for Fae in the entire city. But there are human shelters in these parts where the needy can find a free meal and a bed. Truth be told, we're in a pitiable neighborhood." Fi's blue-green eyes, crinkled at the edges from years of worrying about those under her care, crinkled a bit more. "I can't direct you to any places off the top of my head. I'm sorry to be such poor help!"

"No need to apologize." I reached out to give her hand a reassuring squeeze, a gesture I'd seen Ubiqua make a million times. It felt clumsy coming from me, but my aunt's brand of comfort worked; the strain seemed to lift a little from Fi's frame. "You've been more help than you know. You've given me hope."

Fi smiled, though the expression was tentative, and I realized she wasn't used to being thanked. Seized with curiosity about how this warmhearted woman had come to live among the humans, I raised the issue.

"This shelter does such important work. How did you come to be in charge of it?"

She blushed. "It's a bit of a story. I was born in Chrior but raised here in Tairmor. I wanted to move back to the Realm when I was a youth and study to be a medicine mage, but I kept encountering hurt and sorrowing Fae in the Territory. I knew I was in a better position than most to go about setting up a safe haven for our people in Warckum, so I made it my business to help as best I could. I was struggling something fierce when Luka Ivanova took note and made my efforts count. He's the one who set me up here and gave me a true chance to make a difference."

I nodded, pondering Luka Ivanova and his motives. The Lieutenant Governor seemed almost too good to be true. But questions about him could wait for another time.

"I'm glad you had the inclination to do what you do. It really does make a difference." I gave her my gentlest royal smile. "I'd best be on my way now, but thank you again, for everything."

With a nod, she bustled off, and I hurried to the dining hall to locate Shea. I found her with one foot on the bench of a table, talking with a pair of young Fae men, neither of whom appeared concerned that she was human. She was laughing and joking, more than a match for the two of them. Noting my approach, she used the distraction afforded by my arrival to steal a bowl of pudding from one of her new friends.

"I'm going for a walk," I announced. "I think Evangeline was here, and not too long ago. I'm going to scour the area and see if I can find her. There are plenty of alleys that could offer a place to sleep, and a few human shelters, as well."

Shea swallowed an enormous mouthful of pudding and shoved the bowl into its original owner's hands. After giving the men a sweet smile, she moved a few paces away with me, though there wasn't much worry about being overheard. The men had drifted back into dialogue with one another, our private matters of little interest to them.

"Just let me get my coat from the room."

"Please don't come with me, Shea. You shouldn't be out on the streets—you could be recognized, and that's not a risk you need to take right now. I'll be fine by myself."

Shea scowled, but didn't argue. "You're still healing, so don't overtax yourself. And make sure you're back before dark. Otherwise I'll assume the worst and send out a search party."

"Yes, ma'am," I jested, giving her a salute worthy of Constable Farrier. She narrowed her eyes, the top half of her face attempting a scowl while her noncompliant lips flicked upward in a smirk. Nevertheless, she managed to convey that her warnings had been seriously given.

I took only fifteen minutes to layer my clothing and return to the front entry, leaving the Anlace and my money pouch behind. Given the neighborhood surrounding the Fae-mily Home, I wasn't about to risk losing my most important resources. Stepping onto the street in front of the shelter, I drew my cloak close about me, the chunk of bread I held in one hand serving as breakfast. Nothing about my surroundings looked familiar, so I decided to walk west, having no desire to squint into the sun. Despite the brightness of the morning, it was cold, and my breath formed wispy tendrils of frost that reminded me disconcertingly of a Sepulchre's glow.

The farther I went from the Fae-mily Home, the dirtier the streets became, the more derelict the homes and businesses, and the more frazzled my nerves. Broken windows were boarded over rather than repaired, and garbage was dumped into the alleys. I suspected the only reason the main street wasn't cluttered with refuse was because of the people in shabby coats who huddled together on street corners around trash-heap fires. The air was heavy with a scent that was both fetid and intriguing—more than once I tentatively inhaled an odor despite its putrescence, only the darkest recesses of my mind able to imagine the source.

With no particular idea of how best to approach my task,

I stepped into every shop I passed and peered into every alleyway, intending to blanket the other side of the street on my return. After covering a good ten blocks, I came to a shelter intended for humans. It was more run-down than the place Fi operated—probably lacking the financial support of a donor such as Luka Ivanova—but the smell of food hung heavy in the air, and a plethora of patrons were lined up for a free meal. I studied the hungry who waited outside, then walked through the front door and past the serving stations to check those sitting at the tables. Plenty of girls with blond hair and blue eyes were bent over their food, but none of them held up upon closer examination. Spotting a frazzled-looking woman whose job seemed to be directing traffic—from the street, through the food lines, on to the tables, then back out the door—I approached to tap her on the shoulder.

"Excuse me. Do you have any sleeping rooms?"

She gave me a squinty-eyed glance, jowls jiggling, before returning to her task, pointing and waving her arms to keep people moving, and on occasion curtly calling out a name.

"You must be new," she said when she accepted that I wasn't going to leave. "We don't open the rooms until late evening. Too many people, not enough beds. We wait to see who sorts things out on their own and who's left over. So if that's what you're looking for, you'll have to come back later."

The heartless logic of her words was in stark contrast to the charity being doled out around me, and I realized that one of the impediments to solving the plight of the needy was in determining whether they were to blame for their condition or deserved aid. In my mind, and in the minds of the benevolent, the two weren't mutually exclusive. Nonetheless, when those with plenty would not deign to help their fellow man, those with little to spare shouldered the task in their stead, steeping together kindness and asperity to create a bitter brew that rose near to goodwill. I sighed and pushed these thoughts from my mind, for they were of no use to me in my search.

"Actually, I'm looking for a friend of mine. Her name's Evangeline. White-blond hair, blue eyes, very thin."

"Honey, everyone here is thin. But that name doesn't sound familiar to me."

"Thanks anyway."

I made my way past the poor and the homeless, darting into the street just in front of two men who were being shuffled out in the wake of their meals. Though my search was proving more difficult than I had anticipated, I wasn't ready to give up, and I hurried to the other side of the street to resume scouting shops and alleyways. At some point, I became aware that the men from the human shelter were still in my vicinity, although they were lagging behind. Coincidence or potential threat? Given the number of people on the street and the safety to be found in daylight, I shrugged off the feeling and continued my explorations.

I peered down another disgusting alley and was just about to walk away when I saw movement against the wall under a mound of old packaging materials.

"Hello?" I called, stepping forward, thinking it was likely a false lead, an animal rather than a person. "Anybody there?"

A blond head poked through the pile, then someone scrambled out of the trash and scuttled away. My heart fluttered in my chest. While I couldn't be certain fortune was favoring me, there was a definite possibility I had stumbled upon my missing friend.

"Evangeline!" The young woman stopped, rubbing her forehead with the palm of her hand, but the noonday sun glared down at a blinding angle, interfering with my vision. "It's all right. It's Anya."

I moved toward her, hands held out to my sides, palms up, to show her I meant no harm. If this was Evangeline, she would surely come to me; if not, I was probably terrifying an already-traumatized beggar.

"I'm staying at the Fae-mily Home. You remember Fi, don't you? Tell me, is your name Evangeline?"

"Need some help there, miss?" said a gruff male voice from behind me, arresting my movement and making the hair on the back of my neck bristle.

I swiveled to see the two men from the human shelter, starkly aware of the mistake I'd made in dismissing the feeling they were trailing me. I glanced back at the skinny, indistinct girl, who was now covering her mouth with her hands, her shoulders hunched as though she wanted to disappear. Her reaction, more than anything else, told me I was in trouble.

"No, everything's under control," I firmly told them. "That girl over there is my friend. I came to get her, so we'll just be on our way."

Except for a slight height difference, the men were practically indistinguishable from one another—brothers, without question, and well-known in these parts, if anything could be gleaned from the girl's reaction. Mousy gray-brown hair covered their heads like greasy helmets, and their features were pushed and pulled in various directions by scars that shone like trophies.

The taller one leaned against the wall, using one arm to prop himself up.

"Oh, that'd be just fine, but this here alley's done been closed. If you want out, you'll have to pay the fee."

My stomach seemed to shrivel. Almost every means of protection that came to mind had been taken away by the hunters who had robbed me of my wings. I could try to run toward the girl and the opposite end of the alley, but the way was crowded with trash. And even if I was fast enough to reach the street, I harbored no misconceptions that anyone in this district would bother to help me. Without my magic-induced fleet-footedness and strength, my situation was dire.

"What fee?" I asked, chewing on my lip.

The second man stepped closer to me, his eyes examining my form as though counting the pockets in my clothes.

"How much have ya got?"

"Very little." Having left my money pouch at the Home, I had only a few gold pieces shoved into the pocket of my jerkin. Opening my cloak to retrieve and extend my meager holdings, I added, "Be my guest. I'd be remiss if I didn't donate to the intellectually backward."

I winced internally, knowing I shouldn't have let sarcasm slip into my response, yet unwilling to completely let go of my dignity. Fortunately, my assessment of the brothers was accurate. They had no clue they had been insulted.

"That's it?" the taller man griped, picking at his scalp and flicking whatever specimens he removed at the ground while his brother took the coins from my hand.

I nodded, inching sideways to bring the young woman into my peripheral vision. She was still there, thanks be to Nature. If I'd found Evangeline, I couldn't afford to lose her.

The men didn't like my movement, and the short one gripped my right forearm, yanking me toward him. My shoulder snapped and burned, as though it had popped in and out of its socket, and I gritted my teeth, trying to prepare myself for a pummeling. But the thug only wanted a look at my hand.

"That's a purty ring you've got. Bet it's worth a bit of shine."

I pulled my arm free and rubbed it, stretching my neck away from the offending shoulder.

"You can't have it," I growled, trying to sound menacing. "I can't take it off." This was the truth as far as I was concerned; parting with an heirloom of the royal family wasn't an option. "Just take the money and go."

The man flushed at my audacity and pulled a knife smoothly out of his belt. Numerous pouches, all bulky, hung from the leather, no doubt filled with the money and precious possessions of anyone who'd had the misfortune of encountering the brothers.

"Easy enough fixed," he sputtered with a grin that revealed rotted yellow teeth. "If you won't turn over the ring, I'll just take the 'tire finger."

A scream rushed through the alley like a wicked gale, ricocheting off the walls and scaring me more than the man's threat. We all turned to stare down the narrow passage. Raking in a breath, the young woman I continued to hope was Evangeline released another howl, then darted away from us, clambering over the obstacles and into the street. My courage plummeted. I'd lost her. On top of that, I was abandoned. Though I doubted she would have been much help, I felt strangely more vulnerable without her. Her presence had made her a witness, perhaps a disincentive for the criminals to harm me; now the thieves might as well kill me and be done with the whole mess.

The men closed ranks on me, and I shut my eyes, knowing

I had no choice but to hand over the ruby ring that was not only my birthright, but my responsibility to protect. I couldn't help interpreting this as transcendental confirmation that I was never meant to return to Chrior and the life I'd known there. It might be better to never go back than to face Queen Ubiqua's discontent at the loss of a royal treasure.

"Hey, back off!" a new man shouted, and my would-be attackers pivoted on their heels, running off without even taking proper stock of their competition. Had they recognized the voice? Was I about to be in even more trouble than before? Then I caught a glimpse of the scarlet tailcoat worn by the Constabulary who had entered the alley.

Relief flooded my body like sweet Sale, and I turned to my rescuer. Striding toward me was Tom Matlock, the younger of the men who had escorted Shea and me to the Governor's mansion. He had a walk that dared people to step in his way, yet the expression he wore as he drew near sent an opposite message—like he might drop his life's work to help someone in need, even if that need was as simple as assistance from a carriage.

"Are you all right?" he asked, coming to my side.

"Yes, I'm fine. A little spooked. But I still have all ten fingers."

I held them up, trying to be glib, though they quivered rather embarrassingly. He laid a hand casually on my back while he looked me over for injuries. His cinder-gray eyes were darker than Davic's, and his hair was the color of light chocolate instead of black. Its texture wasn't the same as Davic's, either. It looked as though it took some maneuvering to tame it properly for his job, while my betrothed's hair was smooth and cooperative—I'd played with it enough to know.

I couldn't remember why I'd thought the officer and Davic resembled one another. They weren't the same at all.

Though I was sure Officer Matlock noticed my shakes, he didn't mention it, moving on to a different issue.

"What are you doing this far from the Fae-mily Home? I mean, this area is pretty dodgy."

I laughed weakly. "I noticed." Feeling the pressure of his gaze, I added, "I was looking for a friend who also suffered an injury. Fi told me she was at the shelter a couple of weeks ago."

"Do you have reason to believe she came this way?"

"I think I saw her. I'm not sure—it might just be hope talking—but I think she was the one who screamed and ran out of here."

Officer Matlock's eyebrows rose, and he glanced down the alley as if to visualize the route the young woman had taken.

"She ran right by me. I wish I'd known. I would have stopped her. But, Anya...she didn't *look* like a friend of yours. She was...well, she wasn't in good shape."

I cocked my head and pursed my lips in irritation. "In case you weren't listening, I said something bad happened to her. She's been missing for months."

"Sorry, I didn't mean it like that. Look, if she's still in this neighborhood, I have an idea where she might be. Want me to show you?"

"Yes!"

He jerked his thumb in the direction the young woman had escaped. "This way."

He headed down the alley, and I hurried to keep pace with him, optimism building and making my entire body tingle. *Please, please, please,* I repeated to myself as we left the alley and crossed the street, made a few turns, then marched into an overflowing pub. A ripple went through the crowd at the Constabulary's entrance, and the establishment's clientele swiveled to eye us. Sound and motion ceased except for surly mutterings, as though a frosty breeze had coated everyone's tongue with ice.

"This isn't a raid," Matlock calmly informed the crowd. "Just go back to your business."

The patrons gradually resumed their conversations, and we approached a sleek black bar that spanned one wall of the establishment. A stocky, muscle-bound man with greasy salt-and-pepper hair emerged from behind it, throwing a dirty rag over one shoulder.

"What can I do for you, Officer?"

"I'm looking for someone. She may be here. But not in the pub."

I glanced at Matlock in bewilderment, though the bartender appeared to know exactly what he meant.

"You'll leave me guests alone?" he asked.

"You have my word."

"Right this way, then, sir."

The bartender led us around the far end of the counter and through a door, then down a flight of stairs. Opening another door, he ushered us into a room so dense with smoke that my eyes began to sting and weep.

"Take as long as you need," our guide muttered, heading back to the pub.

"What is this place?" I asked, glancing warily at my surroundings. We were in a room below ground, and the lights were so subdued by the haze that I had trouble adjusting to the dark.

"Just stick close," Matlock instructed. "Folks come here to kill their pain, so to speak. Illegally, of course."

He moved forward, and I took his arm, irrationally afraid of something springing out of the smoke and dragging me off to its lair.

Mimicking Officer Matlock, who was holding a cloth over his mouth, I buried my face in my cloak, then squinted around the room. People were sitting at tables and lying on cots, some laughing, some in a stupor, and some in zealous embrace. As the clouded air fought through my clothing and filled my lungs, I was hit by wave after wave of light-headedness until it became a persistent state. Still I did my best to examine faces in every conceivable corner.

"She's not here," I coughed, my breath so short and the heat of the room so great that I couldn't last any longer.

Matlock nodded and put his hand on my elbow, leading me up the stairs and out of the building. I felt weak, disoriented by the seeming timelessness of the room—with no windows, there could be no sunrise, no sunset, no stars or fresh air. Despite the loss of my wings, I remained Fae in my heart, and these notions were anxiety-inducing at best. That room could have fooled me into believing Nature had disappeared entirely.

"Sorry we didn't find your friend," Matlock said, while I deeply inhaled the cold, crisp air. "That was my best guess."

"Thank you for trying." Though I should have been disappointed, my mood was lifting, and I felt strangely euphoric. Everything I saw was sharp and defined. For a moment, I thought I could float into the air, even without my wings.

"Are you all right, Anya?" Officer Matlock was gazing into my green eyes, concern wrinkling his brow.

"Yes," I said with fervor, accidentally tipping toward him

and almost cracking my head against his. The incident struck me as so funny that I broke into uncontrollable laughter.

"I guess I have my answer."

He steadied me, which for some reason made me laugh harder. His eyes shone like sparkling silver, his hair was rich like the deep earth, and every minuscule aspect of his physiognomy was distinct—the light smile lines around his mouth, the shadow of his facial hair. I could count his eyelashes. I could have memorized him with one blink and carved his likeness into the Great Redwood.

"Keep taking deep breaths," my personal bodyguard gently advised. "I'll see you safely back to the Home."

I had no problem breathing deeply because the scents around me were so potent they transcended both malodor and perfume. It was as though the entire world had turned into a stimulant. We strolled along the streets until my exhilaration faded, and I blinked an odd fuzziness out of my eyes.

"What do you know that I don't?" I asked, latching on to the only explanation I could muster for what I had been feeling. "What was in that smoke?"

"I didn't think you'd be gone so long," Matlock chuckled, letting go of my arm and waiting a moment to see if I would fall over before resuming our walk. "It's a drug called *Cysur Naravni*—Nature's Comfort. On the street it's called 'the Green' because it can dye the skin around your mouth and nose, depending on how you take it. It can make you feel strong, even invincible. Happy, of course. People say it enhances the senses."

"I'd say it does."

He shook his head, grinning.

"What?" I pressed.

"We were only in there a few minutes. I didn't have any reaction."

"So?"

"So I'm wondering if it takes some kind of talent to get sloppy that fast."

I smiled despite myself. "I've never even smoked tobacco. Maybe you have gills, but I'm new to these sorts of things. I didn't think you'd hold my clean living against me."

"I wouldn't dream of it."

We fell silent as we arrived on the doorstep of the Fae-mily Home. I was about to thank him and say goodbye when he caught my hand and drew me around to face him.

"I don't know how that drug made you feel, Anya, but all joking aside, that stuff isn't good for you. And it's illegal. I didn't say before, but Cysur is also sometimes called Black Magic because Fae who've lost their connections claim it makes them feel *normal* again. But it's not worth it—trust me."

I shrugged his warning off, baffled and a little insulted that he would assume I was so weak-willed. "I'm here looking for my cousin, not a stuffy cellar. I won't let anything get in the way of that goal."

"Does your cousin have a name?"

I blanched and my heart beat louder. I'd gotten comfortable and careless, tripped up by my own tongue.

"Illumina," I responded, absurdly thankful that I was searching for two cousins. "That's her name."

"I'll keep an eye open for her," Officer Matlock promised, relinquishing my hand. "I'd best be going, then. I'm still on duty, after all. Take care."

I watched him walk away, mulling frantically over our conversation to determine if I'd damaged my cause, then went inside to find Shea. Ever sociable, she was in the dining room playing dice with a few other residents, but she withdrew from the game when she saw me.

"Any luck?" she asked, coming to my side.

"Yes and no. I saw Evangeline in an alley—at least I think it was her—but she ran away. Officer Matlock was on duty in the area and helped me search for her." My voice grew strident as the events of the day hit me with astonishing force. "I lost her, Shea! I found her and then I lost her."

My spirits sank ever further, their depth emphasized by the exhilaration I'd experienced not long ago. Shea drew me to a chair at a nearby table, took a seat beside me, and placed a hand over mine.

"At least you know she's alive. And you've got an idea of where she's living. You can start again tomorrow."

I picked at the grain of the table and sighed. "I suppose that's true. At least a little good came out of this day."

"Are you telling me everything, Anya?" She wrinkled her nose, her eyes skimming my clothing. "You've brought quite a stink back with you."

I gave her a good-humored shove. "It's just pub smell. I've been in a lot of rather unsavory places."

"You might want to air out your cloak and wash up before dinner. Otherwise you'll find yourself eating alone."

"*You* wouldn't even join me?" I sniffed in mock offense.

"Not a chance."

I grinned and headed to the back hallway off of which the sleeping rooms were located, leaving Shea to rejoin the dice game. I glanced over my shoulder just before I left the dining hall, wondering whose money she was betting.

chapter fourteen

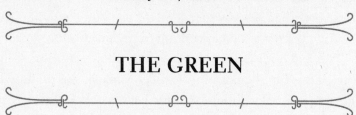

THE GREEN

It was only because the logs in the fireplace had burned to ash during the night that I noticed the crack of light from the hallway—the opening of our bedroom door.

I lay frozen but alert, shifting just enough to slip my hand under my pillow and grip the Anlace I had stashed there. A shadow entered the room, and I tried to think of a way to rouse Shea without drawing attention to myself. I'd been awake all night, rethinking the day and trying to decide the best way to renew my search for Evangeline, so I was certain no one had left the room. This person was not supposed to be here. Had someone recognized Shea despite our efforts to keep her hidden? Or perhaps Spex and Hastings had a contact in Tairmor who'd been sent to finish the work of the Sepulchres in the Fere. What if the men who had tried to take my ring had pursued me? I was sure they'd heard me say where I was staying.

The light and its corresponding shadow all but disappeared when the door closed. Flashbacks to the Sepulchre attacks made me bite my fist to keep silent as I listened for the tiniest sound. Then I heard a whisper amongst the snores and snuffles of my roommates.

"Anya? Are you here?"

The voice was so soft it was difficult to recognize, but the cadence and pattern of the speech were familiar. Tensed for a ploy, I rolled off the creaky mattress to stand barefoot on the floor.

"I'm here."

Cold fingers clamped around my wrist, sending a shiver down my spine. But before I could protest, I was tugged across the floor and into the hallway, where the light of a gas lamp allowed me to determine who had fetched me.

"Evangeline," I breathed, though identifying her was like imagining features onto a skull. Her cheeks were so hollow, her eyes so sunken, her skin so pale that I could hardly believe she was alive. Her white-blond eyebrows and eyelashes had more color than her face, and sleep circles like bruises spread almost to her temples. Her clothing was the same linen that many of the residents of the Fae-mily Home wore, but it looked tattered and uncomfortable, as if it were too small for her, though I doubted even a child would have had a tinier frame.

She fell into me, and I gripped her, thinking she had collapsed. When I realized she was hugging me, I squeezed her as tightly as I dared, standing on my tiptoes to compensate for our difference in height. It was then I noticed the empty space at her back. I closed my eyes and clenched my jaw. *Not her. Not her, too.* But the haunting proof was there. My stomach twisted at the thought of her pain, for I was all too familiar with it.

"When?" I choked. "How?"

"I could ask you the same thing. Only it doesn't really matter, does it? Neither of us can go back." She sniffed and swiped at her eyes. "I'm sorry this happened to you, but I'm glad you're here. I didn't think I'd ever see any of my friends again."

"What happened to us does matter, Evangeline. In my case it was hunters. Right outside Chrior."

"Oh."

Her blue eyes were murky and blank as a seafloor, and I couldn't believe the Faerie standing before me was my once-vibrant friend. I couldn't believe I was talking to Evangeline the nonconformist, the rebel, the girl who'd never let anyone tell her who she was. She'd regularly braided rainbow-colored ribbons into her hair, cut off her dresses at the knees, rolled her sleeves no matter how important it was not to wrinkle them. She'd once been full of life; now she was empty. It was like her spirit had gone into hibernation somewhere deep inside, or worse, had evaporated altogether.

"You?" I pressed, trying to get her to focus. "What happened to you?"

She gave a short giggle, her expression frightening in its hopelessness. Tears, unaccompanied by the usual noises of crying, drained from her eyes, leaving rivulets through the dustings of grime on either side of her slender nose.

"I don't remember." Again, the strange, incongruent laugh. "But somehow I ended up in a hospital here in Tairmor. When I came round, the doctor said I had enough drugs in my system that I'd probably never recall what happened to me. And he was right. Everything before the hospital is just noise in my head. So loud and confused it hurts to think about it."

I took her hand and led her toward the dining hall. Both of us needed to sit down. I felt faint, and I could only imagine the stress her frail body was under. We took a table, settling on benches across from each other, and Evangeline touched the wick of the lamp between us.

"I keep trying to light things. Only the fire is gone from

me. I'm screaming and reaching for it, but it doesn't turn its head or even remember that we were once friends. Sometimes I wonder if my elemental connection existed at all, if it was nothing more than a beautiful dream."

"My connection to the water is gone, as well. But we're both still alive. That's what we have to hold on to."

Not for the first time, and probably not for the last, I wondered if this was a good thing, what being alive meant if we were separated from the current of Nature that connected everything. We were akin to broken treasures, forgotten loves, stones caught in a crag, begging the river to carry us along. But Evangeline needed to believe that *alive* meant something good, and I hoped she would not sense my inner turmoil.

Without Evangeline's spark, it was dark in the room; only the yellowish glow from the street lamps outside assured us we weren't entombed. The gloom was omnipresent evidence of what my friend had lost.

"You must have some memories," I encouraged. "Think about being examined by the doctor. Can you work backward from there? What's the last thing you remember before you were given aid?"

Evangeline shook her head of matted hair, maybe having already tried this approach, maybe not wanting to try at all. The extent to which I understood her apathy was alarming. I certainly hadn't tried very hard to help Tom Matlock and Constable Farrier identify the hunters who had attacked me. But there was something bigger going on in Evangeline's case. Spex was still in Oaray identifying Faeries, and that meant others were in danger. She had to recall something.

"You went to Oaray," I tried again, hoping to trigger her memory. "Roughly four months ago."

"Has it been that long?" she asked, voice tremulous.

I nodded, my heart aching for her, though I refused to drop the subject.

"It was autumn, the leaves were turning color. You met with two men about getting your travel papers. Their names were Spex and Hastings. Spex was about our age and carried a cane. Hastings was big and bald. You probably went up to an attic room with them, just like you were told to do before you left Chrior."

Her brain was working now, her eyes flicking back and forth as she sifted through bits and pieces of her memories. Then she sat up straighter.

"I remember them. Anya, do *you* know what happened to me?"

"Some of it, but not everything," I confessed, emotions divided over what I was doing. Would stirring recollections help Evangeline, or just get me the information I wanted? "I know a few things because I met Spex. When you went to get papers from him and Hastings, he identified you as a Faerie. They probably drugged you—perhaps put something in a drink. You might have felt funny."

"Yes," she interrupted, nodding emphatically. "But it only comes in flashes after that." She tugged at the knots in her hair, eyes frightened. "I could use some water."

I rose to fulfill her request, dread prickling my stomach at the images that might be flooding her mind.

After taking a few sips from the glass I brought for her, Evangeline resumed her tale.

"There were Sepulchres, these horrid white things. I didn't think they still existed, but that's what someone called them. My captors locked me in a room with one of those creatures and…" Evangeline shuddered and met my eyes. "It knew my elemental connection, Anya. Its face glowed in front of me, and it whispered *fire* again and again, even though its mouth was…was…"

"After that?" I prompted, not needing to hear her stutter out a description of the webbed skin covering the Sepulchre's gruesome facial orifice.

Evangeline growled in frustration, hitting her forehead with the base of her palm. Her nails were all different lengths, some chewed, some sharp, all tinged a telltale green around the cuticles.

"That's when everything in my head gets loud and cluttered, and I want to *split it open* because there's too much to hold inside."

"Then tell me. Let some of it out."

She gulped in air and tried again. "There was darkness, unending darkness, and…my body was dragged across the floor, and the ground I think, a number of times." She closed her eyes, letting herself sink into the sensations. "Pain, so much pain. And the sound of water."

There was clarity in this last revelation, and I latched on to the potential clue.

"Here in Tairmor?"

"No, it wasn't constant. There was an ebb and flow. And the air tasted like salt, and dirt, like I might have been underground." She sighed, the light that had momentarily flickered in her cornflower eyes fading away.

"I'm sorry, Anya. I don't know if I'm making this up, or if I'm telling it in order, or really much of anything. The only thing I'm sure of is that I ended up in a hospital in Tairmor. Who knows? Maybe I was in the city the whole time."

Salt, dirt, water, transport—my mind was coursing through possibilities so fast my head grew fuzzy, and a dry nausea made my stomach ache. This was not the time to panic or speculate, though I wanted badly to do both. Instead, I gave my friend a sympathetic smile.

"You have no reason to be sorry. None of this is your fault. The people who should be sorry are the ones who hurt you. They tried hard to make sure you couldn't remember anything, but you did. You survived. You beat them, Evangeline."

"I'll never fly again. I'll never set a spark alive. I'll never cross the Bloody Road and return to Chrior. I'll never be able to pass the gift of magic to my children, which means they'll never know the pleasures I've loved and lost." The blankness was back in her eyes. "It doesn't feel like I beat them. It feels like they took everything from me."

Her epiphany about children hadn't occurred to me, and the insight grated like broken glass against my insides. I fought despair at her condition, at mine, and at the future. She and I had lost much more than our own magic—we'd lost it for all those who would follow in our bloodline. I bit my lip, my thoughts going to Davic. He had the right to have Fae children; he deserved to have Fae children. But he couldn't have them with me. Any child of mine would be little more than human. At that realization, I flushed as though with fever. My bigotry, hidden from me so well for so long, settled on me like crushed velvet, at once too heavy to bear and too comfortable to throw aside. I saw now that I didn't think a human life worth living. I didn't fight for humanity because I saw the need for equality, but because I pitied human existence.

I closed my eyes, appalled at myself, then fixated once more on my friend, for regardless of the turmoil I was feeling, she needed comfort.

"I'm here," I murmured, clasping her cold hands, not knowing what else to say. "You're not alone. We have each other."

"At least I had the chance to tell you what happened to me. You'll tell Ione, if you see her again?"

"You'll tell her yourself. Don't think for a moment that she won't come and visit us."

I was trying to be upbeat, but the words felt stiff coming off my tongue. Still, Evangeline seemed to find some solace.

"I think I can rest now."

"You should stay the night. There's no need to go out on the streets."

"I will. I've already talked to Fi." She came to her feet and walked around the table to give me a tight embrace, then padded off down the hallway.

I laid my head on the table, so tired my eyes were watering, so tired I'd forgotten to ask how she'd ended up in that alleyway or if she'd heard word of Illumina. That could wait until tomorrow, although her tearful reunion with me seemed to negate hope. And even if Evangeline had seen Illumina, I had to wonder how much of the incident she would recall. As I reviewed the things my friend had told me, it occurred to me that fate had never been kind to her. First her parents had driven her out of her own home with their manipulations and abuse; then her much-anticipated Crossing had turned into a nightmare. The scope of her suffering was almost incomprehensible. More than that, it was horribly unfair.

In need of sleep to clear my head, I stumbled back to the room Shea and I shared with the other privileged guests of the Fae-mily Home. Had they also been sent here by Luka Iva-

nova? How many of us did he see in a week, a month? Maybe
he was naive enough not to realize that someone was hunting
Fae—not an opportunistic criminal, but someone important,
someone with a goal. The Governor's son sent us to Fi believing each incident to be an anomaly, but there was nothing anomalous about any of this. These acts reeked of hatred
against my people, of a desire to see us all hurt. And as far as
I knew, I was the only one who had started putting the pieces
together. But what shape would this puzzle take? And what
could I do to stop its completion? Feeling that more weight
had just been placed on my aching shoulders, I rolled into bed
to stare helplessly at the wooden supports of the bunk above
me until I sank into a murky sleep.

Shea shook me awake the next morning, and I frowned, one
hand going to my aching head. I'd slept with my jaw clenched
tight, and it as though I'd driven my teeth through my skull.
I looked around to see that we were the only ones in the bedroom, everyone else having headed to the dining hall.

"Breakfast," Shea said, her brusque manner telling me things
were not altogether back to normal between us, despite the
day that had passed after our fight. I moaned, wanting to keep
sleeping, but the smell of sausage, eggs, and warm bread hung
like a cloud around me, and my stomach insisted I get up. I
began to dress, recounting my conversation with Evangeline
while I did so.

"Someone cut off her wings, and it wasn't hunters after a
trophy. Whoever's responsible wanted to know her elemental
connection. I have no idea what's going on, but I'm starting
to think I was lucky I lost my wings before we got to Oaray."

"And I'm starting to think we should have forced Spex to

come with us," Shea replied, fastening her bullet belt over her shoulder. On one hip she secured her pistol, on the other a hunting knife. Her bed was made, her things packed, and it hit me that she was ready to depart. "I'm positive he knew more than he told us."

"Shea, we can't leave yet. I have to stay for a little while and help Evangeline."

"I have to help myself. I can't stay in Tairmor any longer."

The implications of this statement reverberated in the silence until Shea sighed and slung her pack over her shoulder.

"Breakfast?" she repeated, picking up her cloak.

I nodded and accompanied her to the dining room, where we sat beside each other, neither of us speaking. Guilt and recrimination hung in the air, though I didn't think either of us was especially spiteful. The end of our partnership, which I'd thought I'd postponed, was here after all. I would stay with Evangeline; Shea would go on ahead without me. I searched the faces of the others around us, but did not see my blonde friend among them. No matter—she'd looked so exhausted that she was probably still sleeping. I would catch up with her later. I eyed Shea, aware of how much I would miss her and wanting to tell her so. But before I could open my mouth, a scream rent the air, jolting me out of my chair and causing Shea to spill her juice across the table.

"Damn it," she barked. "What the hell was that?"

"Fi!" the aching cry went on, raising the hair on the back of my neck. *"Fi!"*

The owner of the Fae-mily Home came scurrying from the foyer, then zigzagged among the tables to reach the back corridor and the sleeping rooms, everyone's collective gaze following her progress. At the sound of weeping, Shea and I

locked eyes, then stood and walked slowly after her, not wanting to incite a stampede toward the source of the disturbance.

When we made it to the hallway, we hurried to a bedroom
at the far end, where a small group of Faeries had gathered.
While I couldn't imagine what had occurred, their expressions
of horror and disbelief told me it was bad.

"Nature," I heard Fi gasp. "Go, get it out of here! No one
needs to see that!"

A young boy, pasty with shock, staggered past us, carrying
a flask that he quickly deposited in a rubbish bin, and Shea
and I stepped into the room. Someone pale lay on the floor,
and four others, including Fi, knelt around her. The shade was
drawn over the window, and I bypassed the huddled group to
allow sunlight to penetrate the scene.

I was wrong. The girl on the floor wasn't pale. She was blue.
Her skin was exposed outside the scant cover afforded by her
undergarments, and her limbs were stiff and still. I stood immobilized, not quite able to comprehend the scene. Shea was
in the doorway, the boy who had disposed of the flask trembling behind her. Tears like jewels adorned the faces of the
others gathered around the body. Fi touched the dead girl's
cheek, withdrawing her hand quickly at the shock of cold. And
yet I couldn't make organized sense out of what I was seeing
and feeling. Dead woman. Blue skin. Revulsion. Grief. What
was I missing?

I inched closer, and came to the strange understanding that
facial features in and of themselves weren't reliable for identifying people. At home when I saw Davic, I didn't recognize
him by his physical countenance so much as I did by his soul
full of inner peace, the presence he emanated. With Shea, it
was her fiery, determined spirit; Illumina, her aura of intelli-

gence and her shifting moods. Without Evangeline's life and personality, she was a mouth and a nose and a pair of eyes almost indistinct from everyone else's. Gradually, I filled in what was missing, and I saw my friend lying on the floor, her eyes open, and although I'd thought her gaze empty the night before, I understood now that *empty* was not a word to be used lightly. Evangeline's eyes were waxy, and had they not been so vibrantly blue in life, I doubted I would have been able to discern their color in death.

Still, I couldn't react. All I managed were two shocked and anguished words. "It's Evangeline."

I was barely aware of movement, but Shea appeared at my side, anchoring me and keeping me upright.

"What happened?" she asked, the question directed to the others in the room.

Fi looked up from where she was kneeling by the body, her orange-and-yellow wings curled around her like a blanket.

"We found her like this, with an empty flask in her hand. Undiluted Cysur—you can't mistake the smell. She must have taken her own life."

As the words hit me, I doubled over and lost my breakfast. Evangeline was dead by her own hand, the losses she had suffered too great for her to bear. I hadn't helped her after all. Maybe I'd even hurt her. Or maybe all she had wanted was the peace that came from telling her story to someone who cared, someone who would see that her friends and family knew her fate. If that need had been keeping her alive, I wished I'd never satisfied it.

I swayed on my feet, and if Shea hadn't been there, I would have fallen into my own vomit. Images overtook my senses, and I stumbled away from her to press my back against the wall, closing my eyes against the pain hammering my skull.

I dug my fingers deep into the soil, moist and teeming with life from the ponds all around and the fountain statues that sprinkled water onto everything like dewdrops. The water lilies were pink and ripe, birds chirped their spring songs, and Fae children ran about, chased by their parents, the laughter of both filling the last hollow corners of the woods. Chrior was alive after a long winter spent indoors bundled in warm clothing. Today we were barefoot and free.

Ione and Evangeline made the two remaining points of our triangle, sorting through rocks they found in the mud and speculating about what rare stones they might have uncovered. Even at eight years old, I was aware of how uniquely beautiful Ione was, with her crystalline-clear blue eyes, soft blond hair, and heart-shaped face, and of how unlike the other children Evangeline was. She had a wild appearance—clothes that had been spilled on and not cleaned, and an eager and open expression that suggested she would try anything once.

Evangeline had just finished telling us about the human graveyard she'd found hidden away in the forest, and the angry ghosts that lived there, when a gruff exclamation from nearby caught our attention.

"Illumina!"

The voice was a man's, and I recognized it at once as belonging to my uncle Enerris. I turned, garnering grass stains on the seat of my pants, and saw my little dark-haired cousin frozen halfway across the green to us. Her ears poked through her lank locks, and her lip trembled. She'd been coming to play with us, and her father was annoyed, Nature knew why. My mother always said to be nice to Illumina and include her in our games, but I didn't know how when my uncle, whose presence tended to end games and inspire silence, always accompanied her. I couldn't understand why he brought her to the playing grounds if he didn't want her to play.

"Let her go, Enerris."

In the background, my mother appeared beside my scowling uncle. He was old and gray and hard, while Incarnadine was soft yet resilient like the flesh on my palm. "Excuse me?" he replied, slowly and deliberately.

"You heard me." My mother didn't back down; her vigor made up for what she lacked in height and weight in comparison with her brother. She waved my cousin ahead with a maternal smile. "Go on, Illumina. Go play."

Practically atremble, Illumina took advantage of this temporary permission to be a child, scrambling around me to settle between Evangeline and Ione, as far from our parents as she could go. There was a moment of silence, then Evangeline hugged her and pointed out the pile of rocks she'd accumulated. Things in the triangle—or whatever shape we now made—returned to normal, though I kept one ear attuned to what was happening behind me. I'd never been hurt by Enerris, or seen him hurt anyone else, but there was something unkind about him, and I didn't like him being near my mother.

"She's my daughter, Carna," he snarled.

"Then be a father, for Nature's sake. She's six years old."

"Haven't I warned you enough times not to come between me and my child? I'll raise her how I see fit."

"Giving her leave to play is hardly interfering in her upbringing."

"I say it is. I say all you do is interfere. And one day you'll be sorry for it."

"I'll be dead before I'm sorry for trying to give that girl a little joy."

My mother was unrelenting in her stance, enough so to draw the attention of a few others on the grounds, including the Queen, who came there often to watch the children of her court flourish.

Enerris fell quiet in response to the stares. Though I felt sick with fear in that moment, I was too naive to know what was scaring me, too young to realize my uncle's abrupt silence generally meant an idea had occurred to him.

As the years passed and my mother continued to defy her brother without consequence, I forgot the primal fear of my youth in favor of practicality, arrogance—all the things that replace raw instinct when people grow up. Then Incarnadine fell ill, and her symptoms were unfamiliar to the medicine mage as her body steadily withered away.

And at my mother's funeral, Enerris held Illumina's hand and smiled.

"Anya, *Anya,* snap out of it. You're scaring me."

The voice was Shea's, more shrill than usual, drawing me back from the edge. I brought my eyes to bear on her, forcing them to focus.

"I'm okay," I mumbled. "Just…shocked."

The worry lines in Shea's face formed tiny hills and valleys, and I smiled faintly at that thought, which did nothing to placate her.

"I'm getting you out of here," she informed me.

Taking me by the arm, she hauled me from the scene, through the dining room, and to the walk in front of the Home, perhaps thinking fresh air would bring me back to my senses. Although *fresh* was not a word I would have used to describe the air quality, the chill breeze that buffeted us did help me to focus. At once I was inundated with emotions—anger, confusion, grief, a peculiar sense that Evangeline had betrayed me by taking her own life—so many emotions that it was ludicrous to think I might express them all by crying. I fought my welling tears on this premise. What had happened to my stoicism, the calm strength that was expected of a member of the Redwood Fae? It was our birthright to lead, to offer comfort to others, to display courage in the midst of trying times. This brand of weakness wasn't supposed to be in my bloodline.

I concentrated on the noise and bustle of the streets and let them overpower the chaos in my mind. At last, I turned to Shea, who stood at my side, concern pulling her eyebrows together.

"We should go inside and help Fi," I said. "She shouldn't have to deal with this on her own."

The same boy who'd stumbled past us with the flask of Cysur stumbled past us again on our way into the shelter. This time he was wearing winter clothing and pinning a hat to his head as he tore down the dirty road on his way to the nearest Constabulary station.

He returned within half an hour, an entourage of officers in tow, and the Fae-mily Home became *their* home for the remainder of the day as the circumstances of Evangeline's death were investigated. Constable Marcus Farrier arrived in the late morning to oversee the removal of my friend's body, and it seemed he would rather have been anywhere else, the lines of his scowl as permanent as if they'd been scars. I saw the death litter borne down the hall toward the back door, and Farrier motion for the officers to pause. He threw back the white sheet covering Evangeline's corpse far enough to access her arm, and his pitiless hands lifted her wrist for examination.

"She used all right," he grunted, rolling one of her cold fingers between his own. "We'll never know if the death was suicide or stupidity." Replacing the sheet, he added, "And I'll never care. Get it out of here, boys."

He glanced about distastefully. He thought the shelter a

waste of space and money, that much was clear. What he thought of my people I dared not speculate, for the sake of my fragile state. But I did recall how he'd marched into the Governor's mansion without the hesitation of a subordinate, and as I met his haughty gaze from the opposite end of the hall with my own nearly as dead as Evangeline's, I entertained the notion that his power might be great enough to have moved the players into position for her kidnapping.

chapter fifteen

NO REASON AT ALL

Shea postponed her departure, staying with me throughout the day, and she watched me from the lower bunk as I packed that evening. The other residents of the Fae-mily Home were at dinner, granting us the privacy to talk, but she didn't know what to say, so didn't say anything. I was relieved that she remained quiet. There were no words of solace she could offer.

I looked up from my belongings to catch sight of Shea's reflection in the mirror that hung on the wall. There was apprehension in her eyes, and it told me I wasn't acting like myself. Appropriate, because I didn't feel like myself, either. It was only a matter of time before Evangeline's death would land like the head of a hammer atop my other losses and enfeeble me. I had to travel far and fast before it happened.

"What about your friend's funeral?" Shea finally ventured. "Will you go?"

"She ought to be burned." My voice shook as though the grief I was locking out of my heart had eked into my throat. "She was a Fire Fae. All they're going to do is dump her in the ground. That's not a funeral. I'll serve her memory better by finding Zabriel, and then finding whoever did this to her."

I was cold as the bitter wind outside, and Shea's face in the mirror told me she was beginning to understand my mood. I was done apologizing for the secrets I had kept. She could forgive me or not, come along with me or not—it made no difference. I had a purpose, and everything else was extraneous. There would be no more silent debate over who had suffered more, because what was there to measure? Pain inflicted? Lasting damage? Odds of survival? These things *couldn't* be measured. If we were going to continue journeying together, it would have to be with a clean slate.

Shea pulled her rucksack up beside her and picked through its contents. A tiny knock on the door interrupted our efforts, and Fi slipped inside, her wings still in a sad embrace about her shoulders. She glanced at Shea, then back to me, and I sensed she was hesitant to speak in the presence of my human friend. I gave her a nod to let her know Shea could be trusted, and words gushed from her mouth.

"I know who you are. I recognized the Anlace first, then your ring. You're Queen Ubiqua's heir. I would have let you come and go without mention, but I thought you should be told one of your relations was here."

My mind jumped to Zabriel. Since Illumina had not been to Oaray, I'd assumed the worst of her fate. But Fi's description left no room for doubt.

"A girl with long dark hair and marks on her body, wearing a ring to match yours. She was on a search for her cousin. Don't worry—I won't tell anyone you were here. But please listen."

Fi came farther into the room, her hands closed around something she did not want me to see, at least for the moment. Her eyes were earnest, boring into mine with such intensity that I struggled not to give ground to her.

"Something's wrong in the Territory, dreadfully wrong. I've

only noticed because of my business, but Fae are shorn of their wings oftener and oftener. They end up here or at hospitals without remembering much. I've already sent word to Chrior that Crossings should be stopped. The only human I've had a notion to tell is Luka Ivanova, and he's been investigating the situation with as little attention drawn as possible, trying to track Fae in the Warckum Territory and all that. He's leery of starting a political squall before the timing's good. I sent the girl to him. If anybody can help find the Prince, it'll be Luka."

"We can't trust anyone in the Governor's family," I blurted, my stomach clenching. There was no way Illumina would have gone to Luka Ivanova for assistance, but Fi's knowledge of my quest and her faith in the man were a potentially disastrous combination. "Zabriel's presence in the human world cannot become known to those who would have an interest in detaining him here."

"I understand," Fi assured me. "I understand better than you credit me—just think of the injuries I see every day. Luka doesn't know anything about the Prince from my lips, but he *is* a reliable source of information. If you need him, use him. The same goes for me."

I offered a troubled thank-you, not completely placated. Fi extended her closed fist to me, and I accepted her gift, my brow puckered in bewilderment. When I opened my palm, I held a locket stuffed with the small, fragrant seeds of Tanya flowers that grew only within the boundaries of the Faerie Realm. The flowers gave off a sweet, calming fragrance, and were believed to inspire inner peace.

"I took it from around Evangeline's neck before she was removed," Fi explained. "If you find the Prince, give it to him.

Tell him what became of her. Maybe it will remind him why we need him."

I nodded, uncertain of what to say. Her intentions were good, but already Zabriel's concealment was faltering. Even if word of his presence in the Warckum Territory spread only among Fae, the Governor's son was in a good position to find out. Fi couldn't be the only Faerie who considered Luka an ally. I had to find my cousin, and fast.

Shea and I said little in the aftermath of Fi's departure. My thoughts were fixed on the good news she had delivered about Illumina: not only was she alive, but she'd made it safely to the capital against all odds, and presumably with travel papers obtained from someplace other than the City of False Smiles. How and why she would have gone elsewhere was a mystery, but such had to be the case, for it was risky to enter and explore Tairmor without passable documentation. Once here, of course, she might have seen Zabriel's wanted poster just as I had. Would she have set out for Sheness? With any luck, I'd find her in the port city, and all the royal cousins would at long last be reunited.

As the other Faeries returned from dinner, it occurred to me that the owner of the Fae-mily Home might have made Shea realize, perhaps for the first time, the significance of the mission we were on. When I'd first told my friend of Zabriel's identity, her anger could easily have interfered with her understanding. But now it couldn't be overlooked that Zabriel was more than a runaway princeling—he was a beacon of hope in times that were beginning to darken the vision of many of my people.

Not surprisingly, I had trouble sleeping that night. Every time I closed my eyes, Evangeline's opened, not as they had been in life, but as I'd seen them upon her corpse. Even with this image imprinted on my memory, I couldn't reconcile her absence from the world. Why hadn't she confided her true pain to me? Why hadn't I realized something was wrong when she'd hugged me that last time? Regret was like a vacuum inside me, pulling everything toward an empty core, and things I should have done, could have done, continually roiled through my mind. Across all the scenarios I could invent, one theme was present: Evangeline should not have died.

It was the drink Shea made for me from the herbs in her pack that finally allowed me some rest, apparently working on scarred hearts as well as scarred bodies.

I remained in bed the following morning, allowing myself to drift in and out of lucidity. I had wanted to leave Tairmor before I could be tempted to attend Evangeline's interment, but my brain felt swathed in cotton from the medicine I had taken, creating a distinct lack of motivation. Besides, Shea wasn't pressing for a quick departure anymore.

A knock on the door that I instinctively knew belonged to Fi—no one else could have made the rapping of knuckles against wood sound fluttery—drew me from my musings. I sat upright and threw aside my blankets. Had she remembered more about her encounter with Illumina? Or perhaps she'd heard news about Zabriel. I sighed—what if I'd stayed too long and she was bringing information about the burial arrangements?

I walked to the door in my bare feet, wearing an unbelted tunic over leggings, my auburn hair in disarray, and opened it, not pausing to consider that Fi might not be alone.

Beside her stood Officer Tom Matlock, his hair carefully

combed, the coat of his red uniform unbuttoned to reveal a crisp white shirt beneath. The pistols and knives on the weapons belt around his hips were well polished, glinting at me from their matched leather holders.

"You, um…have a visitor," Fi announced, her eyes wide with surprise and compunction. But there was no going back.

"Come in," I said with all the grace I could muster.

Matlock crossed the threshold, a fleeting smile playing upon his features in concession to the awkward situation. I nodded to Fi, who took her leave with a mouthed apology. My guest had stopped a few feet into the room, and I walked by him to take a seat on the edge of my bunk.

"Sorry," he said with a shy chuckle. "I'll step back out if you want to finish getting dressed."

"What would be the point? You've already seen me at my worst."

"As worsts go, I've seen a lot worse."

His attempt at a compliment helped me relax, and he took my change in posture as a cue that he was welcome to stay, moving to sit in the chair by the fireplace. Still, his presence was troubling. What business could have brought him here?

"I didn't expect to see you again so soon. Is there something I can do for you, Officer Matlock?"

"Call me Tom," he said with a wave of his hand. "I had hoped we were past the formalities. Besides, I'm only an officer when I'm on duty. Off, I'm nineteen, young and foolish."

I laughed, seeing straight through his bluff. Tom Matlock was never foolish; I felt sure of that. I was surprised by his age, though—I would have thought him older simply because of his rank.

"Okay, *Tom*." I shifted position, pulling one leg up and

under me as the low fire hissed, then repeated my question. "What can I do for you?"

"I stopped by to see how you're doing, but… Fi told me about the Faerie who died. The friend you were searching for, I assume."

I nodded, not really wanting to talk about Evangeline. The wound to my heart inflicted by her death was still too fresh. But my silence and downcast eyes did not dissuade Officer Matlock.

"It won't be much help, but I saw the Green around her mouth and nose as she ran from the alley—Cysur residue. If she was an addict, she might not have meant to kill herself. It could have been an accident. I thought it might help you to know that."

"Thank you, that's…" I'd been planning to say "good to know," but the words caught in my throat. The news that Evangeline's death could have been an accident rather than a suicide made it at once more tragic and easier to bear.

"Anyway," Tom continued, "I know *sorry* doesn't begin to cover it, but I am—sorry, I mean. How are you holding up?"

"I'm fine, more or less."

Tom was looking at me with an earnestness that I was used to seeing in Davic, and my heart ached at the memories of my beloved that glimmered on the horizon of my mind. I longed to feel his arms about me. Davic was solid, reassuring, unchanging—all the security I could no longer have. Tom wasn't my promised. But he did seem to care.

"It doesn't feel real," I managed to say. "None of it does. The loss of my wings, Evangeline's death. It's all so…nonsensical."

"Your friend's name was Evangeline?"

I nodded, then found myself gazing blankly through the

window as I told him things I wouldn't have said to Shea. I didn't know what it was about him that inspired confidence; all I knew was that the thoughts and emotions I had been bottling up inside needed to be released.

"She was this vivacious, beautiful Faerie. I've known her— or, I guess, I *knew* her—since we were two years old. How can she be gone? I could easily convince myself yesterday didn't happen, except my stomach is sick and my heart is beating just a little too fast and I can't get comfortable no matter how hard I try because something in my world is just *wrong,* like…like stitches holding a wound together have been torn asunder."

"There's nothing for that but time," Tom said, drawing my eyes to his. "But it's the hardest kind of waiting. You aren't able to fill your days with anything but survival."

"Who did you lose?" I asked without thinking, but he flashed a tiny smile, assuring me he wasn't offended.

"Trust me, that's a long, boring story."

"How could it be?" I pressed, wishing he would share something so the ache I felt wouldn't seem so conspicuous, like I had poured my heart out on the floor between us. But he winked instead, abandoning his reflective mood.

"Because I already know how it ends."

I cocked an eyebrow at him, but there was nothing I could do if he wanted to evade the question. It would have been nice to know how it was he understood my feelings—had he lost his mother or father? A sibling? A best friend, as I had? I pushed it to the recesses of my mind. I would probably never know.

"How long have you been a Constabulary?" I asked, seeking a way out of the silence.

"I was sort of an errand boy for the police force by the time

I was thirteen. I've been an officer since I turned eighteen, so almost two years."

"So old," I joked, and he grinned.

"You won't be young forever, you know."

"That may be, but I'll always be younger than you."

"And just how young is that?"

"Seventeen in the spring." He shook his head, and some of his brown hair fell forward across his temple. I leaned toward him, feeling an inexplicable urge to brush it back into place, much as I would have done with Davic. At the last moment, I came to my senses—this was not my promised sitting across from me—and stopped before I embarrassed myself. He stood, oblivious to the unease with which I was regarding my hands, his manner more businesslike.

"Although I'd like to say this is just a casual visit, Anya, I'm aware you're supposed to check in with the doctor. I thought I'd offer you a ride to the hospital."

I cringed. Upon being discharged, I'd promptly discarded Dr. Nye's directive to return, relying on Shea's ability to re-dress my wounds if necessary. Still, now that Tom had brought it up, it wouldn't hurt to get some more of the painkiller for the road. Maybe it was a good thing we hadn't taken off yet.

"That's very kind of you, but I'm inclined to decline. I'm willing to walk, and I'd hate to ruin your off-duty time."

"I volunteered, remember? Besides, it's a longer walk from here than you realize, and not the most pleasant one."

I bit my lip, wanting to accept, but worried Tom was being a little too kind. What was he after? In the end, I acquiesced, for there were no signs of deception about him.

"All right, if you insist. Now I really should finish getting dressed."

"Not that I don't appreciate this look," Tom said with a wave of his hand in my direction, "but you're probably right."

He stepped into the hallway to wait, and I quickly donned thicker leggings and my jerkin, wishing I had something less drab to wear. When I was ready, I joined Tom, and he escorted me through the Home, giving a quick shout to Fi to let her know where we were going. Then he led me outside, where a buggy complete with a driver was parked, allowing my escort to ride with me inside the cab. Although he sat across from me on the bench seats, his proximity nevertheless set my hair on end—out of mistrust, confusion, intrigue, I couldn't decide—so I concentrated my attention on the sights outside the carriage window.

"If you don't mind my asking," he said after a bit, "how did you and Mary become friends?"

"Her family helped me after I was injured."

"And she just decided to travel with you? Her parents didn't mind?"

Ignoring the second part of his question, I answered the first. "She wanted to see more of the world. In Chrior, when we reach the age of fourteen, we're old enough for a Crossing into the Warckum Territory. It's a journey we make on our own, and it's part of what signifies our passage into adulthood. It also gives us an introduction to how you humans live, sort of a cultural awakening. I suppose Shea leaving her family to travel with me is a form of Crossing for her. You might say it's a personal declaration of independence."

He laughed. "You're careful with your words. If I listen for what you didn't say, I'd guess her parents weren't pleased when she left with you. But that's their business, not mine."

I gazed at him with renewed interest. He was intelligent as

well as kind. I hadn't expected that. In my experience, most questions posed by humans were easily evaded. Officer Matlock seemed to catch me at every exit.

"This Fae Crossing you mentioned," he continued. "You said you're eligible when you turn fourteen. How old were you when you went on yours?"

"Fourteen."

"Left on your birthday?"

"The day after."

"Enjoyed your trip immensely?"

"Certainly did."

"And how many times have you crossed since then?"

"A few."

I was grinning, for though Tom had spent relatively little time with me, he seemed to have gauged my nature pretty well.

Our arrival at the hospital ended our conversation, though I wondered what else he might have asked given the chance. In his gentlemanly way, Tom accompanied me inside for my checkup, then stood outside the door of the examination room while I met with Dr. Nye, who was of the opinion that I was steadily and appropriately healing. He did give me a fresh vial of painkiller, however, along with an admonition to take it slow for a couple more weeks. The former was appreciated, while the latter would be ignored.

Tom and I didn't speak much on our return trip to the Faemily Home, just a bit of small talk. But as we neared our destination, he became more serious.

"How long do you expect to stay with Fi?" he asked, his gray eyes studying me.

"Not much longer. I'm feeling fine, almost completely healed."

"That's good to hear. Are you off to find your cousin, then?"

"Yes, we have an aunt who is dying, and Illumina needs to return immediately." Once more I relied on my younger cousin in my explanation, for this was as true of her as it was of Zabriel.

"Then I can understand your urgency in finding her. Still, the selfish part of me wishes I had a bit more time to figure you out."

I didn't know what to make of this statement, so didn't respond. Then I chided myself for the possibilities that had sprung into my mind. The most likely explanation was that he was interested in learning more about my people and our way of life.

The carriage halted in front of the Fae-mily Home, and Tom helped me from the cab, his hesitation revealing a temptation to walk me inside. But it was nearing dinnertime, and I expected he had someplace else to be.

"I know you'll be fine, Anya, as you continue your travels," he said, sounding more like he was assuring himself than me. "But if you do run into trouble, you can get word to me through any Constabulary station. And don't be afraid to drop my name if you need to open a few doors. I may be young, but as one of Luka Ivanova's handpicked officers, I'm pretty well-known in the Territory."

"Thank you. I'll keep that in mind." I hesitated, chewing on my lower lip. "I probably shouldn't ask this—I mean, it's not really any of my business—but do you like working for the Lieutenant Governor?"

"I'd rather work for him than anyone else." Tom shrugged. He perused my face, then cleared his throat. "I'd better be on my way, but I've really enjoyed our time together. Getting to know someone like you is one of the more pleasant aspects of my position."

With a respectful nod, he turned and approached the carriage, leaving me alone and befuddled. I entered the Home, then turned to watch from the window as he gave one of the horses drawing the buggy a scratch and a kiss on the nose before hopping back inside the cab. With a flick of the reins, the driver sent the horses off at a trot, and the carriage disappeared from sight.

While Tom did have a purpose in seeing me, it now felt more like an excuse than a reason. What, then, could he be after? Concerned that he had muddled my judgment and prevented suspicion from setting in, I tried to clear my head. Then a refreshing idea struck me. What if he'd come all this way *just* to see me? I couldn't explain why that notion made me happy, other than that it was flattering to my ego. Still, I couldn't deny that I wanted Tom to have come here for no reason at all.

Frustrated with myself, I began to pace in front of the window, trying to temper my feelings with logic. Tom Matlock was a law officer in Tairmor, a career man, a human, and there was no reason for me to believe he had any special interest in me. Even if he did, I was promised to Davic. More than that, I *wanted* to be promised to Davic, although I didn't know how our relationship would work out in the long run.

The log in the fireplace in the corner of the entryway broke, and embers sprayed upward, reminding me of the winter solstice festival in the Great Redwood. I stopped my pacing, resolving to find Shea before Tom's visit perplexed me any further.

I turned toward the dining hall just as Fi emerged from a side room with a stack of clean towels that interfered with her vision. She nearly ran into me, the towels almost tumbling from her grasp as I sidestepped her. I caught the one that managed to part from its fellows, and Fi sighed in relief.

"Oh, thank goodness," she said, cheeks flushed. "Young reflexes. Actually, I was thinking about you a minute ago, and now here you are. How was your time with Tom? I mean, Officer Matlock. I suppose I should address him rightly no matter how much I see him."

"It was fine—very nice, I should say. He seems like a good man. Does he come here often, then?"

"Once in a while, more than the other Constabularies in the city. He works with the Lieutenant Governor, and since Luka keeps this place on its feet, Tom is bound to wander in and out. He's kind, dependable. Always asks if I need help before he goes, and won't leave a job half-done. And he's rather good-looking, wouldn't you say?"

I laughed at her teasing grin.

"Come on," she cajoled. "He'd be a fantastic catch for any young woman."

I shrugged and replaced the stray towel atop the stack in her arms.

"Sometimes people your age don't know a good thing when they see one," she said with a significant look, then motioned with her head to the other side of the entry.

I followed Fi into one of the stockrooms, where staff could fetch various supplies for the residents of the Home. Clean laundry adorned the shelves on one side, and woven baskets of dirty laundry occupied the floor space beneath.

"I was going to ask about Luka next," I ventured. "Unless you're thinking of playing matchmaker with him, as well?"

"My dear, I think Luka will be a bachelor forever. Every woman in this city has tried for that man. What is it you want to know?"

"I'm just generally curious. I take it he's not married. Does he have children?"

I was feeling a surge of inquisitiveness about Zabriel's family tree. Did he have human cousins? Or was his uncle the only heir to the family dynasty, making Zabriel highly important on this side of the Bloody Road as well as in Chrior?

Fi began shelving towels. "Luka isn't married and never has been, though of course there are always rumors about powerful men. Plenty of women have gone after the prestige of birthing an Ivanova heir and made claims, but unless you put stock in gossip, he doesn't have children. I believe that. Anything else wouldn't be in keeping with the honorable man I know him to be. Besides, if the Governor had a grandchild, legitimate or not, he wouldn't leave the child unacknowledged. William's death devastated his legacy."

I nodded, struck by Fi's loyalty to the Governor's son. Not having much experience with him, I didn't know if this was a good thing or a potentially perilous one.

"I wish there *was* a human heir in the Territory," I mused, and her eyebrows bounced in agreement, her thoughts tracking mine to Zabriel. "By the way," I went on, diverging from the topic, "have you seen Shea?"

"She left before you and Tom." Fi brushed past me to wave an old couple through the front door. "She said to tell you not to look for her until evening, which I guess is about now. Oh, and she said not to worry."

Shock rippled through me, crawling down my arms in vine-like tendrils. "Did she say where she was going?"

"Yes. She said she used to live in Tairmor and was going home." Fi patted my hand, recognizing the anxiety on my face. "She'll be back, really. She's human, after all, and surely she knows the city."

I forced a smile. "Yes, of course she'll be back. I'm just... on edge."

Fi accepted this and headed off toward the kitchen. I returned to the room where Shea and I had been sleeping, a steady stream of curse words running through my head. Knowing my friend had gone "home" did me no good whatsoever— she'd never told me where her family had lived, and looking for her in the enormous capital would be futile. I tugged on my long hair in frustration; there were so many things that could have happened to her.

Needing a distraction, I sat on my bunk, took the Anlace from its sheath, and ran a rag over its already gleaming length. But my mind refused to quiet. It wasn't just the Constabularies who posed a risk to Shea. As I had discovered, street people and criminal types roamed the poorer areas of the city. But the worst thought was that she could be in custody right now, kneeling in front of Governor Ivanova, and I had no ability to help her.

I cleaned the Anlace more vigorously, shining the pommel and the bright ruby that stared out from it, its beautification offering no assistance despite whatever royal mysteries it contained. Shea had warned me to be home before dark when I had ventured out to search for Evangeline, threatening the formation of a search party if I failed to follow her advice; she certainly would have heeded that advice herself. Yet pink streaks were quickly spreading across the sky, announcing the setting of the sun. What would I do if Shea never came back? How would I find out what happened to her? And how long could I afford to wait before moving on without her?

chapter sixteen

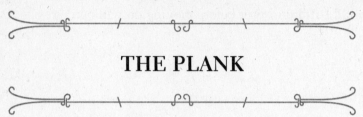

THE PLANK

When the dinner hour arrived without Shea's return, I headed to the main hall. The frequent meals I was skipping were starting to show in my weight and in my stamina, forcing me to pay momentary attention to my health. I scrounged up a tray and dutifully stood in line, then found a secluded corner in which to poke at my food. This day had become impossibly long and dreary, and I wished I had risen with Shea and either prevented her from leaving or gone along with her.

The bang of a tray on the table jolted me to reality, and my head jerked up. Shea was standing across from me, hair windswept and cheeks rosy.

"Sorry, didn't mean to startle you," she said, plopping herself down in a chair as if nothing was wrong. "You were still sleeping this morning and I didn't want to bother you. How are you feeling?"

I gaped at her, then clenched my teeth, trying to rein in my temper.

"How am I feeling? I'm feeling like you need to explain why four days ago Tairmor was too dangerous for you, but today you're suddenly safe on the streets."

"Look, I know it wasn't smart," she said, holding up her

fork and knife in surrender. "But I had to see my home again. I had the impulse and the opportunity and just had to do it. I mean, I'm *here* for the first time in years. If it helps, I thought I would be back before you were awake—those herbs put you into a pretty heavy slumber." Looking a bit guilty, she added, "I didn't talk to anyone other than the officers who stopped me to check my papers. But they passed scrutiny, so no harm done."

It was clear she'd thought about how best to explain her actions, which made me leery of her story. But her almond eyes were innocently wide, and her complexion, honeyed from our travels, was free of telltale pink. I examined her, starting to feel that I was being too hard on her. Then my eyes landed on the shoulder of her cloak, where a ragged tear revealed the navy of the coat she wore beneath.

Pointing to the spot, I asked, "How did that happen?"

She flung the cloak over her shoulders to hide the evidence that her outing had not been as smooth as she wanted me to believe.

"It's nothing. Caught it on a fence is all."

"And you couldn't stop to unhook it? You were running from something, weren't you?"

"I said it's nothing." She crossed her forearms on the surface of the table, a rubescent glow at last reaching her cheeks.

My face, in turn, lost its color. I'd been right to worry—she might have gotten away from whatever danger had pursued her, but that was probably nothing more than a fortunate fluke.

"You got lucky," I sputtered, deciding not to pursue the issue further. She *was* back safe and sound. Sensing she was eager to talk about the day, I asked, "How was the old homestead?"

"Still there. It's just as I remember it, this little place on the northeast side, crammed up with the neighbors' houses. It sits on a slope, so the whole house seems to lean a little. It drove my father insane because he couldn't fix it, no matter how good a carpenter he was."

Shadows crossed her face, and she paused in her tale.

"What is it, Shea?" I prompted, reaching for her hand. "What's bothering you?"

"Everything's exactly like it was; only it isn't, because another family has moved in." Her voice cracked, and she cleared her throat. "I don't know what I expected, honestly. It was stupid of me to think the government wouldn't take our house in partial settlement on my father's debt. I can't believe I let it get to me, but seeing another mother and father with their children was crushing." She paused and recaptured the stray hairs that had escaped her ponytail. "The house isn't ours anymore."

I'd been trying to make her feel bad since she'd joined me, but now it was clear she'd been feeling awful already. Remorse filled my stomach, mixing horribly with my food, and I pushed my plate aside.

"Humans don't know this the way my people do, but trees and just about everything in the natural world have spirits and feelings and memories. There may be new people living in your house, but the wood of the walls and floors remembers you and your family. You'll always belong there."

"Do you really believe that?"

"Believe it? I used to listen to Nature speaking. I know it's true."

Shea smiled a little at this thought. I didn't know for certain that deadwood, which the humans used to construct their buildings, had the same capacity for memory as did living trees, but she needed to believe it right now.

Gratefulness flickered in Shea's eyes, and her mood appeared to lighten. But the moment was short-lived.

"There's more I need to tell you, Anya." She fidgeted, ultimately folding her hands on the tabletop in front of her. "It's been bothering me for a while now, and I think today just made it worse. Should I have left my family? Maybe it was selfish of me. My mother's probably been forced to do most of the cooking, cleaning, and laundry since I left. Maggie and Marissa aren't really old enough to help much with those things. And I doubt anyone's been reading to my sisters and tucking them into bed like I did. I never talked to my sisters about helping around the house before I left. Never helped them to see what needed doing. I never even *explained* to Maggie and Marissa where I was going or why I was abandoning them."

Her use of the word *abandoned* rang in my head. I'd abandoned Davic, my father, Ubiqua, Ione, everyone when I'd taken off. Davic was the only one who'd gotten a goodbye.

"You have the right to live your own life, Shea," I soothed, able to believe it for her but not for me. Not when my loved ones were expecting me to return and I never would. "You forget there was a time before you were old enough to help around the house, a time when your mother and father managed without you. And Maggie and Marissa are of more help than you want to admit right now. I'm sure everything's fine with your family. In Chrior, we have a saying, wisdom handed down by the Old Fae—'the moon rises as the sun sets, so there is always light in the world.' It means there's always hope. That there's something good in everything that happens."

"I wish I could live in Chrior," Shea said, swiping at a few tears that had fallen on her cheeks. "It sounds like people are happier there."

My throat burned, for that was a trip neither of us would be able to make. And I'd had much the same thought the day I'd returned to the Faerie Realm for the winter solstice—Fae were more content and at peace than humans because they coexisted with Nature instead of dominating it. The Realm across the Bloody Road was hallowed, a place where time felt slower, kinder; a place that provided a retreat, a refuge from the outside world. The people in the Warckum Territory believed in a promised land after death, but we didn't have to because we already had our sanctuary. The threads of human religion, similar in all its forms, had never appealed to me before this moment. Now I understood that on this side of the Road, if death didn't offer paradise, there was no paradise to be had.

"Let's move on tomorrow," I proposed, needing to divert my thoughts. "I've had enough of this city."

"That's something we can agree on."

Shea shoveled forkfuls of food into her mouth, and I did the same, hardly tasting my meal. Unsure of the distance to She-ness, I decided we would have to get an early start. Though I didn't say it, the loss of another day, while partly my fault, was eating at me. We needed to make up time.

"Anya," Shea said, recapturing my attention. "I've been thinking. Some of the Fae here in the Home could cross the Road and reenter your homeland. You could use one of them to send a message—"

"No," I interrupted. Shea's eyebrows lifted, telling me I had responded too quickly and too strongly, and I tried to soften my reaction. "All that the Queen and my people want is for someone to find Zabriel, and I'm still capable of doing that. Sending a message would only complicate things."

"For them or for you?"

"For Queen Ubiqua, who may already be ill." I punctuated my words, hoping to discourage further questions. I didn't want to go down this road; I didn't want to hear my own justifications regarding my decision, because I knew they were weak. "And for my father, my friends."

"Aaaand?" Shea twirled a hand in the air, drawing the word out, more perceptive than I had hoped she would be. "No more secrets, remember?"

I sighed. "There's a young man, Davic, who would come after me if he knew."

"And is he just any young man?"

"No." My cheeks were in full bloom, not because I was confessing a relationship but because I was scared of how much that relationship might be influencing the issue. "We're promised to each other. But he's unfamiliar with the human world, and his first Crossing shouldn't be like this. It shouldn't be because of a tragedy, or because he thinks he should be with me, protecting me, grieving with me. He wouldn't see any of the good that's out here, and it's important that he does."

"He doesn't like humans?"

"Davic likes everyone." I chuckled. "But he's happy in Chrior. If he could choose, I think Crossings would be a thing of the past, and humans and Fae would stay on their respective sides of the Bloody Road. We'd coexist by pretending the other race is extinct. It would be the simplest solution, really, except that it's not a solution at all—it doesn't take into account long-term politics. The humans are constantly expanding their population and their land occupation, and we can't ignore how that may affect our way of life. But that's Davic—he lives in the moment, to be happy, to make other people happy. The problem is that the future comes at the same pace whether you prepare for it or not. That's why I want him to learn to love what's out here."

"Is he supposed to be King or something? Since you're the heir?"

I'd forgotten that Fi had let that information slip in Shea's presence, but it wasn't something I wanted to dwell on. "Not a king. He would have been a prince." I automatically corrected the sentence in my mind: Davic would have been a *perfect* prince.

I looked away from her, and she quickly moved on to something else, perhaps sorry she'd pursued this line of inquiry.

"Fi told me about a young, handsome Constabulary who stopped by to see you," she put forth, a mischievous smile curling her lips. "Are you sure *he's* not the reason you'd rather Davic stay at home?"

"Certainly not!" Strangely, however, while the suggestion of another man in my life could have been upsetting, it instead offered a welcome sense of normalcy. Being teased by a friend over the tentative friendship I'd developed with a man who'd been good to me felt like a luxury, and I was relieved to have a lighter topic to dwell upon.

"No matter what Fi told you, Shea, Tom was simply nice enough to offer me a ride to the hospital for my follow-up appointment with Dr. Nye. There was nothing more to it."

"And what did you say?"

"I told him you could take care of my wounds." I leaned forward with a smirk. "Your encounter with that boy in Strong proves how much you like to play doctor."

Despite my jab, she wasn't through needling me.

"But did you go with him?"

"Yes, I mean, it did seem like a good idea."

"And does *Tom* know you only used him as an escort?" Shea was so giddy that her body language almost suggested inebriation—she was leaning precariously sideways onto the table, grinning at me with twinkling eyes, her face radiant.

"Officer Matlock arranged a carriage, and that is *all*," I insisted, standing and picking up my mug to obtain a refill. "Although he did say a thing or two about irresponsibility, a message perhaps better directed at someone else."

Shea's mouth fell open, and I wiggled my eyebrows at her before heading on my way to the buffet line.

"Exactly what does that mean?" she called after me.

I flipped my auburn hair over my shoulder, enjoying her consternation.

By the time I returned to our table, Shea had recovered and was picking at her food. After a few minutes, I realized she was softly singing. I tuned in my ears and heard, "Anya and Davic, will their love be true? Will they have children, maybe one or two...."

I decided it was best to ignore her.

Though we were up early in anticipation of our departure, a full house greeted us at breakfast the next morning. To our bewilderment, Fae were everywhere, some eating, some standing around and talking in groups, others darting in and out of the corridor that led to the sleeping rooms, fetching warm outdoor wear.

"What's going on?" I asked an older man with badly mangled wings who was among those who shared our sleeping room. Though his appendages were still attached, he would never fly again.

He beamed, busily pulling his cloak around his shoulders.

"The Governor's men made an announcement last night. They're executing a Fae hunter today."

My stomach dropped. I glanced at Shea, who stood perfectly still, looking as discomfited as I felt. The man hurried away from us to seek out his companions, but his smile lingered in my mind, for it had been crazed with jubilation. He was hungry for retribution, even while his warped and shrunken wings maintained his connection to Nature and magic. In some ways, he'd been lucky, but that didn't stop him from being vindictive.

I tried not to feel the way he did, for his lust for revenge was not in line with Queen Ubiqua's teachings. It wasn't right to view a person's death as cause for celebration, no matter what he or she had done. In the Faerie Realm, the value we placed on life dictated that we never destroy it out of fear, anger, or hate. The worst punishment that could be imposed in our world was banishment. And yet the twinge that remained in my shoulder blades triggered an ugliness in me that ran counter to my aunt's beliefs. I wanted to see this hunter suffer, too. Damn my conscience; I wanted a reckoning.

We ate our breakfast, and I downed a cup of hot cider, all the while feeling more bloodthirsty than I ever had in my life. I didn't know execution procedures in Tairmor, but however they would dispatch the guilty party, I hoped it would be as painful as having bone sawed through; as painful as hearing the *thud, thud, thud* of a halberd and watching the essence of my being float away; as painful as knowing that no warm welcome waited in the future for me because I would never be going home.

Though Shea looked a bit sickly, she joined me in picking up snatches of conversation among the other residents of the Home, all of whom were palpably excited. Everyone wanted to know who was dying today, and the prevailing viewpoint was that the execution was right—it was necessary. The Governor was driving an evil from the world. As I considered this, some part of me felt incredibly sad; my kinsmen had lost the purest sense of what it meant to be Fae…and considering my inner exultation, maybe so had I.

Only Fi was subdued—Fi with her intact wings and unscarred body making her the sole resident of the Fae-mily Home who had not suffered injury at human hands. She sat in the entry hall at the admissions podium, spotlighted by the morning sunlight that sifted through a high window to land perfectly around her body. Her legs were crossed on the seat of her chair, her head hanging forward, her hands limp in her lap. It was in the winter sun's disposition to bring false warmth to a cold scene.

Though it was questionably ethical, Shea took her pack to the buffet table to gather food for the road in accordance with our plan to leave Tairmor that day. While my friend was thus engaged, I went to Fi and put a hand on the podium to announce my presence.

"What is it?" I asked, startling her. She raised her head, and I could tell she hadn't slept much.

"You've heard the news?"

I nodded and leaned against the lectern, guilt creeping inside me. Fi was a better person than I was. She was capable of feeling compassion for someone who deserved death. The evidence covered her face.

"I can't blame any of them," she continued, gesturing weakly to the chattering crowd in the dining hall. "They've all suffered more than I have. How can I judge them? But I know they won't be merry when the day is out. They'll gather for dinner in those exact same seats, but they won't be smiling and laughing anymore. They'll be weighed down by the knowledge that watching an evil person die didn't erase the evil that person did in life. All these Fae I want to protect think they're about to be fixed, but they're not. Taking satisfaction in another person's death doesn't heal you—it diminishes you. They'll be left with more holes inside than ever."

"But they'll know the law cares about what happened to them," I said, not wanting to listen to her message, so similar to something my aunt might have said. "Retribution isn't evil. Everything in Nature is about requital and balance. Aren't we—they—entitled to some of that fairness?"

"Tell me the last time misfortune struck at Nature's hand and you thought it was fair."

I didn't answer, feeling chastised, and Fi expounded upon her philosophy.

"I don't pretend to understand Nature's concept of balance because it doesn't stop to consider ours. All I know is that it's wiser and more powerful than us, and taking matters into our own hands can only momentarily make us *feel* better. It can't heal us, and it won't bring peace to anyone. There are other ways to show the wounded that they aren't forgotten."

As her message sank in, I took a step back, trying to suppress my conscience. She was but one voice among many, a voice I didn't want to hear anymore. Besides, the decision didn't lie with me; it had been made by the Governor, who surely understood such matters better than I. It was up to him to determine right from wrong in the Territory.

Turning away from Fi, I sought out Shea, and the two of us left the shelter with the other residents of the Home, intending to part company when we neared the "execution plank," as the crowd was calling it. The rolling hills of the city took us closer to the gorge, and river spray made the day colder, but not unbearably so. Shea was careful to wear her hood while we traversed the streets, though with all the hustle and bustle it would have been an extraordinary feat for someone to identify her.

The execution had been turned into a spectacle at the very least; in truth it was almost a faire, with impromptu stands erected to sell food and trinkets. Momentarily caught up in the atmosphere, we stopped to examine some of the wares, and I was tempted to purchase a necklace of stained glass in the shape of Faerie wings. The colors were eerily similar to what my own wings had been, and the proceeds went to various Fae aid groups. Before I could make up my mind, my attention was drawn to the next stand down, where people were gathered in strident debate—the owner claimed to sell baubles and jewelry infused with Fae magic. I rolled my eyes at the notion. If my body, which had been born a vessel for magic, couldn't retain its birthright, I doubted the greatest alchemist in Warckum, or the world for that matter, could coax a rock into accomplishing what I couldn't. Shea and I approached the stand anyway, curious about his salesmanship.

Most of the merchandise looked like it had been found in the rubbish bin of a mediocre jeweler. I turned to Shea, intending to make a joke, only to find her fingering a disconcertingly familiar item. Indeed, her other hand was clutching the small, upside-down looking glass pendant her father had given her, which rested on her sternum, cradled by its chain. I knew without checking that the pendants could have been twins.

"Made by a real scientist, these were," hawked the proprietor, who had sneaked up beside us. He flashed a gap-toothed grin, eager to make a sale. "A *sorcerer*. Buy one and be able to tame magic creatures, not to mention hoodwink the people around you. Your worst enemy could be your best friend! These rings over here will give you luck. The pendants are for protection, and I'll wager the condemned wishes he had one today."

With a tight smile, Shea shook her head and turned away.

"If it's anything like my father's necklace," she confided, "then it doesn't work very well, at least on Sepulchres."

I laughed. "Magic that lets you hoodwink people? It's magic that makes it impossible for Fae to tell a lie. Reconcile that for me."

We moved away from the crowd on the logic that with so many gathered for the execution, we could cross the city uninhibited and make an easy exit from Tairmor. As we walked, my eyes drifted to the gorge, and I realized that "execution plank" was a literal term—made of wood and supported by sturdily built scaffolding, a beam extended well over the ravine carved by the river. Despite my earlier vindictiveness, the prospect of someone being forced to jump to his or her death upon the rocks and frothing water far below was sobering, and I was glad we weren't staying to watch. At a safe but prime viewing distance from the scaffold, I noted a raised and roofed seating box through which well-dressed government officials and uniformed guards were entering, a group that included Luka Ivanova, with a beautiful woman at his side; some other dignitaries; and, most notably, a stalwart and imperial old man in decorated military garb: Governor Wolfram Ivanova.

I stopped, mesmerized, Shea coming to a confused halt a few paces in front of me, as I examined the Governor and tried to reconcile the things I knew about him with the man before me. He was Ubiqua's father-in-law, Zabriel's grandfather, a man who had lost his eldest son to the violent end of a love story. He supported Faerie rights, yet ironically seemed oblivious to the abductions of my people.

What captivated me most, however, were his eyes. My vision was still sharper than the typical human's, so even from this distance, I recognized those warm, trust-inspiring bister eyes—they were the same as Zabriel's. I knew something else, as well: no one who shared blood with my compassionate cousin could possibly be ignoble. I was so fascinated that I might have stared unceasingly had Shea's hand not wrapped around my wrist in a vice grip. With a nod of her head, she indicated where she wanted me to look.

I shifted my attention to the prisoner, a bulky, black-haired man in shackles who stood upon the scaffolding. Then I noticed a second person in shackles being pulled across the half circle that separated the crowd from the abyss. I recognized his keeper before I identified the scruffy young man—Hastings was supporting a weak-legged Spex, holding him up by the arms. They looked curiously intimate, like parent and child, but I knew protecting Spex was a notion as foreign to Hastings as having hair on his head. The man knew nothing about kindness.

Ignoring the guards who stood on each side of him, the prisoner turned toward Hastings and Spex, slowly shaking his head, his mouth forming the word *no*. It was clear that we were indeed seeing a father and son, though Hastings was not a member of the pair. Shea put the pieces together at the same time I did; the resemblance between Spex and the man about to be executed was distinct. The condemned was a Faerie-hunter, arrested and convicted, and his son had likely been implicated as the spotter, his talents for some reason entrusted to Hastings in Oaray. Now it appeared the young man was going to be taught a horrific lesson. He would be forced to watch his father die. But why?

"Oh, God," Shea breathed, her cold fingers gripping me tighter. "What if it's because of the information Spex gave us? Hastings sent Sepulchres into the Fere after us, but what if that wasn't enough for him? What if he wants Spex to suffer, too?"

She clamped a hand over her mouth, eyes stricken. Words now muffled, she squeaked, "Dear God, Anya, are we responsible for this?"

I gaped at the scene, feeling like the blood was draining from my body and leaving me gray and empty. While I had no strong desire to stop the execution, I was vehement that Spex shouldn't have to bear witness to his own father's death. I knew little about Spex, but I'd seen him handled like a street mutt by Hastings and take the abuse without complaint to keep his family alive. He'd done what he could to help me find Evangeline. He wasn't good, but he wasn't evil, either. Fi's words of mercy echoed in my mind, generating guilt that threatened to consume me like a disease.

"We don't have to watch this, Anya," Shea said, her voice desperate. "Let's get out of here."

I nodded, grateful I wasn't alone in wanting to flee. Then Governor Ivanova stepped to the rail of the seating box to address the crowd, a young dog hopping up to sit beside his elbow. A servant reached for the animal, but it growled and snapped at the man's fingers, successfully retaining its position.

"Just another minute," I said, against my instincts. "I have to hear him speak."

Shea shifted foot to foot, then tugged the hood of her cloak close about her face and nodded as the speech commenced.

"A long time ago, you and I began an initiative that was not devoid of challenges, not without opposition, but most of all, not without benefits that outweighed the risks," the Governor said, his voice wavering with age but constant in conviction. "This initiative was to bring two powerful, innovative cultures together, the humans and the Fae, for the betterment of both. Setbacks were inevitable, then and now, some caused by the well-intentioned, some outside of our control, and some perpetrated with injurious intent in order to prevent our progress."

Ivanova's eyes, no longer so warm, went to the scaffolding and the sentenced man. He swept his arm grandly in the same direction, and his dog, a wolflike puppy, began to pace the rail. "This convict before you, Alexander Eskander, is more than a thief. He is more than a poacher. He is more than a deviant from the laws of our great society. He is a *murderer,* and one of the enemies to progress that I have described."

Hisses and curses rose from the crowd. The Governor permitted the sound to swell, then silenced the assemblage by raising his hands.

"Alexander Eskander has caused immeasurable pain to our allies, the Fae, and thus has caused pain to every citizen of the Warckum Territory. He has abused and mutilated them, thus has abused and mutilated us. He has hunted them, and taken and sold their wings for his own personal gain, thus he has sold a part of every one of us. He is a scourge and a plague upon our advancement and, like a cancer, we must cut him out to preserve the health and majesty of our commonwealth."

"The Fae may be *your* friends, Gov'nor, but they're not ours!"

The shout reverberated in the air, to be echoed by several others in the mass of citizens, along with sentiments such as

"Black magic kills!" and "Allies are *all lies!*" Indignation and the desire to counter this prejudice swelled in my chest, and I recalled the day of Falk's Pride, when bullets had rained on my people to protest our dealings with humankind. Remembrance of that incident checked me at once. I'd been shot inside our sanctuary of magic, where guns and bullets and violence were abhorred, and where the elements had been at the ready to defend me. How many times was the danger multiplied in Tairmor, where almost every person carried a loaded firearm, and the public might not support me if I joined the fray?

In answer to this question, eggs, fruit, and rocks flew toward a group of Fae who were huddled together with heads down. I recognized them as members of the Home, and was shocked to see they had dared to drop their shrouds. They shrieked and stumbled, curling their wings around their bodies and yanking their coats and cloaks up to protect their bowed heads. Nevertheless, I saw a stone collide with one man's jaw, and a geyser of blood and teeth explode out the side of his mouth.

Though the group under siege was across the semicircle from us, I shifted behind Shea, hoping to disappear. At least I didn't look Fae. Only a spotter would know the difference. In the next moment, I was awash in shame. My reaction was exactly what the terrorists wanted: to make me hate my heritage and wish to be something different.

Red-uniformed officers were quick to subdue and remove the rabble-rousers, almost as though they'd expected a riot. Other law enforcement checked on the injured and helped a few to medical stations. The actions of the Constabularies served to reinforce the Governor's message, and I was sparked with confidence that Ivanova was genuine in his support of my people. As things quieted, I studied his form, but his expression revealed little of his reaction to the incident, although his dog snarled. Knowing that animals often picked up on their master's moods, I suspected there was more going on beneath the surface. Luka, on the other hand, didn't disguise anything. He looked sick with fury, arms crossed and tensed, highlighting the hard muscles beneath his expensive sleeves.

My spirits improved based on these assessments, at least until the Governor's eyes traveled to Spex, and I could no longer pretend he was compassionate and generous through and through. Now that the disturbance had been subdued, the Governor resumed his speech, acting as if he had not been interrupted.

"Eskander raised his children to serve him in his vile deeds. For them, there is yet the chance for reformation. But only once this man's influence has been purged from their lives. For the sake of his children, and all the children of the Warckum Territory, I hereby send Alexander Eskander to his death by means of the plank."

Ivanova raised his right hand high, then brought it emphatically downward, indicating that the execution should go forward. My breathing became fast and shallow as Spex's father was prodded by the guards to leave the safety of the scaffolding and walk to the end of the narrow board. I huddled closer to Shea, vilely fascinated. Though I wanted to look away, I was not a good enough person to do so. A gate was closed behind the prisoner to prevent his retreat, and the entire crowd held its breath. There was nowhere Eskander could go but into the breach.

In Hastings's firm grip, Spex was panicking. He grappled with the bald man's bulky arms, desperate to rush the scaffolding. But he was small, and Hastings easily hoisted him off the ground, all the while laughing with his red-coated compatriots.

"Dad!" Spex screamed, voice breaking.

Hastings walloped a fist against his charge's stomach. Spex gasped and coughed, doubling over. Meanwhile, the guards on the scaffolding wobbled the plank teasingly.

Eskander went to his knees, urine staining his pants as he stared down at the violent river, the rapids breaking over the sharp, unforgiving rocks of the ravine. His hands were bound behind him, ensuring that if by some miracle he survived the plunge, he would drown instead. Pivoting precariously, he crawled toward the gate, begging for his life. I strained to hear and was able to make out the words, each like a stab to my heart. It wasn't his life for which he begged.

"Not in front of my son," he pleaded, his voice colored by an accent—likely Bennighe, the language Spex had spoken in Oaray. "Please, not in front of my son."

"Drop, drop, drop!" the crowd chanted, camaraderie and anonymity giving free rein to their innermost bestial desires. In the next instant, the plank was released to snap vertically against the gate. Over the sound of the river, not a scream was heard from Alexander Eskander as he fell to his death.

Spex uttered an agonizing cry that resounded in every nerve of my body, but his voice was quickly drowned out by the cheering of the crowd. My heart felt seared, as though it were being stripped away piece by agonizing piece. If any man with a hand in this brutality was able to sleep tonight, I prayed he would never wake up.

Defeated, Spex went limp against Hastings, relying on a man he had to hate more than anyone else in the world to keep him on his feet. His eyes were blank, disengaged, the same way Evangeline's had been the night before she'd died.

Then Hastings picked him up like a child, stealing away the last of his dignity.

Tears ran down my face, not for the man who had died, but for his son who had loved him, no matter his crimes. Queen Ubiqua, who considered these human leaders her allies, her *equals,* never would have stood by and allowed such a ruthless act to be carried out. Alexander Eskander's punishment may have been justifiable, warranted even, but his son's pain gained Faefolk nothing. Memories of my own mother's death inundated my brain, and with them came the words Zabriel had said in somber comfort: *You're still whole, even if it doesn't feel like it. Your mother was a piece of the background.*

Spex didn't look whole to me. He looked like he'd lost every piece of his background and now stood alone against the black.

As the exuberant crowd began to dissipate, Shea and I staggered away. The horror on her face was a reflection of my own. What would happen to Spex now? Having been taught his lesson, would he return to helping Hastings and the others who were hunting my people? This execution, a great show of solidarity with the Fae, would have had an enormous impact on him, but perhaps not the one his keepers wanted—Alexander Eskander had been arrested, charged, and killed for the same crimes Spex was being coerced into committing. How would he ever reconcile that level of hypocrisy? While I didn't know who was behind these troubling events, I was certain that someone with considerable power was involved, for no one else could have pulled the strings to bring father and son together in such a garish manner. And if the Governor was naive in this regard, then he was an unforgivably stupid man.

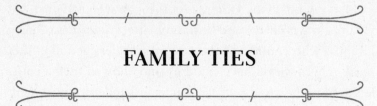

chapter seventeen

FAMILY TIES

Shea and I found ourselves on foot as we journeyed through Tairmor. The horse that had carried us into the capital had been lost by the time Luka Ivanova had summoned us from the hospital. Presumably it had been repossessed by one of the government-sponsored livery stables within the city, the brand on its haunches betraying its ownership. While we could have engaged a new rental, Shea was reluctant to interact with anyone in the aftermath of her individual misadventures. She still wouldn't tell me what had happened on the day she'd returned to her family home, but her resulting hesitance made our journey more arduous.

The capital was asleep by the time we drew close to the west gate, which opened in the direction of Sheness. Of course, the lateness of the hour had its benefits—there was no one about to see us leave.

The omnipresent rush of water stole what little ambiance of warmth could be gained from the gas lamps lining the streets. The snow that had started in the afternoon grew heavier, biting at my skin on impact, and I gathered my cloak more tightly about me. Now and then, eyes set in grimy faces would gleam at us from alleyways, and my hand would drop to the Anlace, but the cold kept even the crazed and homeless hidden in their crannies.

When the bridge to the stone-pillared gate came into view, I realized we were feeling frozen spray from the river and not petals of snow. After glancing at each other, Shea and I pulled our hoods so low we could barely see, providing protection from the sting of the river hail in addition to concealment.

The guards on duty watched us from the window of their tower until the last possible moment. Then two men descended to approach us, their scowls indicating their annoyance at being lured outside, despite their thick overcoats and fur hats.

"Papers," one of them grunted, blowing on his hands for warmth.

We reached into our packs, and the guard who had spoken snatched my passport away from me, letting his partner examine Shea's. While the Constabularies were thus engaged, the tower door opened and a third man, younger and more jovial than the others, came onto the bridge, straightening the collar of his uniform as though he had just donned it. In his other hand, he brandished a book.

"You forgot the log," he called, walking over to join his comrades. "I know your shift is ending, but that's no excuse for you two fools to fall off your game."

I smirked at their exchange, ready to sign my name and pass the quill to Shea, then realized she'd moved behind me. Before I could process what was happening, the new arrival took note of her. His round face paled, seconds ticking by while he soaked in the sight of her, and I had the feeling his mind was turning as quickly as it could. The other guards shifted, cold, ill-humored, and confused.

"You know I have to arrest you," the youngest man at length declared, though to his credit, he sounded regretful.

The other guards perked up, perhaps glad for a little excitement, while shock rolled over me, providing the heat that was lacking from this wintry night. Before Shea could run, one of the men grabbed her arm. Alarmed, I tried to separate them, only to be pushed aside. I stumbled and fell into the railing of the stone bridge, hitting my back hard against it. Gripping it for balance, I turned and gazed into the abyss that had earlier claimed Alexander Eskander, my eyes playing tricks on me as the distance to the glimmer of river far below fluctuated. Had I fallen, the roiling water would have killed me with pleasure if the impact alone hadn't done the job. Shea's voice jarred me back to the present.

"You didn't have to say anything, Nicholas," she spat, struggling against the handcuffs the Constabularies were securing around her wrists. "You could have let me sign the log and walk out of here, you bastard."

I stood dumbly by, knowing I couldn't take on all three guards and break Shea free. Yet I couldn't make my legs move to desert her. His globular jaw set, the man who had identified my friend turned to his fellow guards.

"This is Shea More, daughter of Thatcher More, who is wanted for debts owed to the Governor. Take these two to the jail. And send someone to inform Ivanova."

Skittering like cockroaches, the guards jerked me away from the railing, only too eager to secure handcuffs around my wrists.

"What have *I* done?" I snarled, the gravity of the situation made starkly real by the icy metal branding my skin. "For that matter, what has Shea done?"

The man called Nicholas glowered at me as his counter-parts confiscated our weapons and packs. When one of the guards tried to take hold of the Anlace, I twisted away from him, to be rewarded by a punch in the stomach for my fail-ure to cooperate.

"Be careful," I barked, doubled over, watching him fum-ble with the dagger out of the corner of my eye. Though I couldn't reveal the significance of the knife, if it were lost or damaged, the wrath of the Queen's Blades would descend upon the Constabularies of Tairmor, and the Queen's wrath would descend upon *me*.

The guard looked unexpectedly abashed at my tone; per-haps the nature of the Anlace itself had told him it was some-thing special. Meeting my gaze, he carefully tucked the blade into the pouch at his hip.

"You have aided a fugitive in an attempt to escape the city," Nicholas pronounced in answer to my question. "I'm sure if we examined your travel documents, we'd find both of you to be carrying forgeries. And Shea's crime is clear—under the Territory's laws, she's as guilty as her father."

No longer interested in me, he muttered instructions to his fellow guards, ending with a directive.

"Take them away. And for God's sake, don't tell me what becomes of them."

The men took hold of us, and Shea made a desperate lunge toward her betrayer, face contorted with rage.

"Whether you know my fate or not, it will still be on your conscience, Nicholas More!"

Though he flinched, Nicholas walked off without response. The Constabularies in whose custody we stood dragged Shea and me across the bridge to a barred wagon, which was apparently kept ready for these sorts of occasions. They thrust us inside and attached our handcuffs to eyelets on the floor, then they moved the horses off at a brisk trot, snow and ice cutting our cheeks as the wagon covered ground.

Shea and I sat in stony silence, and I barely staved off panic. What was the punishment for using forged travel documents? Would I serve a sentence at Shea's side? There was no one in the city who would vouch for me or try to see that the law was not executed to its fullest extent. And if I were taken off the streets, the future of the Faerie people would lie in Illumina's hands.

Faced with the genuine possibility that my younger cousin would rule, my mind ran wild. Were Illumina to take the throne, she would shut down our borders, no longer permitting Crossings or an exchange of knowledge; she would institute a campaign of hate as vile as anything Enerris or Falk or the protesters at Eskander's execution had implemented; and she would endorse, perhaps even orchestrate, the use of our elemental connections to bring the destructive power of Nature down on those she labeled enemies. Everything Queen Ubiqua had worked for would be undone, and everything that made our race noble and pure would be lost.

Shea's weeping drew me from my fraught trance. I faced uncertainty, but she faced seven years of labor to pay off a debt to a man who, based on today's spectacle, knew nothing about mercy. Perhaps uncertainty was a blessing.

"Who is this Nicholas?" I asked, wishing my hands were unbound so I could comfort her. The wagon rattled and bounced over the uneven cobblestones, and my shoulder crashed against the floor, shackles preventing me from sitting upright.

"My cousin," she said, and I could tell this was half the reason she was crying. "That pig. He follows and enforces laws that he knows aren't right. He doesn't care who gets hurt so long as he gets in the good graces of the people in power."

"Shea, I swear to you. I will get you out of this."

She choked out a laugh. "I don't think you can, Anya. I don't think anybody can."

Unwilling to concede the point, I yanked and twisted my handcuffs, only proving that we were trapped.

The building to which we were delivered was small and drafty. We entered to stand in a front office vestibule, where our names—my false human surname, Redwood, included—and the details of our arrest were entered into a record book. When this processing was finished, we were ushered down a hallway and deposited in a room with seats along its walls and a putrid smell that suggested it was used as a holding cell for unruly drunks. The place was not equipped with security befitting more serious criminals, but our handcuffs were adjusted to anchor us to separate benches.

We spent the next half hour with our heads hung almost to our chests, listening to footsteps in the hallway until finally one of those echoes turned toward our cell. I'd assumed Nicholas More had been exaggerating for effect when he'd ordered his comrades to inform Ivanova, because surely no one would dare to bother a member of the Governor's family at this time of night. But it was Luka who strode through the door, and I recalled that he was responsible for law enforcement in the Territory—the Constabularies answered to him.

Tonight he was wearing a puffed-sleeved white poet's shirt under a scarlet tunic with gold buttons from top to bottom. Luka came highly recommended by people I trusted, but there could be absolutely no question as to his social class. Looking most exasperated, he gave the door a shove to close it.

"I didn't expect to see you two again so soon."

"Sorry to disappoint," Shea mumbled.

The Lieutenant Governor examined her tear-splotched face with interest, his brow furrowed. I could detect no sympathy in his manner, however. Perhaps because he felt she'd done this to herself.

"Allow me to explain something. There are those fugitives I consider worth pursuing and those I do not. At the time we met, my dear, I had no investment in you. Unfortunately, now that I can no longer feign ignorance, that has changed. Understand, I prefer not to be in the business of enslaving children, but the Governor's laws are unambiguous. If I'm going to be able to help you, you need to help me first."

"Go to hell."

Luka shook his head, then dropped to one knee in front of Shea. He pulled a key from his pocket, unfastening her handcuffs in what I presumed was a show of good faith. After tucking the key into one of his pockets, he gripped her chin, firmly but not unkindly, and forced her to meet his gaze.

"Think carefully about what I'm about to offer. If you tell me where I can find your father, and the information proves reliable, I can justify making the charges against you disappear."

"*No.*"

Coming to his feet, Luka crossed his arms, tapping the fingers of one hand on his tensed bicep.

"I am *handing* you your life, Ms. More. You'd be issued legitimate papers, free of infractions. This is the only chance you'll ever have to walk away from your father's mistakes with clean hands. Once it goes on record that you've been uncooperative, no one in this system will be lenient with you."

Shea vehemently shook her head.

Luka massaged his temples with forefinger and thumb, trying to think of a different way to persuade her. Then he straightened his posture, his manner brusque.

"Fine, if that's the way you want it. But whether you know it or not, you've already told me where to find Thatcher More, and I'll be organizing the hunt tomorrow. A human and a Faerie traveling together is unusual enough, but that same Faerie injured in the Balsam Forest and nursed back to health, well, that's not a coincidence. Your family must have found her, and that means they're hiding in the east."

It was patent from Luka's tone that he regretted the villainous role in which he had been cast. He had extended to Shea her best option, and she'd turned it down. Now she would be charged with not only tonight's crimes, but her father's, unless the search resulted in Thatcher's arrest. Luka and I watched Shea for her reaction, and little by little her anger melted into fear, until sobs racked her form.

He sighed and looked away, too practical for guilt but not for regret. I glowered at the chains that bound me—had the Governor's son deigned to unlock my handcuffs, I could have embraced my friend.

"Please," Shea sniveled, rising and latching on to the front of Luka's tunic with both hands like someone who was drowning. "Please, you don't have to do this."

Luka placed his hands on Shea's shoulders, and that was all the invitation she needed to throw herself into his arms. He stumbled back a step, surprise and discomfort written on his face, but ultimately returned her embrace, probably not knowing what else to do. I'd never seen Shea like this before—broken and begging—and it tore at my heart. I was at fault for this; I was the reason her family was traceable.

"What…what will happen to my father if you arrest him?" Shea mumbled, face half-buried in Luka's shirt.

"He will have to pay his debt, in labor if not in money, according to the Governor's laws."

Shea clung to him for several moments, then wiped away her tears.

"I'm sorry, but I can't tell you where to find him. I just can't." Disentangling herself from Luka's embrace, she raised her chin in an expression of stubbornness that I knew well. "I can almost believe you care about me, yet you would take away my father without a second thought."

Luka plucked at his shirtsleeves, trying to control his agitation—Shea had clearly gotten under his skin—but his voice when he spoke was steady and resigned.

"I have second thoughts, my dear, and third thoughts and fourth thoughts, because this sentence is not yours to serve. Your father is a coward for leaving a girl to suffer in his place, and you don't repay a coward with martyrdom. I know Tairmor is your home. If you would only assist me, I could put you in good standing here, even provide you with a place to live in a nice neighborhood."

"I'll never betray my family," Shea reiterated, sinking down on the bench.

Jaw clenched, Luka snapped the handcuffs around her wrists. Pivoting on his heel, he went to the door. But at the last moment, he turned again to face us.

"I'll give you until tomorrow morning to think about your

situation, Shea. Perhaps a night in shackles without food or water will encourage you to come to your senses."

With that, Luka departed, to my dismay having said nothing about my arrest or what charges might be levied against me.

In the aftermath of his visit, our breathing in the small room was disconcertingly loud, and Shea leaned forward, elbows on her knees. Then she lifted her head, a smirk on her face and an almost manic glint in her eyes. Had she snapped under the pressure? Or had she come up with a plan to fool Luka and get us released? I was about to speak when she held out her closed fist, slowly uncurling her fingers to reveal a key nestled in her palm.

"Is that what I think it is?" I asked incredulously, my heart soaring.

Shea nodded, pleased by my reaction. "I took it from Luka's pocket when he was hugging me."

I rubbed my jaw, laughing louder than was probably wise, but unable to contain myself.

"I can't believe you snatched the key! How did you dare? And where did you learn to do that?"

"We didn't have much to lose, now did we? And I learned the gambit when I was a girl playing with my friends. We used to practice sleight of hand, magic tricks, cheating at cards, that sort of thing. When we got good enough, we would dare each other to pickpocket people in the market. It was stupid and dangerous, and after a couple of us got caught, we had to stop doing it. But...*I* never got caught."

"I'm impressed. I never knew you had such skills. But we still have a problem. The key will get us out of these handcuffs, but what about the door?"

"It would be too noisy to try to break it down, so we'll have to trick the guard in the front office into opening it. And then we'll have to incapacitate him."

I nodded, willing to try whatever it took despite how daunting escape seemed. Shea unlocked our handcuffs, and I searched my brain for a plan of action, knowing we had few resources at our disposal. In the end, only one strategy seemed feasible.

"I think one of us should pretend to be sick. The other can call for help. If the guard comes in, he'll be distracted, and we can knock him out."

"It's as good as any plan of mine," Shea concurred. "Do you want to be the sick one or the rabble-rouser?"

"I'll act sick. You're better at causing trouble than I am."

Shea gave me a pained smile. "I assume you mean I'm the better actress."

"Of course." I rolled my eyes, feeling beads of sweat forming at the back of my neck in anticipation. "Now let's do this. And remember, you'll have to move quickly once the guard comes to check on me."

I rubbed my wrists, gathered a wad of spit in my mouth, then refastened the handcuffs, taking the key from Shea so I could release myself when the time came. I lay down, my arms draped spastically over the bench, my head lolling back but not quite touching the floor. Looking at Shea, who had retaken her seat on the bench, her shackles unlocked but lying upon her wrists, I nodded.

Pulling in a lungful of air, she unleashed a cry that would have reached the ears of the dead and buried. That wasn't enough for her, however, and she began to shout, her voice high-pitched and panicky. Though I was witnessing a performance, I half believed she was in the grip of a demon.

"Help! Somebody! *Guard!* Please, help me! My friend's dying!"

It wasn't long until we heard the rattle of the lock, and I slipped into character, convulsing on the floor and releasing my store of saliva in a bubbling froth. Then our cell door was pushed open to frame a burly, middle-aged man, his bald pate wrinkled with concern and annoyance.

"Damn it," the guard swore, dropping to one knee beside me. "What happened?"

"I don't know," Shea replied in an emphatic whimper. "She's having some kind of fit. Please help her."

The man made a sound somewhere between a sigh and a growl, his arms moving above me as he debated whether or not to pick me up. Seizing her chance, Shea sidled up behind him and leaped upon his back, locking her forearm and elbow around his neck while she pushed his head down with her other hand. I rolled out of the way, wiping my lips, as his fist slammed the floor to prevent a fall. But he was a strong man and lumbered to his feet.

I watched in stunned immobility the scene unfold—the guard gasped, trying to speak, his face growing redder and redder while Shea doggedly clung to him, applying pressure to his throat. Grappling behind him, the man at last found a handhold in her hair. He yanked and wrenched, and she cried out, then he hurtled backward at the wall. With weight on his side, I was sure the impact would injure Shea, possibly badly. He had enough body mass and momentum to squash her like a bug.

Jolted to my senses, I lunged at his knees to impede his progress. He grunted in surprise, Shea's choke hold still preventing him from making real noise, and I rammed my shoulder into his hip, pulling up hard. Realizing what I was doing, Shea beat an escape, but her head smacked against the stone wall with dizzying force. The guard almost simultaneously crashed to the floor, the heavy thud of his body telling me the damage she had suffered was regardless far less than it could have been.

Shea moaned and gingerly touched the back of her head, her eyelids widening and narrowing in a fight to focus, while the guard lay dazed, though still moving. Not waiting for our enemy to regain his voice and possibly his feet, I straddled him and pushed my forearm against his windpipe just hard enough to cut off his air. He flopped like a fish for a few seconds, then gave in to unconsciousness. I scrambled away from his body, frightened by my own actions. The guard was still alive, thank Nature, but he'd feel like a mountain had fallen on him when he woke.

"Are you okay?" I asked, going to Shea's side where she had slid to the floor.

When she didn't respond, I gently tipped her head forward to take a look at her wound. It wasn't difficult to find—the hair around the injury was tinged red, sticky and matted. But experience with the occasional bang on the head had taught me that such wounds tended to be overdramatic, bleeding beyond the scope of actual damage. Already the blood was caking and coagulating. With no time to waste, I took Shea's wrist and guided her to her feet.

"Is he dead?" she whispered, pale and trembling.

I shook my head. "No, this guy's as strong as a bear. It won't be long before he's up and reporting our escape. He'll barrel through that door like it's made of parchment."

With that thought in my mind, I made certain Shea was steady, then scrambled to the side of the unconscious guard.

He didn't look good, which made me doubly regret what I was about to do.

"Sorry," I mumbled, before kicking the man's foot to position his lower leg. I set up my aim and squeezed my eyes shut, then stomped on his ankle. The bone crunched like an egg. I fought back the urge to gag, and when I looked to Shea, I could tell she was in the midst of the same struggle, her mouth slightly ajar, nostrils flared.

"We need to get out of here," I said unnecessarily, not wanting to think about what I had done.

Shea went to the door and peeked through it into the hall beyond while I retrieved the ring of keys from the downed man's belt.

"All clear," she whispered, motioning for me to join her. "Let's go."

We slipped into the corridor, closing and locking the cell door behind us in the hope our flight would not be discovered for several hours. Turning sideways to provide ourselves with a line of sight both ahead and behind, we approached the office vestibule, relieved to find it was deserted, a miracle considering how recently Luka Ivanova had been there. This might have made me chary, except that this jail appeared to be little more than a drunk tank. I doubted it was ever well staffed, and especially not at this time of night.

Spotting our packs and weapons abandoned in a corner, we snatched them up and moved to the front door. We opened it a crack, and seeing no one posted in front of the jailhouse, hustled into the darkness and down the street, not concerned about direction. We only wanted to put distance between us and any Constabularies who might be on duty in the area.

Rounding a corner, I dared to let myself breathe normally,

only to come to an abrupt halt. Without thought, I shoved
Shea against the nearest building, out of the glare of the street
lamps. Her skull connected with the stone, and I winced, having forgotten her questionable balance. She bit back a groan,
raising one hand to her temple to support her head.

Coming down the road was a cloaked man, his hood pulled
up against the cold, hands jammed in his pockets. I eyed him
closely as the wind disturbed the cloak enough to reveal the
double-breasted red tailcoat hidden beneath. I cursed under
my breath, feeling we had started the day with little luck and
were ending it with even less.

Pressing our backs against the building, Shea and I stood
still, willing him to pass on by. He soon did, looking down
at his boots, in all likelihood in a hurry due to the wretched
weather. Still, something about his walk made me uneasy, and
I watched him until he was out of sight.

"That was close," Shea murmured, hoisting her pack once
more. I lifted mine, muscles tightening from our altercation
with the guard, and Shea caught my grimace.

"What's the matter, Anya?"

"Not sure. I probably pulled something in the fight with
our *little friend* back at the jail."

Shea disregarded my attempt at humor, worry descending
upon her face. "Is it your back? Is that the problem?"

"Oh, not this again. I'm fine. You'll be the one needing
those painkillers the doc gave me. Your head's going to swell
up like a ripe mushroom."

Shea acknowledged this with a sardonic lift of her eyebrows,
then spoke my thoughts aloud. "Doesn't really matter, does it?
We need to keep moving."

We hurried on, sticking to the shadows until we judged

ourselves to be outside the zone of immediate pursuit. Huddling against a wall in a clean, covered alleyway between two high-end shops—quite a change from the neighborhood surrounding the Fae-mily Home—we went about determining how to get out of Tairmor.

"When I was younger," Shea confided, "my friends and I heard stories about tunnels underneath the city, caverns cut by the river over the years. It's not too far-fetched a notion when it comes right down to it. Supposedly, you can make your way in and out of the city if you know how to access them."

"Please tell me you know how."

She screwed up her rounded face in a way that wasn't particularly reassuring. "I've never been in them, but I have some idea. We need to get to the river first."

"Where are we now?"

She curled down farther against the shop wall, and I knew even before she answered that she had no more clue than I did.

"I was kind of hoping you wouldn't ask. All I can say is we're in a wealthy section of Tairmor."

I nodded, not particularly perturbed. "It's all right. If we're lost, we're lost, and we'll just keep wandering until we're found again…though preferably not by the Governor's men."

"That's quite a fatalistic attitude you've adopted."

I laughed. "It's about the only approach I haven't tried today."

We gave ourselves a few more minutes to warm up out of the wind, then returned to the street, following the crash of water toward its source. I automatically attempted to unfurl my wings, and my back twinged—how easy it would have been to fly to the rooftops and chart a course. Still, humans functioned without wings. If they could do it, so could I.

The rush of excitement generated by our escape gradually subsided to be replaced by aching tiredness. A foul mood set upon me, growing fouler still as Shea continually bumped into me, either not paying attention to her path or...unable to walk straight. I glanced at her, a new worry taking hold. How serious might her head injury be?

"Are you all right, Shea?" I asked, trying to get a look at her eyes in the light of the gas lamps.

"I'm fine, just cold."

She didn't seem aware of her uneven tracking, the wooly look in her eyes, or the concern behind my question. Though she needed time to rest, that was a luxury we could not afford, and I settled for keeping closer watch on her.

Factories cropped up around us with an abruptness that confirmed the existence of distinct districts in the city of Tairmor. I hoped we wouldn't encounter any alley guards like the brothers who had tried to rob me near the Fae-mily Home. It looked like this was exclusively a work district, however, and not populated at night.

"The entrance should be around here somewhere," Shea said, clutching my arm for balance as she scanned the buildings. "Rumor held there was one inside an abandoned warehouse building."

"Okay. Where should we start?"

"Do you want to split up to cover more ground?"

This didn't strike me as a good idea. Shea could forget where she was or pass out in the street.

"I don't want to split up. What if we lost track of each other?"

"I'm pretty sure I could find you both again. I haven't had much trouble following you so far."

A male voice had entered our conversation, and I pivoted in its direction, muffling a scream with my fist while Shea fumbled for her pistol. I squinted into the snow, and Tom Matlock strolled into view. I cursed the continuing deterioration of my senses toward those suffered by humans—I hadn't had an inkling that he was behind us. Then it clicked into place that he was the Constabulary we'd seen earlier on the street, and I further bemoaned my stupidity. It was my failure to make this connection that had enabled him to follow us. But the most distressing part of his appearance was that I didn't know whether to be relieved, for he had proven himself a friend, or panicked, for he was also staunchly loyal to Luka Ivanova.

chapter eighteen

SAVE US ALL

Realizing that Shea was reaching under her overcoat, Officer Matlock rushed forward to snatch a fistful of her cloak, yanking her so hard she almost fell to the ground.

"Don't," he warned, steadying her before he released her. "The gun—just don't."

"Are you going to arrest us?" I demanded, heart hammering, while Shea shuffled behind me, apparently of the belief that I was better equipped to handle this particular Constabulary than was she.

"That's what I'm trying to decide."

His answer disappointed me, and I didn't bother hiding it.

"Look, *Officer Matlock,* my only offense is carrying false papers, something Luka Ivanova wasn't concerned about when we met him at the Governor's mansion. And Shea hasn't committed any crime—she was only taken into custody because of something her father did. Neither of us is really a criminal, and neither of us is dangerous."

"I assume when you say *Shea* you mean *Mary,*" he said sharply, and I rubbed my temples, only catching the tail end of the smirk that dashed across his face.

"Fine. We're both using false passports. But she's only using one because she's been forced to do so by a law you can't possibly support."

His reaction was unreadable, his face carefully composed, no doubt from practice in his official position. He slowly extended a hand toward me, finally resting it on top of my forefinger and pushing it downward. Until that moment I wasn't even aware I'd been pointing at him.

"At ease," he said, and I forced myself to unclench my jaw, feeling the pressure leave my temples.

He sighed and smoothed the hair on one side of his head, his manner more blasé than when he had intercepted us.

"The law you're referencing is meant as an incentive to the actual guilty parties to come forth in place of their family members. It's really not intended to punish someone like Shea. It's supposed to appeal to a criminal's conscience, which I know is a little oxymoronic. Sadly, that seems to be proven by your circumstances."

He eyed Shea, valiantly trying to disguise that he felt bad for her, and I could feel myself calming down. Sympathy on his part was a good sign. But it bothered me that he was defending the government's rationale. It didn't fit with what I knew about him. Still, he was a Constabulary. I supposed buying into the doctrine came with the job.

"I was called to the jail to talk to the two of you," he resumed. "The Lieutenant Governor thought I might have more success in gleaning answers from you or in convincing you that protecting Thatcher More isn't the best decision."

Shea unexpectedly spoke up, and her vitriolic words did nothing for my case.

"What do you know about it? Absolutely nothing! So consider this—would you betray *your* father?"

Tom shrugged. "I haven't so far. And that's why I tried to tell Ivanova all this effort is pointless. He already knew, of course, and I'm also doubtless that he detests the measures he's been forced to implement with you. If I take it upon myself to interpret that liberally, it means everyone would be better off should the two of you disappear."

I beamed at him, relief rushing through me. I wanted to hug him and tell him that Nature would repay him for his kindness, though I retained enough control not to do either of those things. Shea's reaction was more subdued. She had settled against a doorway for support, clearly affected by her head wound, and I wasn't even sure she was still following our conversation.

"Just one more thing, Anya, and this is important. Please be honest so I don't have to hate myself in the morning. It's obvious the guard at the jailhouse never sent anyone after you. Did you kill him in your zeal to escape?"

"No. I mean, he won't be able to work...or walk...for a while, but he'll absolutely live."

Tom snorted a laugh, then tried to cover his reaction by pretending it had been a mistake, but he ultimately gave in to a grin. He had an open smile, no tension or falsity hiding within it.

"He'll absolutely live," he repeated. "Damn, I knew there was a reason I liked you."

"You do?" I swept snowflakes from my auburn hair, flutters rising in my stomach.

"Sure," he said, so casually that I felt a touch of disappointment. I internally chastised myself, for he and I were nothing more than acquaintances. And he undoubtedly liked a lot of people.

Shea cleared her throat, having tuned in once more. When I looked toward her, she was tapping her fingers on her upper arm. Suitably checked, I returned to business.

"We need to get out of the city," I told Tom. "We're looking for a way into the tunnel systems."

Tom's eyebrows lifted so subtlety I might have missed it. Then he shrugged. "I'm not sure how you two know about the tunnels, but since you do, follow me."

He started down the street and I made to trail him, but Shea gripped my arm and pulled me close.

"How do you know we can trust him?"

"I don't. But I figure if he tries anything...well, he's smaller than the other man we incapacitated this evening."

Shea grinned at this prospect. Ahead of us, Tom paused, swiveling to face us with his palms turned up in an unspoken question.

"Coming!" Shea called, her gait faltering as she set off in front of me.

We were already tired, and the stroll Tom took us on through the tangled streets seemed endless. Shea hadn't even been close in her assessment of how near we'd been to our goal. At last he stopped before a large, desolate-looking building plastered with hazard signs. In disregard of these, he took a ring of keys from his pocket and used one to remove the rusty padlock that secured the door.

"The keys to the city?" I inquired, and a slight smile curved his lips.

"If only you knew."

I had no clue what he meant.

The inside of the building was an empty, grimy, open space, which we crossed to an unmarked pit in the floor. Tom yanked a torch from the wall and blazed it with a handheld lighter, an invention that was gaining popularity in the Territory. Some Fae were concerned that it gave humans too-ready access to the element of fire. A closer look at the little silver object confirmed what I'd always thought—guns were the bigger threat.

Moving to the pit, Tom let the torch's light reveal narrow steps that wound down into virtual nothingness. We began the descent without comment, tackling flight after flight, the temperature leveling off when we neared the bottom—there were no drafts anymore, not at this depth. I glanced at Shea, who was shivering, her eyes blank and staring as though she'd forgotten how to blink. I pulled a blanket out of my pack and wrapped it about her shoulders. Perhaps it was just her injury, or perhaps the heightened peril her unsuspecting family faced had finally penetrated the haze in her head.

Tom stopped at last and scanned the rocks that lay scattered and piled on the floor where they'd broken away from the walls. He located whatever he was looking for and knelt, pushing aside a number of heavy stones. I stooped to assist him, a groan escaping my lips as my sore body protested the work.

"Take it easy," he said, nodding in Shea's direction. "I think your friend could use your help."

She was sitting down, head cradled between her knees, and I went to her, rubbing her back to keep her blood flowing.

Eventually Tom uncovered a trapdoor. He lifted it, and the overpowering sound of rushing water met our ears. I'd known we'd be close to the river in the tunnels, but I'd hoped for the farther end of near. It didn't sound like that wish was going to be granted, and I swallowed the lump rising in my throat. Since the loss of my elemental connection, my comfort with water had violently diminished.

"The caves are safe from the Governor's men," Tom told us, rising to his feet. "Follow the tunnels west—that's to your left—and you'll leave the city without being seen."

"Aren't *you* one of the Governor's men?" I asked, cocking an eyebrow. "Are we safe from you?"

"I'm not one of the Governor's men," he chuckled, the sound weirdly contained within the rocky walls. "I work for Luka Ivanova."

"I'm not sure that's any better."

"You don't have to trust him, only me. I have no intention of telling him where you are or even about our encounter. I'll claim I went straight to the jail and found whatever it is I'm going to find once we're done here."

"Do *you* trust Luka?" I asked, unable to resist one last question.

Tom hesitated, scratching his forehead. "Yes, as much as you can trust any politician." Then he motioned to Shea. "Judging from her behavior, I'd say she hit her head when you scuffled with that jailhouse guard. She probably has a concussion. Try to keep her awake tonight, and don't rush. You won't be pursued, and you don't want to overtax her."

In his gray eyes was a level of caring I did not expect, and I gave him a brilliant smile to convey my thanks. For all I knew, he was risking his career for two young women he barely knew.

"Take care of yourself, Anya. Perhaps our paths will cross again one day, hopefully under happier circumstances."

He lowered Shea and me into the bowels of the tunnels, then let the trapdoor thunder into place over our heads. I shuddered, feeling more like we'd been buried alive than freed.

We set off into the inky darkness, groping about on our hands and knees in order to progress. I led the way, Shea holding on to the bottom edge of my cloak so we wouldn't be separated. The rock floor vibrated under my hands as though the Kappa were raging at us to leave its home, and the noise was so oppressive we couldn't hear each other speak.

At length, the narrow passage widened and the right wall fell away, replaced by pillars of stone that opened windows to the great river and streams of moonlight from far above. Shea collapsed against the wall behind me, and I went to sit next to her, breathing in the fresh, cold scent of river water, no longer feeling so terrified of it. I wondered how far below Tairmor we were, marveling that no one in the city would ever suspect we were there. They would wake and go about their business, but we were in a different world. It was several moments before either of us moved, exhaustion and fear dictating a silent agreement that we rest here until morning.

"I wonder how far east these tunnels go," Shea remarked, spreading out a bedroll and blankets. Her movements were jerky and awkward due to the dampness and cold, which felt like it had seeped into our bones.

"I imagine they run where the river runs. But with all the offshoots, it would be easy to get confused. By the way, Tom said you shouldn't sleep because of your head injury."

"Tom can go to hell," she groused, sitting down on her bedding. "I'll go west with you, then circle around the city once we're aboveground. I won't be much help to anyone if I get lost."

"You must have taken quite a crack to the skull, Shea, because you can't go back to the Balsam Forest."

Her eyes flashed. Yet again they reminded me of flint—with every spark of anger that passed through her gaze there was the potential for disaster.

"I have to get my family to safety. This is my fault, and I owe it to them to warn them."

"Listen to me." I tried to grab her wrist, but she tugged away. "Luka doesn't know where to find your family. The Balsam Forest is an enormous place. His men could search it for months and not find a trace of them."

"I should never have left them—don't you see? If it wasn't for me, no one's thoughts would have turned in Thatcher More's direction. He would have been forgotten, we all would have. I'm the reason we're damned."

"This is not your fault, Shea." My voice was stern, and she swung her sagging head toward me, eyes swollen with tears. "None of you should have to live in hiding. This is the fault of unjust laws and cruel politicians who are happy as long as their own interests are served. It's sick, and it's twisted, but you aren't to blame. And if you go east, your family will be caught for certain. I'd like to believe Tom's motives for helping us are pure, but it's entirely possible we're being followed. Don't let your guilt make Luka's job easier."

Shea trembled with the struggle to control her crying, looking helplessly around and gulping for air. She had become someone I hardly recognized—a scared little girl—and I hated the Governor for having this effect on her.

It took a few minutes, but blessedly the strong-minded woman I knew returned, and Shea slammed her fist against the rock floor.

"The world is so wrong," she ranted, the words raw in her throat. "People starve, and families like mine live in fear. Faeries are attacked, killed, driven to kill themselves. The only people who care are the ones who work in the streets and run shelters and sacrifice their own chances at personal success, while the people who cause all this misery run the world. How did we let this happen, any of us humans? Where were our brains, our eyes? And what's wrong with us that we can't stop it—that we aren't even trying?"

I steeled myself, not wanting to react to her heartfelt speech, not wanting to turn into that little girl I'd just seen in Shea. But I was too worn-out to retain control, and I ended up entertaining tears of my own. What a sorry pair we made, weeping in the old forgotten caverns beneath a great city.

Regaining my composure, I yanked my bedroll loose and opened my pack to remove what remained of our jerky, while Shea pulled bread from the supplies she had taken from the Fae-mily Home. As I rooted through my things, I laid them on the ground beside me, taking inventory—my long-knife, my clothes, my money pouch, the tiny vial of Sale that had been an accidental gift from Hastings.... Then my throat seized, my face flashing hot then draining cold. Shea recognized the signs of panic and sat up.

"What is it?"

"The Anlace," I rasped. My voice was almost gone, lost in the tension of my neck and body. "The guard at the gate took it, remember? And it's not here. Nature, it's not here. It's not here!"

I let out a dry sob, and Shea scrambled over to me, shoving through what little remained in my bag to determine that I was right. When she raised her eyes to me, she looked stricken.

"Is it so important?" she asked in a small voice.

"It's the Queen's Anlace," I responded. My cheeks and arms felt numb, useless. My words had trouble pushing through my lips. "Only the Queen herself is ever supposed to hold it, or the rightful ruler of Chrior. I don't know why she gave it to me in the first place. It wasn't mine to keep. And now I've *lost* it."

Shea placed a tentative hand on my shoulder. She didn't know much about Fae traditions, but my pallor alone was enough to inform her of the seriousness of what had happened. An ancient relic of my people, its cultural—and monetary— value incalculable, was missing in the human capital, likely in the hands of a grubby little gate guard who might sell it for a donkey and thereby abandon it to history. Nothing else as old and exquisite as the Anlace existed in the known world. And I was to blame for its passing.

"It's not your fault, Anya," Shea murmured. "One day, when it's safe for us again, we'll search for it. We'll find it. I promise."

They were empty words, but they were all she could offer, and the only comfort I could take. I took a shaky breath and after a moment returned my things to my pack, with the exception of my long knife, which took the Anlace's place at my hip. There was nothing I could do to fix this. I would have to tell Queen Ubiqua what I'd allowed to happen. I'd have to admit it to my father, to Davic...and somehow I'd have to accept that a significant heirloom of Faerie history was gone because of me.

Shea shuffled to the cavern wall on her knees and leaned back, giving me space while she nibbled on her food. It was then I realized the Anlace wasn't the only thing missing from my supplies. The map that Thatcher More had drawn was absent as well. And that map could give a discerning eye a strong indication of where he and his family were hiding.

I glanced at Shea, my palms beginning to sweat. Should I tell her? It was possible I'd simply lost it somewhere along the way. I hadn't needed to refer to it since Oaray. But what if it was in Luka's hands? Did that change anything I had said? Though my conscience ached, I kept my mouth shut. Shea would panic at the truth, and she would be headstrong and foolish about it. Besides, Thatcher wanted me to protect her. I couldn't give her a reason to run off alone with nothing to guide her but anger and anxiety.

When we finished our meager meal, Shea and I curled up together, and in that moment, we were each other's only friend in the world. But one of us was again keeping secrets.

The next morning offered a reasonable amount of light in the cavern systems. There were dark patches that slowed our movement, but for the most part, our path was open to the river and the narrow piece of sky that beckoned above it. The sound of the coursing water, the river frothing white as it cut through the rock, was our constant companion, so deafening it was a waste of effort to listen for sounds of pursuit.

We traveled primarily in silence, Shea going ahead for a while, then switching places with me depending on our relative strength and fortitude. I had given her some of the painkiller the doctor had prescribed for my wounds, and it helped with her headache, though not much with the dizziness and fluctuating nausea. At least she wasn't dying.

I was watching my feet during a stretch in which Shea was in the lead when she stopped dead in the pathway.

"Anya," she called, her voice dripping with disgust. "Tell me this isn't what I think it is."

I looked up, but a pile of stones blocked my view of the river and whatever had caught her attention. Curious, I went to her side to investigate.

In an eddy between two jutting rock formations floated

something large and slimy, bobbing side to side as water flowed
beneath it. I stared, comprehension coming slowly; the tattered
clothing that barely clung to the flesh and the mop of scrag-
gly black hair that looked ready to fall off led me to the conclusion that I was gazing at a body—the body of Spex's father.
The corpse was bloated with gas, the skin so waxy and pale I
could practically see through it. There were surprisingly few
lesions, considering the fall and the resulting impact, only the
gruesome nibbles of water animals. But the eyes—the eyes
were open and one had been pulled from its socket by a scav-
enger. The rib cage was crushed, and here and there a bone
stuck out of the swollen dermis. I doubted there was a single
bone inside this body that wasn't broken. One thing was certain—his death had been as horrific and painful as I'd originally hoped it would be.

"He'll just…just rot down here," Shea observed with a shudder. "Children play on the banks of this river outside the city in
the summer. People drink from it. *God.* How many…*bodies*…
do you suppose are down here?"

I swallowed with difficulty, my throat closing up. At a loss
for words, I stared at the river in morbid fascination while it
conducted the body in an eerie slow dance. I'd considered
Evangeline's burial profane…yet I'd wanted *this* for Eskander,
however fleetingly. What had I thought would become of his
corpse? How had I ignored that the answer would be an af-
front to Nature, whose spirit I professed to worship? Because
it had been *convenient* not to consider these things.

"We have to go," I said, giving Shea a prod. She stumbled
onward, although she continued to glance over her shoulder
until there was nothing left to see.

"I'm sorry, I'm so sorry," I mumbled, leaving the body behind, though I wasn't sure to whom I was apologizing.

After a while, the tunnel narrowed and we began to ascend. We took our time for Shea's benefit. The climb was steep and tiring, but the way had been smoothed at one time, and it was easier going than it could have been. Realizing there was light emanating from around a bend up ahead, I glanced at Shea, whose pale cheeks and wide eyes revealed that she, likewise, thought it was too soon to have arrived at the end of the cave system.

We pressed against the wall and crept cautiously forward. When we came to the bend, Shea peered around it, only to snap back to my side. I questioned her with my eyes, not daring to speak. She pointed ahead, her breathing fast and shallow, and I stuck my head around the corner.

The path curled around a wide, bright cavern, in which moist gray-brown pillars supported the ceiling, breaking up the open area. Stalactites of incredible circumference dripped clear, cold water from their tips, but the stalagmites that had been reaching to meet their kin had been for the most part demolished—by the colony of Sepulchres who considered the chamber home. Glowing white, they floated to and fro as they went about their business, appearing nearly weightless, moving gracefully despite their deadened, shrouded legs. Their clawlike fingers were enough to propel them where they desired to go.

On the floor of the cavern was a collection of what appeared to be crude treasure chests, augmented with raw gems that had probably been recovered from the recesses of this very cave system. But another moment of observation revealed the use to which the Sepulchres put these chests. Sweeping downward with a knapsack no larger than my satchel, one of the creatures opened the lid of an empty box and deposited the package inside, allowing the sack to fall open.

Bones, stripped meatless, lay within, the skeletal remains small enough to be those of a child. The Sepulchre who had carried the corpse extended one of its overlong fingers to stroke the side of the small skull, with pride or reverence I couldn't tell. My stomach lurched. The chests were coffins where the creatures laid to rest the children they kidnapped and devoured for their purity. The skeleton was hardly as long as the finger that was fondling it.

I must have made a noise, because dozens of sickly green eyes found me with the unnatural speed I'd grown to dread. Like owls, the creatures were able to turn their heads in any direction at the blink of an eye.

I retreated and shoved Shea down the passage in the vain hope we could run. Even with her belt full of bullets, she would never be able to drive off an entire colony of supernatural beings, and the Anlace, our only effective defense, was gone. But already the tunnel was irradiating, telling me we weren't going to get far.

When a Sepulchre came from above us, slipping to the ground as though it were suspended by invisible cords, we halted and spun about to find two more closing in from the rear. Judging from the blinding light that reflected off the walls, the rest of their number occupied the passage that extended all the way back to the chamber.

Shea whipped out her pistol, but the Sepulchre closest to her plucked it from her hand, one razorlike finger hooking the trigger mechanism. The awful wheezing sound the creatures made was now everywhere, almost drowning out the river. As the horrifically scarred and stretched face loomed closer to me, I clenched my fist around the hilt of my long-knife. I was seconds away from taking a swipe at the Sepulchre's mouthless aspect when inspiration struck—Evangeline had thought them capable of speech. I uncurled my fingers, concentration overcoming instinct, and raised both hands. If they could speak, they could recognize surrender.

The Sepulchre who had stopped us tipped its head to one side. Reaching for Shea, it tugged almost gently on her clothing until it rose to come face-to-face with her. She was defenseless, and fear emanated from her like vivid dye disseminating in clear water.

For a moment, we stood suspended in time; then one eerie finger rubbed the looking glass pendant that hung around Shea's neck, the friction causing a high-pitched squeak. Seemingly attracted by the sound, the colony pressed in on us from behind, and I felt hands on my shoulder blades and upon the sheath at my hip where the Royal Anlace had once rested. But I had lost my chance to attack, and could do little more than hold still. Then their wheezing changed to words that emerged from no orifice I could see.

"Magic sings," the whisper said, one voice leading, the others echoing. I was shaking head to toe, so hard I thought my joints might come unhinged. Clearing my throat, I drew dozens of spectral eyes.

"What…are you…doing…beneath…Tairmor?" I asked, strange spaces between my words, for it took great effort to force each one from my mouth.

The reply was more a reverberation in my head than an actual sound, and it felt like the Sepulchres were tapping into my brain to communicate. Shea's hands were raised as though she might cover her ears, confirming that she heard it too.

"We hide. Survive. Unseen, unwanted. Cut off from the Old Fae. Unable to be what we were."

"The Old Fae? I don't…understand."

"Humans and Fae were one." The answer thrummed in the air, and I thought it originated with the Sepulchre who was touching Shea's necklace. "Then we were honored. Now we are banished. And abused."

Abused… Were they talking about their involvement in the conspiracy against the Fae? It hadn't occurred to me that the Sepulchres might be unwilling participants. The earth seemed to undulate beneath my feet.

"Who is abusing you?" I asked, looking at these hideous beings with tentative sympathy.

The Sepulchre wagged its head from side to side. "We are banished. Others are abused. They are changed. Violent. But you are friends, magic-bearers. Save us. Save us all."

The creature released Shea's pendant and slid to the ground, facedown, and I had the impression it was trying to bow.

The wheezing resumed, growing louder, then the creatures backed away, and it felt like part of my soul was withdrawn from my body along with their fingers. The sensation was enough to make me woozy, and, hardly aware of my descent, I hit the hard floor of the cavern and knew no more.

I was in the woods with Davic, holding his hand and skipping. We were likely the only Fae out today—it had been drizzling all morning, and a fog rose around us, heavier the farther we tried to look ahead. I let go of Davic's hand, clamped my eyes shut against the haze of raindrops, and spun in a circle until I was dizzy and had no idea from whence we'd come. I loved the sensation of being lost. There was a surge of the heart that came with not being able to find my own

way home, followed by the security of knowing that Davic would al-
ways lead me back.

He caught me before I could topple, and I beamed into his striking
gray-blue eyes, about to surrender to him when I heard the scream. It
came from all around us, dispersed by the fog. I pulled myself upright
and clung to Davic's jerkin, scouring our surroundings. His body was
taut, while I tried my best to mute all senses except my hearing. When
the sound repeated, a shrill cry that scraped down my spine, I shoved
away from my promised and followed it into the mist.

"Anya!" Davic called. "Don't—let's go back!"

I finished the rest of his speech in my mind: You don't know
what's making that sound, or why. It could be dangerous. It
could be...

"Dying," I murmured to myself, picking up speed. Wet leaves
slapped my face and branches dripped water down the back of my shirt,
but I didn't care. Then I heard the screech a third time—nearer yet
softer, as if the creature was weakening.

At the base of a tree some yards away I found the font of the cries.
A baby fox, fur still peachy with fuzz, was crying piteously. Its leg
was crushed, whether from a fall or an attack by another animal, I
couldn't be sure. It was difficult to tell if it had suffered other injuries.
But where was its mother? Listening acutely, I could detect no sounds
in the bushes. She wasn't coming, perhaps couldn't come, making an
attack the more likely cause. The mother fox had probably fallen to
the same predator. The woods were quiet, at least until Davic came
jogging in my wake.

"Nature, Anya, you can't do that. You don't know what could be
out here."

When he noticed where my attention was focused, his demeanor
softened. He couldn't stand an animal in pain any more than I could.
He deliberated, then slipped his cloak off his shoulders, not about to

leave a wounded creature to die in fear and agony. The kit shivered. Its baby coat was soaked with the day's drizzle, and it opened and closed its mouth, emitting small whimpers. It was wary but sensed our magic. It knew we were allies, even though it had probably never come face-to-face with a Faerie before.

Davic crept up to the whimpering animal and draped the cloak over it before it could run and hurt itself further. It struggled, but he scooped it into his arms. Holding the small bundle close to his chest, he made comforting sounds for benefit of the kit, which gradually relaxed, although I suspected more out of exhaustion than trust. Either way, it was safe.

"Let's go," Davic said, now in a hurry.

When we arrived in Chrior, we took our charge to my alcove in the Great Redwood. A few drops of Sale down its throat sent the fox to sleep. I stroked its neck while Davic examined its tiny leg. He had never been taught medicine, but he had a penchant for putting things back together, and therefore for figuring out how they'd broken in the first place. He could design, build, repair, or deconstruct anything given the proper time, and he could do it all without writing a single step down.

"There aren't teeth or claw marks, and there's no blood," he determined. "But the break can't be from a fall. The angle of the impact isn't right. It's almost like..."

"What?" I pressed.

"Honestly, it looks like this was calculated. I can't rule out that something fell on the leg, but did you see anything nearby that would be heavy enough to do this?"

I shook my head—weeds, leaves, broken branches, the density of twigs. There hadn't been anything that could have caused the injury.

Davic nodded, eyebrows drawn close together. "Then I think someone did this, perhaps with a rock. The poor thing couldn't have gotten far after that."

Blood pounded in my temples, and I grasped for an explanation other than the one that frightened me. "But humans can't cross the Road."

"Right," he replied, meeting my eyes.

Davic had reached the same appalling supposition I had. But how could a Faerie have done this? We were supposed to be friends with Nature and protectors of innocents like this kit. Furthermore...if we were correct about the baby's fate, what cruelty had been inflicted upon its mother?

Regardless of how the injury had occurred, there was nothing to be done at present except straighten and bind the fox's leg, which Davic did deftly.

"It's a girl," he said when he'd finished. "Pretty thing."

"Poor thing," I corrected.

"We can't know for sure how this came about, Anya," he said, seeing the sickened expression on my face. "I'm just guessing. There's no point in worrying about it. We'll just keep her until she can walk on that leg, then let her go where we found her."

"We should tell my father, as Queen Ubiqua's Lord of the Law."

"Yes, of course, but that can wait until morning."

My promised went home for dinner with his family on the other side of the city, leaving me with the patient, for whom I constructed a burrow of sorts with a blanket and some sticks. She was in a corner, warmed by the heated walls on both sides, so I retreated to my bedroom, confident she would feel better tomorrow. If only she could have spoken and assuaged the pit of nerves that Davic's deductions had opened within me.

But during the night the fire in the indentations died, and when I awoke the next morning, the little fox was cold. I scrambled to hold her against me, blanketing her and sharing my body heat, but she was gone. I looked at her face with its beautiful red fur, glassy amber eyes

partially open like she'd died looking for aid—for me. My throat hurt,
and I let it sting, afraid that if I tried to swallow the feeling away, it
would run to my eyes and escape as tears. She'd needed someone to
nurture and protect her, and I hadn't done enough.

When Davic came to check on the kit, he wrapped his arms around
both me and the dead fox, because I didn't want to put her down. He
didn't think it was wrong or ghastly. He understood. A life had gone
out of the world, a life he and I had both cared about, however little
time we had spent with her.

He kissed my forehead, content to stay with me all day if that's
what I needed.

"Anya, I know it doesn't mean much right now, but you can't save
them all. You can try, but you can't save them all."

I woke on my stomach in the tunnel near the Sepulchre cavern, the area around me so empty and dark that it took me a minute to determine which way was up. As my disorientation passed, I felt around for Shea. When my hands met the fabric of her clothes, I found her shoulder and shook her awake.

"What the hell happened?" she asked, nothing more than a voice in the blackness.

"I'm not sure. What do you remember?"

"Sepulchres."

Then I hadn't dreamt it. I'd hoped my mind had conjured the encounter, because this far underground, with no sun and not so much as the superficial reassurance of security from a crowd of people, being asked to *save us all* was petrifying.

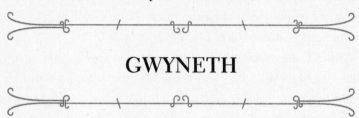

chapter nineteen

GWYNETH

Shea and I resumed our ascent through the tunnels, surfacing at last on the west side of Tairmor. Emerging into the daylight, I wondered if the tunnels were kept by the Governor and his fellows as an escape route in case of an emergency, though Tom had said the cavern system was unmonitored by Ivanova's men. Either way, the higher-ups in the government most certainly did not know the system was occupied by Sepulchres.

A quick assessment of the area around us told me we were already a mile or two from the city gates, a safe enough distance to keep us from being of interest. We were also within sight of what Shea told me was a river station, from whence boats ferried people to and from the ocean. Having never made it all the way to Sheness in my travels, I was unfamiliar with this mode of transport, and not particularly trusting of the notion.

It was late afternoon and the sun was beating down, leaving only a few patches of snow dotting the landscape of dead grasses and rolling hills. The river, emerging from the gorge, widened and flowed more slowly, though its surface hosted no ice. I offered Shea my hand to pull her from the lip of the cave.

"Remember where this entrance is," she advised. "Could come in handy."

Senses on alert, we approached the station, a wooden long-house built half into the hill and half upon the water, where it was supported by thick, dock-like posts. There was no sign that anyone was looking for or following us, and the few people we did encounter were busy preparing themselves or this evening's boat for travel.

The *Nautigull,* so named for the seagulls that flew about the area pestering passengers for food, had two enclosed decks with a railed and canopied sundeck at the top. Though aged, the boat looked well kept and sturdily built. It had an apparatus like a windmill at the back that rested partly in the water to propel it forward; it represented one of those feats of human engineering that impressed some Fae and appalled others. Our boats were operated by Water Faeries, and required nothing more to provide transport than the ability to float. Humans couldn't communicate with the water, and had to employ cleverness and force in such endeavors. They did well with what they had; faulting them felt arrogant.

Though the fee for boarding was hefty, it wasn't unmanageable with the money Luka Ivanova had given me, and the fare included meals and a stateroom, for we would travel through the night. The man collecting tickets scrutinized our passports before reluctantly motioning us on board. We alone among the passengers did not check baggage with him, having nothing more than our packs, and his scowl suggested he thought the money with which we'd paid was stolen. As it turned out, our lack of luggage was but one of ample things that set us apart from our fellow passengers. We were also younger than the rest, far less well attired and, from what I observed, the only females.

Everyone who boarded with us—a club of men in tailcoats

with cigars—proceeded to the sundeck, where they settled in
to await the boat's departure in comfortable lounging chairs
that had been bolted to the floor. Shea and I kept to ourselves,
trying to disappear into the rail next to what appeared to be
a buffet table equipped with an outdoor stove. Instead of so-
cializing, we spent the long minutes whispering guesses about
the men's occupations. I was glad for the amusement, as it distracted my attention from the lapping of the waves against the
sides of the boat. Though the three months Davic had given
me were running out and we needed a fast mode of transportation, I was glaringly aware of the depth and strength of the
water beneath us.

Most of our travel companions looked like moderately successful businessmen. However, Shea and I figured one passenger to be a solicitor based on his pompous manner and leather
satchel, and another, closer to our age than the rest with bright,
innocent blue eyes, we supposed to be on an errand for his
father. Since no new passengers had arrived in some time, I
expected we would be on our way before long, but the boat
remained moored to the dock. I soon learned the reason. The
men around us stood as though called to attention, removing
their hats and adjusting their coats to tidy their appearances.
Shea and I glanced at each other in bewilderment, then joined
the others in beholding the gate beyond which the gangplank
descended. Judging by the reactions of our fellow travelers,
the two people who were approaching were by far the most
important of the *Nautigull*'s passengers.

The young woman wore a dark green travel dress with cri-
nolette, bustle, and matching jacket; an elaborate feathered hat;
black high-heeled boots; and fishnet gloves over delicate, bejeweled hands. Her mouth was painted dark red, her eyes lined

with an autumn glow, and her rosy cheeks were framed by ash-brown hair. Behind her walked a tall, somewhat stocky older gentleman in a black cloak, an aureate cane acting as an extension of his arm, directing the men managing their luggage. Try as I might, I couldn't stop staring, though my interest was not only due to their wealth—they were also familiar to me.

As our fellow travelers bowed and murmured, "Sir, madam," I was finally able to place the newcomers. They had been guests of the Governor at the execution. The woman, my age or close to it, had stood at Luka Ivanova's side, and the man, probably her father, had been next to the Governor during his speech. They drew near, and the other passengers gave them respectful nods, Shea and I following suit, suddenly feeling we had more in common with the moderately successful. With a smile that turned her lips upward but did not crinkle her face, the young woman separated from her father and descended the stairs to the lower decks.

"I'm afraid my daughter is not on the lookout for suitors, gents," said the older man, taking a seat as though he were holding court.

Laughter ensued, the comment enough to break the nervous tension in the air. Taking advantage of the moment, Shea and I stole away and headed to the cabin deck, the lowermost deck where the staterooms were located, and where our tickets indicated we were being housed. The departure horn blew as we found our assigned quarters in the forward section that was reserved for female passengers. Though I wondered if the wealthy young woman was in one of the rooms off the central corridor, I had neither the energy nor the inclination to search for her. Instead, Shea and I entered our tiny cabin—little more than two beds with a bit of floor space in between—and collapsed on our mattresses. Shea dozed off almost immediately, rocked to sleep by the undulating water beneath us, while I found the same movement disconcerting. The noise of the waves was amplified by the now-present hum of the propeller apparatus, and I felt entombed in our tiny space. Was there a way out if the cabins flooded? Not that I could see. But tiredness eventually overcame my discomfort, and I likewise fell asleep.

The sound of voices and high-pitched giggling woke me several hours later, along with an ache in my stomach that could only be attributed to being waterborne. While my elemental connection had been in place, I'd never experienced seasickness, but now nausea played games with me, sneaking close to the top of my throat then retreating like the tide. But the noise coming from down the hall was an even bigger annoyance.

Groaning, I rolled off the bed and glanced out our small window. Night had fallen, and the surface of the water looked oily in the glare cast by the lights of the riverboat. Then another barrage of giggles hit my ears, and I gave Shea's bedpost a swift kick. She grimaced and met my eyes, her expression too alert for her to have been truly asleep. No doubt the obnoxious laughter had disrupted her slumber, too.

"Should I shoot them?" she asked, freeing one hand from her blankets and searching the floor for her pack and gun.

"No, but whoever that is, I'm about to tell them to shut up. Coming?"

Shea got out of bed, her ponytailed hair worked into a masterful mess. She pulled on a pair of leggings, unevenly tucked in her shirt, and followed me into the hallway.

A single lamp hung from the ceiling to illuminate the passage, the motion of the boat swinging it side to side. A steadier stream of light emanated from a room a few doors down the corridor, and we headed toward it, another round of giggles sufficient to convince us that this was the culprit's location.

The door was partway open, and I peered around it, not wanting to be taken by surprise when I barged in on the occupants. I snorted in disgust at the sight that greeted me. The pretty young woman who had a few days ago been on Luka Ivanova's arm had brought the young, blue-eyed chap to her bed. Still mostly clothed, they were nonetheless passionately engaged, the stench of alcohol rank about them.

In my experience, reasoning with the intoxicated was a nonsensical, circular activity. I'd managed, with some amusement, a happy-go-lucky Davic on rare occasion, but I expected interrupting this liaison would reap nothing but frustration. Shea laid a hand on my shoulder, drawing my attention. With a mighty roll of her eyes, she motioned me back down the hall.

We'd gone only a few steps when we heard a muffled grunt, and the giggling ceased. I turned my head, wondering if one member of the amorous pair had succumbed to the drink, and saw a shadow pass before the light in the bedroom. Content that the problem had resolved itself, Shea and I returned to the cabin in the hope that the rest of our night would prove more peaceful.

By the next morning, my stomachache had subsided, and I was hungry for the breakfast the crew served on the open deck. The day was sunny but cold, due in part to the constant movement of the riverboat, and tarpaulin drop cloths had been hung to the west to cut the wind.

Shea and I went through the buffet line, then joined the other passengers who were seated at a large table engaged in deep enough conversation to pay us no mind. It took me a moment to notice that the pretty young woman who shared our corridor was at my right, only she wasn't ignoring us like the rest. She touched my forearm, wearing the same smile I'd seen the day before, the one that didn't reach her amber eyes.

"I'm Gwyneth," she offered, extending her hand. I accepted it with trepidation—Shea and I were not on this boat to make friends, and I was reluctant to give up so much as my name. I obliged, however, afraid that my refusal would stir questions.

"Anya."

Gwyneth then shook hands with Shea, using only the tips of her fingers as though she wasn't conditioned to endure such a coarse gesture.

"And you are?" she asked.

"Mary Archer." Shea looked Gwyneth up and down. "You look well this morning, considering your evening's entertainment."

I coiled my fingers to keep from slapping my forehead. *Why* would she say that? We were trying *not* to draw attention to ourselves. Fortunately, Gwyneth didn't take offense at Shea's remark, perhaps because she didn't want to bring the incident within her father's purview.

"I'm sorry," Gwyneth said, leaning closer to us. "I'm afraid I did have a bit to drink. No more than my companion, mind you. I just hold my liquor better. But you mustn't say a word. The women on this boat ought to stick together."

She spoke as if we were old schoolmates or members of a sisterhood, and an irritated flush crept up Shea's neck.

"It wasn't a woman you were stuck to last night," she grumbled, making no attempt to conceal her dislike for our new acquaintance.

Knowing there was only one way to deal with Shea's tenacity, I jumped in to redirect the conversation.

"And where is your companion this morning?"

Gwyneth shrugged and settled her light brown hair about her shoulders. Her crimson dress matched her lips, behind which white teeth shone in brilliant contrast.

"He must still be asleep," she replied, but I sensed a lie. I also sensed it was a lie I shouldn't pursue.

Showing no concern for Shea's sullen silence, Gwyneth bestowed her company and her conversation on the men at the table. This suited me just fine—she struck me as trouble, and trouble was something we did not need.

Shea and I finished our meals and returned to our state room, where we passed the time playing games with the dice and cards we found stashed in one of the drawers beneath our beds. The air was chilly despite the sunshine sifting through the window, so we snugged our cloaks around us. I didn't mention her horrid manners, because the more I thought about it, the more I wondered if I wasn't a bit like Gwyneth in Shea's eyes. I didn't drink and carouse in the style of a wealthy party girl, but now that Shea knew I was royalty in Chrior, did she imagine my life to have been equally lavish and indulgent? The assumption wasn't *wrong;* I'd never wanted for anything. Maybe Shea's resentment of Gwyneth was in part directed at me.

A couple of hours later, a gong sounded and we joined the others for lunch on the captain's deck, the middle deck that housed a lounge, a galley kitchen, and a dining room. There was no sign of either Gwyneth or her blue-eyed admirer, but her stocky father was once more the center of attention, zealously discussing business in Sheness. I gathered he was the owner of a shipping and trading company that operated out of the port city, an enterprise that had earned him great wealth, the admiration of his colleagues, and the personal friendship of Governor Ivanova.

Shea had been napping when the lunch bell tolled, and was quiet as we settled into our corner of the long dining table. I didn't mind her mood, since it gave me the opportunity to eavesdrop on the others gathered for the meal.

"What of the raids?" asked the pompous fellow Shea and I had pegged as a solicitor, pouring wine into crystal glasses for himself and his companions. "I heard your ships and a few others have been victims of the pirates prowling the water and the ports."

"*Piracy* is a term that hardly begins to describe the tyranny of those animals," Gwyneth's father replied in his deep, resonant voice. "They're far more dangerous than you might imagine. Their attacks are ruthless, their thievery is brazen, and they kill without remorse. We've increased our security and made our operations more clandestine in hopes of eluding them, but the effort has about erased our profits. These men know which of our ships carries the most important cargo, even when the ship's own crew isn't aware of it. I've been in Tairmor updating Governor Ivanova and his son on the state of these affairs. Things have improved with a larger troop presence, but I fear the culprits are lying in wait. The truth is our crusade has resulted in hardly any arrests."

"Surely some of the pirates are in custody," said another of the businessmen, this one thin and fidgety, with a chain on his jacket that led to the same pocket in which he had slipped his hand. When he gestured, however, the chain slipped free, revealing that no pocket watch was attached. I nearly laughed—apparently he felt the need to use a ruse to show he fit in with the social class among whom he stood. "Can't you break them and get the names of their associates?"

"We've tried, but they're a stoic and fiercely loyal lot. And the ones who are ripe for the catching aren't trusted enough to have information we really need. The fellow who offered the most promise committed suicide before we even had a chance to interrogate him."

With this dark twist in conversation, several of the men glanced our way. In an effort to allay their concern over what we might hear, I sent a still-tired Shea to our room, then paid another visit to the buffet table to refill my plate. I had no intention of leaving, for Zabriel might be involved with the pirates in question. And whether he was or not, the information I was collecting could help focus our search once we reached the port city.

I moved to a seat farther away from the congregation of men, hoping to encourage them to resume their conversation. I would have to trust to my faltering—but still keen—Faerie hearing to take in every word.

"What did Ivanova have to say on the matter?" the solicitor began again.

"The Lieutenant Governor is tasked with crime control in the capital, as you no doubt are aware, and he keeps himself advised of serious crime all across the Territory. He's certain that if we catch this Pyrite fellow, the game will be up."

One of the older men noisily rose to his feet, and my heart picked up rhythm.

"Enough," he blustered, the turn in dialogue clearly not to his liking. "That scum is a demon, and not to be discussed while on the water. Nothing but bad fortune can come of giving voice to these matters out here in the open."

The men shifted guiltily, and whether they agreed with the sentiment or not, more than one pair of eyes skimmed the deck. Clearly Zabriel was more than just a thorn in the side of the wealthy shipowners; he had also inspired some superstition.

Alas, the gentleman's portent was sufficient to stop further conversation about my cousin. While the group didn't break up, they did switch their attention to other matters, and I returned to our state room to tell Shea what I had learned. Growing restless in the aftermath, we decided to take a walk on the sundeck, thinking the fresh air might clear our heads. But as Shea pulled on her boots, there was a knock on the door.

I opened it to see the lieutenant who was second-in-command of the vessel. His serious countenance was enough to tell me this was no social call.

"Forgive the intrusion, ladies," he said with a bow. "We've lost track of one of our passengers, a Mr. Trenton. We're checking with everyone on board in order to determine his whereabouts."

"Who?" Shea blurted, pounding her foot against the floor to better position her boot.

"Mr. David Trenton, blond hair, blue eyes. One of our younger passengers. I'm afraid he hasn't been seen since last night." He paused, examining us, perhaps recognizing that we weren't the kind of ladies with whom he was used to dealing and could handle the truth. In any case, he added, "We fear he may have gone overboard."

"I haven't seen him today," I said, scraping my thumbnail against the metal door latch I still clutched and flaking off a little rust. "From what I know of last night, he had a fair amount to drink. If he found his way to the top deck, I imagine he could have gone over."

Though I wasn't sure why I was protecting her, I didn't tell the lieutenant that the young man had fallen asleep in Gwyneth's stateroom, nowhere near the deck or any place else from which he could have fallen. Shea glowered at me, harboring no reservations about causing trouble for the wealthy young woman, but she held her tongue. With a nod, the ship's officer departed, and we sank uneasily down on our beds, walk momentarily forgotten.

"Do you think Gwyneth had something to do with this?" Shea asked, keeping her volume low.

"I doubt it. I mean, what would be her motive? Besides, *both* of them were drunk. If he fell overboard, it's far more likely he wandered up to the sundeck on his own. Maybe he was vomiting off the side and lost his balance."

"You're probably right. I just really don't like her."

"I don't, either. But we don't have to like her. We just have to stay away from her."

Shea leaned into her pillows, laughing cynically, a sign she wasn't sure this was possible.

"Do you still want to take a stroll, Anya?"

I hesitated, thinking that going for a walk ran directly counter to my goal of avoiding Gwyneth. She knew we had seen her the previous evening, and the last thing I wanted was to hear details about her liaison with Mr. Trenton.

"No, I think I'll stay here and try to figure out how best to look for Zabriel once we reach Sheness. We can hardly walk up to any old person on the street and ask for directions to the pirates' lair."

"True enough. But I'm going to stretch my legs. I don't think I've stopped panicking since we were arrested, and now this mess... I need to wear off some energy."

Shea opened the door, peering to her right, then left to make sure the young woman we had been discussing was not in sight. With a small wave, she stepped into the corridor, leaving me behind in our little chamber.

I lay down on my bed, folding my arms beneath my head. How was I to find someone who didn't want to be found? Someone who had managed to elude detection and capture by the Governor's Constabularies? Someone with a reputation as big as Sheness itself, and who apparently had as many hiding places? I wasn't one of the Queen's Blades—I wasn't prepared for a task of this magnitude. I didn't even have a starting point.

I thought back to my conversation with Luka Ivanova in his office. How had the Governor's son described William Wolfram Pyrite? *Young, handsome, daring, some might say philanthropic—sometimes I think he has more admirers than I do.* So my cousin was a person who inspired loyalty. This wasn't surprising, but it did mean that if I wasn't careful in my approach, I was likely to get myself killed, Shea along with me.

My head aching, I closed my eyes, intending to rest for a few minutes. I woke several hours later to fading sunlight filtering through the window. Alarmed, I sat up to discover that Shea had not returned. I scrambled out the door and headed to the captain's deck, imagining that my troubled friend could be miles behind us, cold in the river's clutches. If it could have happened to Mr. Trenton, why not to her?

The scene that greeted me when I burst into the dining room would have been comical were my topsy-turvy emotions not dominated by relief. Shea was sitting at a small round table with four gentlemen, talking, laughing and sipping rich amber liquid from a shot glass. A pyramid of gold pieces lay in the table's center, and Shea rubbed a pair of dice in her hands.

Glancing puckishly at the men, she blew on them and gave them a roll. When the dice settled, she whooped and scooped up the pot amid groans from the other players. I gaped at the gold tower she was piling in front of her. I had played the game with her earlier, and she had won no more often than had I. What had changed her luck?

Catching my eye, Shea came to her feet, knocking some of her coins to the floor, where they gleamed as they rolled and spun. With a giggle, she gathered them again, fashioning her tunic into a pouch to hold her winnings. When she had captured the strays, she brushed her stacks of gold into her make-shift pouch to mingle with the others.

"Thank you, gentlemen, for a lovely afternoon," she sassed, one arm protectively cradling her winnings like a pregnant woman might cradle her unborn child. "And thank you for your donations to my travel fund."

"You can't leave now," the solicitor griped. "You've got half our money!"

"You should be glad I'm leaving now—if I stayed any longer, I'd have *all* your money."

The men laughed uproariously, an indication their insides were well warmed with liquor, and fell into easy conversation. Blushing like a schoolgirl, Shea came to my side.

"Are you a hustler or a cheat?" I muttered, offering my money pouch to take part of her load, which was stretching the fabric of her shirt to its limit.

"Shhh. Let's step away first."

We moved to a corner table across the room from the gamblers, watching the kitchen crew set up the buffet table, for the evening meal would soon be served. Finishing off their drinks, the gentlemen gathered their effects, the fortunes they had lost to my friend seemingly having been forgotten the moment the gold had left their sight.

"I did pretty well, don't you think?" Shea asked, sinking into a chair, her speech much smoother than I was expecting. Unlike the other participants in the dice game, she was nowhere near inebriated.

"I think you're lucky."

"No, I'm not."

She transferred the remaining gold pieces from her tunic to the pouch at her hip. Then she opened one hand below the height of the table, toward the wall where only she and I could see it. A pair of dice rested in her palm.

I frowned. "You stole the dice?"

"Not exactly. These are *my* dice. They're loaded."

I stared stupidly at her, then comprehension dawned. "You really *are* a swindler?"

"More of an opportunist," she laughed, enjoying my reaction. "The opportunity was there, and I took advantage of it. I wasn't given these big, round eyes for nothing." She fingered the dice before tucking them into her money pouch. "My father taught me to play the game, and he used these once as a joke. He let me keep them, and I've carried them around ever since. Sort of a good luck charm, I suppose. If you only switch the dice a few times, you're not likely to get caught. Besides, these folks can afford to lose…and they'd *never* accuse a young lady of cheating."

At the playful waggle of her eyebrows, mirth bubbled up from my belly. I tried to muffle its sound, only to end up snorting like a hog, which set Shea off, our laughter enough to make us both appear drunk. The Fae were the ones stereotyped as charlatans, tricky with our words and deeds, because our inability to lie was hard for humans to comprehend. While it did force us to cleverer tactics if we wanted to conceal something, human distrust was, for the most part, misplaced. Shea was the one for whom they had to watch out.

I clutched at my aching stomach, fighting to regain control, for there was a serious issue underlying her actions that I needed to address.

"You can't do that sort of thing anymore, okay? If you'd been caught, we might both be arrested. *Again.*"

"Don't worry. I'm not about to push my luck. But think about what you just said. We're probably the only ones among this boatload of bourgeois passengers who've ever been arrested, and yet we're indubitably the most innocent of the lot. There's something not right about that." A smile flitted across her features, then she winked. "But you know what? The risk was half the fun."

I rolled my eyes, though I secretly wondered what it would feel like to take such a risk. A strong sense of propriety had been instilled in me from birth, and it kept me from considering such behavior. Traveling, seeing new places, and never knowing what might come next gave me a rush that I supposed might be similar, yet the stakes were higher for Shea, the thrill more immediate, concentrated into a crucial hour or two. I cast a sideways glance at her, thinking a rush that intense was liable to be addicting. Still, seeing the light in Shea's eyes made me want to take that same sort of chance someday. As long as no articulated lies were involved, there was nothing to stop me. Besides, I didn't even know if my speech was restricted by magical law anymore. Maybe I was just relying on habit. And if habit was my only obstacle, a whole new world lay before me, one that was *truly* human.

Gold pieces safely stored away, Shea was smugly watching the servants carry stacks of plates and trays of silverware in preparation for dinner. Judging from her expression, she hadn't taken my warning seriously. I already had enough things on my mind, and didn't want the added worry of what else Shea might consider an *opportunity*.

"Shea, I meant what I said before. We really can't afford to take chances like that."

"It wasn't that risky, Anya, but I know what you mean."

"Do you? Remember that boy in Strong? And when you left the Fae-mily Home by yourself in Tairmor? I told you to be careful after both of those incidents, and you didn't listen then." Under any other circumstances, I would have felt out of place reprimanding her, but Nature ice over and boil if I was going to hazard losing my freedom again on her account.

"I *said* I've got it, Anya." There was irritation in Shea's voice, and her eyes held an almost disdainful glint. "Maybe you should try having fun sometime. And you're not always so sensible, you know. Remember how you almost died in the Fere because you were too stubborn to see a doctor? And I wasn't the one chasing after Spex and Hastings in Oaray. Don't go about pretending you're better than me."

I sighed heavily, restraining my rising temper. "That's not what I'm doing. We've both made misjudgments. All I'm saying is we have to be more cautious from now on. Sooner or later we're just going to run out of luck."

She gave a quick nod, then resumed watching the servants, who were pushing in carts that clanked and groaned under their burdens of steaming food.

Like ants swarming a picnic, the remaining passengers scuttled into the dining room, eager to raid the platters. Catching sight of Gwyneth's father, I felt a surge of gratitude that he had not been involved in the dice game. I doubted he was as gullible as the rest; he wasn't the type to suffer the company of fools.

The announcement that we had lost Mr. Trenton was made at the conclusion of the evening's meal, although most of the passengers were already aware of the situation. Safety protocol was reviewed, and we were told that access to the sundeck would be closed off for the remainder of the voyage. With all eyes on the captain while he issued this last decree, I took the opportunity to find Gwyneth in the crowd of concerned faces. Feeling my gaze, she turned to me, her expression devoid of interest or worry, and it felt like spiders ran down my arms. From her tiny smile, I gleaned an awful truth: Gwyneth knew exactly what had become of Mr. Trenton. The question that begged to be answered was whether or not she had played a part in his disappearance.

chapter twenty

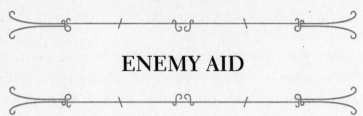

ENEMY AID

"She's crazy," Shea insisted, not even waiting until the door to our quarters had closed to launch her accusations. "Worse, she's evil."

She spun around, eyes wild, then yanked on the storage drawers that were housed under our beds, viciously rattling them several times, but she could not remove them. Finally, she gave one of them a frustrated kick.

"What are we going to use to barricade the door?"

I would have laughed if my mind hadn't been leaping to similar conclusions. I couldn't say for certain whether Gwyneth had done anything wrong, but the circumstances of Mr. Trenton's disappearance were undeniably odd. And her attitude had been much too cavalier. But surely the smile she gave me could have been meant to be reassuring—it could have been intended to convey hope. There were a million ways to interpret a single expression, weren't there? Gwyneth could even have been in shock and reacted inappropriately. Such lapses happened and could be forgiven. After all, people handled distressing news in different ways.

I'd almost calmed myself down when the door swung open, setting my heart to racing all over again. It didn't help that

Gwyneth barged across the threshold, not waiting for an invitation. In our cramped quarters, the heavy floral scent that clung to her was almost sickening, and the midnight blue dress that hugged her curvaceous form was a blatant reminder of how easily she could have manipulated Mr. Trenton.

Shea shouted and jumped back, drawing her pistol and pointing it at our unexpected guest. Not knowing whose behavior shocked me more, I stepped between the two of them, for I doubted Gwyneth had come to kill us. Shea's eyes narrowed, then she tucked her pistol back into her belt, though her hand continued to rest on its handle. With a lift of her eyebrows, Gwyneth gave the door a shove, its slam signifying the abandonment of her girlish, innocent guise.

"I'd hoped you wouldn't be quite so astute," she said, and my hand dropped to the long-knife at my hip. "Yes, I sent that drunkard Trenton over the side of the boat, *with* a life vest and a flare gun, I'll have you know."

"Why the hell would you do that?" Shea all but screeched. "You're insane! I told you, Anya—she's insane!"

"Oh, I certainly am not. You should be thanking me, not shouting at me. You see, Trenton let it slip that he was following you two on Luka Ivanova's orders. Having spent a good deal of my life trailed by people I neither desire nor require, I thought I'd spare you the same annoyance. So the truth is I saved you."

We stared at her, trying to grasp what she was telling us. Shea and I had discussed the possibility that we were being followed, but hadn't seen any evidence to substantiate it. But if Gwyneth was telling the truth, then she had done us a favor— in her own way.

"We could tell the captain, you know," Shea warned, her fingers twitching where they lay against her gun.

"You could," our confounding travel companion agreed, smoothing the skirt of her dress. "But I'm afraid he wouldn't believe you. I travel often with my father on this river, and the captain knows me well, or at least as well as I want him to know me. He would find your claims that a sheltered, well-bred noblewoman could commit such an act ludicrous. Besides, how could I possibly have overpowered David Trenton? The notion is just silly."

"Apparently not," Shea grumbled. She plopped on her bed in defeat, though her expression remained bitter and distrustful.

"Now that we've cleared up that little matter," Gwyneth went on, ignoring Shea, "let me get to the real point of my visit. I've come here to extend an invitation. I've already told my father the three of us have become friends, and he's agreed to let you ride with us from the bay to Sheness, and then on to our home for dinner. You are headed to Sheness, aren't you?"

Shea seemed inclined to deny this on principle, but I nodded.

"Yes, we're going to the port city. And I would happily take you up on your offer if you could give me a believable reason for extending it. What's your interest in us? Why get involved in our affair with Trenton?"

White teeth flashed at me from behind bloodred lips. "Like I said before, the women on this boat ought to stick together. Besides, dinner with just me and my father at the table can be boring. I suspect you two will enliven things considerably. Now then, we should be docking late tomorrow morning. Why don't we just meet on deck?"

She paused, but our lack of response did not faze her. "Grand. I'll be off then. Good night!"

Gwyneth pivoted and departed as abruptly as she had arrived, leaving Shea and me completely baffled. We readied
ourselves for bed in silence and crawled under our covers, but
neither of us could sleep. The restlessness in the room built
until we spontaneously broke into conversation, our voices
low, indicative of a fear that someone might overhear.

"She was on Luka Ivanova's arm at the execution," I said
into the darkness.

"And from what you overheard, her father is connected to
the Governor." Shea's voice was troubled, and the waves thud-
ding against the riverboat's hull were an unrelenting reminder
that we were trapped on the vessel. "Plus he's connected to
Zabriel, though in a far less friendly sense."

I rolled over and hugged my pillow to my chest. "So what's
her angle? Is this related to Luka? I mean, he's shrewd, and
whether I want to think it or not, so is Tom Matlock. Maybe
this is an elaborate ruse so that Gwyneth can set herself up to
keep an eye on us. Or maybe she's going to turn us over to
the Constabularies when we arrive in Sheness."

"I don't think she's working for Luka. Wouldn't Luka have
had to make arrangements with Gwyneth's father to get her
involved? And her father hasn't shown any interest in us. I'd
wager he doesn't even know our names. Besides, in my experience, wealthy businessmen don't make willing lackeys, nor
do they put their pampered daughters in danger."

"There seems to be a lot he doesn't know about his daughter, though," I mused, still unconvinced. "She and Luka looked
pretty friendly with one another at the execution. Maybe she
helps him just for the thrill of it."

"But she wouldn't have gotten rid of Mr. Trenton if she
were working with Luka."

I rubbed my forehead in frustration, my temples seeming to push outward against my skull. "Then maybe she's helping *us* just for the thrill of it? She has to suspect we're involved in something illegal if the Lieutenant Governor had someone following us."

"So is Gwyneth a friend or an enemy?" Shea's voice remained as skeptical as mine, and for good reason—nothing about Gwyneth was simple or straightforward. "And what do we do?"

"I'm not sure. What I do know is that we need to get to Sheness as quickly as possible. And we don't have a better, faster option than the one she's offering us. While I'd love to see the last of her, we may have to trust her for the time being."

Shea sighed, and I heard her sit up in the empty blackness. "I don't think I'll ever trust her, because I still believe she's completely insane. But maybe her insanity has some perks. We'll have to be careful, though. If Gwyneth *is* working for Luka, it means she's trying to find my family."

"We can always lead her on a merry chase through Sheness," I snorted, though the other risk of being tracked by Luka Ivanova flitted through my head. I didn't want to put him on Zabriel's trail, or the trail of William Wolfram Pyrite, as the case may be.

"Then we'll go with her tomorrow," Shea declared, and I made a noise of affirmation. Perhaps Gwyneth represented our first real break on this journey. And if not, Shea and I were sharp enough to elude her. How dangerous could one mollycoddled young woman be? Still, I had to wonder what answer Mr. Trenton would have given to that question.

★ ★ ★

The riverboat made good time, and by noon the land bordering our passage had widened, and we floated in the peaceful Bay of Arvogale. I'd never seen water that stretched on and on, seemingly forever, and its vastness filled me with longing. The ocean glimmered red and gold atop its deep blue depths, reflecting the light in much the same way the jewels on Ubiqua's throne reflected the torches of the Great Redwood. Waves beat against the boat and shore in a ceaseless rhythm, counting out Nature's heartbeat, while the whitecaps on the horizon formed an inaudible chorus.

A visit here while still in possession of my elemental connection would have been intense, with the hum of every water molecule vibrating through my body. But even without my wings, I did not fear the ocean's power in the same way I had the river. The ocean was infinite; I was finite and fleeting. To fear it would have been similar to fearing the aurora. The muscle of those waves was so beyond my control and comprehension that an aversion to it was pointless, leaving reverence the only sensible alternative.

Shea and I left the riverboat station in the company of Gwyneth and her father, whose name we finally learned was Leo Dementya. He had become the owner of DemenTransport upon his father's death, inheriting a fleet of ships so remarkable they'd been lent to the military during the Faerie–Human War, a generation before Governor Ivanova's time. The company had only grown since then, and Dementya was one of the most prominent names in Sheness, probably in the entire Warckum Territory.

How different our accommodations might have been if Dementya had known we were fugitives, that Shea had stolen close to half her weight in gold from his friends, or that my cousin was the infamous Pyrite who had robbed him many times over.

We landed at one of the docks owned by the transport company, and footmen attached to a gold-embellished carriage boarded to claim Gwyneth's and her father's luggage. Shea and I maintained possession of our packs and followed after our hosts to be waved through the military checkpoint where travel documents were examined. Apparently Leo Dementya's endorsement was all it took to negate the Governor's strict laws and security measures.

We ate lunch in a restaurant by the bay, and for the first time I tried shellfish, concluding it was an acquired taste. In the Faerie Realm, river fish might be served, but our Realm did not extend to the ocean. After the meal, Shea and I waited while our host took care of some business matters and Gwyneth made the rounds of friends. I didn't mind being left on our own, glad to be relieved of the pressure to make small talk. Shea clearly felt the same; she cradled her head in her arms on the tabletop, looking desperate for a nap.

It was late afternoon by the time we were tucked into the carriage pulled by six black horses that we'd earlier espied. Trunks and travel bags had been strapped to the top of the coach, although the packs Shea and I had refused to surrender were nestled at our feet. I glanced at my friend, who was fingering the looking glass necklace her father had given her. Thatcher had said it would bring her luck, and the salesman peddling similar items prior to Eskander's execution had claimed the necklaces were for protection; that they could hoodwink people and tame magic creatures. Could there be some power in the pendant? The Sepulchres in the caverns under Tairmor had seemed to react to it, and at times it felt like we were luckier than we should have been. But it wasn't possible. Objects couldn't be infused with magic any more than could wingless Fae. I gazed once more out the window of the carriage, preferring to contemplate scenery instead of fantasy.

We were traveling south, the ocean to our west, the city of Sheness lying to our east, and I didn't know which sight was more captivating. On one side, the setting sun lengthened its arms in pale shades of rose, silhouetting the amethyst clouds and dropping brass tears upon the entire surface of the water until it shimmered so brightly it was difficult to behold. Ships with white sails were frozen specters across the seascape, as though painted on the horizon. There was a salty smell in the air, and gulls dove and swooped in an unending quest for fish.

On the other side, Sheness sprawled, gritty and untamed, her factories belching smoke, her cobblestone streets overrun with wagons, carriages and people, her buildings marked with artwork and scrawled profanities. While Tairmor was stately and organized, Sheness was chaotic and belligerent. Even from a distance, I could hear the clatter and buzz of a city that never slept. She held intrigue, danger, mystery, and more than a few notorious names and faces, but not a speck of Nature's beauty. She was man-made, a portrait of humanity's best and worst, so intertwined they were indistinguishable from one another.

"It's a lot to take in, isn't it?" Gwyneth commented, and I gave her a wry smile. She and her father, seated across from us, had made occasional attempts at conversation during the ride, but for the most part, they had left Shea and me to our gawking. When we turned into a drive marked by a pair of stone columns, Gwyneth drew our attention to a group of buildings up ahead. "Here we are, safe and sound. Welcome to the Dementya Estate."

Gwyneth's family home had the look and feel of a castle, the impression aided by turrets that topped its three-story stone walls. Built on a bluff, it overlooked the ocean, and was as old as the family to which it belonged, though it had been updated over the years to permit gas-powered lamps and indoor plumbing. Servants' quarters, a stable, a groundskeeper's shack and several storage sheds made up the other buildings, forming a small village unto themselves. Tall, glass-shaded lamps sent fragmented orange light spreading across the twilight grounds, and the horse's hoofbeats echoed in the courtyard, giving the impression we had entered into a dream.

We were ushered inside by servants, to be awed by the heavy woolen tapestries, gilt-framed paintings, and marble statues that adorned the large rooms, recalling the lavishness of the Governor's mansion. We were given a chance to wash and refresh ourselves, then joined Gwyneth and her father in the dining room, where the light of a large chandelier with teardrop pendants reflected off the shining floor. Flames crackled in two large fireplaces to add warmth, and a wall of windows granted a view of the water. Winds frequently and audibly battered the house, but it stayed firm on its foundation, as solid and substantial as anything humans could construct.

The meal was served in several courses at a table smoother than the backs of my hands and darker even than the bark of the Great Redwood. Though we did not inquire, Leo informed us that there was no Lady Dementya, his wife having passed away some years ago. He turned out to be a pleasant man with whom to converse, although we were limited to topics he considered appropriate for his daughter. Evidently in the upper echelons of the Warckum Territory, women were supposed to be protected and uninformed, though neither concept seemed to suit Gwyneth. Based on our experiences with her, she had plenty of knowledge and wits about her, traits she managed to keep hidden from her father. She laughed and fawned over him, and I had the impression he thought her ideally stupid, the epitome of a well-raised young lady.

Having been raised in the midst of court life, I was comfortable dining in rich surroundings, but Shea was so nervous her hand shook as she raised her wineglass for a sip. Fortunately, Dementya placed no further demands on us. He seemed to view us in much the same way he did his daughter, and was only marginally interested in our reasons for being in Sheness.

"You're young to be traveling on your own," he commented at one point. "I assume you're here to visit family?"

Though Leo hadn't intended to provide us with a rationale, we embraced it nonetheless. Shea nodded, while I found it amusing to flirt with the truth.

"We're here after a cousin of mine. We hope to convince him to return home with us."

"And where is home?"

"East of here," I replied, although the entire rest of the Territory was east of here. I hoped he would let my foppish answer pass, since if pressed for specifics I would be unable to lie.

"From Tairmor?" he persisted, and I groaned internally, glancing surreptitiously at Shea.

"No," she piped up, accurately reading my plea for assistance. "A small town on the other side of the Fere."

"I see. Is this your first time in our city?"

Shea suddenly looked like her tongue was glued to the roof of her mouth. From what she'd told me, the only other time she'd been in Sheness was when her family had been trying to flee the Territory. Her memories were written all over her face, so I hastily repaid the favor and rescued her.

"Yes, and I'm hoping we'll have time to explore it." Sheness was the only major human city in Warckum that I hadn't yet visited. While I wanted to find Zabriel, part of me hoped the quest would lead us through every inch of the gritty metropolis. "Do you have any suggestions on where to start?"

Leo chuckled. "Why, start in my shipyards. The ships are the most impressive part of Sheness, and mine are irrefutably the best. The rest of the city is, I'm afraid, a bit derelict. But there's history here, if you're willing to look for it. This was the first human settlement in the Warckum Territory. By all means, return here and I'll lay out a guide for you."

"Thank you. That sounds wonderful."

"I'll let Gwyneth make the arrangements for you to tour the docks. Perhaps we can take you out on one of the vessels. If you've never been in Sheness before, then you've never ridden the crest of the ocean. It's a bit more exciting than cruising along in a riverboat."

"We'd like that very much." I dabbed at my mouth with my napkin, the smile on our host's broad face telling me I had made a favorable impression on him. "Thank you for your hospitality. You've been extremely kind to us. But I'm afraid the exhaustion of travel is sneaking up on us, and we'd best find lodging before it arrives."

"You're quite welcome. And I shouldn't have kept you so late. Traveling can be tiring for us all." Leo stood and came around the table to clasp my hand. "I took the liberty of sending one of my men ahead to reserve a room for you and Mary at a lovely inn on the outskirts of the city. I wouldn't want you to end up in an unsavory neighborhood."

"Again, I thank you. But you needn't have gone to such trouble."

"No trouble at all." Turning to his daughter, he added, "Gwyneth, would you make sure the arrangements are in place for these young ladies and see them on their way?"

"Yes, Father."

With a bow, Leo retreated from the dining room, leaving Gwyneth to usher Shea and me through the wide corridors to the front entry. While we waited for a servant to retrieve our cloaks, she picked up two packages wrapped in elegant paper from atop a side table.

"I think you'll find these useful," she explained, extending one of the mysterious parcels to each of us. "Everyone underestimates the wind on the coast. These will keep you warmer than what you've been wearing. They are, of course, my gift."

I thanked her as I had her father, although I couldn't prevent a dubious undertone from entering my voice. Shea was not so subtle and spoke her doubts out loud.

"That's it then? All you wanted from us?"

Gwyneth flashed her white teeth in an unsettling grin.

"I never wanted anything from you. When you have this much to give—" she spread her arms and looked about the massive foyer "—keeping it to yourself is tiresome. Now, if you're ready, there's a hansom cab waiting outside. The driver knows where to take you."

With a stomach full of delicious food, it was difficult to be cynical, and I shook her hand, an apology hidden within the gesture. Shea did the same, and we stepped into the biting wind, rushing to close the doors of the cab around us. Once we had settled across from each other, the driver snapped the reins to move the horses off at a trot, and I waved to Gwyneth where she stood in the doorway of her family's mansion. Then I grinned at Shea.

"What are we waiting for?" I asked, giving my package a shake.

Soothed by the heat emanating from the coal in a grate below our feet, we ripped into Gwyneth's presents, not quite believing her hints about their contents. But our eyes met in disappointment when beautiful red velvet cloaks lined with white fur and embroidered with gold thread fell into our laps.

"Well, she was right," I ventured. "They'll keep us warm."

"Yes, but they're boring compared to what I was expecting." Shea's bottom lip stuck out in a pout. "She threw a man into the Kappa just so she could bring us home and give us cloaks?"

I laughed and patted her cheek. "I guess so. I was starting to think she knew something about our real reason for being here, or at least that she was planning to sacrifice us in some elaborate Dementya family ritual."

"I suppose we shouldn't be let down about that last bit."

"I think I am a little. I've never been a sacrifice before."

Shea's pout was dissipating, and she tugged on her hair with a frustrated growl, drawing a chuckle out of me.

"You think *I'm* funny?" she retorted. "Well, you're *hilarious* around rich people."

"Oh, really?"

"You say things like *you needn't have* and *we'd best* do this and that. You sounded like a popinjay in there."

"A what?" I tried hard to sound offended, but it wasn't working. My cheeks hurt from smiling.

"You know! A dandy. A coxcomb. A carpet knight!"

She flung her wrapping paper at me, particularly proud of this final insult. I huffed, then wadded up the paper and flicked it at her face. My aim was perfect, and it bopped her on the nose.

"This carpet knight got you one hell of a free dinner," I cackled.

"Then please take credit for getting us these boring cloaks, as well, popinjay."

"But what if they're not boring? Maybe there's a map to the pirates' den hidden in the lining."

Though I was joking, we both took a quick look, our enthusiasm a sign that Dementya's wine had gone to our heads. Discovering nothing, we snuggled into our new garments and settled back on the bench seats.

"I guess we'll just have to find Zabriel the hard way," I concluded, thinking that all in all, this had been a good day.

Now that we had left the Dementya Estate behind, traffic on the road was picking up, and lights from passing coaches flitted over our faces. Though we were in good hands, the questionable things I had heard about Sheness began to tinker with my mind. I hoped we would soon arrive at our place of accommodation.

Our carriage wheel hit a rut, and Shea and I emitted matching shrieks as we pitched to one side, a loud bang indicating the door of the hansom had been flung open and closed. Then we threw our hands over our mouths until the carriage had righted itself. Meeting each other's eyes, we broke into laughter at our synchronized overreactions. I was about to tell Shea that we really *were* turning into popinjays when a passing lamp illuminated the interior. My words caught in my throat, numbness shooting like frost all the way to my fingers and toes.

Shea and I were no longer the only people in the cab. A shadow had crawled in beside her and was crouching in wait for its best opportunity to attack.

chapter twenty-one

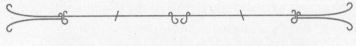

THE GREAT DEADWOOD

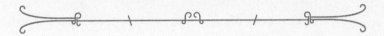

Bombarded by images of Sepulchres, highwaymen or worse, I shouted to alert Shea to the intruder, then jumped up and hit my head on the ceiling of the coach. She sprang toward the door, apparently to leap into the street, but our uninvited guest gripped her arm, a gloved hand sliding over her mouth like a door latch locked tight.

"This is the problem, dear," the interloper hissed, the resonance of the voice definitely male and definitely familiar. "You keep supposing you're going to find Zabriel. You haven't considered that he might find you instead."

"Mother of *Nature*," I breathed, mind reeling.

I collapsed onto my bench seat, eyes unfocused, but not because of the lump forming on the back of my head—because of the form taking shape before my eyes. Temporarily robbed of speech, I raised a shaky hand to calm Shea, who was putting up a mighty fight. Though she didn't understand what was going on, she surrendered, and our new passenger released her. Eyes and hair wild, she scrambled to the opposite side of the carriage.

"It's all right, love," he said to her, removing a top hat from his head of silver-blond hair and tossing it next to me on the bench. "Anya can vouch for me."

Shea was pale and quivering in the disjointed light from outside, but she straightened as realization dawned.

"You son of a bitch," she gasped. "You *son of a bitch*. You're Zabriel."

He bowed his head with a smirk, which served to transform Shea's incredulity into anger. She let out a battle cry and unleashed a kick to his side that would have sent him back out the door had it still been open.

"Shea, don't!" I cried, half expecting the driver to stop the horses to see what was going on inside the coach.

Shea wasn't in a mood to listen. She wound up for a second attack, but Zabriel was quick to divert her blow. In another instant, he was twisting her arm behind her back and pinning her to the wall of the cab. She grimaced, her face toward me, one round cheek flattened against the black-painted wood.

"*Oww,*" Zabriel muttered, feeling his ribs with his free hand, the jest gone from his voice. "Is this how you always say hello? Because I'm guessing you don't have many friends."

"Go to hell."

"Stop it, both of you," I snapped, struggling to come to terms with the unexpected twist the evening had taken. My gaze went to my cousin, silently pleading with him to come closer and prove I wasn't dreaming.

Deserting Shea, Zabriel slid to his knees on the floor of the cab. He took my hands in his, and I looked into his dark, almond-shaped Ivanova eyes, which carried in them so many of my own memories. His hair sprang forward unregulated, and I reached out to touch it, then slid my hands over his cheeks and onto his shoulders. He was real, he was here, and he was safe.

Throughout my journey with Shea, I hadn't considered how I would feel if I actually ended up face-to-face with my wayward cousin, and now I was in such turmoil that I didn't know which emotion would dominate. I was happy—more than that, I was euphoric. But I also wanted to slap him so hard his relations on both sides of the Bloody Road would sit up in their beds. I wanted to scream at him; I wanted him to understand the bedlam of grief and rage and...and *abandonment* he'd left in his wake in Chrior. Yet I was terrified that if I did anything at all, he would disappear all over again.

"Let's see..." Zabriel mused in response to my silence. "I'm taller than you remember, and more muscled. And I'm a heck of a lot better-looking." He swept my thick auburn hair over my shoulder and winked. "That's it, isn't it? Come on, Anya, say something."

I stared at him, thinking of the things I needed to tell him but not knowing where to start. Then my mind skipped to the mutilation I had suffered. How would he react to it? Without conscious thought, I inched toward the back of the seat, hoping he wouldn't notice that I was different. I didn't know how or when I had come to be ashamed of what had been done to me, but my stomach was coated with humiliation.

"For years," I finally managed, "no one's known if you were even alive. And you think I care about your jawline?"

He peered at me through the shades of his eyelashes. "You can play that game all you like, but if I'd gotten uglier, I'd be hearing about it. Don't even try to deny it."

The urge to hit him for being so glib was formidable, but it couldn't overpower my desire to go along with him and pretend the past two years hadn't happened. After a brief, almost physical battle with myself, I hurtled into his arms. He grimaced, and I readjusted my position to put less pressure on his newly bruised ribs.

"I missed you, too," he said, still lighthearted, but I knew the moment of discovery would come, felt it arrive as he tucked his face into my hair, his hands curling into fists over the fabric where my wings should have been. His words became a whisper. "God, I'm so sorry."

At first, I didn't move, didn't acknowledge him; then I gave in and sank against him, willing to be weak in the circle of his arms. He and I both understood that silence could signify more gratitude than a thousand words of thanks, an embrace more support than a million promises. But most importantly, from my point of view, I determined that his wings were still there, the membrane, though shrouded, soft under my fingers.

An eternity later, he cupped my face in his hands and used his thumbs to wipe my cheeks clean of the tears that had appeared without my acquiescence or awareness.

"I'm okay," I assured him, taking his hands in mine, unwilling to dwell on the past, on years that had been lost and misfortunes that couldn't be reversed. Zabriel, the long-absent Prince of the Fae, was kneeling before me, and that meant the *future* could be planned. "I really am. But you could have chosen a better moment for your grand arrival."

I looked him up and down as he reclaimed the seat next to Shea and his smile drifted back into place. He was dressed in a fancy double-breasted coat, which I recalled from the wanted poster in Luka Ivanova's sitting room, and his boots folded down almost at the half, the butt of a pistol extending from one of them. He was tall and lean, and had shed the last vestiges of childish weight, revealing more angular features, as he'd so modestly proclaimed himself: sharp cheekbones, a rigid jaw, a mysterious brow. He was even handsomer than when I'd last seen him, the golden glow to his skin a testament to his health and vibrancy. I couldn't help thinking he'd done well by leaving Chrior.

"You may be right," he answered with a chuckle, then he shifted his gaze to Shea. "I do believe I've paid for my dramatic timing, though. Isn't that right, Smiley?"

"It's no more than you deserve," she retorted, not ready to forgive him for the scare he'd given us. "Where did you come from, anyway? Were you hanging on the back of the cab?"

"Of course. I'm surprised you didn't notice, since you seem to view yourself as quite the little soldier."

"I could kick you again, you know."

"Oh, let's not make a mess. The good man driving this cab has been so tolerant of our rumpus that I'd hate to have him cleaning you out of the grate."

Zabriel's hand played with the shiny hilt of the blade that was barely visible between his hip and the wall of the cab.

"Why don't we pause for introductions?" I interrupted, worried Shea might very well call his bluff. "Then if you'd still like to battle your way to harmony, you can go right ahead."

Though she sullenly dropped her chin, Shea nodded, while my cousin settled back with a smirk.

"Zabriel, this is Shea. She and her family helped me after I was hurt." My eyes met his, but I did not elaborate. The time for details would come later. "Shea, this is my infamous cousin, Zabriel, Prince of the Fae."

"Infamous—I like that." Zabriel stretched out his legs and

planted them on the seat between me and his hat, feet crossed at the ankles. Extending a hand to Shea, he offered, "Truce?"

She accepted his hand without making the requested promise, but he didn't seem perturbed by any ill will she might harbor toward him. Outside the carriage, the city proper was sprouting up, and gas lamps attached to posts cast halos on the still-active streets. Their consistent light unburdened our eyes, and Zabriel's mood shifted toward the serious.

"Now, Anya, before you launch into that interrogation you no doubt have planned, I need to make one stipulation. You won't like it. But I don't want to play any more games, and I'm hoping you feel the same."

His face had hardened, the walls I'd grown used to seeing about him before he'd left Chrior returning like the chill that deadened autumn leaves. He'd become royal and unassailable in the span of a single breath, shrouding his benevolence as easily as he did his wings.

"But first, let me set your mind at ease about Illumina. She's safe."

"Illumina?" My eyes widened and my pulse quickened. "You've seen her?"

"Yes," he confirmed with a dismissive wave of his hand. "I'm aware of everything that goes on in Sheness. She doesn't know my whereabouts, but I have people looking out for her. I figured she was looking for me once I saw her in the city, and assumed there might be more of you on the way. I asked Gwyneth to keep an eye open in Tairmor. She's a friend, if you hadn't guessed. When I learned *you* were on this side of the Bloody Road, I decided I could afford a conversation. But let me make myself clear. I'm not likely to be persuaded of anything, and I will *not* be forced."

This was the Zabriel I remembered all too well—defensive, aggressive, distrustful of his mother. He'd drawn his legs under him, his elbows upon his knees, one hand sealed around the opposite fist. He was daring me to say he had to come home regardless of his wishes, goading me into giving him the justification he needed to disappear again, clearly of the belief that there were more Fae, probably the Royal Blades, waiting to make him abide by the Queen's demands if he refused. But I'd never done anything to earn that cold glower, and indignation rose in my chest like a snake ready to strike.

"The last two years may have changed you, Zabriel, but they haven't affected me much. I wouldn't have tried to trick you then, and I wouldn't now. It's just Illumina and me, and in all honesty, I wasn't even supposed to come. Queen Ubiqua has no intent to force you." I took a deep breath and met his eyes, determined to keep my voice steady. "She's dying, Zabriel."

He stared at me for a few seconds, his expression unchanging. Then his gaze dropped to the grated floor. Though I wanted to reach out and offer some comfort, I sat stiffly by, awaiting his reaction, while Shea examined him with wary interest.

"She's dying," he repeated. "Of what?"

"I don't know. But she's certain. The Great Redwood predicted it."

For an instant, it felt like the whole world was holding its breath, then Zabriel's posture relaxed and he grinned. Appalled, I shifted farther away from him, his response hitting me like icy shrapnel. Shea's head swiveled back and forth between us, her jaw clenching and unclenching until finally she cracked.

"What is wrong with you? Didn't you hear right? Your mother is on her way to the grave!"

"Sorry, but the Great Redwood also predicted I would die on the Bloody Road. And yet...here I am." He slapped himself irreverently on the chest.

"Did Ubiqua tell you that?" I asked, dumbfounded. I'd only been told of the Great Redwood's age and wisdom, never that it had failed in a prediction.

"As a matter of fact I *did* get this news from the Queen herself, and I've been calling that tree the Great Deadwood ever since I danced across the boundary. But if my mother insists on perpetuating this nonsense, well, at least her funeral arrangements will be made early."

I gaped at him in horror, seeing all the features that were recognizable to me but not the Prince I'd known. He was flippant and sarcastic and talking blasphemously about things that were sacred in Fae lore. I wordlessly shook my head. Shea, ever more direct, spoke my thoughts out loud.

"That's just not right."

"Oh, come on now." Zabriel crossed his arms, and temper flared in his dark eyes, his brows poised at an angle every bit as sharp as his cheekbones. "My mother has no reason to believe the Redwood's prediction, if indeed the hollowed-out stump even made one. How about we try to be honest about her motivations? She expected me to have had my fun by now and come home, like any other Faerie on his Crossing. But I haven't, so she's doing whatever's necessary to get me to return so I can become the Prince of Interracial Relations that she conceived me to be."

It felt like he was spitting on me with every sacrilege that fell from his lips. I'd left my home and my family, journeyed across the Territory, risked my life, *lost my wings* to bring him this message, this joke-worthy message that he didn't think merited the breath I'd used to deliver it. And he justified himself by mocking the Queen I revered, the Queen I believed to be dying. Had I really at one time thought him compassionate and selfless? Had living in the human world changed him this much?

His expression dared me to lean forward and smack him, betraying his assumption about what I would want to do. But I wouldn't give him the satisfaction, although it looked as though Shea might do it for me.

"You really have been gone too long. You've managed to justify what you did by re-creating history, re-creating your mother into some manipulative shrew who only wants to use you. But the truth is, you're having fun playing the part of a filthy, murdering pirate because it's everything you weren't supposed to become. But there's one thing I already know about your life out here, Zabriel. You've created a court for yourself, complete with enemies, allies, a city, and a sea to rule. Whether in Sheness or in Chrior, you're a prince because that's the only thing you know how to be. The problem is you want it on your own terms. You want the perks without the responsibilities. You'd rather be a self-styled prince than a real one who helps people."

Zabriel regarded me with one brow raised, his thoughts unreadable, while Shea's normally cherubic face was lurid. Then he clapped, slowly and deliberately.

"That was quite a speech, Anya. My mother chose the right heir if she wants to be succeeded by herself." I had forgotten how deductive and observant he was, the remarkable way in which his mind accounted for his senses, processed details most people dismissed, and turned them into an arsenal. In this case, it was simple reason that had led him to the conclusion about

my appointment by the Queen. I saw Shea bristle on my behalf out of the corner of my eye as Zabriel went on listing my
faults. "Self-righteous, single-minded, pointing out flaws and
making it your business to fix them. In truth, not such a terrible set of traits for a ruler."

He leaned forward, his fingers twined, his eyes glinting at
me in the light from the gas lamps outside, and lowered his
chin without conceding our staring contest.

"I can even respect that, Anya. But I start to have a problem
when you come to *my* city and try to tell me what to do with
my life. You think right from wrong is a single, straight-edged
standard, defined by your ideals. Here's the truth, and trust
me when I say I'm giving it to you gently. I don't give a damn
about your standards, and neither does most of the world. Just
because *you* believe in something doesn't mean it's going to
happen, or even that it should happen. Right and wrong don't
exist—not in the way you see them. They are relative con-
cepts, not absolutes. Tell me, who cared about Thatcher More's
personal moral code when he angered the people in power?"

"How did you—" Shea started, but Zabriel cut her off, still
addressing me.

"Who cared about your values when your wings were cut
off? Who gave a thought to the upbringing and beliefs of that
kid in Tairmor whose father was executed while he stood
helplessly by? Preaching and judging are the habits of people
who haven't *lived,* Anya. So you shouldn't begin your effort
to convince me you know best by proving that you have no
idea what the world is really like."

My thoughts spun, and I grappled for a response, but Zabriel
didn't wait for one. He swiped his hat up from the bench, pre-

paring to depart, then held up a hand, sighing as though with a pang of apology.

"Here's another truth, Anya. You may view me as a disgrace, but in my mind, I'm exactly what I'm supposed to be. And for the record, I haven't abandoned the Fae. On the contrary, I'm doing everything I can for them. Just not the way you'd like."

He locked eyes upon me, and in that moment I realized he *was* pained—maybe a victim of his own cynicism, definitely of his own impulsive mouth. Ubiqua's scolding voice rang in my head: *Irresponsible. Self-indulgent. Childish. You're too intelligent to be that thoughtless, Zabriel. You'll destroy someone with your words someday.*

He could have been reliving the same memory, in any of its myriad incarnations, but I would never know. With a crooked half smile, my cousin swung the door of the hansom open and hopped onto the street without thought to its movement. I scrambled across the seat and stuck my head out the window, not wanting to lose track of him, but he was gone.

"Well, he's precious," Shea said, shocked. "Are you certain he's what the Fae need?"

"He's the Queen's son." I shrugged, not meeting her eyes. I didn't want her to see the doubts that were stirring in my heart and creeping over my hopes like poison vines. "There is no one else."

Shea's piercing gaze told me she suspected I wasn't telling her everything, but she didn't press further. We rode in silence the rest of the way to the inn. The encounter with Zabriel felt like a raw sore in my gut, and I was terrified I'd seen the last of him. He hadn't wanted to hear anything I'd said about Ubiqua, about the need for him to leave Sheness, about the Faerie crown. But without him, Chrior could have a fourteen-year-old queen, and a second, perhaps even more violent, war with the humans. While changing his mind and his attitude might be difficult, the Faerie people still needed Zabriel, the only Prince of the Fae in our world. I also couldn't help but think that, regardless of his protestations, he needed us.

chapter twenty-two

PIRATE HEAVEN

Despite the warmth and luxuriousness of our second-floor room at the lodging house—the best Dementya money could buy, with its separate beds, private bathroom, and large windows overlooking the street—I couldn't relax and enjoy myself. Shea tried once to provide a modicum of hope for my Realm by inquiring after Illumina's qualifications for the throne, but I gave her a short summary of my younger cousin's naïveté and inexperience and left it at that.

I couldn't believe it had come down to Illumina. I wouldn't, not without significantly more convincing. But even with this prospect sneaking nearer, I was relieved by Zabriel's promise that she was all right, that he had *people* looking out for her. Whatever else was the case, no one was dead, and I truly did want Illumina safe. But what sorts of people might those be? I grimaced, imagining the sordid folks Zabriel might be associating with these days. Before I made any other plans, I needed to find my younger cousin. That was something I could manage, something on which to focus in this miasma of worries.

It was strange to think of Chrior as all the way on the other side of the Warckum Territory, enclosed by miles of protective woods. The Faerie Realm seemed like a cradle from which

I'd been thrown like a baby bird before I was ready. Zabriel had left willingly when he'd been younger than I was. Whatever reassurances I could conjure about our earlier exchange, no level of dramatic inclination attributable to his character could belittle that reality.

I struggled to sleep that night, at some point falling into a shallow slumber, only to be awakened by the sounds of Shea moving around the room. I sat up, squinting in the morning sunshine pouring through the window, my eyes as tired and dry as if I'd propped them open all night. She was already dressed and standing in front of the mirror, combing her fingers through her hair, and I tumbled out of bed and over to my pack on the floor. There was a note, rolled and tied, on top of it, and I held it out to my roommate as I rummaged for clothes.

"Is this yours?"

"No, never seen it before." Shea's curiosity engaged, she came to my side.

I tugged at the knot, and a tiny rock fell into my hand. Frowning, I fingered the rough stone, which glittered like gold. Realizing it was pyrite, I unfurled the parchment to scan the scrawled message.

Take Leo Dementya up on his offer.
Ask him about the island.

"Did Zabriel stop by this morning?" I asked, extending the note and fool's gold to Shea. "This rock has to be his signature."

"No, I haven't seen him." She glanced around, her forehead puckered. "He couldn't have been in here, could he? Because that would be awfully creepy."

The particles of dust floating in the mellow air probably made more noise on landing than Zabriel did. I chuckled but tried to be matter-of-fact in my explanation to Shea, lest I double her suspicion of my cousin.

"Stealth is part of his nature. Faefolk move more quickly and quietly than humans, not that you can judge it by me. I'm just relieved I didn't chase him away completely."

"Because you told him off?"

Abandoning her efforts to tame her tangled sable hair, Shea yanked it back, imprisoning it in a bun on the back of her head with her frayed blue ribbon. I knew her irritation with Zabriel had returned when she snatched the end of her coverlet and violently threw it over her mattress so that it resembled a made bed.

"Anya, he deserved it. From where I was sitting, it's way past time somebody told him he's not God. He's obviously been living under a false impression." At my uncomfortable silence, she modulated her hostile tone. "Does his sneaking in and out mean he won't contact us in person anymore?"

"I don't know what his intentions are, but he's going to have to see us because I'm not leaving him a note with the information we gather."

I dressed, then Shea and I went downstairs in search of breakfast. We'd barely set foot in the lobby when the clerk behind the register desk pointed us out to a man waiting nearby. As I apprehensively considered who might be interested in us, Shea took several steps back, her body poised for flight. I couldn't blame her, though the fellow who approached did not look threatening in the least. He was dressed fashionably but understatedly, so he would neither negatively nor positively

stand out in pleasant company, and he clutched an envelope
in one pudgy hand.

"From Mr. Dementya, miss," he said with a slight bow, extending the item to me.

I accepted the envelope with a relieved smile and tore it
open, quickly reading the note it contained. As Leo had suggested yesterday, he wished to take Shea and me to his shipyard.
Given Zabriel's correspondence, I had to assume Gwyneth had
told him the invitation would be forthcoming. But what island
had my cousin referenced?

The servant interrupted my ruminations. "Pardon me, miss.
I was instructed to await an answer."

"Of course." Tucking the note inside my jerkin, I hastened
to the desk for paper and a quill. I wrote a short but polite response indicating Shea and I would be honored to accompany
Mr. Dementya, then gave it to the servant, who departed with
a second bow.

"What was that about?" Shea asked, expression puzzled.

"Dementya will be sending someone for us at ten o'clock.
I figure we may as well do what Zabriel wants."

"Why not? We've got nothing else to go on."

After a bite to eat, we returned to our room to don the
cloaks Gwyneth had given us. On the coastline it would be
cold, despite the late winter sun. I suddenly felt fidgety, aware
that the spring solstice would before long be upon us. I'd asked
Davic for three months of freedom from contact through our
promise bond, and the two-and-a-half-month mark had arrived. I didn't know what to expect when the deadline was
reached. He would realize our bond was gone. He might think
I was dead. Why hadn't I sent a messenger from Tairmor to
spare him that fear? I wished for a way to reassure him and

yet keep him in the dark about my injury until I could meet him at the Road, but there was nothing for it now. I was on the other side of the continent.

"They're here," I announced, looking out the window and spotting a shiny black hansom with perfectly paired black horses pulling to a stop in front of the lodging house. Shea buttoned her coat over her pistol and bullet belt, then pulled her new cloak closed for good measure. At her nod, we headed on our way.

When we emerged from the inn, the driver of the cab hopped to the ground and opened the side door for us. Inside sat Gwyneth, wearing a dress and matching hat in a royal shade of purple, and her father, who stood as best he could inside the coach, unwilling to forgo his manners despite the cramped space.

"Ladies," he greeted us, retaking his seat only after Shea and I had settled ourselves on the bench opposite him and his daughter. "What lovely cloaks."

I returned a courteous thank-you for the compliment, then peered out the window at the grimy port city while Shea talked a bit with Leo and Gwyneth. There was too much traffic in Sheness for there to be hope of keeping the streets clean, and factory smoke clung to everything it touched. The artwork that adorned the sides of many of the buildings, which I'd noticed the previous day, appeared to be noncommissioned, uninhibited in style and taste and, in some cases, message. Anarchism was a popular theme among the talented street painters of Sheness. Foreign tongues, Bennighe plus others I couldn't identify, floated around us like colors completely new. People snapped at one another and were downright rude more often than not; there was none of the finesse of Tairmor in this place.

At length we reached the Dementya shipyard—a series of docks that could have constituted their own bay—and alighted from the carriage. The icy water kicked up a scent that was fresh despite the putrid underdraft of fish. The smells combined into a unique odor that was neither pleasant nor unpleasant, much like the cattle scent that surrounded Strong. For some, the docks smelled like home. Judging from the gleam in Leo Dementya's eyes as he escorted us through the maze of crates being loaded and unloaded from his towering black-and-gold-painted ships, he was to be counted among their number. He was thoroughly at ease, strutting through his kingdom, pointing out the tasks being undertaken by his worker bees as they nodded and called him *sir,* the constant bustle at times making it difficult to hear him. Gwyneth, on the other hand, looked uncomfortable, waving a large purple fan in front of her pinched face. It wasn't warm, so her purpose had to be to ward off the smell.

Before long we approached a schooner. Its shadow loomed over us, although it was smaller than most of the vessels in the yard. Its gangplank was lowered, and men scurried about on deck. It didn't take many to operate the sailing ship, which was designed for fishing rather than cargo. I glanced at Leo, for the schooner looked ready to make way.

"All aboard, ladies," he said with a magnanimous smile, gesturing up the ramp.

I hesitantly led the way, Shea behind me, then we waited for Gwyneth and our host to board. With one hand on her father's arm, the other lifting the hem of her skirt, she looked delicate and helpless, like the sun might be too rough on her skin.

Once we were all on deck, Leo showed us the bowsprit, and the mainsails and topsails, listing off the schooner's attributes in the manner of a boasting parent. For an instant, I understood Zabriel's weakness for this life. It was bold, almost primal in its challenge, an alternate world where nothing existed except the sea, and man's only mission was to dominate it. I instinctively knew it could grip a person like an addiction.

We gathered along the railing as Dementya sailors saw us out of the harbor, and I watched the shore drift away, tuning out our host's impassioned voice. The rocking of the vessel had my heart pounding, and I couldn't bear to glance over the edge at the froth we were creating as we cut through the ocean at great speed. The serenity I'd found with regard to the ocean on the day we'd arrived in Sheness hadn't been permanent, and my stomach gave a subtle lift like I might toss my breakfast. It wouldn't be long before we were too far from land for me to swim to the docks if something went wrong. I gripped the balustrade, trying to resign myself to the fact that I could drown out here, a fatalistic approach the only one that might permit me some enjoyment on this excursion.

To my surprise, I heard Shea laughing with Leo, her guard dropped, and I was glad that one of us was exhilarated by the outing. Gwyneth stepped up beside me, increasing my discomfort even more. Despite her kindness and her connection to Zabriel, I still didn't like or trust her.

"Not a seafarer?" Gwyneth asked, resting her elbows on the carved wood, a tease in her voice that made my skin itch.

"I didn't come to Sheness to tour around in your little boats," I retorted, nerves overpowering my manners.

"I know why you're here."

I cocked an eyebrow, waiting for her to elaborate as the brisk, salty air annoyingly tugged strands of my auburn hair loose from my ponytail. Zabriel must have told her a thing or two about me. Gwyneth sighed, wispy curls breaking free from beneath her pinned hat, the faraway look on her face granting her the appearance of a mythical siren instead of a victim of the wind. This was also annoying. Her beauty was unparalleled, her amber eyes insightful as they rested on me.

"I know his real name, Anya. Doesn't that mean anything to you?"

Her words troubled me. Legend, law, and probably most of Zabriel's acquaintances in the Warckum Territory knew him as William Wolfram Pyrite. Why had he revealed his true identity to Gwyneth?

"We met by accident," she resumed, barely audible over the rush of water and the whipping of the schooner's sails. "This may come as a shock to you, but my father's business isn't always a shining emblem for ethics. I won't bore you with the reasons I oppose certain of his practices, but suffice it to say, Zabriel and I ended up running in similar circles. And once I recognized him as Fae, he wasn't able to ignore me."

"How did you find out?" I hedged. Zabriel would have been careful to conceal his heritage and to shroud his wings.

Gwyneth smiled, the corners of her claret lips dimpling her cheeks. "Because I can *see*. Do you understand what that means? That's why Zabriel and I trust each other. My skills are in high demand among a certain class of people, and I need to avoid those people as much as he does. My own father doesn't know of my talent. So your cousin and I keep each other's secrets, and in return, there are no secrets between us."

"You can see magic, and you help Zabriel rob your father?"

"Say that a little louder, why don't you?" Gwyneth looked over her shoulder at her father, though there was little risk of being overheard as far as I could tell. Leo was still sharing the experience of the open sea with Shea. "I give Zabriel pieces of information here and there. Deals that were going to hurt hundreds of people might have gone through without his intervention."

"So he's a hero, is that it? Because the men on the riverboat were calling him a demon. How many people have been hurt *because* of his intervention? He's a thief, and apparently he's been involved in a few deaths. I'm sure he's convinced himself and everyone else of his noble intentions, but you may as well save your breath with me, Gwyneth. There are other ways to accomplish what he's doing, and the romance of being a pirate won't impress me. I'm not about to be persuaded that this is the life he ought to be leading."

"Zabriel told me you were stubborn." She laughed, clamping a hand over her hat to keep it in place. "Well, don't forget that he is, too. The only difference is that you're a natural politician and he's a man of action. Right now he has a name for himself and a platform he can manipulate to his advantage. His reputation is overblown, which you've probably guessed, but having every act of piracy on this coast blamed on him gives him quite a mystique. You're not just going to drag him away from this."

Shouts from the sailors drew Gwyneth's attention, and she would have let this be the end of our conversation, but I grabbed the fine, crimped fabric of her upper sleeve and brought her back around. Indignation flashed in her eyes, and she laid a hand over mine, warning me to let go. I matched her resolve with my own, refusing to budge.

"I have to see him soon, Gwyneth. Not on his time. There are more factors at play than he knows about. It's obvious that you can get in touch with him, so do it. Right away."

The tension lasted another moment, then we released each other. To my consternation, she offered me an expansive smile. I couldn't tell if it was sincere or for the benefit of those who might have noticed our power struggle.

"I respect you, Anya. You know what you want and you go after it, to hell with the obstacles in your path. But what you or I want isn't going to matter. Zabriel will make up his own mind."

She gazed out over the water once more, and I watched the way she leaned into the blue of the ocean and the sky, thinking she belonged at the helm of the ship rather than on its deck.

"Look out there."

Gwyneth pointed into the distance with one hand, hanging on to her hat with the other. I followed her finger and saw a mountainous isle covered with trees and grass just starting to come to life after the winter. The schooner gave it a wide berth, and I recalled Zabriel's note. *Ask about the island.*

Pushing away from the railing, I scurried to join Shea and Leo. He was allowing her to control the helm, and she was giggling as though they were father and daughter. It was a sweet sight—she looked genuinely happy, and he seemed delighted at having someone to teach about sailing. Either Gwyneth had already learned her fill about seafaring or she'd duped him into believing she had no interest in his pursuits.

"What is that place?" I asked, indicating the island, and the enthusiasm in Leo's face waned. Perhaps the topic was of little interest to him, but with Zabriel's hint in mind, I listened for anything of significance in his reply.

"That's Evernook Island. I'd take us closer, but the tides in that area are unpredictable. There's not much to see, anyway. It's little more than a chunk of rock that's government owned for the public's safety. As far as I know, its only value is for military warehousing."

I squinted across the expanse of water between the schooner and the island, trying to see through the still, leafless trees to the heart of the small mountain. There was something built into the side—a gray structure that melted into the stone.

"Is that a warehouse, then?"

But Leo Dementya was no longer paying heed to me. He was instructing his men to bring the schooner about and return us to the shipyard. We'd been off land for almost three hours, and dinnertime would soon be upon us. I kept my eyes on Evernook, remembering what Evangeline had said about the constant ebb and flow of water she'd heard during her imprisonment. Waves crashed against its cliffsides, and there was something about the way that gray tower glared at me that was ominous. I was willing to blame my imagination for the feeling, although there was another possibility. Maybe Zabriel knew more about what was happening in the Warckum Territory than I'd given him a chance to admit.

As we were preparing to leave the Dementya Estate that evening, having again been invited to dine, Gwyneth beckoned me aside. Shea and I were standing with her in the massive entryway, waiting for the butler to fetch our cloaks.

"Try The Paladin," she murmured in my ear. "I only see him when he wants me to, but he spends time there. It's a sailor's pub."

An image of Zabriel at celebrations in the Great Redwood, smiling and laughing, capturing everyone's attention, flashed in my brain. Then I grimaced, trying to factor drunken sailors into that scenario. I hadn't enjoyed my experiences in pubs thus far on this journey. Despite this, I nodded my thanks to Gwyneth and walked with Shea to the cab that awaited us. With little time left in the day, I instructed the driver to take us to the shorefront rather than the lodge where we were staying.

Shea had, of course, seen Gwyneth whisper to me in the entry. Astute enough to figure things out, she didn't inquire as to the reason we were going off course.

"In what seedy corner of the world are we supposed to meet Zabriel tonight?" she asked when we entered the city, the cab clattering across the cobblestone streets.

"A place called The Paladin. If it helps, I don't think he's expecting us. We may get to surprise him for a change, unless he and Gwyneth have some sort of psychic connection."

Shea smirked, obviously pleased by this notion. Her resentment toward my cousin for his stunt in the carriage had not yet abated, not that I could blame her. He'd scared the life out of us both, and in light of her close call with Luka Ivanova in Tairmor, Shea was especially jumpy.

The shorefront never slept—we passed scores of drunkards stumbling out of questionable establishments along the miles of harbor, along with an equal number of men in crisp, clean uniforms. They weren't Constabularies like Tom Matlock and Marcus Farrier, but captains and lieutenants representing various shipping companies and military endeavors. Despite the hour, the area was brightly lit by lanterns, permitting deckhands ranging in age from nine or ten to their ripe forties to scurry unceasingly up and down shadowy gangplanks, loading crates and preparing their ships for duty.

Our cab slowed to a stop in front of a ramshackle building that appeared to have had its foundation washed away and rebuilt four or five times. Nothing had been done to disguise the evidence of attempted sustainability—I could see a black and charred stone base, topped by a gray stone base, topped by sandbags and logs, as though beginning fresh had never occurred to the owners. Malformed steps compensated for the pub's lack of parallelism to the ground, and a line of eager drinkers spilled from the entrance and down the street. A sign hung at a slant over the arch of the door, barely illuminated by the nearest gas lamp, and I squinted to bring it into focus as I stepped out of the coach. It read The Paladin, and I felt a twinge of anxiety that this was the right place.

"Ready when you are," Shea muttered, stepping down beside me. The door of the establishment was propped open, and she gestured toward it, looking as if she was about to swallow bitter medicine. I nodded, and with a deep breath each, we fought our way to the front of the rabble to enter.

The stench of alcohol, sweat, and halitosis that hit us when we crossed the threshold was gag inducing. The open front door was probably the only thing keeping heat and odor from suffocating The Paladin's patrons, though they shouted and laughed like they were in paradise. There was no line of sight through the crowd, and Shea and I clutched each other's sleeves so we wouldn't be separated on our way to the serving counter. My green eyes and auburn hair, together with Shea's striking dark gaze, made us stand out in this crowd like diamonds amid coal. I wished I'd thought to remove our luxurious Dementya cloaks, yet another reason we'd draw attention, before we'd ventured among these lowlifes.

We didn't get far before male voices caterwauled in our direction. I looked around to see a group of grungy sailors raising their mugs in salute and gesturing for us to join them. They were disgustingly drunk, and one stood on his chair to throw his hand down the front of his trousers, apparently expecting us to be flattered or enticed by the gesture. Furious and embarrassed, I again felt helpless in my own body. Were I still Fae, I could have spilled his drink, making him slip and crash to the floor, shoving the embarrassment he'd forced upon me back down his throat. But the only statement I could make while staying safe was to walk away. And although that decision should have been empowerment enough, the knowledge that it wouldn't make him respect me gnawed away at my dignity.

Feeling a rough tug on my arm, followed by a release, I spun to see what had become of Shea. A grimy, stubble-cheeked sailor had grabbed her from behind, arms snug around her waist, face brushing against her hair. I could smell his breath from several feet away.

"How 'bout a kiss, missy?" he chortled, as though he were perfectly within his rights to be holding her. "Then we'll see where the evenin' takes us."

I went for my long-knife, wondering about The Paladin's policies on killing its customers, but before I could make any other move, Shea slammed the heel of her boot down on the man's foot. He let go of her, yowling in pain.

"Call that the climax of our evening," she seethed, backing away. She surveyed the crowd, perhaps fearful of its response, only to be greeted by raucous laughter. Then the men and scantily dressed women between us and the bar gave way, the sailors removing their hats and nodding as we walked past.

The woman swilling drinks was middle-aged, with a sour expression that told us she didn't appreciate the diversity we brought to her clientele. Nevertheless, she was willing to serve us, drying out a couple of mugs before slamming them down on the bar.

"What'll it be?" she grumbled.

"Something strong," I replied, wanting to sound tough but not having any idea what the pub served.

The woman smirked crookedly and turned to Shea. "You?"

"It would be best if I can see straight." She folded back the corner of her coat to reveal the shine of her pistol, her words heavy with the implication that we intended to cause trouble. I prayed the woman wouldn't take her seriously. Shea was too bold—or too shaken—to realize that flaunting her gun might provoke more problems than it would prevent.

"It'll be best if we're just left alone," I clarified. "We're not here to make friends *or* enemies."

The barmaid's distrustful eyes flickered over us as she sloshed together my drink, then she pushed the mug toward me. I picked up the tankard, and we shuffled through the crowd to a table left of the counter, which offered a decent view of the room. It also positioned us to see anyone who came to the bar.

We watched the endless train of patrons come and go, feeling like pieces of fancy furniture stuck in the corner, off-limits and unapproachable. There wasn't a boring person in the place, but as far as I could tell, Zabriel wasn't among them. I tried one sip of the drink I'd been given and put it down before it could do the same to me. I'd definitely been given what I'd ordered.

A man approached the counter, his swagger drawing a multitude of stares. His weathered face was framed by an impressive hat that would have protected his skin on the deck of a ship, and he wore a brass-buttoned coat that reached his knees, from which observations I determined he was a seaman. Not a mere sailor, though—he stood straight and tall, shoulders back, his bearing that of a man in charge, and greeted the woman tending bar with a familiarity that suggested he was a regular. The two of them chatted comfortably, then their expressions grew serious and she nodded toward someone on the opposite side of the pub from us. I craned my neck to figure out who they were discussing, and the seaman's gaze fell on me. My efforts to determine the object of his attention had been enough to draw that attention. With a flush, I met his off-putting mismatched eyes, afraid to consider what conclusions he may have drawn. Almost as though our silent exchange had been an accident, the moment passed.

"Anya." Shea's tone was urgent, and she pointed across the tavern in the direction that was of interest to the pair at the bar, her eyes fixed on a familiar face.

"Mother of Nature," I breathed, sinking farther into my seat, though the likelihood of our theatrically styled acquaintance noticing us was negligible. He sat at a table of his own, his cane leaning against the chair beside him. His suspenders were in place, his lids lined even more thickly than usual; he lacked only the top hat Shea had smashed in Oaray. He spoke with charming ease to someone I couldn't see, hands gliding like the wings of a bird in flight. He was cleaner than the last time we'd seen him, better kept, so perhaps he'd slipped away from his keeper for good. I searched the vicinity for Hastings, but there was no sign of the bald-headed man who had made an attempt on our lives in the Fere.

As my panic dissipated, questions surfaced in my mind, only to quickly scatter when a waitress throwing tankards and tumblers onto a tray moved aside to reveal the person sitting across from our suspendered acquaintance. Though her face was turned away from me, her slim stature—even slighter than Spex's—and long, lank black hair were instantly recognizable. She was relaxed, her tiny frame shaking with laughter, but I feared he would soon identify her as Fae, if he hadn't already done so. With or without Hastings, I didn't trust Spex's record with regard to my people. What was in the cup she was holding?

I sprang out of my seat and barreled across the room, jostling many of The Paladin's customers and spilling a few drinks. I didn't care. Spex was not going to hurt my cousin. He was not going to sell out Illumina to his masters and land her in the Fae-mily Home—or worse, in a grave next to Evangeline.

Shea clamored after me, but she wasn't fast enough to stop me from snatching Spex's collar. In one smooth motion, I yanked him to his feet and hurled him against the wall. There was a *crack* as his head collided with the wood, and he winced, one hand going to assess the welt.

"What's your problem, *seonnha?* Are you crazy?" he demanded, then recognition dawned and he rolled his hazel eyes. "Oh. It's you. Question answered."

"That friend of mine you identified?" I hissed, glaring down at him. "She's dead. You killed her. I don't care what Hastings is holding over your head—you stop this. No more, do you hear me?"

Most of the pub was watching us, though my words were likely lost in the general chaos of the place. Still, Illumina's sweet, high-pitched voice rang out my name, while Shea vied just as desperately for my attention, the two of them creating a chorus of "Anyas" at my back. But it wasn't my cousin or my travel partner who separated me from Spex. No, neither of them could have picked me completely off my feet with one hand while pinning my adversary to the wall with the other.

"Enough," the man growled, and I could feel the word vibrating deep within his chest, the support of his body the sole force preventing my collar from choking the life out of me. "I came here to have a quiet drink, and you two are ruining my evening."

I was certain no one came to The Paladin for a quiet drink, but I didn't think arguing the point would endear me to him.

"Outside, now," he ordered, setting me on my feet. My mind whirred as my eyes landed on the brass buttons of his coat, then he guided Spex and me to the door with his hands on the backs of our necks. While I didn't know what he had in mind for us, I knew I was vulnerable to a man who had shown an interest in me that had nothing to do with disrupting his plans for the night.

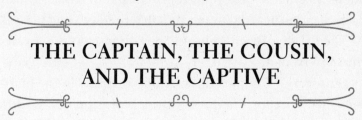

chapter twenty-three

THE CAPTAIN, THE COUSIN, AND THE CAPTIVE

The seaman hauled both Spex and me into the street, The Paladin's milling patrons parting to create a path. I saw apprehension and respect in their eyes, and alarm shot through me. What kind of man did it take to earn the respect of a drunken horde like this one? And did he just want us to leave? Or did he have a nasty fate in store for us?

I would have taken off running as soon as he shoved me forward had I not been worried about the fate of my cousin and my friend. From other nearby pubs, a slew of grungy men had emerged to form a circle around us. Unfortunately, it looked as though our captor had plenty of friends. Spex and I drew closer together, the threat we faced transforming us into allies. My eyes darted around, searching for options, but I could see no way out. I hoped Spex was tougher than he looked.

In the background, Shea and Illumina tumbled through The Paladin's doors, wide-eyed and terrified. My stomach lurched and cramped, and I clutched at it, fighting the urge to double over. Would their involvement in this mess make things better or worse? While Shea's pistol could come in handy if things turned ugly, Illumina would have to rely on her elemental connection in order to help us. Making it known that she was Fae could be more disastrous than the current situation. Meeting Shea's eyes, I raised a hand to tell her to stay back, and she tugged Illumina into the shadows along the wall of The Paladin. Bracing against Spex's back, I forced my dry throat to swallow.

"I'm sorry," I mumbled, watching the man in the brass-buttoned coat for his reaction, the words bubbling forth without much thought. His arms were crossed, and the expression on his leathery face didn't change, offering no encouragement. "I had a bit to drink, but no harm's been done. My friends and I will just clear out of here." I took a deep breath and attempted a smile. "And to show there are no hard feelings, I'll pay for a round of your favorite poison. Fair enough?"

The seaman, finally showing signs of life, adjusted his wide-brimmed hat, considering me with heavy brows that overhung his unusual eyes, one blue, the other brown.

"You had one taste of a very poor drink," he rumbled. "I've seen some lightweights in my time, but none that light."

Spex gritted his teeth and stepped forward, while I suppressed the instinct to pull him back to our defensive position.

"What do you want from us? Money? We have little, but are willing to turn it over to avoid trouble."

"I want you to shut up. You think I don't know why you're here, what you are?" The words were a growl, and the man made a broad sweep with his arm, beckoning a few of his associates forward. "Get him out of here, boys. Before I do something he'll regret."

"You wouldn't dare, Fane!"

The shout rang out from a doorway behind us, and a man

of a different sort burst into the circle before anyone could lay a hand on Spex. He was taller than average, albeit shorter than the seaman who had dragged us into the street. There was a scar across his nose that disappeared into the deep lines etched on either side of his mouth, but the scowl he wore was more imposing than any battle wound. Burly, but without a noticeable ounce of fat, he was laden with weapons. Knives of myriad shapes and sizes protruded from his boots and were sheathed at his hips, while pistols lay snug in holsters that criss-crossed his chest and bullets shone like studs in the leather. His clothing was better tailored and in better condition than that of the sailors, and his face lacked the color and weathering of those who made their living on the sea. A band tied around his head restrained red hair that was longer than was typical or practical. He pointed at the spotter, eyes never leaving the man he had called Fane.

"The boy is *mine*."

"That makes this even more satisfying."

Fane snapped his fingers, and two of his men stepped forward to grasp Spex under the arms. The spotter managed to elbow one of them in the diaphragm, though all he got for his trouble was a cruel wrench to his arm.

The newcomer snarled like an animal. "I'm warning you, Captain. You don't want to interfere with this one. I'm not playing with amateurs."

"If your benefactors aren't amateurs, then why did they hire one?" Fane scratched the scruff on his cheek, studying his adversary. "Look at it this way, Opal. I'm making a simple point. It's nothing personal, and it'll be to your advantage if you take a lesson away from this. Just look 'round. You're outnumbered, you always will be, and when you stick your dirty fingers in my pie, things get lost in the crossfire." Turning to his men, he finished, "Why is that lad still within my sight? Go on and get him out of here."

Spex spat on the ground at Fane's feet before he was dragged, kicking and yelling, down the street.

Opal watched the scene with dead eyes and a jaw so tight his teeth had to be grinding their counterparts into powder. But instead of pursuing the sailors, he shook his fist at the captain, for so he had addressed Fane, the fingers of his other hand dancing between the hilts of several daggers as though perusing his options.

"You'll regret this, and soon," he vowed. "Mark my words."

Whoever Opal was, he stormed off, thinking better of an attack. I watched him disappear in one direction, Spex in the other, my breath coming fast. What lay in store for the young man who'd just been traded off like spoils of war?

I already knew that Opal was not the kind of man I wanted on my tail, but his threat didn't seem to bother Fane, making me wonder what danger I now faced. I poised my body, preparing to spring. I could reach my long-knife quicker than anyone could get to me, and Shea had her pistol. Big hat or no, I wasn't going to let the man in the brass-buttoned coat send me anywhere.

I eyed the captain as he moved toward me, trying to intimidate me. Shea darted out from the shadows, her mouth pressed into a grim line and her hand inside her coat, resting on the butt of her gun. Illumina followed a couple of paces behind. Sweat trickled down my neck—we three were about to have a knockdown fight against incredible odds. But before drastic action could be taken, the man swept his hat from his head in an exaggerated bow.

"Relax," he said with a chuckle, his demeanor transform-ing from that of a strict, unassailable leader to the easy posture of a mate. "One of those lightweights I mentioned before is your cousin Pyrite." He held out his hand. "Captain Fane, at your service."

I wobbled, struggling against both the light-headedness that signaled a faint and my mounting fury. Was it sport to Zabriel and his friends to terrify us? Calling upon every shred of de-cency instilled in me by my royal upbringing, I plastered a po-lite smile on my face and prepared to make peace. After all, I'd wanted to be out of danger, and I'd gotten my wish. But Shea stepped in front of me, exhibiting her usual amount of self-control.

"You couldn't have introduced yourself ten minutes ago?" she castigated, slapping down Fane's outstretched hand. "You people are so goddamn dramatic. Either take us to Pyrite or get out of our way."

For a moment, silence greeted Shea's outburst, then the crowd around us erupted in laughter.

"I like this one," Fane announced, surveying his men. "But lads, the excitement's over for the night. Time to be on your way."

The sailors dispersed, shaking their heads and chuckling, and the captain motioned us down the street, whistling to himself in a self-satisfied fashion. The sound was strangely beautiful, especially in light of the tension of the past moments. Tingling with both excitement and relief, I grabbed Illumina's arm, un-able to believe she was actually with me.

"What happened to you?" I breathed, letting Shea and the captain move ahead of us.

"I'm where I should be," she smugly responded, looking

me over, her malachite eyes wide and curious. "You're supposed to be in Chrior with Aunt. Did she send you after me?"

I shook my head, zeal faltering as memories of my injury crashed down on me; then I fortified myself for the coming revelation. Illumina needed to know what had happened to me, but I didn't have to live through it again—I could dissociate from her response, just disappear behind the barricade in my mind.

"I left against her desires, Illumina. I was worried about you. But listen, I—" My voice broke, my barricade cracking and crumbling, and I took a shuddering breath to recover. "I can't go back to Chrior. Not ever."

The ache in my tone delivered my message without the need for further words. Illumina had always been sharp, and she peered carefully at me, lips parted slightly, their pinkness setting off the pallor of her skin. Her face was devoid of emotion, and yet she looked sick, as though a poison was roiling beneath her skin. There was a second—a split second—during which I couldn't tell if that sickness was empathy or judgment. Then she broke her silence, chasing away my misgivings.

"Nature, Anya," she murmured, shaking her head, her hair moving in flat ripples under her chin. Her face was thinner, her cheekbones more defined, with shadows beneath her eyes. Her travels in the human world could not have been easy. "What are you going to do?"

"I've already told Zabriel," I replied without thinking, intending to shift focus from my tragedy to the reason all of us were here.

Illumina's jaw tightened and her spine stiffened, her body language revealing that the Prince hadn't bothered to contact her.

"You've seen Zabriel?"

"He found me," I clarified, not wanting her to feel she had failed in her mission. "Found you, too. He said he had people looking out for you—probably our escort and his men."

I gestured discreetly to Fane, who was still whistling, swinging his feet out in a little jig as he walked to go along with his music. He'd shown no interest in our conversation, but despite his nonchalant manner, I doubted he was indifferent to the arrival of William Wolfram Pyrite's extended family. Shea was watching him like a mother bear eyeing a wolf, so I didn't concern myself with him. She'd alert me if he did anything threatening.

"I would have found him, you know," Illumina asserted, staring straight ahead without blinking. "Zabriel's not as clever as he thinks he is."

"He does think he's pretty clever," I acknowledged, hoping to bring a little humor to the conversation. Illumina's dispassionate delivery was more suited to someone tracking an animal than to a person close to reconnecting with a long-lost family member.

She continued without acknowledging she had heard me. "That fellow in the pub was going to help me find him."

I stopped walking, the color going out of my face. "You told Spex about Zabriel?"

"No," Illumina scoffed. "Of course I didn't. I'm not stupid, Anya."

"I never said you were."

She sighed and halted, the wind playing with her hair, letting it rise and fall in wisps and sheets. Confused, I met her gaze.

"I'm sorry for being rude," she said, her voice softer, less challenging. "It's just been a difficult couple of months. But I wasn't going to tell the spotter—Spex—about Zabriel. I was only going to use him."

I cringed at her word choice, though it didn't make sense for me to care about Spex. Still, his forced presence at the execution was close to the surface of my memory. Did anyone ever look at him without trying to figure out how to use him? Not wanting to dwell on the thought, I resumed walking before Fane could notice we'd stopped.

"You're working with humans now?" I asked, wondering if Illumina's experiences in the Territory were opening her mind. Was this what Queen Ubiqua had intended when she'd set my younger cousin this task?

Illumina gave a high-pitched giggle that drew questioning glances from Fane and Shea, and she looked so giddy I thought she would clap her hands together. In the next instant, her expression had cleared, with no transition. Perplexed, I wondered if she had forgotten what she had found humorous.

Her composure regained, Illumina leaned close to me. "Using the spotter isn't the same as working with him."

I gazed into her eyes, which were but inches from my face. The perimeters of her irises were almost black, emerald saturation creeping in across the distance to her pupils. Sometimes dead like stagnant water, other times vibrant like Nature itself, my cousin's eyes were as variable as the rest of her.

"If you know what Spex is, why would you risk talking to him?"

Illumina shrugged. "I was willing to take the chance that he wasn't interested in me. There are things more important than my safety at stake in this game."

I didn't know what to make of this statement, but she was

right about the stakes. Zabriel was the priority in this task we now shared.

"How do you know the spotter's name?" my cousin queried, shrewd as always.

"I met him in Oaray and saw him again in Tairmor. How do *you* know about his talent?"

"I pay attention," Illumina vaguely replied, an unsatisfying answer, one that shed no light on what route she'd taken across the Territory. Could she have gone through Oaray after all? Had Spex simply forgotten her face?

"Keep up, lads!" Fane shouted, and it took me a moment to realize he was speaking to us. Since there was no one else to hear or obey his directive, Illumina and I hastened to join him and Shea. "We're a good ways from any savory part of the city now. Being an unsavory type myself, I'm not worried about my own skin, but you lot ought to stay close."

We were leaving the harbor behind and entering a maze of dark, pitted streets in a part of Sheness that looked unfriendly at best. Though discomfort prickled my nerves, one thing seemed to be true—Captain Fane was at home in our seedy surroundings, strolling along with hands hooked in his coat pockets. He even skipped over cracks and puddles without looking down. A glance at Shea's cramped and tense posture told me she didn't appreciate his lackadaisical manner, while Illumina glared upward at the clouds of pollution that separated us from the stars. The walls of the buildings on either side of us were slick with grime, and walking these narrow alleys felt almost like being underground again.

Fane continued onward, leading the way to a dilapidated two-story house that was alive with light and unpleasant noise—drunken cackling, shouting, even the yowls of a disgruntled cat. There were a couple of sailors on the front porch, but no neighbors about, or at least none who dared complain about the racket.

With a nod to the pair whom I presumed were on watch duty, Fane hopped up the steps to open the door for us, and we crossed the threshold into a large parlor. To my surprise, the place was warm and clean, with a fire smoldering in the hearth and plenty of faded sofas and chairs for seating. A woman nearing her elder years was leaning out of a doorway to yell at some sailors who were lounging about. With a jolt, I recognized them as the ones who had taken Spex.

"You should wash up before you come into my home," she squawked, brandishing a dirty dishrag. Her admonishment only served to draw rough laughter.

"Welcome to Aunt Roxy's," Fane said, winking his blue eye at us. He strutted ahead and took the woman's hand, spinning her into the main room and finishing with a dip. "She feeds us and sews up our clothes and wounds, and does absolutely none of it with a smile on her face."

The dishrag knocked Fane's hat off his head, revealing gray hair plastered against his skull. Now that he was in brighter lighting, the age that his lean and nimble form belied was apparent. He couldn't be much younger than the grumbling woman in charge of the place.

"Should've taken the damn thing off when you came inside, Captain," Aunt Roxy snipped, bumbling out of his arms and straightening her clothing. She was dumpy and round, gravity unfairly pulling her features downward, but it was her attitude most of all that gave her an unpleasant countenance. While she wouldn't have been pretty even with a smile, she could have risen into the ranks of the homely. She displayed no interest in learning our names, instead waving at the sailors with both arms like she was herding cattle, barking at them to finish the dishes. They scurried off to the kitchen, one of them good-humoredly giving her a kiss on the cheek.

Now that Roxy had cleared the room of all but Fane and the three of us, the atmosphere changed, growing more serious.

"Upstairs," the virago pronounced, though no one had addressed her further.

"He up there?" Fane asked.

"Him and the boy. Locked the little shit in a cupboard to muffle his whining."

Fane grinned. "I assume you mean Opal's kid, not Pyrite."

Roxy rolled her eyes. "I'll bring up some food when the cleanup crew has finished earning its keep."

Though it felt disrespectful to be a stranger in someone's home, Roxy didn't appear to mind our presence. Either Fane's endorsement was enough, or she had grown accustomed to a lot of peculiar comings and goings. As she vanished into the kitchen after the sailors turned kitchen help, I became aware of weird noises coming from above—a thump as if someone was abusing furniture, followed by a curse-heavy complaint. With a jerk of his head toward the stairway, the captain led us upward.

There were two rooms on the second floor: Roxy's bedroom, and the room for everything and everyone else. The latter space was floored with knotted wood and held half a dozen beds, two wash tables, a coal-burning stove, and a desk at which Zabriel lounged, boots propped on its surface. His copious blond hair was sticking up and out over his forehead, and one hand rubbed his bristled chin. To my shock, his shroud was down, and his black-and-green wings glistened in the lamplight. I stared at them for a long time, at the smooth, effervescent membrane that ticked every so often, the movement natural and involuntary. Wings wanted to fly. My concentration was broken by a fat tabby cat near Zabriel's feet who growled out a nasal crescendo at a floor-level cupboard whenever its locked doors buckled from the inside.

"Can he breathe in there?" Fane asked, hooking his thumbs in his belt.

Zabriel glanced over his shoulder at the cupboard. "Hey, Tiny, can you breathe?"

Spex's response was loud and rude enough to be taken as an affirmative. Zabriel shrugged at Fane, who took a seat in the only other chair in the room, motioning for us to make similar use of the beds.

We acquiesced, though Illumina perched on the edge of a mattress at greater distance from the rest of us than was necessary. Her arms were crossed, and she was observing the goings-on like she did the crowd during celebrations in the Great Redwood.

"Hello, cousin," Zabriel greeted her before giving me a nod. He tapped a quill pen against the desk. "Nice cloaks, Anya. I assume they came from Gwyneth?"

Before I could answer, his gaze shifted to Shea and he made an expression that was somewhere between a grin and a grimace. "I see Smiley came, too. Wonderful."

"I'm Smiley. He's Tiny," Shea rejoined, eyes sparking as she pointed to the cupboard. "What does that make you? Unoriginal?"

"Where did you find her, Anya?"

Shea huffed, grinding the heel of her boot into the warped

floorboards. "I'm not a lost puppy, you know. And frankly I'm beginning to wonder why we bothered finding *you*."

Zabriel's dark eyes widened, comically indignant, while Fane hooted and slapped his knee. But Illumina, looking pale and dignified, interrupted the exchange to address me.

"Accepting gifts from humans outside of official circumstances is not proper for Faerie dignitaries. You shouldn't have taken that cloak, Anya, let alone be wearing it. Or do you no longer consider yourself a representative of the Fae? I suppose that would be understandable under the circumstances. Appropriate, even."

I gaped at my cousin, struck dumb. Out of the corner of my eye, I saw Fane examining his hat as though he'd never seen it before. A stuttering sound came from Shea, likely because she wanted to defend me but couldn't figure out how to do it. I was used to Illumina saying inflammatory things in the same tone she might have used to recite a recipe, and even I was struggling to pull my wits together.

"I see you've inherited your father's tact."

It was Zabriel who had spoken up in my defense. He tapped his pen on the desk a few more times, its rhythm consistent with rising irritation. Then he flicked it away, and it landed in the corner near Spex's cupboard. All traces of his egotism were gone, and his gaze sliced across the room like a throwing knife, permitting Illumina no reprieve. She shifted her position, a reaction I'd never elicited from her; neither to my knowledge had Ubiqua. There was something special about facing an accusation from Zabriel, an underlying message that seemed to say: *You've been seen, and you can never be unseen.*

"The loss of Anya's wings makes it necessary for her to adjust to life in the human world," he went on, "but it in no way supplants her heritage. You prefer to be underestimated, Illumina, to have people think you're young and misguided so you don't get blamed for the assertions you make. But I'm not that gullible. And since your Queen and the majority of the Faerie people seek peace with the humans, your objections are transparently personal. Don't masquerade them as political. Unless, of course, they embarrass you, which would be understandable. Appropriate, even."

Illumina was trembling, her snowy cheeks so flushed that it looked like blood had been smeared on top of her skin. She wasn't humiliated; she was infuriated. A blow against her politics or her dignity was the worst kind of insult she could be dealt.

"Just because an opinion is popular doesn't make it right, Zabriel. Or do you think it's right to attack Fae and sell their wings? After all, that's a popular pastime here in the Territory."

Having repaired a bit of her dignity, Illumina raised a hand to brush back her hair, her expression sullen.

"Relax, cousins. I meant no harm." Peering up at us from under her brows, she sulkily added, "Though I'm not sure the same can be said of you."

"That's enough squabbling," Fane declared, slapping his hat against his leg. "This is getting us nowhere."

"You're right," I piped up, ready to put our disagreement behind us. "We shouldn't be arguing. We should be making introductions. Captain, I'm Anya, and this is my friend Shea. I assume you already know Illumina, since I suspect you and your men have been keeping an eye on her. And Shea, this is Illumina. Illumina, meet Shea."

Fane stood and extended a deep bow. "My pleasure. At your service, lads."

Though Shea and I exchanged a look, no one corrected the captain, probably sharing my presumption that we were simply victims of his vernacular. As he retook his seat, Shea opened her mouth to say something to Illumina, but Zabriel jumped to his feet, interrupting her.

"Good to have that out of the way," he declared, rubbing his hands together. "Now let's focus on the business at hand."

My older cousin's bright and passionate disposition was back, and though it was not his intent, Illumina was once more relegated to the background.

"You, you, you, and Tiny," Zabriel continued, pointing at those of us seated on the beds before waving dismissively at the cupboard, "are all here for the same reason. To find me." He paused, crossing his arms over his chest, his aptitude for showmanship on full display. He loved to be at the center of attention, which was fortuitous, because others loved putting him there. "In case you haven't already realized this: no one finds me unless I want them to."

"Here comes the speech," Fane interjected, drawing a scowl but not a comment from Zabriel. The older man's words had some effect, however. My cousin's posturing diminished, and he cut to the chase instead of embarking on whatever self-gratifying monologue Fane had referenced.

"The point is having the lot of you looking for me has become inconvenient. So I figured I'd save you the effort and the embarrassment, as well as keep you from getting hurt, and just bring everyone together."

"Spex was looking for you, too?" I asked, drawing a series of agitated poundings from inside the cupboard. "Zabriel, he's a Faerie spotter. This could be serious. Do you know who sent him?"

Before Zabriel could deride the notion that his enemies were near to pinning him down, Fane leaned forward and gave an actual answer, one that wasn't geared toward establishing William Wolfram Pyrite's reputation for his new audience.

"It took the Ivanova family long enough, but they're finally coming round to the possibility that your cousin may be Fae. The man who tried to get in our way outside The Paladin—Opal's his name—is a bounty hunter who's had his eye on Zabriel for a while. He must have called in a favor from someone higher on the food chain to get his very own spotter, unless the government is straight-up employing mercenaries now."

"Adrien Opal." Zabriel fell back into his chair and hooked one leg over the arm, gazing at the ceiling as though reminiscing about an old friend. "His game's getting better, I'll admit that. He's still not clever, per se, but he might get there one day. I feel like he's learned a lot since we started."

Fane cackled, then winked in my direction.

"He's out of the way for the time being," the Captain reiterated. "But he'll be back for Tiny in due course. I assume we'll give him up in the name of good sport?"

"I don't know what else we'd do with him. I've already got myself a spotter."

My eyes darted between the two pirates, irritated at their callous attitudes. Spex might represent a deplorable cause, but he was still a person, not a chess piece.

"You can't give Spex back! I watched the Governor kill his father in Tairmor. He's a slave. But since Opal witnessed his abduction, right now he can't be blamed for running off. This might be the best chance he has to be free."

"I'm right here," Spex growled amidst a fervent clatter inside the cupboard. "And I'm *not* free!"

"All right." Fane sighed, and he crossed the room to flip the latch on the cupboard door. Spex, black hair a mess, tumbled onto the floor, the tabby cat hissing and barely scrambling out of the way. With remarkable quickness, he got his feet under him and dashed for the door. But Fane was quicker, grabbing a fistful of his shirt, popping a few buttons off in so doing. Not ready to give in, Spex swiped at the captain like a feral animal. Catching hold of Spex's arm, Fane produced a pair of shackles and snapped one end around his wrist. The other end he attached to the leg of a nearby bedpost in a way that would require our prisoner to drag the bed with him were he to attempt escape.

"Take a break, spitfire," the captain instructed, leaning against the closest wall to supervise Spex. "Is that any way to thank me for letting you out of there? You might have scratched my pretty face."

Spex was still poised for flight, straining against the metal band that held him. But however avid his fury, he wasn't going anywhere. With a glower, he slumped to the floor and pulled his knees against his chest.

"Anyway, the deal is this," Zabriel said, regaining our attention. "I won't return to Chrior—"

"But your mother is—" I stuttered.

"*Until* I've taken care of my business here. I've thought about what you said, Anya, and it's possible that I was hasty in drawing my conclusions. You're right. I owe my mother an explanation. At least, I owe her a visit."

A thoughtful pause ensued, and Zabriel's dark eyes flickered to Fane, searching, I realized, for approval. Whatever their relationship, the captain was part of the reason my cousin had reconsidered his decision. I wondered how they'd met and what bond they now shared that prompted my independent-minded cousin to turn to Fane for approval.

"You'll come home then?" Illumina echoed, eyes round with a mix of emotions far exceeding surprise. But it was beyond my ken to identify what the news meant to her. None of us had really expected this outcome.

Zabriel put an elbow on the desk and ran a hand along his jaw, nodding despite his obvious reservations.

"And will you stay?" Illumina pursued.

"My reasons for leaving haven't changed, so no, I don't expect I will."

Zabriel once more rose to his feet, almost knocking over his chair in the process. He couldn't stand the silence that invited him to consider the implications of his choice, and so he compensated, erasing that silence with his vitality.

Though I was disappointed by the second answer he had given, I was heartened that he was at least going to reenter Chrior, for it meant I had won half the battle. And once he saw the Faerie Realm again, remembered its beauty and its promise, he might well stay. I glanced at Illumina, who was studying our cousin carefully, and I thought a little tension left her posture. Perhaps she, too, believed she had won half the battle. What worried me was she believed it to be the ultimately decisive half. What would happen if my vision of the future materialized and Zabriel thwarted her ambition?

chapter twenty-four

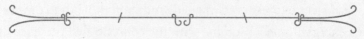

GRAINS OF TRUTH

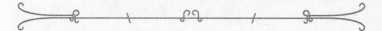

"So, Anya," Zabriel exclaimed, obviously relieved to have the discussion about his obligations to his mother out of the way. "That business I mentioned in the note I left for you. What did Leo Dementya tell you and Smiley when you asked about Evernook Island?"

"Nothing," Shea grumped, speaking on my behalf, perhaps a little annoyed that the question hadn't also been directed to her. "He said people don't go to it and its only use is for military warehousing."

Zabriel pointed at her and grinned like he was a teacher and she his sharpest pupil. "That was true six months ago. But there's been a marked increase in traffic around the island since then. There's more than warehousing going on there— or, at the very least, whatever is being warehoused has grown in importance. Evernook is owned by the government, but there's been no announcement of an official initiative that would explain the activity we're seeing. In conjunction with how out-of-the-way and inaccessible the island is, that tells me whoever's authorized its use is trying to keep things out of the public eye. The captain and I have been looking into the matter, and, well…we don't like what we've uncovered."

"Does this have anything to do with the Fae abductions?" I asked, biting my lip.

Zabriel's expression darkened, and though he didn't move, his energy homed in on me with the concentrated presence of someone's breath on my face.

"What do you know about that?"

I'd almost forgotten the locket Fi had given me, but now I pulled it out from under my shirt and unclasped the chain that held it around my neck. I extended it to Zabriel, feeling as though Evangeline had slipped from my protection a second time when I laid it in his palm. He fingered the heart-shaped pendant, perhaps finding it familiar, perhaps sensing there was a sad story attached to it.

"It was Evangeline's," I explained. "She wore it on her Crossing."

"It *was* hers?"

He slowly let out his breath, having guessed her fate. He met my eyes, and some wall inside him shattered. For the first time since our reunion, I felt connected to him the way I had when we were children, a closeness I'd never had with Illumina. In moments like these, we not only understood each other; we felt each other's pain.

"Evangeline was abducted in Oaray and taken to a place where they cut off her wings. She was drugged and could only remember bits and pieces—being transported, the sound of water, the smell of salt in the air. When they were through with her, she was dumped in Tairmor, where I ran into her. We talked, and I thought she was going to be all right, that she was going to fight...."

I swallowed hard, trying to erase the image of my friend's

corpse crumpled on the floor, barren of clothes and the dignity she should have been afforded.

"By the next morning, she'd overdosed on a substance people in the capital called 'the Green.' The Faerie who runs the shelter where we stayed wanted me to give you that locket. She was aware I was looking for you, and she hoped the necklace, and Evangeline's story, would help you see how much you're needed."

Behind me, Illumina struggled for air—this was the first she'd heard of Evangeline's fate, and considering her contemptuous opinion of humankind, she had to be reeling—but I didn't try to comfort her. Instead, I fixated on Zabriel, since his reaction might give me a sense of the duty, if any, he still felt toward the Faerie Realm. He closed his eyes, his breath, though steady, quick and shallow. He wasn't as removed from our people as I feared.

"Evangeline," he murmured, pinching the bridge of his nose. His muscles were tensing little by little, evidencing the untamed spirit which his mother continually credited to his father. "For the love of Nature, why *her?*" he asked at last.

"She must have had the right element."

Spex's voice, though soft, cut through the sorrow that filled the room. All eyes went to him, and I could tell from his unfocused stare and his defeated slouch that his good sense was screaming in his head for him to shut up. Yet he persisted in telling us what he knew, endangering himself and his family with every word, a strong indication of the level of regret in his heart.

"At least, I think that's what it was about. Sometimes they were after one element, sometimes a different one. It was luck of the draw for Fae traveling through Oaray, or wherever else spotter checkpoints had been set up. You can be sure there are a number of them since Hastings was willing to loan me out. When I was working Oaray, a Fire Fae might come through on a day when we were after Earth Fae instead, and we'd let them pass."

Becoming agitated, Spex twisted the shackle encircling his wrist with the opposite hand, and a pleading note entered his voice.

"You just… You have to believe me that I didn't know what would happen to your friend. I didn't know what would happen to any of them. I've just been trying to keep my family alive."

"Your family who made their living by preying on Fae," Shea sneered. "They're in prison where they belong. They're not victims—they did that to themselves."

"If you're about to tell me you wouldn't forgive the people you love for just about anything, don't bother. You'd forgive them genocide, and you know it, so take yourself off that pedestal, *seonnha*. Or at least get rid of that pendant hanging around your neck."

"What are you talking about?" Shea demanded, her fist closing around the looking-glass pendant that had become a point of curiosity during our journey.

"Hastings and everyone I ever saw who's involved in this thing wore a necklace just like it. So don't be so quick to assume the people *you* love are innocent."

Shea got to her feet, looking as though she might hurl Spex out the balcony door. Ironically, her attitude affirmed his assertion that she might support her family no matter the cost.

"My father isn't part of this," she snarled.

Spex was not willing to surrender and seemed pleased to

have exposed a nerve. "Maybe he isn't right now, but I reckon he was at one time."

Before Shea could escalate their argument, footsteps creaked in the stairwell, and we all turned to see who was about to join us. I tensed, my eyes landing on Zabriel, whose regal wings vanished beneath his shroud. Apparently not everyone here was privy to the fact he was Fae.

Her jowls jiggling, Aunt Roxy puffed straight into our room to deposit a large tray of deliciously unhealthy-looking snacks on the writing desk near Zabriel. She also slapped down a jug, flapping one hand at the mugs she'd included on the tray.

"Don't you ever make sure this boy eats, Captain?" our hostess groused, referring to my grinning cousin, her tartness insufficient to conceal her well-meaning heart. "You're thin," she went on, a finger dangerously close to Zabriel's face. "And there's no excuse for that when you're at port. Now quit your gawking at me, all of you, or get the hell out of my house."

"Thanks, Rox," Fane said with a chuckle, moving toward the desk. "You know I love you."

"I know you *owe* me," she grunted, heading out the door.

By this time, Shea had retaken her seat, careful not to face Spex, her countenance glum. I left her alone since I couldn't comfort her with promises of Thatcher's innocence. What did I really know about the man? If asked, all I could say was I thought he'd recognized my royal ring, and was aware of the damaging effects of sky iron on Fae magic. That was too much to dismiss Spex's assertions, yet not enough to prove them. Besides, I doubted Thatcher's past had any bearing on our present circumstances. It was best to let Shea grapple with the flood of questions that were no doubt running through her mind, for she was the best-qualified person to answer them.

I crossed to the desk and picked through Roxy's food offerings, taking bread and meat and a few olives. Fane, on the other hand, seemed more interested in the drink.

"Hey, Fane, toss one," Zabriel called.

I turned to see what was going on, and an olive zipped by my head, aimed at my cousin. He caught it in his mouth, pounding the air with one fist in celebration, and I laughed. Despite the heavy issues we were confronting, it felt good to be around him after such a long period of time.

"Now I understand why you're the terror of the seas," Shea snidely remarked, gulping down her second mugful. "I knew it had to be something to do with your mouth."

Fane whooped, enjoying Shea's feistiness. Rising to the challenge, Zabriel grabbed an olive and threw it into the air, then drew a pistol and shot it to bits, causing the rest of us to press our hands over our ears.

"Thought you could use more than one reason. I'm a damn good shot."

"Don't be blasting holes in my ceiling!" Aunt Roxy yelled from below as my cousin the pirate holstered his weapon. "Or you'll be fixing the roof rather than sailing the sea."

Everyone except Illumina laughed, even Spex. I couldn't decide if my younger cousin had lost her sense of humor, or if she just didn't want to partake in anything enjoyable having to do with humans. The latter was more in keeping with her rhetoric.

"What are you planning, Zabriel?" I asked, bringing the conversation back to the important issues. "What exactly is this business you have to finish before you come home?"

"As you're smart enough to deduce, I think whoever is behind the Faerie abductions and mutilations is working out of

Evernook Island. Given the number of children who have gone missing from the port over the last few months, Sepulchres are involved—there's really no other workable explanation. And law enforcement hasn't made any progress with their investigation. Humans and Fae alike are in danger as long as that island's secrets stay hidden.

"But thanks to the reconnaissance done by the captain and his men, we know Evernook is expecting an important shipment within the next few days. Fane's going to intercept that shipment, which might shed some light on things. Meanwhile, I'll infiltrate the island and find out what's going on there, hopefully put a wrench in whatever plans are in place, and then reevaluate. If the timing makes sense, that's when I'll go back to Chrior."

"You're crazy if you think I'm going to let you charge into the center of enemy operations and get yourself killed. I just found you!"

Zabriel and I shared a long look while everyone else stilled, then he picked at a tooth with his thumbnail.

"No problem. Come with me."

His words weren't defiant or meant as a challenge. It was the obvious solution. And so I nodded.

Shea sprang to her feet, and what was left of her food tumbled to the floor, her mug along with it.

"What? Anya, don't be stupid! Zabriel's a pirate, but you're not. You wouldn't be of any use on Evernook. You can't fly, or move silently, or scale mountains. You're basically human, only you don't even carry a gun. I wouldn't stand a chance against a bunch of military men, and you wouldn't, either."

I stared at her, feeling my confidence tearing apart. While I normally would have been insulted by her assertions, she didn't settle on any one point long enough for me to digest it, much less react to it. I'd never seen her like this—she could be a bit tactless, but she tended to keep a cool head. A quick glance around the room told me Shea's outburst had taken everyone by surprise. They were all staring at her in silence, except for Spex. His shoulders were shaking in controlled laugher. Judging from his expression, this was the best party he'd been to in a long time.

Through scolding me, my best friend next turned her fury on Zabriel, moving to stand toe-to-toe with him, despite the crook this put in her neck.

"And you!" Shea jabbed at his chest with her forefinger. "You're not talking about taking her for a stroll or out to dinner. Are you a pirate or an idiot? If you're any good at what you do, Mr. William Wolfram Pyrite, you don't need her. And you damn sure shouldn't put her in danger for no good reason."

She stopped to inhale, and I laid my hand on her arm, turning her toward me. Zabriel took the opportunity to step away, eyebrows and hands high, expression a mixture of amusement and trepidation. He didn't know whether to laugh or run.

"I'm sorry, Shea. Calm down," I said, trying to defuse her anger. "You're right. We need to think things through very carefully. But try to understand. I've struggled long and hard to end up here with Zabriel. And the people who are being hurt by the Fae hunters are *my* people. It's also my responsibility to help them."

"There's more than one way to help," she sullenly answered.

"True, but you and I have proven more than capable of taking care of ourselves. Remember the Sepulchres we fought off in the Fere? And the guard at the jailhouse we knocked out to escape from Luka? And our trip through the river caverns under Tairmor?"

"Hold on a minute," Fane interjected, scratching his head. "You two were in Luka's custody and took out a prison guard to escape? I'd like to hear about that!"

"So would I," Zabriel concurred. "I never thought to ask you about your trip across the Territory. Sounds like I should have."

"Damn right you should have," Shea retorted, eyes only slightly less wild, then she drew her gun. "Still want to shoot olives?"

"Maybe another time." Despite how dangerous this situation had become, his voice was calm, his manner relaxed. He was trying his best to mollify her. "But I have a better idea. Since you clearly can protect yourself, why don't you come with Anya to Evernook? I think that would solve the little problem we're having here."

He looked to me for confirmation, which I was only too happy to supply.

"Sure, Shea, come with us."

She smiled and handed her gun to Zabriel. Then she fell down, spread-eagled on one of the beds.

"She's been drinking, you know," Spex volunteered. "Seems partial to whatever's in that jug."

I approached my friend and caught a strong whiff of alcohol. "I think she's drunk."

Zabriel laughed. "That explains a lot."

"Yes, it does." Fane joined in. "I wondered what had become of the rum!"

The men chuckled, which I found a bit irritating, while Illumina looked disgusted. But then, she generally found human behavior objectionable. I ignored their reactions, however, not about to start another fight. I doubted Shea knew the effect the drink would have. I rolled her onto her side lest she vomit and choke, then threw a blanket over her. There wasn't anything to be done but let her sleep it off.

When everyone was talked out for the night, I discovered that Captain Fane had sent someone to fetch our belongings from the lodging house. Apparently we would be staying at Aunt Roxy's from now on. Illumina was staying, too, since she'd been carrying her pack at the time Fane had swept us away, and she fell asleep with a sketchbook in her hands, charcoal smeared on her fingers and face. There were plenty of beds to be had without the need to disturb Shea. I chose one near her in case she needed help in the night, then attempted to get some rest, dozing intermittently at best.

At some point, I noticed a cool breeze and sat up to find the balcony door ajar and faint light slinking in from outside. Fane was snoring, sprawled across his bed; Illumina was curled into a tiny ball near her headboard like a cocooned creature. Even Spex was lost to the world, curled up on the floor with a measly blanket, still shackled to the bedpost. He must have been accustomed to making do in stark environments because he didn't stir as I tiptoed past.

Zabriel was outside, seated with his legs through the bars of the balcony railing and surveying the street below. It was surprisingly quiet except for the occasional animal's yelp or beggar's scuffle. I went to join him, moving aside the gas lamp he had brought so that I could scoot close and dangle my feet over the edge, too. I leaned my head against his shoulder, not caring what differences and hurts hung between us. I'd spent a lot of time missing him these past two years.

"Thanks for agreeing to come back to Chrior," I murmured, not sure if the words would be welcome. He rolled his thumb across something he held before him, over the street. When the object caught the light, I recognized it as Evangeline's locket. He let my expression of gratitude hang unanswered in the air.

"How was she when you left? The Queen, I mean," he finally asked, trailing a finger down one of the rusty metal posts.

My breath seeped out of me, slow and reluctant as an apology. After so much time and conflict, it hadn't dawned on me that he would, of course, still care. Ubiqua was his mother. He could think he hated her, and choose to leave her, but even those sentiments involved the heart. Indifference was the thing he would never be able to feel toward her. How many memories had risen to the surface for him since Illumina and I had arrived?

"She was fine. That was almost three months ago, though, during the winter solstice. She didn't know how quickly to expect death. All she seemed certain of was that she's going to die."

"And you believe it?"

I readjusted my position, wanting to look him in the eye, but he refused. Instead, he leaned his forehead against the railing, leaving me with no way to decipher the emotions that lurked behind the question.

"Yes, I do." I would have taken his hand, but he was examining the locket in earnest. "But, Zabriel, listen. This business with Evernook Island—it's important, too. The people of Chrior and Warckum need to know what's happening, and you're in the best position of anyone to find the answers. I think Ubiqua would want you to investigate."

"I'm not doing it for her approval." Zabriel raised his head to meet my gaze. "Anya, I know what kind of ruler you and my mother think Illumina would be, but she's been spending a lot of time in human company. I think there's hope for her, in spite of what happened earlier. She's only fourteen, after all, and nobody's ever really given her a chance."

I gave a dry, quiet laugh. "What you're really saying is that you won't rule. Not under any circumstances."

He paused, not wanting to admit it, not wanting to disappoint me. "The Fae wouldn't follow me, anyway."

"Yes, they would," I fervently contradicted. "Don't you remember any of the good Fae? What about Ione and Davic and all your mother's supporters? The people who were your friends? They're the ones who are waiting to greet you back home. Is that so bad?"

"No. But my mother pictured me as the ultimate liaison between humans and Fae, and at the moment, the humans consider me a criminal. That *is* bad, and it *does* prevent me from ruling like she envisioned. I won't tell you that I find this state of affairs upsetting, but whether or not it's convenient for me doesn't change that it's true."

"But in the Territory, you're William Wolfram Pyrite. Don the garments and demeanor of a prince, and I doubt they'd ever make the connection. Besides, from what I hear, the average citizen idolizes you. If you want to walk away from the Laura a second time, then do it, but don't make excuses."

Zabriel pulled his hand back through the rail and shoved the locket into his pocket, and I thought he was going to go inside, tired of gnawing on this subject. But he turned and looked me over the way a scientist approaches a specimen—curious, a little apprehensive, but approving, perhaps even fascinated.

"It really is too bad about your wings, Anya. I have no doubt that out of the three of us cousins, you're the best choice for ruler."

"And I'm the only one who unequivocally can't rule. But perhaps you don't understand the extent of the Queen's objections to Illumina. Before I left Chrior, my father hinted that Ubiqua might have sent Illumina out here to die."

I made the grisly statement as fast and unfeelingly as I could, not wanting to think about it and not quite ready to believe it. Zabriel didn't have such problems.

"It wouldn't surprise me. The Queen has always been willing to make hard decisions without regret."

"She wouldn't," I responded automatically, but my exclamation was rhetorical and Zabriel knew it. Was his cynicism designed to make me see things as he did? Why else would he feel the need to sow seeds of doubt? His relationship with Ubiqua had always been different from mine, but our opinions were more disparate now than ever. Being apart from her had permitted him to cultivate his resentment and ignore the good. She was one of the most celebrated rulers in Chrior's history. More than that, her campaign for peace and integration was in line with his personal values. Mother and son weren't opposite people, whatever he wanted to believe.

Aunt Roxy's cat waddled onto the balcony and jumped to the railing, pacing above our heads in the discomfited silence that had fallen.

"When did Illumina get to Sheness?" I asked, redirecting the conversation to the subject with which we had started. "I knew she had a good lead on me but you talk like she's been under surveillance for a while."

"I first heard she was asking after me almost three weeks ago." Zabriel soaked up this simpler topic with pleasure. "I'm

not going back on what I said about her having potential, but
she is a strange one, I'll grant you that."

"Why? What's she been up to?"

"For the most part, she's been hanging around The Paladin.
If she had any intelligence on me, she was probably just following bread crumbs, but...I don't know." He laughed with
fleeting humor. "Let's just say she's a bit too comfortable there."

"Do you know how she got here?" I threw the question
out as a matter of curiosity, since I was sure she hadn't come
through Oaray. "I don't think she took the same route I did."

"I know she has travel papers like you and me. In this part
of the Territory, you can't go far without having your identity checked by an officer of the law. Or at least without being
forced to pay for an officer's silence."

"She couldn't have papers."

"Why's that?"

"Because Spex was working as a documents supplier in
Oaray, and he told me he hadn't seen her. He took over for
Deangelo a while ago, though Nature only knows what hap-
pened to the old man to clear the post."

"Maybe Spex lied."

"I don't think so. He told me he spotted Evangeline."

Zabriel cocked an eyebrow. "Well, she made it somehow.
I suppose Enerris could have gotten her papers when he was
alive."

"Maybe," I allowed, not having entertained that possibility
before. "She didn't say anything about it, though, not to anyone. My father and the Queen are under the impression this
is her original Crossing."

I found it difficult to conceive that Illumina's father would
have taken her beyond our homeland's borders, which were

protected to the west and south by the Bloody Road and to the north and east by impassible mountains. But in retrospect, anything was possible when it came to Enerris. He had, after all, tried to poison his own nephew with the Queen seated not fifteen paces away. If he had ushered his daughter on a secret and unofficial Crossing, what could have been his purpose? He'd been a human-hater, reviling the Warckum Territory. He'd done everything in his power to keep Illumina's mind closed and her hatred alive. Providing her with experience in the human world ran counter to that goal. It didn't make sense to me.

"Do you feel bad for her?" I asked, the question springing from my own memories of her father, one of the few adults I had feared as a child.

"Because her father was a madman?"

"That, and…because she carves herself up. I can't help worrying about her."

"You don't worry about *her*," Zabriel corrected, bringing one leg up beside him so he could face me fully, dark eyes binding me in place. "You worry about what she could do. There's a difference. When I ran away, I had to come to terms with a lot of things…including more than a few unpleasant truths about myself. My guess about you is that if Illumina died, you would be more relieved than sad."

I sat unmoving, letting his assertion sink in. It was a revolting notion and, I realized, more than likely true. Being around Illumina made me nervous. I couldn't recall ever really enjoying her company. My hopes that she'd stop scarifying herself and that she wouldn't hurt anyone else didn't equal love. They equaled distrust and pity. The worst part was that she'd told me time and again, "You're good to me, Anya. I know you care, Anya," which had to mean I treated her better than most people did. And yet I wouldn't be sad at her loss if she died—only sad that she hadn't had a better life.

"That doesn't make you a bad person," Zabriel resumed. "And you can't help the way you feel, so you may as well be honest about it. My mother never was. She always acted like Illumina was normal and ignored all the things Enerris did to her. It begs the question, which is more harmful to a little girl, causing her pain or failing to stop it?"

"Enerris hurt her, then." It was a statement because I couldn't justify making it a question. The words scarred into her back that she couldn't have written herself—*belief, strength, power, perseverance*—were proof enough. But there were also the messages marring her skin that read more like indoctrination than philosophy, messages like *keep silent your screams and never look back*.

A breeze, salty even this deep into the metropolis, tousled my cousin's silver-blond hair as he nodded.

"Illumina wasn't born the way she is. She's a victim, and not just of her father. My mother should have protected her, only she chose to look the other way."

"Are you saying Illumina blames the Queen?"

"I'm saying *I* blame the Queen. I don't think Illumina even knows the extent to which she's been wronged. I mean, no one's ever told her she didn't deserve it."

"Somebody must have—"

"Not if that's what *everybody's* been assuming. Think about it. We can all pass the problem on to someone else, and so on, and so on, until in the end no one does anything."

I looked at my hands, bleak and ghostly against the dark rail tinged with rust, feeling my gut was similarly tinged with shame.

"My mother would have," I murmured, my voice barely audible. I didn't know if that was true or if I just wanted to believe it.

"Your mother was always doing things that other people never thought to do."

"Did she for you, too?"

He smiled despite himself. He could smirk and grin and make light of a hundred situations, but this smile emerged unrestrained and uncalculated. All Fae had elemental connections, but that was my mother's unique form of magic.

Though I wanted to keep talking, Zabriel was getting to his feet. There were other things I needed to ask him, I realized with a jolt of desperation, things that deserved attention and conversation. Though the question that rolled out of me deserved an introduction, I couldn't lose this opportunity. I didn't know when I would next have him to myself, especially in a divulging mood.

"Zabriel, I saw your wanted poster in Tairmor."

He froze in a crouch, as though he'd almost walked away clean.

"It said you were a murderer. Is that true?"

He glanced out over the street. In a rickety house a few blocks down, a light flared, and somewhere in the distance glass broke and dogs barked, neither sound loud enough to wake a soul under Aunt Roxy's roof.

"Gwyneth told me how a lot of things you never did have been blamed on you," I ventured, heart threatening to leap into my throat. "You can say she was right if you want and I won't ask again."

He swiped at the hair that stuck out over his forehead, then knelt beside me.

"Gwyneth was right, Anya, but not about that. When I left the Faerie Realm, I ended up in Sheness, since that was the farthest I could go from home. After I was here for a while, I found that my *skills,* so to speak, offered me certain advantages, and so I became a pirate. You wouldn't really have expected me to become a butcher or a blacksmith, now, would you? The tale might be one of pure adventure if this was a child's storybook, but in the real world, the best lies and the worst reputations all start with a grain of truth, something nobody can deny."

He offered me his hand, and I took it because I wouldn't have been able to stand without help. I was gripped by fear, already sure of the answer he would give me. I wished I hadn't asked the question, and whether he was Fae or human, I wanted him to lie.

"It's true, Anya. I killed somebody. And that's the foundation for my reputation, the reason the name *Pyrite* means what it does."

I closed my eyes, dumbstruck by his unflinching honesty, terrified of what it meant if I could look past *murder* when it came to him. I was either a hypocrite or I had to open my mind to the possibility that murder was forgivable. Would my mother have been able to do *that?*

Incarnadine was the one who would have had the answers; she should have ruled Chrior upon Ubiqua's death, preventing the burden from falling too soon upon my generation. While I wouldn't generally admit it, we were still children…however capable we were of horrific deeds.

I walked toward the door, but Zabriel gripped my shoulder. Did he want to explain? I faced him, but instead of elaborating, he wrapped his arms around me, tucking my head under his chin.

"One of these days, I'll tell you what I'd be giving up if I became the Prince of Chrior again. In the meantime, I missed you, too, Anya."

I squeezed him back. Whatever had happened before and whatever would happen after, at least my cousins and I were together tonight, safe in this little house in the heart of Sheness. The rest could be sorted out another day, by people smarter and more experienced than we.

We went inside and I lay down on my mattress, staring up at the ceiling. The moon had shifted enough to suggest Zabriel and I had spent a couple of hours together on the balcony. I sighed, no more tired than I'd been before. Catching a slight movement, I spied Zabriel, little more than a shadow pausing by the stairs, reaching into his coat pocket. He withdrew the chain of Evangeline's necklace, letting it stretch and spin as he brought the pendant into the open once more. His countenance was invisible in the dark, but the token Fi had charged me to give him was eating at him; that couldn't be denied. Eventually, he collected the chain in his palm, clenched his hand into a fist, and lifted off the ground to float down the steps on Faerie wings, silent as any specter.

I landed on the lip of Illumina's alcove amidst the lower middle branches of the Redwood, tucking my wings securely against my back. Though my father had offered her a room in our home in the aftermath of Enerris's banishment, she had refused the invitation. Worried that she might be lonely now that her only living parent was gone, I had adopted the habit of checking on her twice a day.

There was a flurry of noise from inside, and I listened intently to the bumps, clangs, and rustles. At the sound of something being dragged across the floor, I went in without knocking, both concerned and curious.

Illumina was surrounded by several large burlap sacks that overflowed with possessions—clothing, knickknacks, letters and other correspondence, and what looked to be the entire contents of the desk in the corner.

"What's going on?" I dared to ask.

My voice startled my young cousin. Her green eyes glowed wildly between the black moss curtains of her hair, and her hand dropped to the dagger at her hip. A stab of panic went through me, accompanied by an image of her pulling her knife to attack. Then recognition came to her and she straightened, arms spreading, welcoming me to take in the scene.

"I'm removing my father's belongings," she explained.

She was indeed—all of his things, so not a trace of him remained outside of those burlap sacks.

"Why?" I pressed, more than a little unsettled.

As far as Illumina knew, her father would be coming back. Queen Ubiqua had couched her decision to exile him in terms of sending him on an assignment to learn more about life in the Warckum Territory. Granted, after Enerris had tempted Zabriel with Sale at the Queen's birthday, few Fae were dense enough to believe that's all there was to the story, but we kept up the pretense for his twelve-year-old daughter's sake. She didn't need to know the full extent of his punishment. Not yet.

Illumina brushed her hair away from her face. "I appreciate what you and the others are trying to do, Anya. Especially you. I know you want me to be all right. I won't forget that. But I'm not stupid."

"I never thought you were."

I came farther into the room, my gaze never straying from my cousin's visage. Her incredible intelligence shone brighter than the gold of the royal ring on her finger. Her speech alone, so beyond that of her peers, was enough to give it away, without the sparks her ever-active brain sent into her eyes.

"My father isn't coming back," she continued. "The Queen banished him for trying to kill her son, which was the right thing to do, the only thing to do."

"But that doesn't mean you'll never see him again. And it certainly doesn't mean you need to erase the evidence that he existed. He's only been gone three days, for Nature's sake."

Illumina had already considered this perspective and had an answer at the ready.

"What my father did was unforgivable. It was idiotic. If Zabriel had died, did he think Faefolk would admire him? No. They would have wept for Ubiqua if not for the Prince himself. If I kept trinkets that belonged to him, they would just be a reminder of his failures. And as for seeing him again…" Illumina gave a wispy smile as she tied the sacks full of memories closed. "Well, cousin, I know my father better than you do. He won't live among the humans. His dignity won't stand for it."

Though I understood her implication perfectly, I wished I didn't. How could a little girl be so stoical at the loss of her father, a loss she believed to be more permanent than even our aunt knew? How could she contentedly throw away every reminder of the man who had raised her? These questions plagued me, even as I helped her carry the sacks away, effectively leaving Enerris in the past.

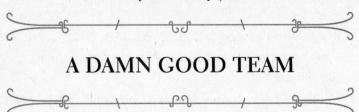

chapter twenty-five

A DAMN GOOD TEAM

When I awoke the next morning, Shea was gone. Filled with foreboding, I tugged on my boots, worried that she'd gone off on her own like she had in Tairmor. She was less likely to be recognized here, but it was unclear whether or not the neighborhood we were in was safe, even in full daylight. It certainly didn't feel inviting. But before my concern could send me crashing down the stairs, she strolled in with Captain Fane, bearing a tray full of breakfast items that had been thrown together by Aunt Roxy.

"I went to the market," she told me, though there was a hint of evasiveness in the way her gaze skirted mine. "I needed a little fresh air." Then more surreptitiously she added, "Next thing I knew, Fane and Roxy were putting together a grocery list for me."

I laughed as quietly as I could at the image of a ruthless pirate making shopping requests, then eyed the captain in question, who hurled an apple at Spex. Some of the questions I'd failed to ask Zabriel during our conversation last night pertained to this man. He definitely dressed the part of a pirate, with pistols at his hips and clothing that was expensive in taste but eccentric in style, by all accounts falling short of an official uniform.

If Zabriel was wanted by the law, I had no doubt Fane was, as well. So was he trustworthy? I viewed him the same way I did the neighborhood around Roxy's house—I couldn't say from experience that it wasn't reliable, but my instincts told me to be careful.

With these thoughts playing in my mind, I went to pick through the breakfast offerings before everything had been devoured. Zabriel was back from wherever he'd gone after our talk, and seemed none the worse for wear. Unlike with Shea, I hadn't thought twice about his safety, but then, this was his city. Illumina was huddled on her bed, hoarding food like she had no idea when she'd receive another meal. I was about to grab a plate when an apple rolled by my feet. Frowning, I traced its directionality to Spex, who looked pale and miserable where he leaned against the bedpost to which he was chained. Though I wanted to hate him, the emotion was exhausting, and trying to sustain it in the face of a young man Zabriel's age wasn't easy. I picked up the apple and returned it, settling across from him on the floor with my own meal.

"You like to play fetch?" he asked, taking the apple and rolling it away from me. It bruised against the cupboard and ricocheted out the open balcony door.

"You're just trying to get rid of me."

"Right you are."

I nibbled a piece of cheese while I struggled to decide how best to start a conversation with him. He had the potential to be an ally, despite his family's business. He'd already given us information he shouldn't have. If not for his fear of losing the people he loved, I was sure his instincts would put him on our side.

"You must know," I finally began, "that what I said yesterday is most likely true. Hastings, that bounty hunter, and whoever else has been using you think you've been abducted, which means you're free of them. They can't blame you for not doing what they say, and they can't punish your family on your account."

"You're assuming they operate by traditional rules. Under normal circumstances, that's not a chance I'd take." He lifted one manacled wrist and looped the chain around it, giving it a couple of tugs. "But as long as I am, quite literally, tied up here, it doesn't make much difference what I'd choose to do."

"What are the stakes?"

Spex looked sideways at me with heavily lined hazel eyes. His clothing was dirty, his suspenders torn, his hair matted. But despite his physical appearance, his spirit wasn't broken.

"Why in hell would I tell you that? The last time I talked to you, they executed my father."

"Your father was slated for the plank, anyway," Zabriel said, hopping onto the back of the desk chair, his feet on the seat, and cutting into our conversation. "Now he's one less thing that can be held over you."

At Spex's stormy silence, Zabriel came to sit cross-legged on the floor beside me, his keen eyes narrowed as he evaluated the prisoner.

"I know exactly what the stakes are, my friend," he resumed. "It used to be about spotting Fae in Oaray, but now you believe that if you turn me in, your mother, brother, and sister will be released. Is that right?"

Spex glowered at him. "How could you know that?"

"Leo Dementya was at your father's execution. I don't get information directly from him, but I do cultivate a few sources in my line of work. The heavyweights in the Territory talk, and I make a habit of listening. Word is that more hunters will soon be executed."

Spex shifted onto his knees, cheeks paling even more, if that was possible. "Then you know why you have to let me go."

Zabriel hung his head in a show of silent sympathy, then met Spex's gaze.

"Whoever's behind this business is manipulating you, and it's time you understand how these people work. Your entire family is condemned, and that's not going to change. Governor Ivanova's stance against Fae hunting is solid, and your mother and siblings have been duly convicted and sentenced to death. Your handlers have just been bending the rules, delaying the inevitable in order to string you along. When you stepped out of line, they let your father's sentence be carried out. They're going to do the same thing three more times—use you, get what they want from you, then let the plank claim its victims."

Spex's face flitted through a variety of emotions, and for a moment I thought he might retch. But he clenched his jaw and stubbornly shook his head.

"Someone in the government's involved in this. That means they can get my family out of prison."

Zabriel squeezed his temples in frustration and tried again.

"I'm sorry to break it to you, but delaying an execution is a whole lot easier than overriding someone's sentence. Only the Governor can extend a pardon, and I don't see his hand in any of this. Clearly someone with connections is involved, but everything they're doing is carefully calculated *not* to draw the Governor's notice. And that includes using Evernook Island as their base of operations. They're eventually going to step out of the way and let justice take its course. They won't have a choice, and they've known it from the beginning."

"Are you saying Spex will be executed, too?" I mumbled, my eyes widening, for this possibility had not occurred to me before.

"Depends on his sentence. By my reckoning, our friend here was never convicted of Fae mutilation. Am I right, Tiny? He's the youngest, and I suspect his only involvement in the family trade was spotting. You don't kill off someone with a rare talent like that."

"So what?" Spex snarled, putting his forehead none too gently to his knees. "Being right about that doesn't make you right about the rest of it."

"Just give it some thought." Zabriel shoved his plate and the food that remained on it toward Spex. "I think your family is damned if you cooperate and damned if you don't, so you might want to consider if there's good reason to keep helping Hastings and Opal. Maybe it's time to get back at them for jerking your chain."

Spex smacked the lip of the plate, overturning it as though to show he wasn't powerless. "Seems to me you're the one jerking my chain at the moment."

"It might seem that way, but I don't gain anything by lying to you."

My cousin stood and offered a hand to me. "Come on, Anya. Let's give Spex some space."

I nodded, letting him pull me to my feet, my thoughts chasing one another like a dog in pursuit of its tail. What would I do were it my family at risk? Cling to feeble hope despite the logic of Zabriel's arguments, and continue to undertake a task I knew was wrong? Or accept the inevitability of my loved ones' fates and hit back? Either way, I'd end up living with tremendous guilt. I shuddered as I crossed the floor to join the others, for one thing was clear: whoever was behind the Fae mutilations, the manipulation of Spex, the abuse of the Sepulchres, and whatever else was part of this scheme, was heartless and utterly self-serving. Evil was loose in the Warckum Territory, and it was up to us—a mistreated and confused fourteen-year-old, a maimed Faerie, the daughter of a fugitive, two pirates, and possibly a Fae-hunter—to stop them.

By the next afternoon, plans were in order for our attack against Evernook—Zabriel and Fane had been organizing the operation long before the rest of us had come into the fold. At their request, the group of us met upstairs to learn the roles we all would play.

"It's straightforward," Zabriel began, inviting us to gather around a map he had spread upon the desk. "Captain Fane and part of his crew will raid the Dementya ship and steal the cargo. The rest of his men will cause a distraction on the island's shore, as though an invasion is under way. That should draw the guards away from the warehouse." He pointed to the sections of the map that were relevant to the different facets of the plan. "In the meantime, Anya, Shea, and I will land on the opposite side of Evernook and sneak into the fortress."

Illumina brushed her hair aside, preparing to interrupt, and Zabriel met her eyes.

"I'd like you to stay here, dear cousin, and keep an eye on our prisoner."

Illumina's mouth opened and closed, and an angry flush colored her cheeks. "You'll take a human with you, but not your own flesh and blood?"

Everyone stilled, her commentary as divisive as ever, but especially unwelcome during a time when we needed to be united. Zabriel was first to recover, and he gave her a caustic look.

"I'm taking Shea because I think she can handle herself in a fight, and because I'd like to keep one member of our family out of harm's way."

"Thank you for your thoughtfulness," Illumina said with a sugary-sweet smile. "But perhaps you ought to consider that I'm the only Faerie here who has an elemental connection. I think that could be of more use to you than another gun."

Not about to be bumped from the mission, Shea threw her hands up in protest.

"Anya and I have been through a lot, and we make a damned good team. I don't think this is a good time to split us up. Tell them, Anya. Who do you think should go with you to the island?"

I grimaced. I would have preferred Shea's company, but Illumina had a point. "She is a Fire Fae. That type of magic could prove useful."

"Well, I don't care. I'm going to that island if I have to swim there."

"Great," Zabriel snapped, punching the surface of the desk. "I'm going to end up handling all the amateurs."

"Two of them are your cousins," Shea shot back, "so the only one you ought to *handle* is me. And that'll only happen in your dreams."

Zabriel chuckled, caught off guard. He turned away for a moment to rub his hands over his face, and I glanced between the contentious pair, considering for the first time that their bickering might hide an attraction. Composure regained, Zabriel mussed his hair and leaned over the desk, his bowed head hiding his smile. I caught sight of a chain under his collar, but it was silver instead of gold like Evangeline's, and I cocked my head, not having noticed it before. As though obeying my curious gaze, the chain's heavy ornament slipped forward and fell through the open top of his shirt, hanging for a second in the air before he automatically replaced it. It was his royal ring, ruby stud bracketed by golden laurel leaves. He might be hiding it, but he still had it.

"What do you think, Captain?" Zabriel asked, oblivious to the fact that anything had transpired in the past second, though for me, the world had shifted.

"I'd take Shea with me if you Fae want to stick together. We can chain the lad up real tight and leave him in Roxy's care."

"My name is one goddamn syllable," Spex grumbled from behind us. "Can't anyone around here remember it?"

"I'm not above putting you back in the cupboard while we're gone," Zabriel cautioned, and Spex laid his head against the bedpost in surrender.

"Would I be on your ship?" Shea queried, addressing Fane.

"Yes indeed. And there'll be plenty of action."

"I'll go with you, then."

"Now that things are settled," Zabriel jumped in, "the captain and I will go downstairs to talk to Aunt Roxy and send final instructions to the crew. Join us after you're dressed."

He motioned to a stack of dark clothing, then he and Fane departed. After sorting through the items, which belonged to some of the sailors judging from their generous sizes, we slipped them over our regular leggings and tunics. I glanced at my companions, wondering if I looked as much like a child in her parents' garments as they did. And that reminded me of the gift Thatcher More had given his daughter.

"What about your pendant?" I said to Shea. "We might run

into Sepulchres. It couldn't hurt to have it with us in case it really has some power."

Shea gave me a cantankerous look, one hand clutching the looking glass that hung around her neck. "It's just a keepsake, Anya. You said yourself that magic can't be infused into objects."

"I'd take it if I were you," Spex interjected in a singsong tone. "I know what I've seen, and it's made a believer out of me."

"No," Shea persisted, and I fought back the urge to mock her defiant expression, not understanding her objection.

"We'd just be borrowing it."

"It's important to me, Anya. It was my father's. What if you lose it?"

"Enough." It was Fane who had spoken. Our arguing had blocked the sound of his footsteps on the staircase. "One shiny bauble is not going to make a difference one way or the other in tonight's outcome. Now let's get going."

Without another word, Shea, Illumina, and I grabbed our travel cloaks, which were darker and more conducive to concealment than the pair of vibrant capes gifted by Gwyneth, and went downstairs with the captain to join Zabriel and carry out our missions. Shea paused and gave my hand a squeeze before she went out the door with Fane, perhaps in apology, but more likely out of fear that she wouldn't see me again. My heart raced, but it wasn't for my sake—I was bizarrely calm at the prospect of being in danger myself, but I couldn't stand the thought of something happening to her. She was only here out of friendship, with nothing personal to gain or lose. None of us could predict what this night would bring, but if all of us made it back, it would be some kind of miracle.

chapter twenty-six

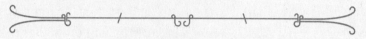

EVERNOOK ISLAND

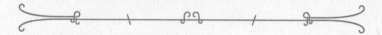

Zabriel, Illumina and I set out that evening like we were on any other stroll across the shorefront, but as we left behind the military vessels and trade ships, the seedy establishments in the area were replaced by boarded-up shacks, some releasing a stench like fermenting excrement. I covered my nose and mouth with my sleeve, wondering how Zabriel and Illumina could stomach it. Zabriel seemed annoyingly at ease; Illumina at least had the decency to look disgusted. Her nose was upturned as though it might escape the smell if only she could get it high enough.

At last we came to a boat that was little more than a dinghy, bobbing in weed-heavy water and slackly tied to a rotted stump sunk into the sand. It had one redeeming quality, and that was its ability to carry us away from the filthy shore.

"This is the best you and Fane could do?" I asked, hating the idea of being afloat in that tiny, unsteady vessel. I'd feared the ocean would swallow us in Leo Dementya's schooner—in this skiff we would be little more than an appetizer.

"Fane is doing a lot better," Zabriel answered. "But that's because he's running distraction. Once that cargo ship is looted and fails to show up on schedule, whoever's in charge at Ever-

nook will send a few bodies to investigate. I'm hoping the island isn't well staffed and most of its population will be looking
the other way when we tie up. It wouldn't do us any good to
arrive in a freighter, waving a pirate flag, and draw them all
back, now, would it?"

"No," I grudgingly admitted, pulling my cloak tighter.

"This boat's a surprisingly reliable little thing—I promise."

Zabriel held the dinghy level while Illumina and I boarded,
then hopped in after us. I sat in front as lookout, leaving him
to row. Though I no longer possessed my connection with
the water, I still had a certain insight into its whims. With
the unpredictable tides around Evernook, I was the best person for the job.

To our surprise, the water in the bay was quiet tonight,
which would normally have been a good thing. But I fretted
that someone would hear the rhythmic rippling of Zabriel's
paddle as we glided nearer to Evernook and be alerted to our
approach. I need not have worried. Out of the west a light
flashed, breaking the tranquility, and a *boom* shattered the air.

"Cannon," Zabriel explained, rowing a little faster. "That
should stir things up."

"Does that mean Fane is in trouble?" asked Illumina.

"Not at all. The captain does this for a living. My guess is
his men have already overrun the transport ship's crew and
seized the cargo. Now they're just announcing it to the world
and giving us a chance to sneak onto the island."

"You killed the transport crew?" I blurted, nausea swelling
under my words.

"I haven't done anything. I'm here with you. But there is a
mission at stake, remember. We're pirates, not keepers of the

peace. Fane will do whatever he deems necessary. Hell, he tried to kill me when we first met."

I swiveled about in alarm, but Zabriel brushed me off.

"Just because he was nice to you doesn't mean he's a nice person. Let's just say he has a rough outer shell when it concerns people who come without references."

I huffed, pulling my hood up to hide my growing fear. I shouldn't have suppressed my instincts about the captain; I shouldn't have let Shea go with him. She had no business on a ship full of pirates. Unable to restrain myself, I asked the obvious question.

"How can you trust him if he tried to kill you?"

"He's straightforward. If he'd wanted to kill me that day, I'd be dead. No playing around. Besides, that was almost two years ago. He's grown fonder of me since then."

"As long as the two of you are happy."

"We are, thank you. But now I have to ask both of you to be quiet. We're getting close."

A few moments later, the stillness of the bay vanished. I gripped the sides of the boat, sure that every muscle in my body would turn to mush. If only I could have calmed the water with my hands. Eddies swept us this way and that, always away from the shore. Rather than directly fighting the current, Zabriel rowed across it, bringing us to anything but a soft landing upon some boulders. We climbed onto the slippery surface of the rocks, spray from the waves drenching us. When our feet finally found the sand, I sank to my knees, limbs trembling. I'd never felt so happy to be grounded. Illumina rested, as well, but Zabriel dragged the dinghy by its rope to a more sheltered area. We would need the small craft to get off the island.

"This way," he called, heading into the trees and the dense

forest beyond. Illumina and I followed, knowing we would have no road to guide us, only our senses and our persistence.

As we moved away from the shoreline, the soil on the island became damp and springy, giving beneath my feet like the vines that made up the floor of Ubiqua's dwelling. In my clumsier human form, I worried that I would stumble or fall. I tried to calm my wildly beating heart, despising the anxiety that had gradually been taking up residence in my psyche ever since my injury, making me more cautious and fearful by nature than I'd ever been in Faerie form. If Zabriel hadn't valued my mind, I had no doubt he would have left me behind. Without me, my cousins could have taken to the treetops and gone twice as fast with a fraction of the effort, and that knowledge was downright embarrassing. But we managed, Illumina leading our party with a flame in the palm of her hand, while Zabriel flew up periodically to check our progress.

Wind was intermittent, but when it blew, it was cold and powerful, ripping between tree branches that reached out to one another, blocking all other sound. When it rested, cannon fire rent the air, and my heart pounded painfully at the thought of Shea. Fane and his crew were creating the distraction we needed, but what might their losses be?

The warehouse was hidden from view until we were almost close enough to touch it. It seemed to come out of nowhere, distinguishable only by the light of the torches at its narrow perimeter and upon its high walls. It loomed over us like a castle, turreted and made entirely of stone.

"Why was this built?" Illumina asked, awe in her voice.

Zabriel stole forward until he was pressed against the wall. "By all accounts it was here when the Warckum Territory was settled. If you believe the lore, it was formed by the original

Fae more than a century ago. That's why it's part of the mountain. I seriously doubt that's true, but it would be a bit ironic, don't you think?"

We crept onward, keeping to the shadows, Zabriel every so often holding up a hand to shush us so he could listen to the night. So far we had seen no sentries, which made me almost more nervous. When we came to an oaken door without encountering resistance, I cast around, not trusting our luck.

"Shouldn't someone be here?" I hissed, but Zabriel motioned Illumina ahead, silently instructing her to melt the door latch. A fire so hot could only be conjured in this environment by a Faerie—whoever discovered the evidence of our trespass would know one of my people was responsible. I couldn't stop to consider the political ramifications this might generate.

"The island is under attack," Zabriel reminded. "The guards are fending off pirates at the opposite shore. Besides, I doubt whoever's running this place has more than a minimal staff—the more people, the harder to keep them quiet."

The door swung inward, creaking loudly, and I cringed, expecting someone or something to jump out of the dark and attack us.

"If only we had an Oil Faerie," Illumina whispered, breaking the tension and bringing a fleeting smile to my face.

"Just keep moving," Zabriel muttered, no longer in the mood for humor.

We followed Illumina through the door, still relying on the tiny flame in her palm for guidance. The darkness inside was heavy, but we seemed to be in a storeroom filled with pots and pans. We'd no doubt made use of a servants' entrance. We proceeded slowly to avoid crashing into the wares and eventually reached the corridor, where feeble torches flickered in a row. There was dead silence aside from our ragged breathing.

"This can't be normal," I apprehensively noted.

Zabriel scowled at me. "It's the middle of the night on an island nobody frequents, and there's a siege going on. Stop worrying, Anya. Either that or stay put and be on watch duty."

"Sorry," I mumbled, irked by his condescending tone. He didn't have the right to chastise me for being wary. Before I could say anything to that effect, there was a clang that echoed off the stone, and I could have sworn I heard the rumor of voices. We looked at one another, our alarm unspoken, then Zabriel darted down the corridor. Illumina trailed him, her fist closing around her flame to extinguish it. For a split second, I couldn't move, terror freezing me in place. Then I forced myself to look over my shoulder. Seeing no one in pursuit, I gulped in air and rushed after my cousins.

As we hurried onward, I tried to pay attention to details so we could find our way back out, not wanting to end up trapped within these cold stone walls. However, the infrequent and irregularly spaced torches made it almost impossible to do so. There seemed to be no right or wrong way to go within the labyrinthine halls. Everything was identical in the castle on Evernook Island. If this place had been carved out of the mountain by Fae, I couldn't fathom what purpose it had served.

Too much time was passing, and in my rising trepidation, it struck me that I could no longer hear the sound of cannon fire. Had it stopped, or had we ventured far enough into the massive structure that outside life no longer penetrated its walls? If the latter were true, did it mean there might be soldiers inside this sanctum who hadn't responded to Fane's attack? Sweat broke out on my forehead despite the chill in the air, and I was almost immobilized once more. Then my thoughts went to the scars on Illumina's body—*belief, strength, power, perseverance, never look back*—and to fifteen-year-old Zabriel's boldness in crossing the Bloody Road to live in the Warckum Territory on his own. I hastened onward, struck by the thought that I might be the only member of our trio who wasn't inclined to be reckless. We needed to leave now, while we still could.

"Zabriel, if Fane has confiscated the shipments, we have enough," I said in an undertone. "You can determine the nature of a predator without walking into its lair. I think we should go."

"No," he flatly responded. "We've come too far to quit now."

We'd passed through a number of doors in our advance through the corridors, their dark gray stone absorbing torchlight to a discomfiting degree. For the first time, Zabriel put his hand on the latch of one and found it locked.

"Open it," he instructed Illumina.

He crossed his arms, black cloak thrown over one shoulder, and leaned against the wall, allowing her to brush past him. She stretched out her hand, but despite her efforts to concentrate, no flame appeared.

"Well?" he prompted, ruder than he needed to be, his forehead creased in concern.

"I can't do it," she carped, staring at her palm, willing a spark to appear. "I can't feel the connection."

"There's only one substance that can affect Fae that way." Zabriel kicked at the metal rimming that adorned the door, cursing under his breath. "Sky iron. Someone has gone to a lot of trouble to safe-keep whatever is on the other side of this barrier."

Numbness stole over me, followed by a sudden rush of heat. Sky iron had been studded into the bindings used by the hunters who'd taken my wings. It deprived us of our connection to the elements, took away our powers and defenses. To Fae, it was the most treacherous substance on earth, and its presence instantly altered my thinking about our mission. Caution now seemed overrated.

"We have to get in there." I lay my palms against the door as though to push it open, but unsurprisingly it didn't budge.

Zabriel cocked an eyebrow at me. "It's good to have you on our side again. I thought for a moment you'd lost your sense of adventure."

"I probably deserved that. But how do we get through?"

Zabriel dropped to his knees and pulled two long, thin metal implements from his coat pocket. He shrugged and began to pick the lock.

"I brought them just in case. They're like old friends. They even have names. I call them *Breaking*...and *Entering*."

Illumina and I peered over his shoulders, watching him manipulate the tools, and it wasn't long before we heard a satisfying *click*. I bit my lip as the door swung inward, only to stop after a few inches, its movement inhibited by a thick chain. My heart pounded, for either this wasn't the only entrance, or someone was already on the other side.

"Really?" Zabriel declared, staring at his new foe. Frustrated, he pulled out his gun and fired twice in rapid succession. I'd never seen a pistol capable of a double shot without some fussing in between, and it felt like my eardrums exploded in the confined space. Pain reverberated like a shrieking echo, and I clutched the sides of my head. Illumina did the same, but Zabriel didn't flinch. He simply kicked the door the rest of the way open.

There was no point asking him to explain his actions, or in trying to convince him that stealth would have been a better approach. Zabriel plunged forward, and not a force in the world could have prevented him from descending the seemingly endless and winding staircase that lay before us.

We hurried after him, dodging pitfalls of crumbling stone. When at long last the three of us reached the bottom, Zabriel snatched an unlit torch from the wall. He held it out to Illumina and it came brilliantly to life, signaling that we had left the sky iron far enough behind.

The room that sprawled before us was lined end to end with bookshelves bearing journals with unmarked spines. Here and there stood locked glass cabinets that held vials of strange-colored potions and concoctions, along with desks that were littered with research tomes and notes. The scent of chemicals and decay was rank about us. I coughed when it invaded my lungs, and resorted to short, unsatisfying gulps of air.

Zabriel walked the perimeter of the room to light other torches fastened to the walls. When he neared a desk, he flipped open one of the research volumes that rested upon it, while Illumina hastily scanned the shelves. I peered at the contents of a cabinet, covering my mouth and nose with my sleeve to block out some of the odor.

"Medical journals," Illumina called.

"And these are books about Fae," Zabriel added. "By the titles, I think whoever is working here might be studying our magical affinities."

I knew they were waiting to hear from me, but I couldn't manage to produce a sound. They had discovered information, while I had discovered a monstrosity: vials were set out on the shelves inside the cabinet like a macabre dinner buffet with the courses labeled—*Blood of the Fire Fae, drawn the twentieth day of spring; Blood of the Air Fae, drawn the third day of fall; Marrow of the Water Fae, supplied the thirty-fifth day of summer.*

Then there were the jars, filled with liquid preservative to sustain their contents—pieces of Faerie wings, a heart taken from the chest of one of my people, and some body parts I couldn't identify. There were slides, as well, which I could only assume contained tissue samples, slices of skin, and Nature knew what else. The vials, jars, and slides were innumerable.

The room moved in and out of focus as I strove to keep my head. *How long? How many?* The dates given did not identify the years.

Seeing my distress, Zabriel hastened to my side. "For the love of—" he swore, surveying the atrocities I had discovered. "Is this…real?"

"Are you happy now?" The voice, low and solemn, snapped me out of my daze. I blinked and looked up at Illumina.

"Happy?" I dumbly repeated. "Why in Nature's name would I be happy?"

Illumina's black hair blended into the background, although the flame she protectively cupped in her palm reflected in her green eyes. On her back, wings the color of dark bruises spread to points, her shroud temporarily forgotten.

"We left the humans alone. We gave them peace. We even tried to manufacture friendship between their race and ours through Aunt's marriage to William Ivanova. And all the time, my father warned that the humans shouldn't be left to their own devices, that they are betrayers by nature, always seeking to conquer and destroy. You and Aunt and all the human-lovers turned a blind eye, hosting your parties while they *tortured and experimented on us.* If any of you had taken the time to look, this place wouldn't exist. So I repeat, are you happy?"

"No, I'm not happy." I took a step toward her, balling my fists. "Our trust has been broken. But you can't make me feel guilty for trusting in the first place, not when it was the right thing to do. You're just saying these things because you need someone to blame."

Before I completely lost my temper, Zabriel stepped between us.

"Not all humans would approve of this, Illumina. There's a reason this *research* is being conducted in secret."

Illumina's petite frame shook, and it looked as if her entire body might burst into flame. "Are you too blind to see that the government has a hand in this? What does that say about your precious humans?"

Zabriel glowered at her as he gently pulled me away from the contents of the cabinets, then he resumed the argument.

"If the whole government was involved in this, the facility wouldn't be located in the middle of pirate-infested waters, secret or no. Yes, Evernook is government owned, but that only means someone made use of government resources that were available to them. That much we already knew." Zabriel's eyes flicked between Illumina and me as he let us process this. Although he was right, my stomach flipped, for logic meant little when standing inside a house of horrors. "We don't have time right now to consider who that someone might be, but we will find answers. I swear it."

"Maybe we'll find them here in the castle." Sorrow and anger were coursing through me, and I needed to focus on action lest my heart break right there and then.

"Plus the evidence to prove it." Zabriel held his torch high and proceeded toward a door at the other end of the hall. "This way, cousins."

We followed the spiraling steps farther downward, deeper and deeper until it seemed we were entering a cavernous new world. After a while, the steady ebb and flow of waves covered up our quick footfalls, and Evangeline's descriptions ominously returned to me—the sound of water, the smell of salt. I shuddered. This was where she'd been held captive. She'd heard these same waves as she'd been tortured, interrogated, and stripped of her wings and dignity. But why had she been let go? Why had any of them been let go?

A light appeared below us, and Zabriel immediately snuffed out his torch, singeing his cloak in the process. The slightly acrid odor burned my nose and throat, and I stifled a cough, fearful that there might be someone stationed in this pit who would hear me.

We pressed ourselves against the stairwell walls, moving more slowly onward. A short distance ahead, an eerily familiar glow danced across the stones on one side, revealing an opening. I pushed off the wall and started forward, knocking aside Zabriel's hand when he reached out to stop me.

"It's not guards," I hissed. "It's Sepulchres."

"How is that better?" Illumina demanded.

"Shea and I ran into a whole nest of them in the tunnels under Tairmor. They seek magic, but I don't think they hurt magical beings. Fae magic is their key to survival, so if they destroy us, they destroy themselves."

"But they do hurt humans," Zabriel cut in. "The children who have gone missing in Sheness—they're being fed to these creatures, remember? And you and I aren't far enough from human to make me comfortable with that."

"We're not little children, Zabriel. And I don't think they otherwise attack without instruction. Besides, if they're here, they must be confined. The Sepulchres in Tairmor said the ones working for the humans are corrupted. Made violent or something. So they'd be dangerous to those who work here if they weren't caged."

"More victims," Illumina concluded. "When we're out of here, the first thing I'm going to do is vomit."

For once, I couldn't disagree with her.

Zabriel was again the one to make the decision for us. "We really have no choice but to proceed if we're going to find out what's going on here. So let's continue, but no more noise than necessary."

"So you won't be shooting off bullets like a madman?" Illumina responded, earning a scowl in return.

Dropping our conversation, the three of us crept past the last of the inner wall. In a flash, at least twenty pairs of eyes were on us, and it felt like the breath was sucked from my lungs.

"Well, that was pointless," Zabriel remarked.

As I'd suspected, the Sepulchres were locked in a cage that filled the cylindrical room like a cork in a bottle. The sky iron from which the bars were made evidently subdued them, and they stared helplessly at us with pupil-less eyes. Zabriel stepped closer, and I snatched at his sleeve to pull him back. These Sep-ulchres weren't like the others I'd seen, not even the ones that had attacked Shea and me in the Fere. These creatures were sickly gray-green, barely luminescent, and their eyes were a dull, watered-down brown. They pressed against the grillwork bars, reaching through with jaundiced fingers. Something unspeakable must have been done to mutate these creatures.

We inched down a few more stairs, and it was then they started whispering.

"Water," the hollow voices said.

I scrunched my forehead, perplexed. Was it possible these creatures were thirsty? Then a jolt ran through my core. They were all staring at *me*. As my stunned mind tried to process this, I remembered what Evangeline had said—Sepulchres could identify our elemental connections. They were doing the job they had been coerced to do, and announcing that I was, or had been, a Water Fae.

"Fire," they said next, in a chorus, and Illumina shivered. To my knowledge, she'd never seen a Sepulchre before, and if their malformed faces and bodies weren't enough to fill you with fear, their voices were even more unsettling.

The Sepulchres moved on to Zabriel, every pair of deadened eyes fixated on him. Unlike with Illumina and me, the creatures hissed and stretched their arms through the holes in their enclosure, reaching for him, whether to break him or beg for food and liberation I couldn't tell. Considering the abuse they had suffered at the hands of nonmagical creatures, their reaction was understandable. But when they started whispering again, my body went cold at their collective words.

"Save us," echoed in my head. "Save us all."

In the grayish, fluid light that emanated from beneath the Sepulchres' skin, I saw Zabriel's jaw clench, and he stumbled back a pace. The plea issued to him was immense in its possible meanings, confusing and daunting. I knew, having heard the same request from the Sepulchres under Tairmor.

Every blank eye beyond the bars was glued to Zabriel, every

aching desire for deliverance thrust upon him. His own dark eyes wide and feverish, he moved away until his back was to the wall. Gone was his arrogance, along with every bit of certainty and flippancy he'd brought with him to Evernook Island. What remained was the boy from Chrior who had been afraid of expectation, who had run from controversy, and who had tried to lose himself in a criminal's life in Sheness. His disguise lay broken around him because these creatures could see straight through it.

Zabriel pitched toward Illumina and me, breath coming fast. Then he pressed his hands over his ears, struggling to shut out the hisses and pleading that besieged him. He shoved past us, but I knew he would not escape the memory of them so easily. Illumina and I hurried after him, making more noise than was probably wise.

"Zabriel, wait!" I called, worried that the intensity of the Sepulchres' need had reminded him of all the reasons he'd left Chrior, worried he would renege on his promise to return. "Zabriel, please!"

"No," he growled, footsteps echoing as he made his way down the next round of stairs. "We need to find out what's going on here and stop it, so everything can go back to the way it was. You never should have come to Sheness, either of you."

"You can't have that life anymore, Zabriel. Don't you see that?" The words flew like barbs from my mouth, but our circumstances did not allow time for compassion. "The game is *over*. There's only the future now, and there's no running away from your heritage this time."

At that, he came about, pointing a finger dangerously close to my face, almost forcing me to retreat. "You don't know anything, Anya. There were things I never told you, things I didn't want you to—"

He clamped his mouth shut, lips compressed into a thin line, eyes nearly manic. Then he looked to the ground, taking several deep breaths. When he once more met my gaze, the fire of anger had left him, revealing a sort of wretchedness.

"Just be quiet, Anya," he said, his wild reactions almost more frightening than the rest of our situation. "You're not helping anybody right now."

The Prince was off again, delving deeper into the dungeon, but it took Illumina's prod at my shoulder to get me moving. My mind was whirring at the prospect of the secrets hinted at by Zabriel's words, yet I had no time to consider them. Instead, I was running to keep up with him.

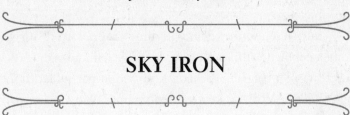

chapter twenty-seven

SKY IRON

We entered another long corridor, leaving behind the glow of the Sepulchres, and Zabriel's disembodied voice reached us from the far end.

"There's airflow behind this door."

Without waiting for us, Zabriel once more tossed caution aside. The corridor flooded with pale light as he threw open the door, and for a moment he stood in silhouette. Then he disappeared from view. By the time Illumina and I caught up to him, he had entered the room that lay on the other side. His mouth was agape, a condition that soon afflicted us all, and we slowly revolved as one while we took in the wonders that surrounded us.

We stood within a forest. Plants, flowers, and trees grew from wall to wall, and what looked and felt like daylight grazed our shoulders, though we were far underground. Birds chirped, toads croaked, and water babbled in fountains buried amongst the flora. The atmosphere was rejuvenating, empowering. Above us, I caught a glimpse of the light source—bubbles or bulbs filled with an undulating golden liquor. As I stared at the floating specimens, they shimmered in that subtle manner that could only be associated with magic.

"They did it," I announced, pointing upward, half impressed and half aghast. "Nature, they found a way to infuse magic into objects."

"Nature has nothing to do with this." Zabriel strode forward along a pebbled path, shoving aside plants left and right. "Why foster life in a brig?" he asked of no one in particular, frantic for answers. "Why make a garden in a pit? Why is this *here?*"

As the three of us struggled through the mass of branches and leaves that crowded in on us, excitement and apprehension battled for prominence within me. We had to be close to finding an answer. But when we emerged into a clearing, I came to a dead stop, turned to stone by the sight that greeted us.

"What is that?" Illumina breathed.

Before us stood a gleaming, oval-shaped silver fountain, a massive work of art, and at its summit a platform upheld a box—one with a great door covered in poor imitations of Fae love-carvings. Zabriel tentatively stroked the lip of the fountain with his fingers.

"A magician's box," I replied, struggling to spit out the words. I knew instinctively that this was what Shea's father had been asked to build, what he'd refused to finish. Those involved must have found someone else to do the work even as they tried to silence Thatcher.

Zabriel stepped back to examine the challenge, dropping his cloak on the floor, then hopped onto the fountain and scaled the tiers with intermittent help from his wings. I climbed after him, struggling at the last until he offered me his hand and pulled me up beside him on the platform. The beauty behind us was in stark contrast to the dark wood of the box, which had the deep vacuity of obsidian. The chirping of birds and other sounds of life seemed far away.

"Stay there," I warned Illumina, and she retreated a few paces. Zabriel kicked at the bolt, and the wood splintered loudly. Palms sweating, I reached across to help him tug open the door.

Inside, machinery clicked and clacked like a music box, but there was no beautiful dancer among these cogs, only a person, suspended in profile, wrapped in loose garments that barely covered the body. I couldn't even determine gender from the emaciated form or the head of short, scant brown hair. Several needles punctured the person's skin, which was so pale it looked bluish-green from thinly veiled veins. The machinery was somehow connected to the needles, monitoring and regulating Nature knew what. As my eyes traveled over the bindings that held him or her in place, I saw raw skin beneath the leather, and at the bare shoulder blades were great, swollen stitches, grafting to the bone a pair of wilted Faerie wings.

My stomach lurched, but I could not move, could not look away. The sight was unholy, the smell of illness and infirmity spirit crushing. I wanted to reach out, but though it shamed me, I couldn't make myself do so. I was afraid. Afraid that someone so afflicted could only be evil or violent, that its outward appearance was indicative of its putrid interior.

I heard the cock of a pistol beside me, and turned toward Zabriel. He was intently examining the thing suspended in front of us, and a flicker of sympathy crossed his face. In the next instant, he raised his gun, aimed it, and shot the unconscious being through its exposed temple. Blood and brain matter trickled down the inside of the box, and it was several stunned moments until I noticed the same thick substances slithering down my face and arms. I raised my hands, studying the remains with appalled fascination, trying to come to terms with my cousin's action.

I locked eyes with Zabriel, seeing there a prince, a rogue, someone merciful, and someone vengeful, all underneath a layer of blood and sweat. I wanted to say something to him, to reach out and touch him, but in the end, I stood silently by, daunted by his courage.

Illumina's shout broke the trance that seemed to bind the two of us together. Past the fountain, water now tainted red, stood Hastings, a goodly number of men at his back.

Zabriel's shroud went up the instant he realized we were not alone, but it was too late.

"No need for that," Hastings called, spitting out a wad of tobacco, eyes only on Zabriel. "We already knew about you and your filthy Faerie blood, Pyrite. Some of the stunts you've pulled made things pretty clear."

Spex's former keeper squinted at my cousin, and my mind raced. What was he doing here?

Everyone with Hastings was heavily armed. We had lingered too long, and now were trapped by a man who was more than the lackey Spex thought him to be.

Zabriel holstered his gun, not wanting to antagonize his adversary. Putting a hand on my waist, he guided me behind him, ironically shielding me with his body. This was wrong— it was my responsibility to protect the Prince.

"You really are just a boy," Hastings scoffed, running a hand over his bald scalp. "Some said so, but I wasn't sure I believed them. You don't have a damn scruff of hair on your face, do you?"

"How does it feel knowing a boy had you and all the Constabularies in the Territory running in circles for so long?"

Zabriel was taunting him, keeping his attention held fast so that Illumina could dart toward the side wall.

Hastings grunted a laugh. "It feels good, considering the money it's made you worth. The sailors have you talked up like you're some sort of avenging sea spirit, but you don't look like all that much to me. I'd keep you as a trophy just to show everybody how wrong they are, if you weren't such a prize for my pocketbook. You are slippery, though, I'll give you that. Almost thought I'd lost you when you weren't with the raiders at the shore. Of course, once you started breaking down doors with bullets, you were easy to corner."

"If you thought you'd lost me, then you were expecting to find me."

The significance of his words hit me hard, and a moan that formed the word *no* escaped from my lips.

"I won't spoil things by saying how I came by the information," Hastings went on with a grin. "But someone ratted you out—you can be sure of that. Not all your allies are so loyal."

One of the other men lurched forward, having spotted Illumina, but Hastings held out a hand to restrain him. Confusion gripped me. Why was he giving Illumina the chance to get away? He had to suspect she was Fae. Then a dreadful thought came to me. Was he leaving her alone because she was his informant? My heart pounded like a drum inside my chest, so forcefully I thought my ribs would shatter. Then my good sense returned. No, she couldn't be responsible. She had always hated humans. She wouldn't betray one of her own to help them. More likely he didn't want to bother with her, for she carried no price on her head.

"What's all this?" Zabriel asked, ignoring Hastings's attempts to rile him as he gestured to the evil contraption at our backs.

"An experiment. But don't worry—that fellow more or less volunteered."

"Like Spex volunteered?" I spat, peering out from behind my cousin, unable to hold my tongue.

"Prisoners of the Territory bargain for what they can," Hastings told me, examining the corpse hanging behind us with something akin to gratification. "This poor sap preferred the box to the plank. But he wasn't treated so badly. Look around—the man lived in his own little oasis. I've been told it calms them down when they need a break from the pain."

"And what was the purpose of this *experiment?*" Zabriel pressed, his disgust apparent.

"Don't know for certain. But from the looks of him, I'd say whatever they were trying to do wasn't working. Yours was a mercy killing, Pyrite, plain and simple. I won't hold it against you."

"I would so hate for a little thing like that to interfere with our friendship."

"Don't flatter yourself, kid. I'm just here to arrest you."

Zabriel's eyes narrowed, and he crouched like a wild animal readying itself to spring. "Try it."

He was carrying his usual weapons and was ready to fly, to fight, to do whatever was necessary by whatever means he had at his disposal. My spirits lifted and I moved away from Zabriel, preparing to make the descent to the floor. We three cousins would somehow make it out of here unscathed.

A harrowing *crack* rent the air, and at first I couldn't identify the sound, though I'd certainly heard it often enough. The bullet tore clean through Zabriel's left shoulder and wing, lodging in the wood of the magician's box. He slumped forward, blood pouring through his fingers as he clutched at his wound.

I screamed and went to him, wrapping him in my arms, but I wasn't strong enough to hold us both up. We fell hard onto the tiered fountain below, then crashed to the floor, my body breaking the worst of Zabriel's fall. The pain of impact was intense and sent a shock wave through my frame that left me wondering how many bones I had fractured.

I torturously raised my head to look at Hastings, whose pistol was stretched before him like a divining rod, steady and smoking from its report. I would never have anticipated such impeccable aim from that beast of a man. Nor could I have foreseen his action. I had thought he'd want to take my cousin alive.

"Zabriel," I managed once Hastings began to lower his firearm. I squeezed my cousin's good shoulder. "Zabriel, we have to get up. We have to get out of here. *Come on.*"

I glanced at Illumina, who looked ready to come forward, and shook my head. Our situation was already desperate. I didn't want a bullet ripping through her, as well.

"I don't think he'll be moving much," Hastings jeered, sauntering toward us. "That bullet's made of sky iron. It won't make the wound any worse, but it'll double the pain. I know—I've used it on Fae before. It'll keep him from causing me trouble."

With a mighty effort, I scrabbled to my knees and wrenched Zabriel's gun from its holster. I aimed it at Hastings, though I had no idea how to use it. He paused, thoughtfully chewing, then shot another greasy ball of spit at the ground.

"Go ahead. Take your best shot."

Despite the shake in my hands, I tried to cock the weapon, knowing that much was necessary. Before I could make more progress than that, Hastings laughed and crossed the rest of the distance between us.

"That's what I thought," he sneered, tugging the gun from my hand.

With no other recourse, I threw my body over Zabriel's, forcing Hastings to pry my fingers free of my cousin's quivering form. The Prince of the Fae, Chrior's greatest hope, was dragged away from me by a brute, and I was too pathetic to prevent it.

Hastings hoisted Zabriel to his feet, eliciting a closed-jaw scream that was brimming with fury and defiance, a noble sound that no one but a true prince could have mustered. It was at once terrifying and heartrending, and for a second Hastings hesitated, fear registering on his face. This expression, this moment, was the one I'd have to cling to for consolation.

Slick with blood and water, I tried to stand, focused on stopping Hastings and his men from leaving with Zabriel. But someone grabbed me by the shoulders and yanked me backward.

"Stay *away!*" Illumina shrieked, and in spite of the fact that she was keeping me from my goal, I smiled. I knew how foolish the men had been for writing her off as nonthreatening.

Hastings's followers made to close ranks around Illumina and me. Features so contorted they were almost unrecognizable, my cousin thrust forth her hand, and, in an elemental rage that would have outshone the Queen's Blades, summoned a wave of fire that heaved forward and turned two of the men into human bonfires. They howled, their skin popping like fireworks. The others who had been intent on arresting us immediately retreated, spreading away from each other as though to create less appealing targets.

Helping me to my feet, Illumina compelled me out the door and down the hall. The pain in my chest was temporarily blocked by the terror and exhilaration pumping through my veins. We retraced our path to the spiral staircase in the center of which the Sepulchres whimpered—the tumult Illumina had created was more than sufficient to keep the humans occupied—before I halted, reaching vainly for her arm.

"Zabriel!" I gasped. "We have to help him!"

My cousin whirled about, green eyes toxic. "No. We can't save him. We need to get off this island."

I closed my eyes in sad acknowledgment that she was right. We did not know our way around the castle, and even if we had been able to intercept Hastings, we would never have been able to haul the incapacitated Prince away with us.

Unwilling to wait for long, Illumina moved off, and I followed, up stairways and down corridors until by some miracle we found an exterior door in the fortress's stone wall. Without hesitation, Illumina blew it off its hinges. It landed in blazing glory along the tree line. Panting, I clutched at my side, stealing a moment's rest.

A rush of wind heralded a massive crackling, and I turned to see a cluster of trees erupt into flames, lit by the door Illumina had set on fire. The devastation on Evernook Island would be massive, and it would take us with it given the chance. I could only hope Zabriel—and absurdly Hastings and his men—would get out safely.

We pushed through the weald with flames roaring after us, shouts and the sounds of weapons growing nearer. Several times I tripped, my near-human form lacking its former strength and agility. I glanced at Illumina, wondering how deep her hatred of humans really ran. Would she take to the air and leave me behind if I slowed her down too much? And could I really blame her if she did?

The fire was spreading with incredible speed, fed by timber that was dry from winter and age. When we finally broke onto the beach, I swerved away from the men lunging at one another, the clattering of their swords at times drowned out by the reports of guns. Smoke hung over everything like thick fog, dulling my senses. The boom of cannon fire added to the chaos, Fane and his ship apparently close enough to join the fray. Illumina clutched at my arm, offering no assistance now that she'd gotten us this far. She'd done her part; it was up to me to guide us the rest of the way.

I took the lead, skirting obstacles and scrambling through rocky terrain. When at last the water came into view—inky black with a shimmer of moonlight across its surface—I wanted to collapse in relief. But the whiz of a bullet past my ear negated that idea. Grabbing Illumina's cloak, I hauled her behind the shelter of a pile of rocks. At least a dozen men were on the shorefront, crouching behind stray boulders while they fired pistol shots at each other. And some among them had surely set eyes on us.

"Any ideas?" I hissed to Illumina, wrapping an arm around my ribs to give them support, breath coming in pained gasps.

"Fire is always an option." Anger simmered in her voice, as if these men were the sole cause of our troubles.

"No! Some of those men are Fane's. Besides, you can't reach them when they're shielded by stone."

"I can fly," she retorted.

"And they could shoot you down. Those guns have good range, you know. Even if you survived, you could lose your wings and end up like me. Is that what you want?"

The ricochet of a bullet off the rubble at our feet added a

jolt of reality to my words, and forestalled Illumina's reply. Nevertheless, our problem remained.

When two of the men stood to rush their foes, a round of bullets from their hidden comrades providing cover, I seized the opportunity.

"Let's go!" I coughed, my lungs burning from the smoke that descended from the air like a blanket.

With Illumina stumbling in my wake, we disappeared into the haze, covering our lower faces with our sleeves. We headed toward a cliff face I had spotted that lay farther up the shoreline, abutting the water. Just when I thought I might pass out, we emerged onto the sand once more, the battle at last behind us. I limped toward the water, my lungs clamoring for fresh air. While I didn't know where we were, one thing was certain—we were nowhere near our boat.

"What do we do?" I croaked.

"Swim," Illumina grimly suggested.

I stared at her, wanting to cry. Not into those freezing eddies and bone-crushing waves. Please, anything but that. Yet we had no choice. Steeling myself, I stood and floundered into the water, praying my fresh injuries and fear wouldn't defeat me. Illumina rushed forward, not tentative in the least.

My teeth began to chatter, and it wasn't much longer before the ill-famed currents around Evernook took hold of us. I kicked hard and fast, the cold numbing my pain, and we shed our cloaks to make it easier to keep our heads above water. Just as Zabriel had rowed the dinghy across the eddies, we likewise swam at an angle to their pull. But they ultimately proved too strong, and the distance to the mainland too great. We wouldn't make it back, even if we'd known in what direction we needed to go.

My body was deadened from exhaustion and shock, and my remaining clothing weighed me down. I struggled, sculling with my arms and legs but making no progress. Illumina's black hair made her difficult to see, but as the inferno on Evernook gobbled up more trees, moving ever nearer the island's rocky perimeter, the water lit up. For a moment, I thought the sun was rising, then I shook my head and the illusion cleared. I bobbed like a cork, my strength giving out, and Illumina pulled my arms over her shoulders in a surprising display of willpower. Feeling a churning in the water, I realized she was using her waterlogged wings to keep us afloat.

It was because of the fire that we were found. We could easily have vanished into the ocean and been lost forever, but a short time later, Illumina was filled with renewed energy, loudly hailing a vessel of some sort. I peeled my eyes open to see a longboat tossed about on the waves, Shea at the helm, directing the sailors where to row.

"Thank God we saw you," she panted, helping to balance the boat so one of the strong-armed men could hoist me to safety. He then reached for Illumina, whose shroud had already risen, picking her up by her clothing to rescue her, as well. "What the hell happened?"

I tried to answer, but my jaw, like the rest of my body, was stiff and uncooperative.

"Here," Shea said, shifting to my side and stripping wet layers from my torso, deftly replacing my clothing with a warm, dry blanket and her own cloak, pulling the hood over my head. She did the same for Illumina, while the sailors rowed in a united effort to bring us home.

"Hastings was there," I finally managed, and the color

drained from my friend's face. "He shot Za...Pyrite. He didn't even hesitate."

"Is—is Pyrite... Is he..."

"No, he's not dead. Not yet, anyway. It was through the shoulder. But that ogre has him now, and he'll take him to Luka or the Governor to collect the reward. We'll never get him out of there, not without revealing who he really is. And that's the one thing my aunt wanted to avoid at all costs."

I'd given up caring what the sailors heard. I doubted they were listening, anyway.

"What do you think they'll do with him?" Shea's voice trembled, and she turned her face from me. Concerned, I laid a hand on her arm in comfort. Unfortunately, I had no words that could do the same.

"They could execute him, Shea. That's what they do with criminals and pirates." A worse thought struck me, and I gagged, digging my fingernails into Shea's skin. "Hastings knows he's Fae. And someone at Evernook has been experimenting on Faeries. Mutilating them, killing them. What if they..." My throat was too tight for me to finish the sentence.

"None of this was supposed to happen," Shea murmured, closing her eyes and steepling her fingers over her mouth.

"I know." I tried to muster some hope. "We'll talk to Fane. He'll have an idea what to do."

She nodded, gazing out at the sea, despair written all over her face. I likewise glanced around, realizing that the surface of the water was filling with other craft headed to Evernook either to assist or observe, for there was little possibility of putting out the fire. In her zeal to escape, Illumina had likely

destroyed every trace of evidence that the horrors we'd discovered existed, and whatever the stone walls of the castle
managed to preserve would be discarded. Still, she'd ruined
everything the Fae-haters had been working on, and I could
take satisfaction in that.

"How about you?" I asked, suspecting Shea would also
have encountered danger this night. "How did things go with
Fane?"

A touch of dramatic thrill entered her voice, despite the
overall wretched outcome of this night.

"I've never seen anything like it. The captain maneuvered
his ship to cut off the Dementya vessel, then disabled it with
cannon fire. The pirates clamored over to the transport ship,
and a lot of brutal fighting ensued. In truth, everything happened so fast I had no idea which side was winning. But in the
end, Fane's men confiscated the cargo and sank the Dementya
ship, putting the surviving sailors into longboats. In some ways,
it was the most awful thing I've ever seen. And yet, I'd do it
again. It's sick, but addicting. I know that already."

"Do you know how many died?"

"No, just that there were casualties." Shea leaned toward
me, rubbing my arms to warm them. "The Dementya crew
took more losses than the pirates. I heard Fane say he only
lost one man, though a lot of them were bleeding when they
got back on deck. I suppose the numbers make sense, though.
Raiding ships is more or less a pirate's occupation, so they'd
better be good at it."

"Sounds terrible," I muttered, not wanting to accept that
Zabriel had undoubtedly been at the helm in similar skir-
mishes. "Not what I'd consider a fine way to live."

Shea and I hunkered down in the longboat to be rowed ashore, while Illumina continued to gaze at the chaos she had wrought, a proud tilt to her jaw. Evernook Island looked as though it would crumble into the sea, taking all its secrets with it.

chapter twenty-eight

TRAITOR

I awoke early the next morning to shouting and only a vague recollection of the events following Zabriel's capture. I pushed myself upright, and gasped in pain. Sharp, breath-stopping radiations threaded my ribs, and I went stock-still until the hurt had abated enough for me to open my eyes and look around. I was in a bed at Aunt Roxy's, blankets and hot-water bottles piled around me. Illumina was curled at my side, having just roused with an expression as bewildered as mine. I studied her, the fog in my head gradually clearing—we had been found by Shea, ferried back to shore, and carried to the house. Sleep had been Illumina's and my retreat from the cold, shock, and exhaustion we'd suffered.

Spex was the only other person upstairs with us, occupying a bed for a change. I supposed with the vacancies last night had provided, Roxy had opened her heart a little and let the spotter be more comfortable. Not too comfortable, however. He was still shackled by one hand to the bedpost.

Heavy footfalls resounded from the main floor, and the shouting that had dragged me from unconsciousness recommenced.

"I want to know what happened!" Fane's voice thundered. "Where the hell is he?"

Aunt Roxy spoke at a normal volume and I couldn't quite make out her words, but it was no mystery they were discussing Zabriel. I eased out of bed, trying to be gentle to my cracked and bruised body, and tossed one of the many blankets around my shoulders. I was the one who had the answers Fane was seeking.

I descended the stairs at the quickest pace I could manage. By the time I reached the bottom, I was gripping the rail for support.

Roxy was beating an old rug in the middle of her living room. I didn't question the logic in transferring dirt from one floor surface to another—perhaps she just needed to be busy. Fane had one hand on the mantel above the fireplace and was looking downward, his body as tense as the words I'd heard him exclaim moments before. Aware of my presence, Roxy ceased what she was doing, and both she and the captain turned my way.

"Where's Shea?" I asked, for she had not been upstairs. Surely she would have already told them a few things about last night.

"Pyrite never made it back," Fane announced, as though I had not spoken. "Where is he?"

I frowned, not quite comprehending the situation. "But hasn't Shea—"

Fane slammed his hand against the mantel, shocking the whole house into stillness. I could have sworn the clock on the end table missed a tick. "I don't give a damn about her right now! Do you know what became of Pyrite, or should I be out searching the water for his body?"

I bristled, my overwrought mind and body rebelling against the old pirate's tone, which seemed to imply he cared more about Zabriel than I did.

"We were ambushed in the warehouse. A man named Hastings was in charge. My cousin took a sky iron bullet in the shoulder before he was captured."

Fane sank into a chair, more aware than I was of the significance of Zabriel's capture on all fronts. Whether he was convicted of piracy and executed or the Fae managed to secure his life by revealing his identity to the Governor, his days as William Wolfram Pyrite were over. We couldn't discuss the ramifications in front of Aunt Roxy, but that conclusion required no corroboration.

"Hastings?" Fane repeated. "That's not a name I know."

"He's a Fae-hunter, used to oversee Spex in Oaray. I've had the misfortune of a few run-ins with him."

"Then we need to find out where Pyrite is being held. If he's still local, we may be able to spring him."

I hid the sympathy from my gaze, suspecting Fane wouldn't appreciate it. No part of me believed Hastings would have dawdled in taking Zabriel far from his allies and fellow pirates in Sheness. If Fane didn't recognize it on some level now, he would when he calmed down. I still had worse news to deliver.

"Hastings was able to take Pyrite into custody last night because somebody told him where to look. The only thing I'm sure of is it wasn't me."

I let my words resonate in the air, examining Fane's glare, made twice as disconcerting by his bloodshot, mismatched eyes. Roxy looked equally distraught, her mouth agape, the rest of her features drooping more than usual. I watched for signs of guilt, but saw nothing except manic fervor in the old pirate, and a crestfallen loneliness in the house matron at what she instinctively knew was a permanent loss. She'd cared for Zabriel, really cared for him, even though she didn't know his real identity.

A banging on the door startled us all back to life. Dropping her rug in a pile on the floor, Roxy went to answer it, her scowl revealing she wasn't expecting company. She'd opened it no more than a crack when Gwyneth blew across the threshold with the urgency and grace of a diving hawk.

"I just heard it from my father," she announced, removing her black lace gloves one finger at a time, elegant as ever, although her hands were noticeably trembling. "The men are saying Pyrite's out of the way. That he's dead or captured. It's all speculation, and Luka Ivanova won't confirm or deny. What's really going on?"

"He's been arrested," Fane told her. "We don't know the complete circumstances yet."

"Goddamn it," Gwyneth murmured, punching her gloves into the basin of her flowered hat and throwing the whole package aside. "Damn. What went wrong?"

"According to Anya, somebody turned, sold him out."

Though usually ready with a rejoinder, Gwyneth had no swift response to Fane's proclamation, lips parted in the silence.

"How do you know that?" she asked at length, her amber eyes landing on me.

"Hastings told us," Illumina called from the top of the stairway. She had emerged from the bedroom, fully dressed, and now sat on one of the upper steps. "He's involved somehow in the Fae abductions, and he rubbed it in our faces. But he wouldn't say who snitched."

"Please, what would I gain by turning Pyrite in?" Gwyneth

snapped, catching me off guard. I'd been searching her pristine features for secrets, much like I had with Aunt Roxy and the captain, and she'd noticed my stare. "The whole bounty on his head wouldn't have paid for this ring on my finger. I already have money and power, the best of both worlds." She hesitated, her point already established, then added one final thought. "And he's my friend. One of the only people who actually knows me. I wouldn't want to be rid of him. Not ever."

She seemed sincere enough, vulnerable even. But I'd seen her blatantly lie to her father with an innocent smile, the epitome of a loving, doting daughter, and I wasn't sure I was immune from falling for her act. In the end, her logic was what steered me toward believing her. I couldn't imagine anything she would gain by having Zabriel captured.

"If I'd gone to the authorities, I'd have been arrested myself," Fane offered. "Think what you will of me, but you know that's true."

Roxy picked up her rug and laid it by the door, pushing the corners into place with the tip of her slipper. With her back to us, I was probably alone in noticing the movement of her arm. She was wiping her nose with her sleeve.

"I've got a hundred men coming in and out this house with a hundred prices on their heads," she grumbled, voice betraying none of her emotion. "If snitching was my game, I'd be living high and mighty, not in this dump."

My thoughts strayed to Illumina, perched above me like a sharp little bird. She wanted the throne upon Ubiqua's death, and Zabriel had been her only remaining obstacle until last night. For a fleeting moment in the underground garden, I'd considered her as a suspect. But I'd decided in the same breath that her ambition couldn't stretch that far. And she might well be the reason I was alive today to suspect anyone. After everything she'd done to see me safely off the island, I couldn't think of accusing her.

Fane lumbered to his feet, having no such reservations. "What about you?" he bellowed up to her. "What's your story?"

"I didn't betray him," she calmly responded, descending the stairs to join us.

"She can't lie," I reminded Fane before he could say anything more. "It's not her."

"The little shit's been chained up since you brought him here, so it couldn't have been him," Roxy piped up, curtailing all inquiries about Spex, the next obvious culprit. That left only one person among our immediate company who had known the details of our plan.

Fane reiterated the question I had asked upon coming downstairs. "Where is Shea?"

"I'm right here," she answered, coming through the kitchen door. She was carrying a sack of supplies, having entered the house by means of the back door. "I've been out on the streets, listening for word. I'm as worried about Pyrite as the rest of you."

"But did you hand him over?" Fane shot back, unwilling to accept anything but a direct answer.

"No," Shea scoffed, shaking her head emphatically, eyes drilling into Fane. "Wasn't I out there risking my life on your ship last night?" She glanced around the room, looking for someone to indicate they believed her. "What the hell are you thinking, anyway, pointing fingers? I thought we were supposed to be one crew, or did I mishear you last night, Captain?"

For a moment, I could hear my heart beating, louder than

any other noise in the room. Shea was defensive, too much so, and I couldn't help but think she was overcompensating for something. On the other hand, how was one supposed to respond to a roomful of accusing gazes? With a smile? Calm consideration? I appraised her, noting how alone and helpless she looked. She certainly didn't need to face my accusatory glare in addition to everyone else's. Shaking off my doubts, I spoke up on her behalf.

"It wasn't Shea. We've been through a lot together, and she's proven over and over again to be a stalwart friend. If you won't believe that she has loyalty to Pyrite, at least trust that she wouldn't endanger me."

"Sometimes that don't matter," Aunt Roxy said, her gristly voice softer than usual. "There's only three outsiders here I can't vouch for myself, and two of you are relation to Pyrite. That leaves her."

She tipped her head at Shea, and I could feel animosity growing in the little house. Annoyed that the others hadn't accepted my word, I hobbled across the room to stand by my friend.

"It's not her. I know her better than the rest of you, and if I had any doubt about her innocence in harming *my* cousin, I'd tell you. Back off."

"Maybe you're blind to her duplicity precisely because of how much time you've spent together," Gwyneth offered, the calmness in her voice designed to defuse my temper failing to do so. "Sometimes our enemies hide close to us."

"Believe what you want to believe," I snarled, clenching my hands into fists, my jaw like a vise. "But tell me this. When is she supposed to have contacted the authorities? Shea and I have been together day and night for months. And Fane—you and

Pyrite have kept us hopping ever since we arrived. She didn't have the *time* to betray us!"

I looked at the people in the room one at a time, daring them to contradict me. Feeling that the tide was shifting in Shea's favor, I added one last argument.

"Besides, Shea doesn't know her way around Sheness. She'd have no idea how to contact disreputable bounty hunters or the Constabularies."

Silence reigned for a moment, everyone shifting their eyes away from me, presumably in embarrassment over their zeal to accuse my friend. Ironically, now that I had everyone convinced, doubt ate at my stomach like worms attacking a corpse. Despite my assertions, my memory whispered that Shea *had* left the house alone on the first morning we'd been here, giving her an opportunity to track down Hastings. And though she wasn't native to Sheness, she had been here before, with her family when they'd attempted to flee the Territory by sea.

"Who then?" Fane thundered. "'Cause whoever it is, they've just made enemies of the entire underbelly of Sheness."

Six pairs of eyes darted around the room, each of us secretly suspecting one of our other comrades. Then another possible suspect occurred to me, and relief flowed through me like a cool drink of water.

"What about Opal? He seemed pretty keen on getting back at you, Captain. Maybe he bribed one of your sailors for information. He is a bounty hunter, after all. He'd do whatever it took to have a shot at the reward on Pyrite's head. And he could be working with Hastings. They're sharing Spex, after all."

Fane rubbed his unshaven chin. The stubble, coupled with the gray circles under his eyes, suggested he hadn't slept last night. He sighed, not apologetic but less eager to blame our troubles on a member of the present company. "I'll see what I can find out."

"Can I go now?" asked Shea. "Are you done accusing me?"

"You can go upstairs," Fane responded, annoyance at her attitude still quick to emerge. He didn't like the fact that we hadn't yet ferreted out the traitor. "Don't leave the house. Roxy here will keep an eye out to make sure you don't."

Shea glanced at the owner of the house, who nodded her head vehemently, and an angry glow spread across her cheeks and nose.

"Whatever you say, Captain," she snipped, then she turned and stormed up the staircase.

In the aftermath of Shea's departure, I foolishly thought suspicion would no longer be cast on her. But as soon as she'd disappeared from sight, Fane was on me, pinning me to the wall with his forearm. The impact was enough to make me cough, and I groaned, my raw muscles protesting the treatment.

"If Shea did this, you can't protect her," he snarled, mismatched eyes narrow and distrustful. "Even I couldn't protect her, assuming I'd want to. Pyrite made himself a symbol in this city, a symbol that took the heat for a lot of things your cousin didn't do. With that light extinguished, some very dangerous people will be left out in the open, and they won't be grateful for it."

I clawed at his arm, more affronted than afraid, although rage simmered deep inside me at my helplessness. With a cry of pain unrelated to my efforts to free myself, Fane stumbled backward, and I fell the few inches he'd lifted me from the ground. Illumina moved close to my side, blowing on her fingers while the captain examined the blistering burn around his wrist.

"We don't know that Shea or anybody else gave Hastings information," Illumina said in her honey voice, staring down the dumbfounded pirate without blinking. "He could have invented the whole thing."

"Isn't that sweet?" Fane scoffed, trying not to reveal fear or alarm, though he moved away from us. A human's first violent encounter with a Faerie's elemental connection was always eye-opening. "Guess you Fae stick together."

"That's more than can be said for you humans," Illumina replied in a wispy voice that was somehow terrifying.

The captain had the decency to allow shame over his prejudicial statement to creep into his expression. The rest of us were quiet, and I wished Aunt Roxy would leave, since she was preventing us from talking openly about Zabriel and the fallout from his capture. But I could hardly insist she get out of her own sitting room. Gwyneth stepped forward in her expensive boots, making herself the center of attention, and I held my breath—this could be good or bad.

"You see, Fane, some people really can trust their friends," she scolded, and I exhaled more loudly than I intended. "It will be a sad day indeed when you take the word of someone like this *Hastings* fellow over the word of our companions. Now, if that's quite settled, my father mentioned he expected a raid at The Paladin to follow last night's disaster. You'd best warn your men, Captain."

Fane nodded curtly, and I dared to add, "We'd be better served right now by focusing on how to help Pyrite. Unless you *want* to see him executed."

For a moment, I thought the captain might lunge at me

again. He didn't welcome having his loyalty challenged. Instead, he picked his hat off the mantel and stuck it on his head, glaring at everyone except Aunt Roxy. Still, his reaction was reassuring. It told me he'd do what he could to slow down the Territory's march toward justice, perhaps even launch a rescue attempt if Zabriel were yet in Sheness. He remained our ally, however much he might resent us. He strode to the door, but before he disappeared into the street, he tossed a report over his shoulder.

"By the way, the shipment we intercepted was sky iron, from what I could tell. Most of it sank with Dementya's ship, but that's what was in the cargo my men managed to retrieve. There was a foreign transport stamp on all the crates, but it didn't say where it was coming from. That's all I got."

Stepping outside, he violently slammed the door, and I was thankful he was taking out his wrath on an inanimate object.

"Upstairs," Gwyneth muttered, giving my hand a squeeze. "We need privacy."

Gwyneth, Illumina, and I mounted the stairway, leaving a wide-eyed Aunt Roxy behind. Spex was sitting up in bed as we entered the room, watching us with a serene expression that belied his awareness of the troubled dynamic of our group. Who was responsible for him now? He had been Fane and Zabriel's little joke, but now Fane had walked out and Zabriel was in custody. Spex's hazel eyes met mine, the same question on his mind. Not knowing what to say, I took the simple approach and ignored him.

"What are we going to do?" Gwyneth asked, cutting straight to the point. She didn't or wouldn't believe the game was up, that there was no way to help my cousin. "It's for the best Fane is occupied right now, but I don't see any point in *us* pretending

Zabriel's still in the city. The people who have him are smart enough to get him out of here before announcing his arrest. Otherwise, half of Sheness would try to free him."

"There's only one thing we can do." I turned to Illumina, who was already nodding her head, anticipating my decision. "You have to go back to Chrior and bring our aunt to Tairmor. There's no time to waste."

Petite features as hard as diamond, my cousin snatched up her leather travel pack and began to stuff her possessions inside.

"I need to return to my family," Shea inserted from behind us.

I jumped, having nearly forgotten she was there. She stood by the balcony, staring across the street. The sun afforded her still form a strange shine, like she were a mirage instead of flesh and blood.

Gwyneth scowled at her, presumably because this was not an ideal time to desert our ranks, while Illumina looked smug, probably expecting this sort of behavior from a human. Neither of them was aware of the More family's predicament, and there was no real reason to tell them. At the same time, there was a very good reason to keep them in the dark. Shea's history might be all it would take to convince them of her guilt, for she would have derived quite a benefit from the bounty on Zabriel's head. It was far less problematic if I was the only one aware of her background. The truth about Shea was my business, my heart insisted, my personal business.

Truth. What a terrifying word. Why was going back to her family suddenly so urgent? Fane had told her to stay put, and she had stuck with me thus far. Why run off when the worst imaginable had happened, and I was in greater need of her support and friendship than ever? My stomach prickled with

uneasiness. We Fae were stereotyped as deceptive and manipulative, yet if you asked us a specific enough question, you
would have no grounds to doubt the answer you were given.
Humans were not bound by such rules. What answer would
I get from Shea if I asked her the question that burned in my
gut? And did I know her well enough to discern the truth regardless of her words?

"Right, you should see your family," I responded, brushing
aside my qualms like cobwebs, and with about as much success.

I dragged my gaze from Shea's silhouette, aware that Gwyneth's eyes were darting between the two of us, keen to navi-
gate the undercurrent in our exchange.

"I'll go with Illumina to Tairmor," I informed Zabriel's
wealthy cohort. "I'll stay there and wait for her and the Queen
to join me. I don't know what influence you have over your father and in the capital, but use every ounce of it to keep Zabriel
alive. Most of all, keep your ears open. If you hear anything,
anything at all, send word to me. There's a woman named Fi
who runs the Fae-mily Home in Tairmor. I'll reconnect with
her, and you can use her to get a message to me."

"I know the place. But, Anya, I'm not sure going to Tairmor
is wise. What if you've earned *yourself* a wanted poster? You
were discovered in that warehouse right alongside Zabriel."

"I'll find a way." Though I had little desire to travel the tunnel system again, it would take me safely into the city. I would
do what had to be done.

Gwyneth bobbed her head, then bobbed it again, recognizing her cue to depart but for some reason wanting to disregard
it. When her tawny eyes landed pleadingly upon me, seeking
some form of reassurance, it came to me that she was scared.
She was vibrant, powerful, unstoppable—and afraid of losing

my cousin. All I could offer her was a smile, but it seemed to be enough. She headed down the stairs, shoulders straight, her usual guise of confidence firmly back in place.

"Are you sure you should go now?" I asked Shea, undertaking the next bit of unfinished business. "The captain seemed opposed to you leaving, remember?"

"My family's in danger and I've waited long enough. I'm not going to stay here for Fane."

Though her reasoning was plausible enough, she wouldn't meet my eyes, breaking out of her statuesque pose to scurry about the room, gathering her things.

Illumina placidly watched Shea, then fastened the clasp on her travel satchel.

"I'll go see if Aunt Roxy can give us any provisions for the trip," she said, with atypical social sensitivity, and I nodded my thanks.

The moment Illumina disappeared through the doorway, Spex reasserted his presence.

"If you want to be alone, you're going to have to do something about me." He held up his chained hand and tugged a reminder. "You can't keep me forever, despite how much you love me."

"That doesn't mean we have to let you go," Shea retorted. "We could let you starve to death. Or just shoot you. Then again, Roxy might have some use for you—perhaps turn you into a potato peeler in the kitchen."

I smirked. Shea was shameless in her enjoyment of Spex's distress. It took him a bit to notice the smile playing on my lips, but when he did, his entire face scrunched in irritation that she would poke fun of him at such a dire time.

"Think that's funny?" he spat, his anger as laughable as his

injured pride. He was like a kitten on the attack—tiny, fero-
cious, and totally ineffective. Realizing he was getting nowhere with us, he sat back to try a different approach, adopting
a more nonchalant attitude.

"I'm way too talented to be kitchen help, and you know
it. I'm a spotter, remember? And you don't have the guts to
kill me."

"I wouldn't go underestimating our guts," I warned.

Thoughts of the previous night flashed through my mind.
I'd watched Zabriel shoot someone in the head and Illumina
roast two men alive. And if I had known how to handle a
gun, I would have shot Hastings in whatever manner of heart
was trapped in his chest. But I had no desire to deal with Spex
that way. What I needed was to have him gone, no complications, so that I could be alone with Shea. There were bigger
matters at stake, and it was hard to imagine he could make
things *worse* for us than they already were. I strode to the desk,
yanked open the top drawer, and withdrew the key that would
set Spex free. I set about removing his shackles none too gently, and in one final endeavor to influence him, was none too
gentle with my words, either.

"You've hurt everyone I love in the Warckum Territory.
You know everything that's happening, and unless I really do
kill you, I can't stop you from reporting to Opal or Hastings
or whoever will take your information. But you've suffered,
too. They've made you suffer, and that's why I can't take your
life. Maybe you'll find it in you to be a little grateful for that.
Now go out that balcony and disappear."

Spex rubbed his wrist where the shackle had bound him.
Almost as though he expected my action to be a trick, he hesi-

tated; then he was out the door, over the railing quicker than any cat, and sprinting down the street.

"I'd better be on my way, too," Shea said, picking up her pack and scanning the cluttered room one last time. I wasn't fooled by her behavior. She couldn't bear to look at me.

"I'm not going to stop you."

Maybe knowing the ending would combat the coward in her and allow her to be honest with me. My heart was pounding and my legs were trembling, though I couldn't have voiced the reason. I already *knew.* Was I really so averse to hearing the truth out loud?

Nervous, I continued to fill the silence between us. "I mean, I just let Spex walk out of here. If there's anyone I should have done away with, it was him."

"Anya…please."

"Please *what?*" I shrilly laughed.

I closed my eyes, trying to rein in my wildly surging emotions. I needed to focus, something with which I was experiencing difficulty of late. But this time when I reopened them, I, at least, was calmer. Shea's restless movements had continued, however, and she looked toward the door like she'd missed her opportunity to escape.

"The truth doesn't scare me, Shea. I think I deserve to hear it."

Shea finally looked straight at me, tears brimming and spilling down her cheeks. My stomach lurched at this confirmation of my fears and suspicions. I retreated from her, hands going to my hair, tugging hard to make sure I was actually awake, actually living what felt like a scene from a farcical play.

"I did it for my family," Shea said, taking a meager step toward me. "The price on Zabriel's head was enough to pay my father's debt. Luka promised he'd arrange for us to move back into our house in Tairmor. So I really had no choice. I had to do it, for my sisters, for Maggie and Marissa."

This time she was bold enough to come near, but I stopped her with an outstretched arm, my anger rising and reaching like a living thing, wanting to lash out at her, to strike her, to hurt her.

"Stay *away* from me."

I couldn't make my breath come normally. I hated her. I hated her so much, and yet there she stood, offering comfort as though she really believed her words, her excuses. I was repulsed. My temples throbbed, my teeth ached from grinding them hard enough to polish rock, and my body heat soared. I felt certain I would explode, my skin unable to contain this much fury. Yet when I spoke, my voice was dangerously subdued.

"You...you *killed* him."

"No!" Shea exclaimed, her tears starting anew. "I didn't know Hastings would be there, or that he'd—that he'd *shoot Zabriel*. I didn't know what was happening on Evernook, the evil that was being done there. I never wanted anyone to get hurt."

"How can you say that?" I seethed. "You know they execute murderers and thieves. You've known that from the beginning. You can't sign someone's death warrant and then say you never meant them harm."

Shea didn't have a response; she just floundered there, clenching and unclenching her hands, round cheeks splotched by sorrow, hemmed in by the lies she'd told to me and to herself.

"I don't understand it," I relentlessly continued. "Why did I defend you when I knew in my heart what you'd done? Why didn't I just let Fane go after you? Why should I care about you at all anymore?"

"Fane would have killed me." Shea's voice was small, her eyes downcast, perhaps in acknowledgment that my devotion was stronger than hers.

"Maybe that's what I should do." Contrary to the violence of my words, I collapsed on the corner of one of the beds. "My Realm is ruined. The Queen I love is dying…my wings are gone…the Prince will be executed. Chrior and the Faerie Realm are finished."

Shea was utterly silent—even the sound of her breathing was muted. She had no understanding of the sweeping power of politics, of how her existence with her family would be impacted by whatever happened next in the Realm of the Fae. No one would be immune to the repercussions. We were looking at an interracial catastrophe if the humans executed our Prince, especially with Illumina taking the throne in the aftermath. Zabriel's loss would stir up all the righteous anger the young Queen would need to cultivate the support of a majority of my people for her campaign. Thanks to Shea's initiative, the Mores would have their house back, yes—and two races of people might engage in a bloody, hateful war that would rip our two worlds apart.

"I'm so sorry, Anya. God, I'm so sorry."

I didn't know how long it had been since one of us had spoken, but Shea's words seemed to wake me from a nightmarish maelstrom of thoughts.

"I wish we'd never met," I told her through clenched teeth. "I wish I'd left you behind with your criminal family. I should never have let you get close to me, never have risked the future of my people on our friendship. You're a cheat and a liar, and I was fool enough to trust you, anyway."

"I don't expect you to forgive me."

"Good," I snapped, coming to my feet. "I'm not going to try."

Shea bit her lip hard, nostrils flaring as she tried to stave off more tears. She knew I meant it. I was incapable of lying.

"For what it's worth," she mumbled. "I'll never forgive myself, either. But I'm willing to live with that, for the sake of the people I love."

Seconds passed, but I refused to acknowledge her justification or lend any credence to the idea that *she* had made a sacrifice. Both notions were repulsive and equally intolerable, and when it looked like she would say something more, I cut her off with a wave of my hand.

"Just go. But travel fast. If Fane finds out you betrayed Zabriel, you'll be dead. And though I'd love to see you suffer for this, I'm not sure that's the punishment you deserve. So *leave,* before I change my mind."

"Thank you, Anya. I know I don't deserve to walk out of here, so thank you."

She seemed lost for a moment, almost melancholy that this was the way things were ending between us, even though this was the ending she herself had wrought. Then she threw her pack over her shoulder and walked toward the door, wiping her face on her sleeve. Coming abreast of me, she halted, reaching out a hand in a natural way that would once have been welcome, only to let it fall to her side.

"I don't know why you would, but...if you ever want to see me, you can find me in Tairmor."

Shea left the room, but I heard her halt at the top of the stairs, then turn around.

"Anya," she said, tentatively reentering the room. "Roxy… Fane has her keeping track of me. I don't think I can go downstairs."

"That's not my problem." I gazed into her frightened eyes, and though I despised myself for taking pity on her, I added, "I suggest you follow Spex."

Shea nodded, grateful I'd come around to aiding her this one last time, and approached the balcony. I didn't know how she'd manage the drop, nor did I care. If she were too meek to try it, she'd just have to face Roxy. And if she fell and broke her neck, life would carry on just fine without her. When silence once more descended upon the room, I looked over to see that she was gone.

I sat motionless in the aftermath of her departure, my lips quivering as the tension brought on by confrontation left my body. But despite the heavy devastation I felt, I tried to process Shea's actions, rejecting, then embracing, then rejecting her rationale in an endless circle of pain. What hurt the most was the feeling that there were other choices she could have made. She could have confided in me as friends should do. We could have found another way to deal with her father's debt. And she should have respected the trust I had in her. But friendship apparently meant nothing next to family loyalty. Or more likely, friendship meant nothing next to the easy way out.

Remembering that Illumina was waiting downstairs, I shoved anything that was important into my satchel. I didn't want to think anymore. Thinking would weigh me down to the point I'd never be able to get up again, and there were still people counting on me. I had to see Illumina safely to Tairmor, and somehow I had to undo what Shea had done. That was my priority.

Roxy had put together enough food to see us through a few days on the road. Though any attempt at normalcy felt stilted, I managed to thank her for her kindness. I also penned a quick note for her to give to Fane that explained our plans, mentioning nothing about Shea. While we were more or less deserting the captain, even he couldn't have argued we were needed in Sheness. This was his turf, his domain to mobilize, and it was imperative for Illumina to reach Chrior. Zabriel's best hope now lay in the mother, the Queen, he'd for so long strived to forsake.

chapter twenty-nine

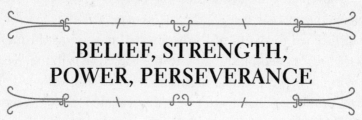

BELIEF, STRENGTH, POWER, PERSEVERANCE

Before leaving Sheness, my cousin and I rented a single dappled gray horse with part of the money we had left. He was a strong-looking animal, and both Illumina and I were lightweight, so we had faith he could carry both of us and our possessions to Tairmor. I assumed she had never ridden before, but she surprised me with her comfort in settling behind the saddle while I took the reins. I supposed her magic, which had a calming effect even on wild animals, prevented her from feeling as vulnerable as I had my first time on horseback. It was also possible someone had given her cursory instruction during her travels, much like the boy in Strong had aided Shea and me. The thought lifted my lips into an actual smile, an expression I thought had abandoned me—that was the sort of experience she ought to be having on her Crossing, which was essentially what this journey meant for her.

Even though travel by horseback would be less efficient, it was a very real possibility that we had been labeled criminals, and we couldn't risk boarding a riverboat. Zabriel would have to last however long it took for help to arrive.

Illumina had never been a fool. Though she asked me no

questions, I was sure she had inferred Shea's guilt. I was grateful for her restraint, especially with regard to a human. She did, however, glance at me every so often with extra pensiveness in her stare.

I listened for word of Pyrite in the little towns through which we passed on our way to the capital, but didn't even catch a whisper. I had no means to decide if this was good or bad. On the one hand, were he to be executed, the Governor would likely make it into a similar spectacle to the one we had witnessed with Spex's father. But the law's silence could mean Zabriel was already dead, that he'd never made it off the island, or that he was undergoing Nature knew what manner of interrogation.

One sleepless night along the way, I remembered that Zabriel had been wearing his royal ring on a chain around his neck at the time of his arrest. What might the consequences of that be? His identity might be determined before Queen Ubiqua arrived; he could be accused of robbing or murdering one of the Redwood Fae; the ring could be confiscated without its significance being discovered and be lost to history. Did any of these scenarios make things better or worse? I had no idea. I was perhaps most terrified that the Governor hadn't been told of Zabriel's capture at all—that the Prince of Chrior could be locked away in another research facility, the subject of ghastly experiments, and we might never find a trace of him.

We entered Tairmor via the tunnels I'd taken with Shea, leaving the horse behind at the river station where Shea and I had originally boarded the *Nautigull*. While there was no need for Illumina to accompany me into the city, she was anxious for news of our cousin, and Tairmor was more likely than any roadside town to have the latest word. This time, passage through the cave system was unremarkable—there were no Sepulchres, and I therefore received no forbidding messages, which was a welcome relief considering the nightmare we were already living. I listed the facets of that nightmare like a mantra, one misfortune for every footfall in the tunnels: Zabriel was gone; Ubiqua was dying; my body was mutilated; Illumina was set to rule; there was a conspiracy against the Fae; Shea, my friend, was a traitor.

Traitor. The term was so foul. It felt good to stamp it across her memory.

It was no small blessing that Illumina had rope in her pack when, after some circling, we spotted the ceiling trap through which Shea and I had first entered the tunnel system. My cousin flew up and pushed it open, disproving my fear that Tom would have restacked the stones that had covered it. After carrying our packs through, she dropped the rope down to me, straining to haul me up beside her. By the time I scrambled through the aperture, we were both laughing through our exhaustion. I wasn't heavy, but neither was she especially strong, and the effort involved in extricating me from the tunnel had put quite a strain on us both.

We sat across from each other, regaining our breath, and a sort of melancholy descended on me. Illumina was pretty when she smiled, but it was an expression she rarely wore. To most in the Faerie Realm, it looked like she'd been born with everything a child could need, but Zabriel and I knew better. The physical scars to match her emotional ones were hidden under the dusty purple tunic she now wore. As I watched the simple joy of a moment spring from Illumina's aspect and settle around her like sunshine, I said what should have been said years ago.

"No one had the right to hurt you when we were growing up, Illumina. I'm sorry no one ever put a stop to it."

The smile that had inspired my declaration faded, replaced by confusion. She gazed at me, and I thought for a moment she might reach out to touch me. Her eyes were green like spring and envy, but they didn't hold their usual wariness. After collecting her thoughts, she found her voice to respond.

"If my childhood had been different, I wouldn't be who I am."

I pondered her words, for her fatalistic tone implied she had no regrets. Still, I thought she had missed my point. She could have been *more* than she had become; she could have been happier; she could have been content. She could even have made a good successor to the Queen. But I let the matter drop—if I had mentioned these things, she might have felt bad about herself, and that was not my intent.

We hoisted our packs and climbed the staircase to city level, emerging onto the streets in late morning. We spent the next several hours traversing the business districts, looking at posters and pressing people we encountered for news and rumors. Occasionally, someone made mention of the incident at Evernook Island and the reverberations its destruction was causing in Sheness, but we didn't hear one bit of gossip involving William Wolfram Pyrite. We chose to believe this was a good sign, lest we drive ourselves crazy.

As daylight waned, Illumina and I said our goodbyes on the thoroughfare. She didn't have any more time to spare.

"Try to get out of the city as inconspicuously as you can," I advised. "You shouldn't have trouble with your passport. I doubt Hastings even knows who you are."

She smirked and gave a haughty little laugh. "I can handle myself, Anya. You should realize that by now."

"Of course. That's not what I meant. There's just a lot at stake."

"I'll rest a little during the day and fly by night. I'll reach Chrior in no time at all."

Her words made me long for the ability to go with her. Would the ache of being flightless ever recede? Then another worry gripped me.

"Illumina, if Ubiqua has fallen ill and, Nature forbid, can't travel, then bring my father."

"Yes, I will. Should I also bring Davic?"

The question surprised me, and I looked away from her. I wanted to say yes, but it felt selfish to make the request—my promised should stay where he was safe.

"No, Davic can't help us. But as the Lord of the Law, my father has the position and authority to speak on the Queen's behalf."

"I'll do whatever has to be done," Illumina assured me. To my surprise, she took my hand, and I met her earnest gaze. "Everything is going to be all right, Anya."

I pulled her into my arms, giving her a light embrace, which she at first fumbled to return. Eventually, she figured out what to do with her body, and her tension eased, but my thoughts went to Enerris. Judging by her reaction, he had not only hurt her physically, but had starved her of the warmth of touch.

Illumina picked up her satchel from where it sat on the ground next to mine and walked away. I stared after her, then scanned the area to get my bearings, feeling unexpectedly miserable. I was companionless, almost moneyless, and had no idea when to next expect a friendly face. I would find

Fi soon enough, but I dared not stay at the Fae-mily Home, since Luka Ivanova might very well have it under surveillance. Worse, I didn't entirely trust Illumina to convey the urgency of Zabriel's situation and bring the Queen to Tairmor. In the end, I comforted myself by thinking that the three months upon which Davic and I had agreed were almost up. When he realized our promise bond was missing, he would notify my father, who would likely enter the Territory to find me. With that as a backup plan in case Illumina didn't carry out her instructions, I warded off a looming attack of near-immobilizing anxiety. The best thing to do was to focus on solving some of my immediate problems.

I ate a lukewarm meal that night at a human shelter in one of the poorer sections of Tairmor, then was fortunate to be able to claim one of their cots. Though the weather was improving with the coming of spring, temperatures still dropped considerably at night. I was grateful for the shelter's presence, for though the food was tasteless, it filled my stomach, and though the cot sagged, it was clean and off the ground.

The next morning, I trudged south, moving into more dubious neighborhoods, looking for landmarks that would tell me I was close to the Fae-mily Home. I didn't stray far from the river as I wandered the streets, finding the rush of water improbably comforting. I couldn't feel its spirit without my elemental connection, but during my time in Tairmor I'd grown accustomed to the sound. It was faint but ever present, like Davic's breathing when he slept or a cat's purr. It lulled my mind into a state of complacency that I greatly desired.

It was late afternoon when I recognized the area in which the Fae-mily Home was located. I approached the shelter, pulling up the hood on my old cloak—I'd left the one gifted to

me by Gwyneth at Roxy's, fearing its scarlet hue and fur trim
would draw attention. Not wanting to run into a Constabulary, I found a niche across the street in which to hunker down,
keeping an eye on the Home for comings and goings. When
darkness had thickened enough to provide cover, I dashed
across the street and through the front door.

Warmth, the smell of food, and the sounds of laughter and
conversation greeted me like an old friend, and I felt I had
come home. Wanting to wallow in the sensation, I asked myself if there could really be danger here, if it could hurt to stay
just one night. Unfortunately, the answer was *yes,* and I determined to stay firm in that resolve as I looked around for Fi.

She found me. Upon hearing the door open and close with
her attuned ears, the petite Faerie, orange-and-yellow wings
aflutter, bustled into the entry from the dining hall.

"Anya," she sputtered, hand over her heart. She rushed to
me, wide-set blue-green eyes examining me for signs of injury or illness. "It's good to see you. Not a day's gone by without me thinking of you. Did you get to Sheness? Did you find
that missing cousin?"

"Not here," I murmured. "Somewhere private."

Fi took my arm and led me into the large storage closet off
the entry, where the staff sorted dirty laundry and shelved
clean. Here we would be safe from prying eyes and ears.

"What's gone wrong?" she asked, pushing her short wild
hair from her forehead. She always looked a little bit frazzled.
"I can see in your face that something no good's happened."

"What I'm about to tell you is confidential. You can't speak
of it to anyone, all right?"

"Of course. The Prince, is he safe? Have you seen him?"

I nodded, then whispered a partial truth. Without Ubiqua's

counsel, I wouldn't reveal the whole of Zabriel's circumstances to anyone.

"Zabriel's left Sheness, and I believe he's here in Tairmor. I need you to keep your ears open for word of him. I've also heard that the pirate Pyrite has been arrested. You'll be doing me a favor if you listen for information on him, too. And a young human woman named Gwyneth may send you a note or two to hold for me. It's extremely important that these notes aren't seen or read by anyone but me. I'll check in with you every couple of days to see what information you have."

"But, Anya, I can house you here."

"I'd like that—I really would. But I was caught with forged papers, and an arrest warrant may have been issued. I'm afraid this is one of the first places the Constabularies would look if they wanted to track me down."

Fi's eyebrows twitched. False documentation laws were rarely enforced against Fae; it was thus fairly transparent that there were facts I didn't want to share.

"Whatever you think is best," she nonetheless responded. "How about at least seeing you off with a hot meal?"

Though my mouth watered at the thought, I declined, nervous that I might have already stayed too long. What if Luka had his men watching the house? In the best case, I was an accomplice of William Wolfram Pyrite, but if Zabriel's identity had been compromised, the Ivanova family's interest in me might have increased tenfold.

After a quick goodbye, I left the Fae-mily Home behind. Fi stood in the doorway and watched me go, worry lining her face. She'd probably worn the same expression when Evangeline had walked out of the shelter to live on the street and nurture her addiction to the Green. While I didn't expect to be on the streets for long, I knew all too well the dangers that lurked in this part of the city, and I quickly searched out an alcove in an alley where I could catch some sleep.

I continued my wanderings the next day, wary of the squalid neighborhood in which I regretfully had to remain for easy access to the Home and Fi's resources. Memories of Evangeline and the brothers who had attempted to rob me kept me slightly on edge, feeding a slowly building sense of apprehension.

To blend in with the other street people, I warmed myself at trash-heap fires and accepted proffered smokes that the homeless called cigarettes, all to avoid the notice of the Constabularies who occasionally sauntered by. Every hour or so, I made the rounds of lampposts and storefronts where news and posters were displayed, but there was nothing about Zabriel.

As my third night alone approached, it began to rain, and I groaned at the handful of coins I had left, having shared half my funds with Illumina. Another human shelter was probably my best option, so I cut through an alley and headed in the general direction of one of the places I'd stumbled upon in my search for Evangeline. Instead of facing a shelter, however, I found myself staring at the raucous pub with the smoke-filled basement that I had searched with Tom Matlock.

"Anya?"

The male voice came from behind me, its questioning tenor telling me I was not yet positively identified. Without looking around, I hastened across the street and into the pub, hoping the gentleman would not follow, or that if he did, I could lose him among the patrons. There was no doubt who had called my name, since I knew few men in the city, and only one who could be so compelling with just a single word.

When I'd pushed well into the seedy, unpleasant crowd,

mugs clacking around my head and drinks spilling everywhere, I finally dared to look back. Near the bar, Constable Matlock was scanning the throng. I ducked, yanking my hood so far forward it almost covered my face, and held my breath, willing him to go away. I counted the passing seconds, my worry abating as their number increased. Perhaps Nature was on my side after all.

At the touch of a hand on my shoulder, I almost bolted. Any attention earned in a place like this was poor luck. But it was Tom's gray eyes I met when I turned around—I should have known he wouldn't be easy to shake. He wasn't in uniform, which meant he was off duty and not required to report anywhere else. At this realization, panic, embarrassment, and giddiness fought for dominance on the battlefield of my emotions. In the midst of their war, they left me with no recourse other than to offer a nervous smile, uncertain as I was whether he would arrest me or buy me a drink.

"I wasn't sure it was you, Anya," he confessed, his voice upbeat. "Why did you run? And what are you doing back in Tairmor?"

I blushed, though the deepening color of my cheeks would hardly have been visible in the hazy light that contributed to the establishment's bawdy atmosphere.

"Interrogating me already?" I joked, searching his face for a sign of his intentions.

Tom chuckled. "I confess I'm surprised to see you. Surprised but happy, that is." He glanced around, dark brows raised at our surroundings. "Would you like to go someplace more, uh...pleasant to talk?"

"You don't like this pub?" The giddiness had won out—he wasn't going to hurt me or turn me in. Why had I doubted him? He was the one who'd freed Shea and me from Tairmor in the first place.

"Actually, I don't think the folks here like me. It's a strange feeling I get." He smirked. "I'm fairly recognizable, whether I'm wearing my uniform or not."

"Then show me a place where you are liked—as long as it's out of the rain."

He grinned and took my hand, leading me through the mass of swarthy patrons and back onto the street. Though it felt like I was being unfaithful to Davic, the warmth of his touch was welcome, and I buried my other hand as deeply as I could in my clothing in an attempt to ward off the clinging chill.

"We'll have to walk a bit," Tom told me, twining our fingers together and sending a tingle up my arm. "Leave this neighborhood behind."

"Okay by me."

We strolled in silence for a few blocks, and my senses automatically evaluated the hand I was holding. It was bigger than mine, just big enough to fit like armor. His skin was tough, reflective of his work as a Constabulary, yet soft and near flawless. The grip was strong, but the way his thumb brushed mine was coyly sensitive.

"So what *are* you doing in Tairmor?" Tom asked, reiterating his earlier question.

I shrugged. "I visited Sheness and liked Tairmor better. I missed the sound of the river rushing through the gorge." It wasn't a lie.

"Did you find your cousin?"

"Yes, and she's on her way back to the Faerie Realm. For obvious reasons, I couldn't go with her."

His fingers tightened against mine. "I know the Territory isn't what you're used to, but life here can be pretty good."

"I'm sure it can be. It's just a big adjustment. One I didn't expect to have to make."

He ruminated on my words, but I appreciated that he didn't express his condolences. He was practical in the same way I was. Condolences weren't helpful, not at this point.

"And...why did you run away from me when I hailed you earlier?"

I took a deep breath. There was no avoiding the truth when it came to such a straightforward question.

"I thought you might arrest me."

"Arrest you? I more or less had my chance at that, didn't I?"

It was raining harder, and he tugged me across the street and beneath the overhang of a nice-looking inn. His hair was damp and his cheeks had the faintly bluish tint of cold, but he put me between the wall and his body to block the wind. I could feel his warmth the same as any hearth fire. He gazed into my eyes, all dark lashes and sincerity.

"Look, Anya, I've thought about what you said last time we were together, and I've come to realize that enforcing the law can be unjust, that it can be the wrong thing to do." He kicked at the ground with the toe of his boot, then went on, "I've never really questioned authority—it's not exactly encouraged in the ranks, believe it or not—but it occurs to me that following orders without a context for them can be dangerous, every bit as dangerous as disobeying them without a good reason. And then, of course, there's what you said about Luka Ivanova, that he knew your papers were forged when you first met but wasn't concerned about it."

He reached out to play with a strand of my wet hair, then

brushed the backs of his fingers along my jaw. Again, I felt both uncomfortable and enticed. It was probably the way his gray eyes reminded me of Davic.

"I figure if overlooking an infraction is all right with the Lieutenant Governor, it's all right with me. I mean, who am I to question one of the great Ivanovas? Besides, I'm partial to redheads. On that basis alone, I could never arrest you."

I grinned in relief, then impulsively threw myself into his arms. He didn't hesitate to return my embrace, nor did he seem inclined to be the one to end it. Eventually, I stepped away, abashed at my brazen behavior. Wasn't I a member of a royal family? Didn't we have manners and dignity and principles to think about? But all of that felt irrelevant for the time being. Ubiqua probably would have hugged him, too, if she'd found out she wasn't going to jail.

"You're a very interesting gentleman, Constable Matlock," I announced, clasping my hands behind my back as though in penance for my indecorous act. "But you would tell me, wouldn't you, if my face was on a wanted poster?"

"Please. You'll have to best yourself a few times before you merit a poster and a bounty."

"I think you've insulted me."

"If it makes you feel better, *I* consider you notorious."

I smacked him lightly upside the head, and his brown hair, impressionable with dampness, stuck up agreeably. He reached around me to open the lodging house door, and we went into the dining room to claim a table. I took in the rich woodwork and sparkling chandeliers, feeling like I owed the other patrons an apology for my plain attire and wildly tangled hair. Compared to Tom in his crisp white shirt and coal-gray vest, I looked like the vagrant I had become. He didn't seem to notice, but when a smartly uniformed server handed us menus, I realized this was the first decent inn I had visited in Tairmor.

"Order whatever you want," Tom told me. "I just got paid."

Hungrier than I realized, I ordered plenty of food, then consumed it all, Tom watching me in bemusement as he more decorously ate. Wiping up the last of the gravy on my plate with a bit of bread, I pushed back my chair and slowly chewed the final bite, for once fully sated.

"Yet another skill you have," Tom remarked. "You're a champion eater."

I dabbed my lips with a napkin. "I couldn't very well waste your money, now could I?"

"Certainly not." He smirked, then settled his forearms on the table, manner more serious. "But I wouldn't have you waste my time, either, Anya. So why don't you tell me what you're really doing back in Tairmor?"

My silence was enough to confirm that his question was warranted, but I responded with indignation, anyway.

"Are you calling me a liar?" I asked, dropping the napkin next to my plate, steadying my breathing and my gaze. Maybe I could intimidate him out of pursuing answers. If he'd been pretending this whole time to be happy to see me, then he was a very good actor, but now seemed like a stupid time to abandon the ruse. I was aware of how defensive my manner had become, and so was he, cocking his eyebrow in answer to my aggressive stare as he trailed his finger around the rim of his wineglass.

"Are you a liar, Anya?"

I examined him carefully, at long last deciding I didn't like how guarded and cynical I'd become on this journey, and that his aspect of innocence was probably not feigned. Forcing my body to relax, I leaned into the table to engage him.

"When I was in Sheness, I kept hearing about this pirate, name of Pyrite. I actually saw his wanted poster in Luka Ivanova's office when I was here before, and it listed a reward of thirty thousand gold pieces. That was money Shea and I could have used, and we kept our eyes open for him while we were in the port city. Anyway, we heard he had been arrested, so I returned to Tairmor out of curiosity, hoping to find out what's going to happen to him."

"And Shea? Where is she?"

"I'm not sure at the moment. She's around."

I wondered if he knew Fae couldn't lie, although we could evade, and if he was falling for any of this. Though he maintained eye contact for a few more moments, expression discerning but gentle, he dropped the matter. He clearly didn't want me to view him as an enemy.

He stood and offered me his hand. "I have an early day tomorrow, so I should be on my way. If you'll come with me to the lobby, I'll rent you a room for the night."

"You don't need to do that."

"You're right. But I'm going to procure a room anyway, and if you don't make use of it, my hard-earned funds will have gone to no good use. Remember, you've already told me you don't want to waste my money."

I laughed, allowing myself repose. I was happy to pretend that the awkward portion of our exchange hadn't happened, especially in light of his kindness. He picked up my satchel and led me to the front desk, where he handed over some coins in exchange for a room key.

"I'll walk you upstairs," he said, indicating the way with a sweep of his hand. "This place is enormous. If I hadn't all but grown up terrorizing this neighborhood, I'd think this building was a maze."

He accompanied me to the second floor, then down a carpeted hallway to my door. As he unlocked it, setting down my satchel, I laid a hand on his arm.

"Thank you, for everything. I overreacted downstairs. You've been very kind, and generous, and forgiving, and helpful, and…"

His soft, strong hands caressed my face, and I lost track of what I was saying. I could see the moment he made the decision; something came together in his expression with the surety and rightness of opposite polarities, and he kissed me full on the lips, his mouth gentle and just distant enough to leave me aching. I tucked my body against his, seeking the comfort and security of his arms, and when he obliged, I entwined my hands in his hair and pulled him tighter, earning a nearly inaudible moan that I felt in his chest. I didn't want him to leave; I didn't want to be alone. What I wanted was passion, to feel fully alive, my senses engaged, my heart overflowing. I wanted to experience the sensations of which I'd been deprived since the loss of my wings.

And then my mind reengaged. What was I doing? I was betrothed, and Davic was somewhere missing me, right now, ever trusting and faithful. I put my palms on Tom's chest and backed away.

"I'm sorry," I mumbled. "I can't do this."

"Can't do what?" His voice was lazy with bliss. "It's only a kiss, Anya. I'm not expecting to be invited inside."

I nodded, wishing that changed things. I met his silvery eyes, and the yearning I saw in them told me he would have said yes had I posed the question. My knees weakened, and had he not taken a step down the corridor, I would have fallen into his arms all over again.

I cleared my throat, gripping the door frame. "Good night then, Tom."

He smiled tenderly at me, then subtly licked his upper lip. Judging from his eyeline, he was imagining it was mine.

"Good night, Anya," he said, ever the gentleman. "I'll stop by midmorning tomorrow to check on you. If you don't mind, that is."

"Not at all. I'll even try to be awake."

He was grinning stupidly now and he knew it, opting to depart before he said anything to go along with his expression. I stood in the hall for another minute, my thoughts and feelings in disarray, especially about Davic. But no part of me was upset with Tom.

With nothing else to be done, I hoisted my pack and carried it into the room, which was clean and spacious, with a bed, a dressing table and mirror, and a separate washroom. Feeling I'd been delivered into paradise, I emptied my travel pack on the floor, found the clothing that looked cleanest, and took a much-needed sponge bath. When I reentered the bedroom to dress, I noticed that the contents strewn on the carpet were not what I had brought. Illumina and I carried identical leather satchels, courtesy of Queen Ubiqua's generosity, and my cousin must have grabbed mine by mistake the evening she'd left. As this was the first time since arriving in Tairmor that I'd had a safe place to shelter, I hadn't discovered the discrepancy until now. I shrugged and dressed, for it didn't make much difference; we carried the same basic supplies.

I set about replacing Illumina's things in her pack, breaking into a grin when I discovered she carried a hefty money pouch. I wouldn't be sleeping on the streets after all, though my cousin might find her journey less luxurious. Spying a small, leatherbound volume, I opened it to discover it was her journal and sketchbook. I hesitated. I didn't have the right to read her innermost thoughts. Then again, the book might contain the answers to how she had gotten travel papers and what route she had taken to Sheness. What was the harm, really? Curiosity winning out against judgment, I started flipping pages.

The typical contents of a diary were interrupted by a pair of pages devoted to a simple, beautiful sketch, much like the ones Illumina drew in her alcove in Chrior or gave to our aunt and me as gifts. This sketch was of a girl lying on the ground in the woods, a dark fog rising around her. In the background loomed a heavy thicket interrupted by a single pathway. I stared, trying to make sense of the drawing, and my hands trembled. The scenery was too familiar, even the tree under which the girl was lying. And there was a dark stain in the snow surrounding her body.

The tree was the one against which I'd been pinned by a Faerie-hunter's arrow. And the path was the Bloody Road. And the girl had to be me.

Illumina had drawn me in the aftermath of my attack. But how? I couldn't remember telling her the details of my injury. I had, however, told Shea. Perhaps Illumina had asked my former friend about the loss of my wings, sensing I might not want to talk about it, and had conjured this horrifically accurate depiction with the aid of her imagination.

I once more examined the pages. There were footprints all around the scene, and at the bottom she had scrawled the words that were also scarred onto her breast. *Keep silent your screams and never look back.*

More unnerved than I wanted to admit, I snapped the journal closed and let it fall to the floor, not sure how well I would sleep with the memory of my maiming revived. Body tired and brain muddled, I blew out the oil lamp and tucked myself into the luxurious double bed for which Tom Matlock was paying. My thoughts roamed in the dark until the recollection that had been clawing at the back of my mind made it to the forefront.

"I didn't betray him," Illumina had said to Fane. Such deliberate words. Why hadn't she said, *"I'm not a traitor"*? Or *"I didn't betray anyone"*?

And then another memory sprang forward, this one from the night my wings had been taken.

"Shhh," a female voice had whispered in my ear.

One woman among five men, her moonlit silhouette slight as a child's, her hand lightly stroking my hair. Suddenly her face came into focus.

I sat up in bed, screaming like never before.

★ ★ ★ ★ ★

ACKNOWLEDGMENTS

Well, this was a tough one. Without the following people, this book wouldn't have happened:

As always, Mom, Cara, and Kendra. You put up with me, support me, and push me in the right direction, even when I can't see it for myself.

My superagent, Kevan Lyon, for being the first line of defense (and offense!) even when I'm being a flake. Taryn Fagerness, foreign rights guru, for her passion and dedication. What a blessing it is to work with you two.

At Harlequin, which these days is feeling less like a publishing house and more like a home: Natashya Wilson and Annie Stone, for their invaluable editing insight. Lisa Wray, whose marketing skills are rivaled by none, except perhaps Mary Sheldon, Melissa Anthony, Amy Jones, and Siobhan Clayton. Jennifer Gould, who somehow deciphered my scanned-in scribbles and turned them into a beautiful map design.

Mr. Larry Rostant, for the stunning cover art.

And of course, everybody who's reading. That means you. Until next time,

Cayla

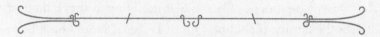

QUESTIONS FOR DISCUSSION

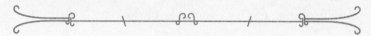

1. What are the motives and goals of the Anti-Unification League? Why does Anya disagree with their goals, even after experiencing personally the violence against Fae being perpetrated in the Territory? Based on what you know about the history of our world, do you think that closing down the borders between Chrior and Warckum completely would be an effective strategy for the long term?

2. The author describes Fae who have lost their wings as often feeling as if there is nowhere left that they belong. Can you think of any examples of peoples in our world who feel this way?

3. Assuming that Anya finds a way to return to Chrior, who do you think would be the most effective leader for the Fae: Anya, Illumina, or Zabriel? Why?

4. Why do you think that Hastings and the men working with him are trying to manufacture a creature with Fae magic? What implications do you think this will have for the relations between the humans and the Fae?

5. From what we know of Illumina, it seems that her extremist political leanings are at least in part a result of her father's treatment of her as a child. Do you think the rest of the family, including Queen Ubiqua, should have been responsible for Illumina's well-being? In your opinion, how much of our personality and beliefs is a result of our upbringing, and how much is inborn?

6. Rather than turning himself in to the authorities, Thatcher More chooses to take his family into hiding. Would you have done the same? Are there any other options that you might have considered?

7. When Anya hears about the upcoming execution of Alexander Eskander, she and the other Fae feel vindicated, even excited at the prospect of his death. But as Anya quickly learns when she sees Spex at the plank, there are two sides to every story. How do you feel about Eskander's execution? How do you think it affected Spex, his son? Did it benefit the Faerie people? Should Eskander have been killed?

8. Shea must make a difficult decision between her loyalty to her family and her loyalty to her friend and companion, Anya. Do you think she makes the right choice? Why or why not?

9. If you were Anya, what would you do next after making the discoveries that she does at the end of the novel?